Breathe
with
me

The Breathe Series: Book Three

WENDY L. WILSON

Printed in the United States of America

ISBN: 978-0-9962379-4-9

Cover Design by *DCP Designs*
Cover Photo by *K Keeton Designs*
Models, *Dusty James and Gabriela Marie*
Author Photo by *Ashleigh Pettis*
Editor, *Jeremy Thompson*
Formatting by *Champagne Formats*

Dedicated to...

Grandma

I love and miss you every single day and although I wish you were
here to celebrate the completion of another book with me, I know
you are in a happier and healthier place now. Thank you for being
such a huge part of my life and for always believing in me. I've always
tried to relay emotion and feelings into words and I do it much better
on paper, but I don't believe there will ever be enough words in the
world to tell just what you mean to me. I love you so much Grandma.
I hope I always make you proud.

Breathe

with

me

A Friend

Evan

SLINGING MY BAG ACROSS MY back, I make my way across the gravel parking lot, immediately feeling at ease with my surroundings. This place has always seemed more like my home than anywhere else.

Feeling the sharp, shifting pieces of rock beneath my feet, I let my eyes wander about. Ribbons of sunlight bouncing along the surface of the water catch my attention. As a kid, I'd spend hours sketching pretend treasure maps in hopes of discovering some long-lost, forgotten booty at the bottom of that lake. After a couple of years passed by, the maps were history and it was a different type of booty that had me on the prowl.

The tranquil sounds of water splashing at the shore and against the edges of the dock along with choppy waves alerts me to early morning boaters that are braving the cold weather for a little fishing. How many hours have I spent there boating with my brother and Grandpa? I'm sure it would add up to years. Not to mention all the times I went out on the lake with *her*.

Shaking my head to brush off any memories that are likely to sneak up on me, I step onto Grandpa's new front porch, taking a few strides to the door. A creaking noise draws everyone's attention to my presence as soon as my feet cross the threshold.

"Evan." Grandpa nods his head as he reclines in his chair in front of the fireplace.

"Hey, Grandpa." I smile then throw my bag to the side of the door.

"Evan, why don't you toss that out in your camper rather than cluttering up the cabin?" My father's commanding tone fills the air and it takes all the willpower I have to not turn around and leave.

So much for greetings. No, Hello son, good to see you, or Hey, Evan, long time no see. I've missed you, Nope, not our family. It's only been two months since I've seen him.

"No problem," I say, turning to head back outside.

I reach down to grab my bag and a cold blast of air hits me as my brother walks inside.

"I think some of your buddies just showed up across the way." I stand back up and nod, holding my bag at my side.

I'm already aware that Judd and Alyssa are headed here for Christmas break, but I still made up a lame excuse that I had to visit Dad while he was in town. I really just want to be where she is; a part of me still feels protective when it comes to Piper. I could not care less about the whole family thing.

Aside from Grandpa, our family is beyond dysfunctional. Lord knows there's never been a group of guys that needs the stability and good graces of a woman around more than us.

Mitch is a complete ass. He only knows how to treat a woman like shit. He's steering in the same direction as Dad, putting his career as a recruiter to the top of his priority list, but doing it all for the wrong reasons. I've always thought being in the military would be a humbling act, but I'm thinking my dad and brother didn't get that memo. It only aids in their cockiness and fuels their thoughts of viewing themselves as God's gift to women and above everyone else.

Dad, much like my brother, has gotten good at using women then tossing them to the curb which is how he acquired two sons and no mom willing to hang around long enough to put up with his shit.

Mitch's mom split when he was only two, unwilling to take on the hardship of moving from military base to military base.

Mine, however, didn't even give it a chance. My father received a call from the hospital in Vegas stating his name had been listed as the father of a new baby boy. She apparently skipped out on the hospital bill before the doctors even had time to discharge her, leaving only me and a sticky note with Dad's phone number behind. After a paternity test and a mountain of paperwork, he says he left with a new born baby and not a clue what he was going to do. He claimed he tried to find her repeatedly, but she had disappeared.

After that, Dad hung up his dogging around for a while to raise us boys and lug us around the country for years before we had the mindset to ask to come live with Grandpa. I was ten when Dad finally settled us in with him, before taking off again. It is the one thing in life that I am the most grateful for.

Grandpa is the only decent one among us. He, at least, had my grandma around until 6 years ago. He always tells me that she's the one that kept his ass in line, and she did. I never got to know her as well as Grandpa, but I remember when she would say jump, Grandpa would smile, give her a little hell then carry out whatever she asked of him. She's the reason he started the construction company and why it continues to thrive after all these years. She was also the brains behind investing in this land which was a damn good idea, if I do say so myself. What started out as a measly piece of property with all of two cabins on it, now houses thousands of campers through the summer, and is Grandpa's bread and butter during the warm months.

"Who all is joining them?" Mitch's cocky tone jolts me out of my train of thought and reminds me that I have to deal with him for a whole week. *Yippee-freaking-yay!*

"I don't know," I mumble, knowing Mitch's only concern is what single girls will be arriving.

Turning back as I pass my brother and open the door, I see Dad heading towards me.

"Is the radiator heater out there?" I ask, wanting to just collapse down on the bed for a couple hours of shut eye but only if it's warm, of course.

I am definitely not a lover of cold weather; I can suck it up if need be, but I prefer coming out here during the peak seasons when the sun is beaming over the trees and the water has just the right amount of chill to it. This time of year, I try to stick to hibernating in my apartment.

"I already cranked it up a little over an hour ago. It was making a strange noise so you might want to check it out and make sure it is putting out heat."

Heading out of the cabin, I scan the parking lot quickly and notice Piper hasn't arrived yet, only a dark green vacant pick-up truck that looks unfamiliar. A cool breeze sweeps through the air, slightly rocking my grandmother's old white wicker rocking chair that still adorns the front porch. The tree branches near the lake shore rattle and crackle like a storm may be brewing, yet the inviting rays of sunshine that soak the beach not far ahead brings a warm glow to the day. For December the temperatures have been pretty mild, thankfully only dipping as low as the 40's.

The screen door slams behind me and I turn, firmly gripping the rustic log banister and gritting my teeth. I'm already in a lousy mood and not sure I'll be able to tolerate my brother the entire Christmas break.

"Your grandpa wants me to show you those heaters that need to be installed in the shower houses," Dad's smooth voice calls out behind me. He makes his way down the stairs and around the side of the cabin before I have time to move. "You coming?"

I shrug my shoulders to no one in particular and bounce down the three steps, joining him right as my ears pick up on the sounds of crunching gravel across the parking lot. Walking over by my camper, I glance around, catching a glimpse of Piper's dad's van. *Here we go. Let this torturous winter break begin.*

After Dad shows me the three units I agreed to install in the shower houses, I make a quick run into the camper to check the heat and drop my bag, then head back to the porch. From here I have a great view of Piper unloading her bags. *A tad bit creepy maybe, but from afar is about the only time I can enjoy her presence anymore.* This past summer, she probably had no idea how much I watched her, wishing things could be how they used to be.

Her long, jet black hair catches in the wind and her arms immediately fold across her chest in an effort to warm herself. I can't help but envy those arms; it used to be mine that would be wrapped around her.

Lifting the hatch of the old white van that her dad has driven for the past seven years, she pulls a red duffle bag out and hoists it over her shoulder along with a black case that looks like it houses her laptop. She crosses the lot and disappears into the cabin for a minute or two, only to return for more stuff. My eyes stay glued on her, waiting and wondering if she can feel my presence like she used to; if somehow she may be able to sense that I'm watching her.

At last, my curiosity is satisfied as she lugs a large navy suitcase out of the back of the van before slamming the hatch shut. The loud clank of the hatch echoes across the lake and back to me, but instead of turning and carrying on in the direction she has taken the last two trips, she comes to a dead stop, turning her head to look right at me. Standing a full twenty yards away, the anger in her piercing, deep brown eyes cannot be missed. Her dark brows dip down into a scowl as she stares right into my eyes as if she is shooting an arrow directly into my heart. *How do I make her not hate me, if she won't hear me out?*

I stare back in a deadly standoff, refusing to look away. Her gaze wavers as she looks down and then flicks her sights back up with a different expression; softer, almost sad. My heart is shredded by that look; torn from my chest, lying motionless on the ground bleeding out from the pain I have caused her. *She'll never trust me again.*

Once she turns and her sad, angry eyes leave mine, I watch her walk away with the suitcase rattling along behind her and I am reminded of the first day I ever saw her. The day I knew she needed to be in my life; in any way possible.

"Hey, did Grandpa tell you anything about the family that he sold cabin one to?" I call out to my brother as I hoist myself up onto the dock, feeling a sting in my biceps, and the heat from the sun already sucking up all the moisture that is dripping down my body.

My brother flops about in the water like a dog desperate to get to dry land. "A little. I know they have two kids, or well…I think one of them is their adopted nephew or something like that. The other is a girl around your age."

I'm only thirteen, but my ears perk up at the mention of a girl my age. "Really?!" I ask, totally psyched to meet our new neighbors now. "When are they supposed to get here?"

Swimming around to the other side of the dock, my always-flexing-and-bragging-that-he-is-a-stud brother climbs up the metal ladder that is attached to the floating dock. I snicker to myself at what a wuss he really is as I sit on the edge, kicking my feet through the cool, misty lake water.

"I'd say that is probably them, now," Mitch says, as he plops down beside me and vigorously shakes his head, spraying me with drops of water.

I snap my head up to the shore, instantly raising my hand over my eyes so that I can block the sun and get a better view. An older lady steps out first, followed by a man on the driver's side then a guy that looks to be my brother's age, from the back passenger side.

Then she steps out. Dark, black, tangles of hair hang down her back and nearly touch the waist of her jean shorts. She spins around as soon as her feet hit the gravel and gazes out to the lake, more than likely taking in the breathtaking beauty of this property.

Her ghostly pale skin tells me that she may need to invest in a boat load of sunscreen and her scrawny, boyish figure is a complete contradiction to the bright red girly bikini top that she is sporting.

As her eyes sweep the scenery beyond me, her mouth curves into a slight smile and I see a flash of color across her teeth; braces maybe. Her eyes continue on their journey until at last they land on me. Me; sitting on the edge of the dock, dripping wet in a pair of cut off jean shorts, my chestnut brown hair in bad need of a cut, a chest that has yet to discover puberty and legs that would make a chicken feel beefed up.

For a moment, our eyes lock and her smile grows, which instantly draws my mouth up at the corners to mock her expression.

"Piper, come on!" A shout sounds from the shore and she turns away from our trance.

My brother bursts out in laughter beside me and hops up. "Well, she's a beaut! Good luck with that one! I'm out of here. Catch ya later." With that he hops back into the water with a huge splash that soaks my nearly sun dried shorts and causes me to flinch, but I still don't look away from the shore.

The girl runs off with a suitcase nearly as big as her, bumping along behind her. Once she gets to the cabin door, she turns back one more time; I assume for another look at the lake, but instead her eyes look to me and that amazing smile flashes across her face again.

No sooner than it happens, she darts inside, leaving me puzzled, curious and smiling from ear to ear with the hopes of finally…

…making a friend.

I remember

Evan

COZYING UP IN MY GRANDMA'S rocker, I kick my feet up on the banister and watch as yet another vehicle pulls across the lot and parks right on the bumper of Piper's van. The car door opens no sooner than it slams into park and out hops Abby. She hollers something into the car and the passenger side slides open. I would assume maybe Alyssa drove with her sister, but I know better. Judd had big plans and no way would they be driving separate; not unless his surprise didn't go as planned. *That would suck! Here I have big plans for a quiet apartment soon!*

Right then a muscle-bound, sandy-haired guy steps out of the side door and walks around to the trunk to join Abby. He looks familiar. I think I've seen him in a few of my classes and maybe even at Alyssa's Halloween party. He and Abby gather gifts and bags, giggling and carrying on as they make their way to Piper's cabin.

Once the door closes behind them something occurs to me and has my face crinkling into a disturbed frown from the thought. *Whose green truck is that, then?*

Abby scurries back out, over to her car and happens to catch me watching. Fixing her eyes on me, she slams the trunk closed and crosses the lot as another car pulls in. I follow her eyes as she waves at the silver car with Skylar bopping her head like a freak to music I can't hear. *Just what I need.*

After this past summer, Skylar has become relentless in her pursuit of me. It's not a bad thing. We did hook up a couple of times and she is completely insane in the sack, but it put me in an awkward position wondering if she has disclosed this information to Piper. I guess in the back of my mind, I haven't closed the door on that, yet.

"Hey, Evan!" Abby's spunky voice calls out as she walks up the stairs on the porch.

All of Piper's friends are pretty cool, but Abby has always been my favorite; probably because she was around the summer that Piper and I became an item. She more than likely knows more details of our past relationship than anyone else, including Judd. I haven't even told Judd all that happened that summer, three years ago. It was a memorable one for us all; the year Judd's mom died, the year Tristan and Mitch became pals and even bigger jerks, and the year all hell broke loose here at the campground, thanks to my big mouth…

I smile and get up from the rocker, looking out in the distance as Skylar waves her arms in the air to get my attention.

"New guy?" I casually wave at Skylar and then nudge my head toward the blonde brute that had unloaded from Abby's car earlier, which is now helping the rest of the girls with their bags.

Abby looks back and a warm smile covers her face as soon as she makes eye contact with him. *I guess so.*

"Oh yeah, I think you met him at the Halloween party at Alyssa's old apartment. That's Hayden." She looks back at me and there is no hiding that she is crazy about him.

Abby always seemed to fall hard, though. Hopefully, this time the dude is a good guy. She also has a knack for falling for the wrong ones as well.

I nod my head, remembering that I had indeed seen him briefly at the Halloween party before I had stormed out. "So, I guess it's serious?" I smirk glancing back at the guy. At least she is moving up from my brother.

She looks at Hayden and shrugs her shoulders. "Who knows, but I like him," she pauses and steps up a stair to smack me on the shoulder. "I better go. You gonna join us later on the beach? We're going to have a huge bonfire."

I nod my head, not knowing what my plans are for the evening, but I'm sure I'll make an appearance.

"I'll see you later then!" she hollers over her shoulder, racing off to join her guy.

The screen door slams shut behind me and I hear Mitch let out a low whistle.

"Mmmm…I miss that tail."

I grit my teeth; he's talking about gallivanting around with Abby a couple years back, when he treated her like complete crap.

Another snap of the door sounds and I glance back, seeing Dad.

"So what are we going to do today?" he says, stretching his arms above his head.

Mitch nudges his chin towards the beach where everyone has gathered, busy throwing logs in a pile. The girl's giggle and laughter kicks up, bringing forth an array of flashbacks of this past summer; of just how miserable I was watching Tyler paw all over Piper. The same pain bolts through my heart as I put two and two together of who the owner of the green truck is, as he lazily arranges his hands around Piper's waist. My jaw tightens and anger starts to surge through my veins as he slides his hands down further to her hips. *I know that shit isn't going to fly with her.*

One…two…three…

Piper spins around and shoves him away playfully, but I know better. I can tell she is playing off how uncomfortable she was when he touched her. I know all about it; been there.

"Well, well…I think I see something that could take up my time. She seems feisty." I snap my head over to Dad, who has walked up beside me against the banister, currently eye-balling Piper. *Not cool!* He smirks, and the anger I was feeling only seconds ago magnifies.

Dad has always had a thing for younger women, but he can sure as shit take his eyes off this one. My blood boils when I see him staring at Piper like she is some slab of meat. I take a step back, ready to bolt inside and deter his attention away from her. I know he wouldn't try anything, but just thinking about what is on his mind is enough to drive me insane with jealousy.

"That's one hot piece of tail," he says as I try my best not to choke him out.

Mitch chuckles and walks in front of me to stand beside Dad, no doubt so they both can ogle the girls that are too young for either one of them, and sure as shit too good for both of them.

"She's not that interesting. Actually, she's kind of bitchy, not feisty and she has a boyfriend, I think," I say, hoping this will knock his mind away from mentally undressing her.

I'd really hate to punch Dad when I haven't seen him in over two months, but as my eyes go back and forth between him and the target he has sighted in, my heart slams in my chest and it becomes harder to breathe.

Mitch laughs and looks back towards me with an evil glare, pretty much his normal expression, but I know he is going to say something that pushes me over the edge.

"They sure don't look like they are taken. Those tight jeans and sweaters look like an invitation to me." He grins, shifting his eyes back out to her.

Dad laughs and I cannot hold back any longer, "Maybe you should try looking at some girls in your league and maybe you should check out women your own age," I say in a condescending tone that I know may get me thrown across the deck.

Dad finally looks away from Piper and over to me with his eyebrows drawn and a frown on his face. *Yeah, that pissed him off! At least he isn't looking at her anymore!*

Mitch takes a swig from his beer, completely unaffected by my comment, then sputters out a laugh. "Oh yeah, I wouldn't go after that one…she's already tainted!" Mitch sneaks a sly grin in my direction, knowing he just touched down on a sore subject.

"Shut up, you asshole!" I spit out about ready to lunge over Dad and knock my brother to the ground.

Dad opens his mouth to intercede, but Mitch nudges his arm to stop him. "Don't mind him. Besides I think he already plowed that field." He laughs harder and I can no longer hold it together.

My eyes widen in rage and I shove Dad out of the way, slamming him into the banister as I lunge at Mitch. Swinging my arm, I knock his beer bottle to the ground with a loud shatter and his ass soon follows, landing right in front of my grandma's rocker.

But I'm not finished.

He screwed things up for me then and although I wasn't big enough or tough enough to do anything about it, I sure as hell am now.

I slam down on the porch, a slice of pain shooting through my knee as I feel the spilled beer soak through my jeans. Gathering a handful of my brother's shirt, he shoves at my chest forcefully as I raise my fist to make him pay for his comment. My brother swings first, grazing my nose with a burst of air right as a pair of strong arms wrap under my armpits and clasp behind my head so that I can't move. My chest heaves up and down as I am pulled to my feet.

Kicking my leg at Mitch, who is still on the ground, I grind my jaw and yell with more venom than I've ever felt in my life, "Don't ever talk about that again! Ever!"

The screen door slams and my grandfather's stern tone jolts us out of the heat of the moment, "Knock it off, boys. I will not tolerate this under my roof." His keys rattle as he makes his way past us and ventures to the drive behind the cabin. He knows none of us will disobey him. When Grandpa puts down his foot, we listen.

Mitch slowly stands up and casts a shitty grin, not the least bit concerned with my anger. Placing his hand on his jaw and wobbling it back and forth with his mouth open, I see a bruise forming. I didn't even realize I hit him. A bit of satisfaction rises within me and I look him straight in the eye, challenging him.

"This is done, boys! Your grandfather is right and I will not tolerate this, either…you hear?!" Dad shouts.

I nod my head and Mitch holds his hands up in retreat. Dad lets go of me and I smooth my shirt back down. Gazing out past Mitch, my eyes make contact with Piper as she looks up in my direction. *She saw the whole scene unfold.*

As Dad and Mitch head inside, my brother laughs under his breath and I step down off the porch. Gritting my teeth as another slice of pain splinters over my knee, I quickly bend to inspect the damage, finding a tear in my jeans with a few droplets of blood. *Great…just great!* I'll have to take a look later; right now, I need to go apologize to her for the chaos. She already thinks I'm despicable, now she's probably afraid of me, too. *Great.*

She keeps her eyes on me as I walk towards her with cautious footsteps, fearful that she may bolt if I move too fast. *Dammit! I just want to talk to her!* That's all I've wanted to do for the last three years, just to talk without all this animosity and hate between us. She watches me the whole way; studies me until I reach the edge of the beach, then folds her arms over her chest, turning in a defiant stance with her back to me. I blow out a sigh, ruffling the hair hanging down on my forehead.

Right then my saving grace comes as Judd's truck pulls into the gravel lot between our cabins and distracts me from getting completely shot down. I turn to wave at them, but when I glance back to the bonfire, Piper has already walked away and joined the guy that she apparently came with. *Better damn luck next time, I guess!!* I shake my head to get her off my mind and head over to help Alyssa and Judd with their stuff.

"Hey, man!" Judd hops out grinning from ear to ear. "What happened to you?" he asks, looking me over.

Glancing down, I immediately notice the small rip with a trace of red is now a full on scarlet soaked hole. "Shit."

I bend, scraping my forefinger over the torn, wet tear and immediately crumple my face in pain. Clamping my jaw down, a splinter of stabbing sensations shoots through my knee as I realize a piece of the beer bottle must be lodged in my leg. I look closer, using my fingers to open the ripped fabric. A shard of glass no bigger than my pinkie nail juts out of my skin.

"Well that's just perfect," I mumble, pinching it carefully with my finger and pulling it out as another painful tingle emerges; this time almost a relieved sensation.

Staring closer with the glass still grasped between my fingers, I check to make sure there are no more visible pieces lodged in my skin. Straightening up, I shift my weight over to my other leg and frown. Judd stares back, waiting for my response, probably wondering what the hell.

"Oh well…my brother and his big mouth happened."

"I completely understand that." The excitement in Judd's tone cannot be missed as he smiles at Alyssa, who is climbing out of the passenger side.

I glance back and forth between the two of them. *They are way too giddy. He must have already done it.*

"So, did you show her?" I say quietly, not wanting to ruin his surprise if he hasn't.

Judd doesn't even answer, but the goofy ass smile that crosses his face says it all as he stares over at her.

"Yes! We are now proud renters of our very own apartment in Fairview," Alyssa squeals, jiggling a key between her fingers. "I can't believe it," she giggles, scrunching up her shoulders in an excited gesture and bouncing on her toes all the way to Judd's side.

I laugh. I'm glad they're happy; at least some of us get lucky.

"Heaven help your neighbors. At least bolt your bed frame to the wall so they can get some sleep," I joke with them as Judd hands me a bag and we begin walking towards the cabins. "Oh, here." I hold up a set of keys. "Grandpa reserved cabin three for you, so you guys will have some privacy, even though he said he does not approve."

I chuckle as Judd snatches the key out of my hand and gives me a sheepish look. He's not used to any type of parental rules, but he's an adult so I say what the hell. A conclusion that Grandpa came to when he handed me the key with a shake of his head. I got a good run down on how 'back in my day', but in the end he didn't want to load his cabin down with more people.

"Thanks, man, but seriously, I want to pay for it," Judd urges for probably the hundredth time.

I hold my hand up to stop his thoughts as we make our way onto the porch of the cabin immediately to the left of my camper.

"I told you Grandpa said he doesn't need you to pay. Just make sure all messes are cleaned up and by messes, I mean…"

"Yeah, I got it," Judd quickly cuts me off before I can dig into the aftermath of having non-stop sex. *I swear they're rabbits.* "So?"

Swinging his head around as he unlocks the door, he nudges his head towards my leg, eyeing my knee. The three of us walk in, Alyssa immediately to the forefront like a little kid that's never seen the inside of a hotel.

"My knee? Oh, same ole shit. My brother's relentless persistence of getting under my skin and saying crap that he knows will light my fuse."

Judd sputters out a laugh, clearly flabbergasted at my statement.

"Well that sounds familiar. Isn't that what you do…all the time?"

"Hell no! I am nothing like him, and you better bite your tongue from saying anything like that, unless you want me to start calling you mini Tristan." I raise my eyebrow, challenging him.

"Touché."

"Hey, this cabin is set up just like the one next door where you guys stayed in this past summer." Alyssa sidles up to Judd; he quickly tucks her into his side like that's where she belongs.

Clearing my throat, I shake loose the tinge of envy that tugs at me and look at her. "Yeah, cabin three, four, five and six are set up for families, hence why they are down on this end. The further down you get the cabins that are more geared towards honeymoon suites..." I raise my hands and crook my fingers to air quote my words. "...and couple's cabins with either a king or queen bed and then the hideaway."

"Oh..." Alyssa looks at me perplexed, biting her lip as Judd totes one of their bags to the bedroom. "So, if this is the second cabin, why is it called cabin three?"

I laugh at her question because I, myself, have even questioned Grandpa on this topic. "Well, when Grandpa first bought this property, Piper's family's cabin was the first one on the plot of land. Then Grandpa built a second cabin, which is the one he stays in..." I point my finger to the right wall, towards the cabin. "Eventually when he added a few more, he numbered the cabins starting with the first one. When he sold that one to Piper's father, he just never changed out the cabin numbers on the doors. I think it's some sort of symbolic bullshit for it being the first big purchase he made with Grandma. So I guess that will always be cabin one."

"Hmmm...makes sense." She smiles, sinking back into the couch with her feet kicked up on the rustic barn wood coffee table.

"What makes sense?" Judd walks out of the back bedroom as I step over to the couch, kicking my bent knee up on the arm in front of me.

"Nothing...she was just asking about the cabins." Raising my eyebrows, I direct the conversation back to the topic of his brother. "So, how's Tristan doing? Have you heard from him?"

Judd shakes his head, looking down to the ground as he leans against the back of the couch, diagonal from me. "No, I haven't. I've called and I've went by the house, but he is always at therapy or locked in his room."

"You know I can help with that lock, right...all you need is a hanger." I nod my head with a wink and a popping noise from my tongue to the roof of my mouth. "Just bust in on him, like I did to you."

"Nahh…" Judd furrows his brows. "We had a good talk last month and last thing I want to do is wreck that. Jake said he needs space and time…so that's what I'm giving him. I'm hoping he'll come around. I just wish he would trust me above all."

I ponder on that for a second, curious. "So you still have no idea what happened to him in the wreck…like not a clue of whether his back was broke or he's paralyzed or anything?"

Alyssa flips around on the couch, eager to join the conversation.

"Judd said he couldn't see anything except the blankets piled up on the bed."

Summoning up everything Judd told me after his visit with Tristan, I nod, agreeing. "Yeah, but you said there was a wheelchair." I snap my finger out to point at Judd, to spark a bit of skepticism. "So, it could be broken legs, a broken back, a broken vertebra, paralysis… literally anything and I'm telling you, if I was confined to a wheelchair my whole life…that would seriously screw my shit up."

Judd shakes his head quickly, not jiving with something I said, "Yeah, but there were no casts or braces on his back that I could see and he was sitting up. Looked to me that he could move just fine."

"Hmm." I press my lips into a straight line and stare ahead. "I guess we'll find out someday. It's not like he can hide it forever."

"Or maybe if it will be healed soon…like if he has two broken legs," Alyssa throws her never ending optimism on the table, but I don't buy it.

I glance over to Judd and he looks right back at me with an unconvinced expression. "I hope that's it."

Eager to find out plans for our break, I shift gears on our conversation. "So when does Jake get here and what is the plan…err, well, what all are you doing?"

Judd strides around the couch and plops down beside Alyssa, cozying up like they are about to play footsie. "Whatever we're doing, you're doing, too." I start to disagree, to step away and shake my head; to escape before he can rope me into being stuck in a cabin with pissy-Piper, but he goes on, "Don't even, man…we are having Christmas at her cabin and Alyssa's mom is even coming down to join the fun."

Oh shit. Now I'm second guessing what I was going to give Judd. I don't normally join in on the sentimental gift exchanges, but I seem to remember a certain someone challenging me at one point and keeping my ass up all night long as a payback for busting in on their romp in the sack. *Yeah, I'm not backing down now.* I have something that is sure to have Judd thinking twice about all the disgusting moans and groans he makes when someone is sleeping only one bedroom away. If Jake stays in their cabin this week, he will be praising my name.

"Whatever. So is Jake going to stay with you two?"

"Oh, yeah…he'll be here tomorrow," Judd answers my question, but doesn't even look up as him and Alyssa get way too comfy side-by-side, eyeing each other like it's mating season.

"Ok well, on that note…I'm out of here." I spin around, taking five paces to the door before turning back to look over my shoulder.

Judd and Alyssa are half way making out, with barely an inch of space between them. *Yeah, I'm no longer even here. What the hell.* I roll my eyes and turn back to the door, throwing my hand in the air as I head out.

"Later."

A muffled bye and a few giggles is all I hear as I pull the door shut and let my eyes instantly wander towards cabin one with a stinging sensation rising into my gut. I can barely even remember what it was like to have that; to want someone so bad you could practically taste it. *Ahhh, who am I kidding…I remember it all too well and it haunts me every single day.*

Grand Slam

Evan

ACAR DOOR SLAMS AS I step down onto the first step of Grandpa's porch, take a seat and then casually lean back onto my elbows so I can take in everything around me. Looking over, I'm surprised to see Skylar hopping out of her small burgundy hatchback. I quickly tally up the vehicles in the lot, counting two trucks that I have never seen, and then glance down towards the beach where a massive pile of brush has been gathered. Squinting to see better, my eyes land on the guy from earlier.

Abby runs up in the distance, colliding with her burley boy-toy, Hayden. She laughs and waves her hands in the air, obviously talking about something dramatic while Piper settles up beside the other dude who also looks vaguely familiar; maybe from the same party. Gritting my teeth as he pulls Piper closer to him, I lean my head back and close my eyes. *I better get used to this shit; she's done moved on years ago. I'll break his arms if he hurts her though.*

"Hey, what are you doing out here all by your lonesome?" Skylar's smooth, sexy voice hits my ears and I snap my head back up with a grin immediately falling across my lips.

"Just waiting for you."

She laughs, tossing her head back along with a mass of brown curls that hang over her shoulder. "You didn't even know I was coming."

Raising my brows with a you're-damn-right sort of smirk, I hold my hand out and glance past her for a second. "That you are right...I didn't, but now that you're here, you want to take a walk with me."

Her eyes light up just as another pair of eyes in the distance seem to be throwing daggers at me by the handful. It's basically the same look I gave the dude that won't keep his paws off her only minutes ago.

"Sure, let me go throw my bag in Piper's cabin and I'll meet up with you," Skylar yells, already on a mad dash across the parking lot.

I jump up, sliding my hands into my back pockets with a shove. Stepping forward, I wander downhill to the path that runs along the shoreline. My feet tread slowly over the dead grass and hard ground that is littered with soggy leaves and small twigs.

Taking a deep breath, I look back up and Piper's penetrating stare is almost more than I can take. *Why does she torture me?* I mean, I'm all too aware of the games chicks can play to entice a guy, but this is definitely not one of them. She looks at me like she has something to say, yet for years all I've managed to get out of her is a few bitter words, pissy ass comments and a back-the-hell-off attitude. Never in all that time did I get out of her what happened after she left that summer; no explanation why she was no longer going to Rosemore High, where the hell she moved to and up until last summer she never dared to set foot on these grounds. I know without a doubt that my face was shocked when she drove up that day; hers was an astounding sight for me. *Damn, she had changed so much.*

Kicking a stray pebble out of my way with the toe of my shoe, my disheartening thoughts are interrupted with soft thuds coming up behind me. I sneak a quick look and see Skylar's deep blue-gray eyes, subtly freckled nose and high cheek bones.

"Ok, I'm back. I had to grab a jacket. It's chilly," she huffs and puffs, out of breath from her sprint to meet me.

Pulling her thin black zip-up hoodie across her chest, she falls into a gentle stroll along side me. My eyes drop to her hands and automatically, I reach out to pull one of them into mine. Although my heart isn't fully on board, I really like Skylar and have grown accustomed to her company in the past several months. She's well aware that I'm not out for any sort of fall-in-love-and-get-married type of relationship. I think that's why we get along so well. She's easy going, laid back and everything between us is cut and dry; no damn games. She has no hidden agenda or expectation and I sure as hell am one hundred percent honest with my intentions.

She grips my hand back with a smile and starts to swing her hand like we're two little kids out on the playground. I cock my head to the side and give her a sarcastic glare from the corner of my eyes. *What are we, thirteen?* She arches her right eyebrow, leveling me with an assertive look that says, 'I can do whatever the hell I want to do' and 'act whatever age I want'. I chuckle and resign myself to swaying my arm along with her silent beat.

A brisk wind blows through the air, swinging bare branches with a swoosh above our head and creating a steady ripple pattern over the dark lake waters.

"I really like it out here." Her chest expands as she gulps down a lung-full of the calm country setting that I have come to call home.

"It's nice, huh?" I look out at the water, gently lapping against the muddy shoreline. "Back when Grandpa bought it, it was nothing but an empty plot of land where people would come and pitch their tents. Even that over there," I point over across the large body of water to the hint of cabins that you can barely see. "Even those weren't built yet. He has a big aerial map in the cabin from before everything was built… just grass, trees and water."

"That does sound nice. Maybe you can show me the map some time."

I sigh and take a quick discreet look her way. "I have something better I can show you later." I keep a straight face as she laughs, but she knows I'm totally serious. "First, I need to check something out."

Letting go of her hand as we get a few more cabins down, I make a bee-line for the second shower house on the property.

"I just need to check out the breaker box really quick."

She follows along behind me as I jog onto the dock, pull the keys out of my pocket and unlock the storage closet right outside the door to the showers. Pulling it open, I scan the wall until the latch comes into sight.

"So what are you looking for?" Skylar wedges herself into the doorway behind me, a rich sensual perfume fragrance quickly filling the room.

Scanning the board for an empty circuit that I can connect the new heater to, I run my finger over the few that are on the small board until I see an available one.

"There we go," I say, slamming the small metal door to the box. "We're adding heaters to the shower houses since Grandpa is starting to see some mid-season traffic. Don't want everyone out here freezing their asses off for trying to smell good, do we?"

I flip around, standing nearly flush against her in the small room. Mischief sparks behind her eyes as her hands fall to my arms.

"So, how about that thing you wanted to show me?"

I laugh, shaking my head at how she isn't afraid of being absolutely direct with me. Grabbing a fist full of her jacket with one hand, I pull her an inch closer and lean over her shoulder, brushing my unshaven face across her ear.

"Patience," I speak softly, making Skylar's face flip around directly in front of mine.

"You know patience isn't one of my strong points."

Her eyes glaze over with a playful hunger as her hand starts a slow decent over my stomach. For a split second, I glance around taking in the space in this closet. It's jam-packed with shelves of toilet paper, cleaning supplies, extra fixtures and a huge ass water softener and wa-ter-heater against the back wall. If it weren't for all those supplies and equipment, there would be ample space to get our freak on. A chilly gust of wind blows through the doorway and has my mind abandoning all thoughts of baring anything until I'm in a heated room.

I chuckle and slide out the door, hearing a frustrated gasp huffed out behind me. Reaching over, I grab her hand and pull her out of the room.

"Later," I enlighten her as she steps behind me on the dock while I lock up. "Come with me a little further so I can check one more breaker box."

She nods, always easy going and quick to agree.

We wind along the secluded dirt pathway that runs the length of Grandpa's property and make one more pit stop so I can mirror my actions from the second shower house. Skylar keeps the trip lighthearted and interesting, discussing the land and appealing to my love for this place. Being around her is simple; uncomplicated, like hanging with Judd, only I've never had a wet dream about him or fantasized about taking him against a water heater.

Rounding the bend, my camper comes into view and I speed up our pace, eager to get back to the warmth of my small little metal home. As soon as we turn under the skeletons of trees that usually canopy the entire property with a lush green umbrella of foliage, my eyes are automatically drawn back to Piper who is dragging a big log to the brush pile. My lip twitches at the corner as she wrestles with it, but I quickly stare back at the ground in front of me to fight off the flood of emotion that comes with thinking of what has become of *us*. *Screw that.*

Looking to my camper and then quickly to a couple of the vacant cabins to the left, I'm conflicted with where to go.

"Come on," she hollers, dragging me towards my camper.

I suddenly want to root my legs into the ground, unable to imagine another girl in the one place that became mine and Piper's private haven years ago. Unhinging my hesitations, I look up at Skylar's giddy and excited expression, and relent. *There's no reason to let the past hold me back forever.* Staring dead ahead while refusing to look over my shoulder, the familiar presence of her gaze tiptoes over my skin, silently nudging me to look her way, but I don't.

With quick hands, I swing the rickety camper door open and motion for Skylar to lead the way so that I can partake in the view of her round ass, thick thighs and curvy hips all crammed into a pair of skin tight jeans. A smile crosses my face as I watch her luscious frame sway through the doorway with me a good arm's length behind her.

She glides over the deep brown carpeted floor of the tiny apartment-style living area that I usually enjoy while out here, to the bed at the far end. Plopping down, she lets out a sigh and looks around, her hands out to the sides slowly petting my unmade bed. I squint, crinkling my brows with unease as I glance behind her to the picture of Piper back when she was fourteen.

"Hey," I take two strides and lean over her, pressing her body back with mine flush against her. "Time to show you that…ummm…thing." I wiggle my brows while subtly removing the picture and sliding it beneath my pillow.

"Oh yeah?" her hands fall to my jeans and it's obvious as usual that we are on the same page.

Standing back up, I pull my wallet out, fiddling with the contents until my hand lands on a single foil package. I keep a good grip on it, but carefully tug at her elbows to pull her up with me.

"Hey, come here."

"Where? I'm thinking this is where we should be."

Her eyes glimmer with curiosity and honestly, I see no need to lie, but I also don't have to make her feel like shit by pointing out that every time I look at this bed, I see Piper's face.

"Let's just get up and move this party to another location." I slide my hand over her elbow and down to her hand, lugging her to her feet and across the room. "That doesn't feel right over there. How about…" I look around and my eyes land on the small kitchen table that juts out from the side wall surrounded by two soft, ugly-ass plaid cushions. "…right here."

Pressing her into the table, I fling the package onto it and slide my hands around her waist while kissing the back of her neck. *This is much better.* No way had I ever been in this sort of position or situation with Piper, ever; I wouldn't have dared.

"Ohhh..." she breathes, dropping the back of her head on my shoulder as my mouth and hands feel their way across her body.

I lean against her, slowly sliding my hand to the button of her jeans. With a quick flick of my fingers, I loosen the painted on denim and gain access to more thrilling areas of her body. My hand dips further down, her zipper scraping the back of my forearm and pinching the hairs on my arm until my fingers make contact. She pants and whimpers as I tease her with my chest pressed to her back while grinding my hips and pelvis hard against her ass.

With my hand buried in her jeans, a slight warm weight settles on top of my wrist as she excitedly tries to quicken the pace of my hand with her own. I hold tight to her waist with my other hand, the animalistic urge inside of me wanting nothing more than to shove her pants to the ground and take her against the table, but something about that seems forceful and wrong. *I will not be one of those guys; ever.*

Moaning louder as I thrust my fingers along her tender flesh, something springs up and not what I was hoping for.

"You didn't go to Weinerville with Tristan, did you?"

I haven't a clue in the universe where the damn question came from and why the hell I would bring up another guy when I'm in the middle of this, but nonetheless, it spills from my mouth before I can think. I really don't care what her answer is, but something about girl talk suddenly strikes me as this potentially becoming a discussion. If they trash talk anything like guys in a locker room, then I want to know if my bedroom skills or anatomy size may be up for comparison with the biggest player around. That shit needs to be nipped in the bud and I might have to work overtime.

Skylar pulls away from me slightly and shifts her head, her profile turned in front of my face. Her eyebrows are raised and her mouth falls open, sparking a bit more arousal from me.

"Are you serious?"

Eager to continue in on my pursuit of making her call out my name in absolute blissful delight, yet unable to concentrate on the tempo of my finger during a conversation, I slow my pace and move my focus to talking.

"Just curious…no big deal," I blow it off, but now I'm definitely interested.

"Ummm…well…" she stutters as I barely shift the location of my fingers.

"Oh, that's a yes," I grin into her shoulder, gently biting her skin playfully. Lifting my chin, I slide my face against her cheek as she moans again, lost in the rhythm of my fingers. "He's not any good though, huh?"

She snaps her head to the side, sweeping her lips around to my unshaven face. "Whaaaa…" she says on a deep breath, nudging her hand back to mine which has slowed even more to a slow, teasing strum of her chords. I snicker, enjoying the torture I'm putting her through.

Pressing my lips to the hollow behind her earlobe, I outline the delicate slope with my tongue, release a warm breath over her skin and whisper, "So did you slam into home with him?"

She drops her head forward and I can barely make out a hot lustful, needy expression as she scrunches up her face and turns to me with a sexy ass glare.

"Ummmm…" she tries to speak and her frustration tickles the hell out of me.

Her chest vibrates in and out beneath her shirt as she answers, "Well yeah, I did."

I pause, now curious on his delivery. "So, what…he swings, runs the bases, comes into home and then goes back into the dugout?"

She blows out an exasperated breath, frantically pushing at my hand which has unknowingly become idle. *Oh shit, forgot about that.* I slowly flick my fingers, picking up where I left off and immediately igniting a jumpy reaction from her as she melts back into me.

"Well…ahhhhh…" she hums and my fingers pick up pace over

her soft skin. With quivery words, she goes on, "Are we really discussing this now?"

I smile, wanting to crack up. I don't give a damn if we're discussing another dude during this. I can rock her world from one end of this place to the next if I want to and she knows it.

"Sure."

She groans and drops the back of her head to my shoulder. "Well, he more like hits a homerun and then steps up to bat again."

My eyes go wide. *Stamina, huh? Figures with the way he gets around.*

"Reeeeally? So, he doesn't stop at the bases or anything…just hits a fielder and rounds back to home?"

A shaky laugh moves over her lips. "Actually, he never even kissed me, but he stopped at a few bases," she gasps as I press my face into her shoulder, now concentrating on the goal at hand. "Like with you… ohhhh," she moans again and I nearly stop, curious at what she's going to say, but I keep strumming. "You're more concerned with my reaction and my needs, but he was just working towards the end game… ummm…all," she breathes out sounding sexy as hell, "…all six times." Her face falls with a laugh.

Oh, that's it! I jerk my hand out of her jeans with the zipper catching on my knuckle and determination spilling through my veins. She spins around on her heels, placing her hand on my chest and with a shocked, ornery look dancing in her eyes at my abrupt action. *Two can play at this game. We'll see if she'll be laughing in a second.*

"Six…seriously six?" I say on a chuckle while my hands flick the button of my jeans followed by quickly pushing the zipper down. I cannot even fathom how that is possible. *Six?* After dropping my jeans to the floor, I pull my shirt over my head and waste no time finishing the job until I'm standing there buck ass naked.

"Get it off." I raise my eyebrows with a smile as I motion my finger up and down towards her clothes.

Her eyes sparkle and she complies, taking less time than I did to strip down. *I'm impressed.* Free of any articles of clothing, I grin and take her by the waist, gently pulling her with me to the cushioned bench seat to our right. She falls back with no help from me and lays there looking at me excitedly with her legs dangling to the ground. My brows quirk up and down playfully as I slide onto her, my lips instantly finding a nice warm slice of skin at her neck to nibble on.

Nonchalantly reaching up to the table with one hand, I feel around the flat surface until I find the condom package I placed there earlier. Thankfully I snagged a good handful from Judd's dresser before I left. *I'm gonna need them.*

My fingers fumble as I slip it on, but I keep my mouth busy gliding over her skin. Free of any further tasks rather than getting busy, I bring both hands up to get a good two handfuls as my mouth dips lower to enjoy the plumpness. Her mouth goes wide on a moan and I dive in, devouring her succulent skin as I thrust forward to make full contact with her body. A shock wave of sensations moves through me shooting up to my lower abdomen and down both my legs. The sparks continue, immediately growing and I am more than ready to rock this boat, but suddenly my mind hits a road block.

"Wait," I steady my breaths and she looks at me like I've done lost my mind. "You didn't do my brother, did you?" *Why have I never wondered this before, and why the hell am I thinking about it now? Just say no.*

"Eeeew…no!" she snaps and my confidence in sealing this deal soars. *Finding out she got it on with my brother may have been a show stopper.*

Extremely aroused and still focusing on keeping my hips idle, a sneaky smirk rises across my face and I breathe out anxiously, "Ok, good. Now hold on tight, because I have several grand slams to hit."

Keep me safe

Piper

MY EYES KEEP WANDERING OVER to his camper; to our place. I can't help it; I can't even focus on any task at hand through the overwhelming surge of heartache that is drowning me with the thoughts of what could be happening right now. Another portion of my heart chips away as I stare at it, hoping they'll come right back out or maybe even see Skylar leave by herself. *God, doesn't he know how bad that hurts?*

"Hey, you need help with that?"

Chris' hand runs the length of my back as he walks up beside me and tries to take the muddy log out of my hand. My skin jumps and I gasp with the contact. As bad as I am tempted to flinch, I keep it under control; I've learned to.

"No, I've got it." I jerk the piece of wood to my opposite side, twisting away from him and dislodging his hand from my body. Looking back at him with a guilty smile, I try my best to erase all forms of bitterness in my tone. *It's not his fault I'm screwed up.* "Sorry, control freak here," I laugh, widening my eyes.

He laughs with me and his hand falls back to the same place, making me take a deep breath.

"You say this like I don't know you." He winks and my guilt climbs. "Give it up."

He takes the log out of my hands, immediately easing the ache in my arms and freeing my forearms from the overbearing stress of the bark jabbing into my skin. Looking down, my fair skin is already sporting a zebra-type embedded print of red lines from where it managed to dig in. I glance back to Chris as he dumps the log into the pile that we have collected, then automatically peek to the camper in the distance.

Why do I let it bother me? Do I really expect him to sit around and pine over me? That's definitely not Evan's style. I'm the one that chose to stay away and not forgive him, so what right do I have to begrudge him a chance at finding someone else?

"You think that's enough or should we get some more?" Chris asks, pointing back at the massive collection of drift wood, logs and twigs we have arranged in a woven nest of limbs.

"Dude, that's enough for us to burn down the entire forest," Hayden pipes up from behind us.

"Guys, I really think this is enough," Abby calls out from my left, "Geez, Piper, do you plan on having a bonfire till the end of the week or were you hoping we wouldn't need the fireplace in the cabin tonight if this one was raging enough?" she teases, igniting a burst of laughter from Hayden.

I glance up at the heap of branches and shrug. Honestly, I wasn't paying attention to what I was collecting each time I came back to the beach with an armful. Ever since I saw Skylar race over to the shower house and disappear into the woods holding Evan's hand, my mind has had one strategy: get back to the beach as fast as I can to see if they came back. I could see them for a while walking down the property line; walking the exact path he and I would every time we went on one of our fishing or swimming excursions in his grandpa's boat. *Oh, just the thought of him doing the same things with someone else kills me.*

"Pie…" Abby draws out my name as she walks up beside me.

"Yeah…" I push my thoughts aside for the moment and snap my head around, making eye contact with her.

Her eyes, however, have gravitated to the same location mine have been most of the morning; to where Evan is. She smiles, an all-knowing and sympathetic expression masking her face. She knows what happened that summer and afterwards. Not even Evan knows the aftermath of his screw up; how could he? I've never had a thing to do with him since. The closest interactions we have had in the last few years, was last summer and this year's Halloween party, needless to say, neither were friendly reunions.

"Everything ok?"

She dips her chin to level her gaze with my barely five foot four-inch frame and although she's not saying as much, I know she's curious.

"No, I'm fine," I bite out with a false snippy yet playful tone. "How are you?" I counter, and Abby relents in her worry as Chris and Hayden make their way to our side.

"Ok, so is it time to light up?" Hayden rubs his hands together, clearly psyched about torching the mound.

I nod, while Hayden and Chris take off for the cabin.

"Ok, dish it out. You are looking at his camper like you didn't expect this. You know he has been seeing Skylar off and on for a while."

"I know…" I sigh, unable to control glancing up to see if he is coming out yet. *Dammit…stop looking.*

"There you go again." Abby points to my face, looking ticked off at how I'm acting. "Piper, you have been dating Chris for two months now. It has been years and you've never even tried to talk to Evan, so until you decide to man up and give him a chance to explain, don't get pissy when he runs off with another girl. He has to move on just like you do. If you want him, then you need to tell him."

I stare at her, my mouth gaped open as usual when she puts me in my place for acting like a whiney baby. She's right. I have no business punishing him, but I still do and I'll probably continue to do it. I don't have the nerve to confront him and all that happened. I do good to push the thoughts and images away each and every time Chris and I get close.

"Do you even love him?"

My eyes nearly bulge out as I snap my neck around to look at her. Her hands are defiantly at her hips with her eyebrows drawn up expectantly with her lips stretched into a thin line.

"Evan?" I spit out immediately confused by her question.

"No!" she bites out with a shake of her head. "Chris."

This loses me even more. Glancing back to the house afraid if anyone can hear our conversation, I confirm that Hayden and Chris are not within earshot as I speak up.

"Well, no…I don't…" I stumble. *Why is she asking this?* "I like him, but I mean, isn't it a little soon to be confessing my love for him. It's been two months."

She doesn't budge, looking at me skeptically while she slides her hands from her hips to fold across her chest.

"What?!"

"Piper, where did you put the lighter?" Chris yells from behind me, but I don't even turn. I keep my eyes glued to Abby with hers also on me, both of us silent. One thing about Abby is she doesn't choose sides and if she has a problem, she's not afraid to let you know it.

I start to turn to go back to the cabin, unsure of what else to add to this conversation. I don't have a leg to stand on. *I'm wrong to still hold this grudge.*

"Hang on, I'll show you," Abby directs her voice to Chris, then looks back at me standing in front of her. "You, sit here and think about what the hell you are doing. This is the same as last summer… you need to get this crap under control. If you're not going to talk to him, then leave him alone and stop with the dirty looks and for God's sake, stop looking so damn miserable every time he goes somewhere with another girl. It's going to happen." She arches a brow and tightens her hands across her chest, before softening her stance. "I love you and I understand this is hard, but you need to do what's right. This isn't good for you anymore than it is good for him. Ok?"

I nod, feeling defeated and like a coward. My shoulders slump as her arms engulf me in a squeeze-the-life-out-of-you Abby-kind-of-hug.

"Ok, I'll be back," she whispers in my ear before darting off.

"Ok, Mom," I mumble glumly.

My legs give out and I slide to the sand. Tugging my knees to my chest, I look between the tangle of branches in an attempt to peer at Evan's camper. *What am I doing? Why can't I let him go and just move on?*

My mind twists and turns, flipping through pages of memories with him and me until it lands on the moment in time when he made me feel the safest. The day I needed it the most, yet he had no idea that he was saving me. He still has no idea what that night was to me.

Carefully shutting the front door of the cabin with my heart beating on the walls of my chest, I take off in the darkness, not even thinking of where I'm going. I don't care. Right now, jumping in the lake with the heaviest rock I can find in my hands sounds like the most suitable solution for my grief. I don't want to think; I can't. Running wildly, my arms flop around at my sides, the air burns my lungs and tears sting my eyes and chap the skin of my cheeks.

A whimper echoes in my mind and I squeeze my eyes shut as my feet catch on something sharp. My body flings forward and instantly I throw my arms out on instinct. I hope I break my neck. Maybe I'll hit my head and bleed to death before anyone finds me. My chest hits the ground with a thud as a dull tingle stretches up from my knees. I scrunch my face and slowly lift myself to my hands and knees as gravel grinds into my palms. I'm still alive. My head throbs and no matter how I try I cannot shut off my mind.

Another whimper sound, mixed with heavy breaths in my ear. God, no! I push up from the ground, still on my knees and slam my hands over my ears.

Stop it! Stop it! Stop it, my mind screams.

Just stop it!

I shake my head wildly, losing my balance and falling to my butt, more pebbles scraping into my skin as the pain gives me a sense of relief. My knees throb and more tears come. I have no control. What happened? Why? Was it my fault?

Pressing my eyes closed as I lie still in the middle of the parking lot, just steps away from a white truck with a side sticker that reads Jansen's Construction, I listen to the sounds of the night. The frogs croak, the crickets chirp and tiny splashes sound farther away until little-by-little a serene image of peace and calm starts to break through all the dreadful thoughts that keep swallowing my mind whole. Letting out a breath, the shooting pain in my side begins to subside as my lungs welcome a steady, easy flow of air once again.

Just as my trembling legs muster up the energy to support my weight and as I swing them around to stand, another sound fills my eardrums; I cringe.

"Hold still," the whisper is laced in pain and regret.

My chest swells as my mouth drops open in a sob, filling me with adrenaline and the need to run; run away from the voice, the breaths, and the memories.

No, no…stop!

I run and run and run, running so fast that my mouth is unable to take in air fast enough. Twigs snap and my feet stumble, barely catching myself a few times, until they find a solid surface. Where am I? I look around, my mind panicked and my heart thundering out for a reprieve from the anguish. Fumbling for the handle, my hand grips to a hard metal knob and I pull, doubting I may even have the strength to get it open. To my surprise, I swing it forward with a stealthy force I didn't know I had; with hidden strength that should have been used to fight earlier, however, I was frozen; too scared to move, to do anything except be a victim. Is it my fault?

A crackle sounds behind me and I look up, aware of my surroundings for the first time. My eyes are fogged over and more streams of water continue to fill them as I stare ahead at the cracked mirror above the sink in the shower house. The light is on, yet the room is still dull; dark and filled with the dusty odor of mold and mildew. My throat wobbles and my stomach clinches as I run forward, throwing myself over the sink as I hurl. Emptying my stomach, one painful catapult of my body at a time, I cry harder, letting exhaustion, shame and sorrow consume me.

After a few minutes my stomach stops ripping me apart, I look down at the mess in the sink as the smell of the pizza I ate earlier takes on a whole new image in my mind. I'll never eat that again. It takes me a few minutes to clean up my mess, too embarrassed that any sign of me being here will let everyone see the dirty images in my head. I toss the wad of paper towels into the trash and take a deep breath. Calm down, calm down, I repeat over and over to myself, hoping it will take my heart and head to another place; a moment in time that was beautiful, not ugly. Everything is ugly now.

Glancing up, I look at my reflection. Is that me? My lip curls into a snarl and I'm disgusted by the sight that looks back at me. I want to scream at it. Flinching as I continue to stare, I fight to resist shouting that it is all my fault; that I'm to blame. How'd it happen? Did I say something that made him think that it was ok, or do something that offered it up as an option he felt was available to him?

I drop my arms to my side, all energy and emotion slowly dripping out of them. I look down for a second, sure that there will be a puddle at my feet; a small river of tears and possibly even blood from my heart being torn from my soul. On top of all the pain and agony inside of me my bladder screams, but I don't even want to touch myself. I'm scared. I can't tell anyone ever.

After minutes of more sobbing, gagging, shaking until I swear I'm suffering from seizures and after painfully wiping any traces of the incident away, I make my way out of the shower house, numb and not knowing where I can go. I glance over to my cabin and a surge of vomit begins to quake in my stomach. Immediately dismissing any thoughts of going back home, my eyes catch sight of a light suddenly appearing right ahead of me; Evan.

I wipe at my eyes, rubbing them with the back of my hands so there is not a single sign of my tears as I race for his camper. I think this is where I saw him go the other day. My mind speeds faster than my legs can carry me, running through possible things to say if he doesn't answer the door and even things to say if he does.

Are you busy? At midnight, I'm sure he's just hanging out waiting for company.

I was just going for a walk and wanted to say hi. Again, it's after midnight.

Panic rises to the back of my throat, but it's too late. My knuckles hit the door with a quick tap-tap before limply falling back to my sides. The silence is deafening as I listen to the thud of my heartbeat, wondering if somehow it could be his footsteps moving towards the door.

With a loud grating-creak sound, the small metal door comes open and I step out of the way.

Evan's eyes widen in surprise. "Piper. Hey...what's up?"

He stands in the doorway in a loose tee shirt and baggy black gym shorts. I tremble, unable to form words. The smile that usually adorns his face falls, and a look of absolute concern and alertness takes over as he steps down the three steps and places his hand on my shoulder.

"Hey, are you ok?"

I look over at his hand; my heart jumps and my skin crawls as I slink back from him a bit.

"I'm ok. I was just..." I glance around, nervously fidgeting with the hem of my shirt and struggling not to cry.

"Hey...hey..." He moves closer, but keeps his hands at his sides. I suddenly feel like a deer during firearms season, ready to bolt at the tiniest sound. "Have you been crying?"

My eyes search the campers outside walls, the beige, brown and rust stripes merging into one blurry mess between the darkness and the glaze of tears that have cropped up. Don't cry, don't cry.

I don't say a word just stare around for an escape. This was a bad idea.

"Hey, you know what? I was just going to play a card game or something by myself. Lame, I know, but it'd be more fun with two players."

He steps backwards, carefully up just one stair as his hand comes into my line of sight and his other foot steps up onto the next.

"You wanna come in for a bit and kick my butt at cards?"

His laugh fills my ears and it's comforting; it's beautiful as it always has been. I look up immediately, my eyes wide as I see a smile shadowing his face. His hand remains held out and I don't even recognize my own movement until I feel a grip on my own hand. My feet move without me telling them to and before I know it, I am sitting on the edge of his bed. He sits beside me and I look around. I should be scared. I should want to bolt, to run, but I don't.

"Ok...let's see." He gets up and walks to a table in the middle of the room. Reaching above it, he opens a set of cabinet doors and pulls out a stack of old board games, complete with dingy, ripped up boxes. "We have Monopoly, Clue, Chess..." He sticks that one back into the cabinet. "Sorry, I hate that one..." rifling through a few more, I watch his movement, comforted with my heartbeat finally steadying to a slow rap. "Monopoly is a good one. It'll keep us busy." He smiles and I snap my head to take in his expression, curious of whether he can see in my eyes what happened only minutes earlier.

After shuffling the other games back into the cabinet, he heads back to the bed.

"Hang on," he says softly.

He reaches around me with deliberate slow and careful movements as he does his best to flatten his comforter around me. I stand up for a second and he takes the opportunity to finish the job before spreading the board out on the mattress.

Minutes stretch by as we busy ourselves in an old-school board game.

He is relentless at working to get a laugh out of me and even though I find it hard, my lips curve up in a familiar shape once or twice. He never once pushes to know what is going on, but I can tell he can see the pain. He probably assumes I got in a fight with my parents or had a bad dream, and I'd rather keep it that way. I never want Evan to know.

With another roll of the dice, Evan grabs my game piece and moves it for me, counting the steps out loud as he taps it to the board.

"Look at that…I told you, you'd kick my butt."

His smile stretches as he looks at me and I stare back, our eyes locked in an innocent friendship, comfortable acceptance and timeless concern of each other's welfare and happiness. I breathe out a truck load of gratefulness as I fight every ounce of emotion inside of me that is threatening to break free. It surges through me like a typhoon practically forcing me face down and buried in his pillow as I yearn for Evan to rescue me…

To make it go away….

To protect me…

For him to do anything and everything to save me and keep me safe.

Walk away

Evan

COMING OUT OF THE CAMPER, I grip Skylar's hand as we sneak stupid ass grins at each other.

"So you're absolutely sure that you never messed around with my brother?" I twitch my brows down, a little grossed out thinking about her and him. *Oh shit, that's disgusting.*

"Wait a minute...you never asked if I messed around with him. You asked if I had sex with him, point blank." She looks at me straight-faced before breaking into a smile.

Jerking her into me, I wrap my arms around her back and slap her lips with a kiss, letting them linger with our warm breaths mixed to create a trail of heat over my skin.

"Ok, you may just have to pay for that joke."

She squeals and bucks in my arms as I dig my hands into her sides, still grasping her in an unwavering grip.

"Wait a minute..." she laughs, throwing her head back, but I just use that as an excuse to dive in and indulge in more of her soft delectable flesh. "Wait...wait," she gasps, "I am going to have to pay for that? I thought you owed me six and from my count that was only three."

Pulling back with a disbelieving grin, I chuckle at her bluntness. "Those three were damn near equivalent to six, actually maybe even nine. Yeah, nine! That was triple the job any home runner like Tristan could manage. I mean come on…" I lean back and look at her. The trace of amusement creases the corners of her mouth. "I not only stopped at each base, but I spent quality time there, played in the damn dirt, polished every damn base and then licked it clean before sliding into home like a pro."

She cracks up and nods just as I look past her to the beach.

"Ok, ok…you got me…you're a stud…you totally…"

Her voice trails off as I see Piper sitting in the grass all snuggled up close to the ass-wipe that I guess she's dating, and then there is the other dude pawing at Abby. Judd and Alyssa sit across the fire, leaning against a huge tree stump, lost in their own world as usual, but my eyes fall back to Piper.

"Come on, let's go join." Skylar tugs at my hand and I fly forward, my head jostled as I snicker at her enthusiasm.

We race over and I immediately settle myself beside the two love-birds.

"Hey Evan." Alyssa leans around Judd with a greeting, round cheeks and bright eyes reflecting the orange and yellow glow of the fire.

"What have you been up to?" Judd turns to look at me, pulling himself away from Alyssa.

I shrug, unable to tell him what is on my mind as Skylar fidgets to get comfortable beside me.

"Not much, I was just checking the breaker boxes at the two end shower houses to make sure they have an available circuit. Those heaters that Dad showed me earlier are by no means brand new. I think he probably picked them up at an auction and they are ancient. I'm going to hook them up but it's pretty much a waste, and Grandpa should know that. They may have to be replaced by next winter, but whatever. It's his money."

"So why are you checking the breaker?"

I clear my throat and subtly glance over to Piper, who is looking right at me. *Shit.*

Casting my eyes right back to where they were, I go on, "Those older units usually have to run on a larger circuit and I may need to use two."

Judd nods his head slowly as I start to bounce my crossed feet that are stretched out in front of me. He frowns for a moment, then looks over to her. I'm positive he is reading me like a damn book. It's not like I'm obvious; I always am where she is concerned. *How is it that I can keep cool with everyone, keep emotions from affecting most of my decisions and most definitely not give a damn about drama, except when it comes to her?*

"I'll be back," Skylar announces as she joins Piper, Alyssa and Abby all running off towards the cabin.

The two other guys jump up and head to the parking lot.

"God, this is driving me crazy," I erupt as soon as they are far enough away.

"What, Piper?"

"Of course, Piper…who else?" I roll my eyes on a sigh as I pick up a stray twig that escaped the wrath of flames. Tossing it into the fire, I grit my teeth, hoping my frustration has been discarded along with the twig. *Nope…no such luck.*

Judd snickers, pulling his knees up and resting his forearms over them with his hands clasped between them.

"Well then, talk to her."

I look at him sarcastically, like he just proposed an all-time dumbass, award-winning suggestion that I knew he would.

"Yeah, right…let me race over and try that so she can tell me to piss off for the hundredth time."

He spits out another chuckle like this is funny. "Well, have you actually ever tried…I mean really tried?"

"What?!" The question floors me. "Of course I have. Did you not see me at the Halloween party? She went ballistic as soon as I said a word and I won't even go into the 'go to hell' look she gives me in class. Seriously, have you ever seen someone that can give a look that damn hateful." I sigh, looking at the roaring blaze. "It's pretty hot, actually," I quip back to myself more so, raising my brows and cocking my head to the side as I conjure up her glare. *Oh yeah, that is pretty hot.*

Judd shakes his head and laughs. "Yeah, pissed off looks pretty good on some girls, but a lot of good that'll do you. You should talk to her...like actually talk to her and maybe try listening instead of trying to glamour her with your quick wit and endless sarcasm."

Snickering at his evaluation of our run-ins, I notice the women making it back towards the fire armed with packages of hotdogs and the fixings for an old-fashion Boy Scout camp fire.

Watching her, a strange sense of dread creeps over me. I'm unsure of what to expect if we actually do talk. She has every right not to trust me; I wouldn't trust me if I were her.

"I'll try," I pause, studying her face from afar as she walks closer. *Damn, was she always this beautiful?* "But if she tears me a new one, expect me to drag your sex-addicted ass out of bed to kick it."

"Oh shit...I'm not agreeing to that, because I'm sure she'll eat you alive," Judd jokes and I grin, leaning my head back against my clasped hands.

"That she will." I smile, but on the inside I'm dying.

Not even Judd knows the whole story. I already betrayed her faith in me; I won't do it again. It was an act on impulse, but nonetheless, I screwed her over in one single minute, then my brother did the rest.

The rest of the evening carries on pretty smooth with the group in a sort of division; Abby, Piper and their hunks on one side and Alyssa, Judd, me and Skylar on the other. Thankfully, my brother is a no show.

So far the main topic across the fire has been football and makeup. I stay out of both subjects, tormented by playing with Skylar's thigh and gritting my teeth every time that jerk-off touches Piper's leg. Her comfort level with his grubby hands bothers me even more, but I'm not sure why. After what I saw this summer, I'm confident she is over any phobias she had with men. That's bittersweet for me. I in no way want her tortured for the rest of her life, but I thought I was the key to fixing it; she made me feel like I was anyway.

"I'm heading in, unless..." Skylar stands beside me, flirtatiously running her foot over my thigh.

I glance past her, not quite bothered by her public aggression, but curious. Piper stands swiftly, mumbling something to the others before jetting off across the parking lot. She doesn't once look back or look in my direction, but the way her arms swing at her sides and her feet stomp into the ground as if Mother Nature just pissed her the hell off, tells me that something is definitely under her skin. Dipping my face into a frown, I take a quick look at her "stud". A bit of anger festers inside of me with the thought that he did something inappropriate or without permission. I've sat here all night with them in perfect sight, and although I kept my focus away from her as much as possible, I don't see how he could have gotten something like that past me.

"Soooo..." Skylar draws out in a questioning tone as if she just asked me something, only I haven't a clue what.

"Huh?"

"Do you want company?"

I stand up in front of her as everyone else starts to disperse.

With a fleeting look towards the path on the other side of the property, I can no longer see Piper. My mind is distracted with where she went; all I want to do is chase her down and put Judd's advice to work.

"Ahh, no. I actually need to get to work super early on the heaters."

"Oh hey, you want me to join you in the morning?" Judd asks as him and Alyssa make their way around the once blazing fire that has been reduced to a pile of coals.

"Yeah, that'd be nice. Do I need to swing by and get your ass?"

Judd laughs as Skylar continues to stay in front of me, one hand on her hip and the other playing with her hair. I glance around again, over her shoulder, to the light at the shower house and then further down the path. Nothing.

"No please don't, because I know you won't knock and I'd like to wake up gracefully instead of to the sound of your mouth."

Alyssa giggles, hugging herself to him.

"Well you better wake up to the sound of your alarm, because I need you down there at 5am."

Judd gives a quick salute and takes off.

Skylar crinkles her nose with a goofy little smile, then spins around, deliberately shaking her ass as she walks off.

"Careful! I'm not ashamed to throw you down right here for four, five and six."

She slowly turns her head with a challenge in her eyes as she waves. Damn…if I wasn't so determined to put this whole thing between me and Piper behind me, I'd chase her ass back to the cabin and kidnap her for the night.

Once she's out of sight, and the faded camp fire has dulled to a quiet crackle with the sputter of a few spare moist sprigs of wood, I turn and look back at the shower house. My feet move beneath me hesitantly, as if I am being marched towards my own execution. What I'm going to say gets pushed to the back of my mind as I draw nearer to the dock and see nobody there. *Where the hell is she?* Knowing for certain that her return would not have escaped me, I amble further down the property, staying on the unlit path. The moon is hidden beneath a cluster of clouds in the sky, but peeks out every few minutes to barely light my way. As the soft, crumbly ground begins to glow, I pick up my pace and look up, secure in my footing.

After walking a good while and searching, a dark shape comes into view that I know all too well; I've made it to Grandpa's boat dock. I don't have the keys to any of the boats, no fishing supplies or even a jacket, but I still continue in on my quest. This is the only place that I would think she may have gone. I've never felt so driven to talk to her. Most of the time, I hold back out of fear of what all she will say to me and how shitty she could make me feel, but not tonight. Judd made a good point. I've never just listened when she starts in on her rants. Yeah, I try to talk, but I don't stop. I keep trying to get a word in to defend myself; to make sense of it.

Stepping onto the dock with a quiet knock of my boot against the wood surface, I stare forward, making out a small silhouette positioned on the edge, looking out to the water. *Just as I thought.* I take a deep breath and my heart stumbles, completely lost in my memories.

"Catching anything good?"

Sitting quietly with my feet swaying below the edge of the dock, the squeaky voice comes as a surprise. I turn my head, keeping my hands gripped to my fishing pole. Standing above me is the same girl I saw earlier today. Her black hair hangs in a mess over her bony shoulders and pale white skin. A ruffled brown swimsuit hangs around her neck, topped off by blue jean shorts with frayed white strings suspended along the entire circumference of her leg.

"Not much," I say, looking up through my eyelashes.

"I bet there's some big fish in there. What all do you do around here?"

Her question strikes me as odd given there is a lake to swim in, boats and jet skis to rent, a beach and docks to jump and fish off of.

"Pretty much this," I shrug.

"Oh...everyday?"

Now she's just being silly. "No, I mean, well yeah, I guess I do most days. Me and my brother go out on the boat and fish, but we go swimming too."

She glances over at the boats with a spark of excitement in her eyes.

"Can I go out on the boat sometime?"

With a cramp sneaking up in my hand, I shift my pole and loosen my grip as I stare at her surprised by her question. Those are Grandpa's boats, definitely not the ones they rent.

"*Those are my grandpas,*" I snap out before thinking about it. "*He doesn't let anyone rent these, but there's ones for rent at the first dock over by The Snack Shack.*"

Glancing back to the boat, her shoulders fall and she cocks her lips to one side as if she is biting the inside of her mouth.

"*But I could take you out in the boat sometime,*" I add, not wanting to hurt her feelings.

This ignites a huge grin as her face springs back to level me with a thankful expression.

"*Really? Ok...maybe later today?*"

I don't have much going on, but Grandpa won't let me take it out after dark. "*Ok,*" I nudge my shoulders up undecidedly. "*But not too late.*" I point at her with one hand before bringing it back to my pole.

Her lips curve into a wide grin showing off a mouth full of braces as she sticks her hand out between us. I look up, surprised to see a girl wanting to shake hands.

"*I'm Piper, by the way.*"

I snap my head back up to her face, a sense of excitement swallowing me up at her introduction. After years of bouncing back and forth from Army base to Army base and then even the last few years since I've been settled here, through it all, I've never found a friend. I've never had one. Sure, I've played with the other kids on base and talked to a couple in my class at school, but this...

I look back at her hand and a smile rises over my lips. My heart pounds and my fingers fumble to keep the grip on my pole as I release one hand and take hers in mine. Keeping in mind on how Dad always says that handshakes should be firm and authoritive, I tighten my grip, immediately noticing how soft her skin is compared to mine. With that in mind, I look back at her and move my hand up and down with a slightly less sturdy hold than I would normally have. I bet she's more fragile than a boy; besides, Dad will never know.

"*Hi, I'm Evan.*"

Her smile grows and so does mine with the thought of having a fish-

ing buddy or someone to dunk into the lake. She takes a seat as if invited and even though there is a sign on the dock that states this is private property I don't say a thing. If she hadn't sat, I would have asked her to.

Staring over at me, I draw my attention back to the lake water and the small colorful bobber that floats along the surface with a peaceful solitude coming over me. Just like that, she becomes my best friend; my only friend; someone whose face I look forward to seeing each summer and every single day she's out here. If I go out in the boat, she goes out. If I go for a swim, she comes with me. I can't take a breath without her by my side. Through pretend voyages to sea, made up shark infested waters that we can't escape and endless nights roasting marshmallows, we play together, smile together, laugh together and never go anywhere apart. We're inseparable; every single breath she breathes with me.

Glancing to the side where I hold tight to the dock, I see the bright orange sign that under normal light reads 'Private Property'. The subtle moonlight and dark night has turned it to a blurred black square, but I can still make it out; I know it's there. My hand squeezes at the rough barn wood post that houses the entrance of the boat dock and I take a deep breath of courage. She doesn't turn and may not even be aware of my presence, but she will soon enough.

With shaky footsteps, I make a move to get closer to her. About twenty paces separate us and with each footfall, a massive wad of anxiety expands in my stomach and up into my throat, making me wonder if I'll even be able to speak when I get there. Her head barely turns and I stop; I freeze. She knows I'm here. But then she turns forward again, the silence screaming at me to say something; anything.

"What do you want, Evan?"

The sudden sound of her voice startles me and I swear every frog and insect within twenty miles of this property suddenly hushed or maybe her icy tone blew my hearing to an oblivion.

I open my mouth, but nothing comes out. Swinging her head around with her hand placed behind her, she glares at me. I can't even see the features of her face, but I can feel the fierceness in her stare. It's slicing through me like a rusty old knife with a colossal amount of force at the blade.

"Well?"

Her arms rise over her chest as they always do and I struggle to find something to say. *Why the hell didn't I think this through?* Judd said to listen, but I'm no dumbass. I know now is not the time to go silent. My chest rises as I suck in a deep soothing breath then release it, letting all wavering thoughts out with it.

"I thought we could talk," I throw it out there plain and simple, and prepare to hold on for dear life.

"What!" she blusters, in an outraged tone like this is the first time I've said a word to her in the past few years. *This is it. This is when I need to keep my mouth shut and listen even though it's pure instinct for me to speak up.*

"Why do you think I would have anything to say to you?" she spits out.

I have no doubt if I could see her in plain sight, her top lip is probably curled up leaving a crease at each side of her nose like it usually did when she was disgusted at something.

I press my lips together to hold my tongue and wait, but she says nothing. *Shit…I wasn't prepared for this. Damn it to hell, did Abby give her the same damn advice or something? Freaking figures.*

I muster up a few more civil words, refusing to turn this into a battle of *how could you* versus *I didn't do it on purpose.*

"Piper, I just wanted to sit and talk." I gulp down my fear of this escalating once again. "…calmly."

Through the darkness, a quick intake of air catches my attention so I take a step forward, confident that maybe the hurricane has done its damage and moved on. She has to know every single interaction we've had this past year has torn into me and deepened the never-healing wound in my soul.

"Evan, just go away." The bitterness in her tone has faded, leaving a defeated hint of exhaustion from any sort of communication between us.

Conflicted, I shift from foot to foot, widen my eyes and bite my lips between my teeth in thought. Above all, I do not want to argue when she says no, or stop, or go away, but leaving will just keep this barrier between us and she is not the only one exhausted. I'm tired of it being this way. She was my best friend; the only one I ever gave my heart to.

"Would you just talk to me?" I say gently, hoping she can hear the urgency and distress in my voice.

"Talk to you? You're the last person I want to talk to," she belts out.

I flinch back, hating the animosity that she exhibits like I did that to her. I betrayed her, yeah, but I am not the villain here.

"Stop making me the enemy," I raise my voice mistakenly.

That's all it takes to elevate the whole thing. Piper shoots up to stand, stomping across the rickety boards till she is only a few feet in front of me with her hands defiantly at her hips and her chin rose up confidently.

"Me?! Oh, you did that yourself, Evan, or don't you remember?" she slams me with the exact thing I knew she would. *Dammit!* "Because if you don't, I sure can remind you."

I deserve for her to say all of this to me. I deserve for her to hate me and I deserve for her to never speak to me again, but I can't keep my mouth shut. Frustration on our lack of being able to just talk courses through me and elevates my voice to a pissed off tone.

"Of course I remember, because you won't ever let me forget! Don't you believe in forgiveness, because maybe if you would calm down…just once…maybe…just maybe, we could put this behind us."

"Forgiveness!! Were you even there? Do you know what that did to me? Because I will never forget and I have a hard time forgiving that!"

I stop for a minute and blow out a monstrous wind of anger before this blows up into a bloodbath. *I hate fighting with her. I hate that she hates me. I miss her. God, I miss her.* A whole chunk of my heart falls with that observation as I look at her figure under the dark canopied dock. Her small frame is straight as a board with her arms still at her side as if she's a super hero. I glance at her from head to toe and back, and my whole body aches for her.

Keeping bitterness that could be misconstrued as hatred out of my tone, I speak up remaining stern and exactly how I've always been with her; completely myself.

"Damn it, Piper...I've said I was sorry and I know that doesn't take away what happened, but I didn't mean..."

"Wait...don't even go there. Don't even claim that you didn't mean to tell him!"

I take another guzzle of air, trying to remain calm, but also wanting to let her talk.

"You hurt me! No...no...you killed me!" she shouts it out and if words could kill, those would have me laying on the boat dock with my blood spilling between the boards into the murky waters below.

"You betrayed me. You were the only one I trusted...the only one. I counted on you..." she stops talking and I can feel her eyes on me. They pin me down and keep me from running away from the guilt. I look down, too ashamed to let her see my face. "I thought you..." she pauses and my head snaps up with what she's thinking. "You said that you...you know what? It doesn't matter what you said, because you took it back the second you told your brother. I should have known it was all a joke to you."

Now this I cannot stand here and listen to. "What?! You know how I felt about you back then?"

"Felt about me?! Oh please! Go tell that to one of those bimbos that you take home on the weekends, or wait...maybe Skylar is the flavor of the week!"

Whoa, if it didn't strike me as pure jealousy, I'd walk away from this conversation and say screw putting this behind us.

She goes on with her rant and I stand quietly, listening as I was told to do. *Judd, you owe me!*

"Besides, I was far from someone that guys pined over, Evan! What was it that made you want me the most...my flat chest..."

I glance down, unable to make out her body in the darkness but know damn well that it is no longer flat. Not by a mile.

"...or maybe it was my crooked smile covered in colored rubber bands..."

I think back to the times around the camp fire this summer when she would laugh. The image is clear in my head, letting me know that I was watching her much more than I thought; so many times more than I should have.

"Oh, maybe it was the way I flinched anytime anyone laid their hand on my back or brushed against my hips. Was it maybe that, that made me so appealing?" She quiets, probably searching for more ways to put herself down, but I am not going to stand for it.

"Would you shut up and listen to me." My stomach churns, talking to her like that, but she needs to stop, and the only way to do that is a quick jolt. I've never spoken to her like this. "I didn't care about all that. Maybe that is what you saw when you looked in the mirror, but that's not what I saw...that's never what I saw. I never gave a damn about all that bullshit, because all I saw was you." I think for a minute about when I first saw her this summer, how she had colored her hair from the jet black locks that I was used to. How when the sun hit her hair, how it took on a cherry red tone. How her boobs look like they've been altered to twice their size. I stop and second think that. *That's not so bad after all.* "Actually, I think I liked you better with the braces and flat chest. At least you weren't afraid to let me touch you back then."

"That's because I trusted you!" she screams and I just know the entire camp ground heard her. "And look where that got me! The laughing stock of Rosemore High! I had to switch schools because of you or do you not remember that either! I had to move. My parents got divorced."

I gasp, bringing my hand up to my mouth. I knew she moved and I knew she changed schools, but I've never understood it. How could it be because of me? To get away from me, I always assumed, but that always seemed so drastic. Her parent's getting a divorce is new information, and I desperately need her to explain what I did to contribute to that.

"No, I didn't know that or well, I knew you left, but I never understood why. Did you hate me that much? Why didn't you just come scream at me back then or kick me in the nuts or pull my pants down in the cafeteria so everyone could make fun of me?" The corners of my mouth tick with a smile, hoping I can get a laugh out of her; I always could before.

Her voice softens, "I'm tired." Dropping her hands, she walks past me and my first instinct is to grab her.

My hand rises and, it's only centimeters away from touching her for the first time in forever, but I drop it to my side and speak, needing to reach her.

"Piper...please. Can we just talk?"

She turns and faces me and all that races through my mind is how bad I want to see her face; to see if this has made a dent; if we have possibly passed the threshold of anger and hate.

"Just leave me alone."

She spins around, but this time I obey her request and watch her walk away.

Forget

Piper

HOW COULD I JUST WALK *away like that? I didn't even give him a chance!* I lie in bed completely still and feel the mattress shift. Turning slightly, I see Abby get up and walk to the door.

"Where you going?" I whisper, but I already know.

She lets out a soft laugh and pulls the door open before slipping through. "Go back to bed." She shuts the door quietly behind her. I really should have just given this bedroom to Hayden and her rather than thinking the girls would stay in here.

"Skylar," I whisper shout into the darkness. *No response. Hmmm.*

Crushing my head back into the fluffy pillow, soft giggles reach my ears from the front room. I grab up a ball of fabric in my fist and pull the pillow out from under my head, shoving it on top to drown out the noise, or potentially suffocate myself in the process.

Inhaling a deep relaxing breath, I close my eyes again and try my best not to think of Evan; to not dwell on all the angry words we said earlier. Being mad at each other never used to be one of our strong suits; we would get in friendly little spats when we were younger, but his obnoxious smirk and charming wit would no doubt win me over with just a few smart aleck words he would throw together on a whim.

My eyes spring open at the sudden whine of the bedroom door, as though someone just came in. I loosen the weight of my hand from pushing the fabric over my ears and listen. Soft footsteps along with the quiet rustling of fabric rise into the air, letting me know Abby is retreating back to bed before things get too out of hand. Chris has been sleeping in the living area too, and Abby had just mentioned earlier how she would prefer not to have an audience when Hayden and her get frisky. Dropping my hand back over the pillow above my head, I resume my comfortable position curled up on my side with my knees bent and my hip, shoulder and head digging into the mattress.

"Piper, you awake?"

A wave of nausea rolls through me, making my whole body vibrate and chills to spiral down my spine. I know the voice, but nonetheless I become deadly still, fear of the past, of the unexpected…possibly even the expected…paralyzing me. My tongue knots in my mouth and my throat closes in as a soft touch runs over my hip. *Breathe, breathe.*

I suck in…

and in…

and in…

and in again and again, not ever feeling oxygen reach my airways. *Breathe, breathe* echoes in my mind as if someone is saying those very words to me.

"Piper…Piper…"

"Piper…" Trent says in the darkness.

A smile creeps over my face as I hear him walk across the living room. I turn my head slightly in the direction of his cot which is slid over to the corner of the living room. The lumpy hide-away mattress shifts with his weight and a sudden draft moves over my body as if the covers have been lifted.

"You awake?"

My smile drops and I nod slowly as if he can see me. Why is he getting into my bed? Mom and Dad crashed hours ago to the back room. Trent and I shut off the TV a few hours later and went to bed, but as I flicked off the living room lamp he looked perfectly tucked into his sleeping quarters. Maybe he had a dream?

"Hey..." he softly says, placing a hand under the covers along my hip.

I tense up and take in a huge gulp of air, baffled and suddenly scared. His hand drops and the mattress shifts, instantly allowing me to let out the breath I was holding and relax my whole body. I move my head to the side, not enough for him to notice, I hope, but curious at the muffled sound that I now hear only inches away; a tearing like paper being ripped. I stop any movement, clueless but still knowing he is beside me. A strong plastic-sort-of-smell reaches my nostrils and I'm even more baffled. Why is he in my bed? Something about it all doesn't seem appropriate, making my insides flip and spin in panic.

The mattress moves beneath me, jostling about until his hand lands gently along my hip again with his body pressed against my back. He pushes his stomach and chest against me harder, aligning himself with me and I freeze, noticing things I shouldn't. My chest pulses in and out with each breath as I fear what is happening. Do I get up and run? Do I scream? Do I ask him what he's doing?

"Hey...you awake?" he says in his soft sweet voice that he usually uses when he talks to me as if I am just a kid and so much younger than him, when I'm only three years beneath him in school.

"I'm sleeping." I squeak out, my entire body reeled so tight in terror.

His hand moves slowly from my barely developed hips to my legs and forward. I squeeze my eyes shut; not understanding, yet somewhat comprehending what is going on. My eyes seal closed so tight that I fear the tears welling up may have nowhere to go, but they fall anyway, seeping through somehow one after another as pain slices through me and makes me gasp.

"Shhhh...it's ok. I won't hurt you, I promise," he whispers against my ear through thick, hot breaths that make the skin on my neck clammy

and dirty.

My mind fogs over at his words. You are hurting me. Stop, please stop, but the words are lodged in my mouth, on the tip of my tongue and ready to jump off, but they won't budge.

Stop, please stop. My head is on a constant repeat, but all vocabulary I have learned in the past nearly thirteen years of my life are lost. My shoulders shudder and my chest heaves in and out and a strangled cry reaches my ear from under the pillow as I am jostled around. My hands ball into fists and although I want to use them to slap him away and stop him, I'm scared; I don't know what to do. The fabric drifts away from my face and his head falls against my shoulder. I remain still; so still with all movement from him completely ceased and the unbearable odor of rubber still lingering in the air.

"I'm so sorry," his words pierce my eardrums, but I still cannot move, think, feel or comprehend why this happened to me; why he would do this. "I'm so so sorry," he breathes through a muffled sob. "I shouldn't have done that...it's just, I thought that's what..." the bed shifts beside me as I remain frozen in shock.

Barely glancing over my shoulder as the blankets tug and shuffle around me, I make out Trent's shadow settling at the edge of the bed. His head hangs down as quiet sniffles fill the air.

"I'm so sorry. I didn't mean..." his voice trembles, matching the vibrations of my own.

My eyes glaze over, blurring his already barely recognizable silhouette lit only by the presence of a full moon shining through the window in the kitchen. I suck in a strangled breath and drop my head back to the pillow, slowly pulling my knees to my chest. My bikini bottom slides further down on my left hip and the untied strings tickle at my skin. Quickly lowering one hand to pull it up, I grip the fabric in my fist as another stream of tears dampen the pillow.

Trent gasps as the bed shifts again, making my heart plummet and my breathing go into an overactive frenzy. My head whirls, but I am completely frozen once again except for the rapid motion of my chest, trying to keep up with my quick intakes of air. Is he going to do it again? Fear grips every inch of my body and a strange drowsiness engulfs me. In the already barely lit room, blurred black dots bleed into my vision and a dizziness that feels as if I stood up too fast swarms in my head. My chest sinks in on a breath and another and another, making it impossible to exhale.

"Piper..."

Slowly tugging my eyes open, the cool, clammy touch of a hand on my shoulder along with Trent's whispers, once again way too close for comfort, resigns my efforts of being calm and gentle as a rush of adrenaline kicks in and catapults me to my feet. My tee shirt falls around my body automatically as I spin around to face him. He's crouched at the edge of the bed again and for the life of me, I cannot place when he moved back beside me. A throbbing sensation drums at the back of my head as I take a huge intake of air.

"Are you ok?"

He reaches his hand out towards me and my heart jumps into my throat as I jolt backwards, wrapping my arms around my waist as if they can make me invisible. I wish they could.

"Oh God, I'm so sorry. Are you..." he whispers with an unusual tone to his voice; compassion or sadness maybe.

The strings of my swimsuit bottom dangle loose, grazing my thigh and nearly making me jump again. I glance down and quickly grip the hem of my shirt to ensure that I am covered. My suit slides at the other hip, but still stays held up. I lay one hand along that hip to keep it in place, but am too scared to pull the other side up; too afraid that my shirt will rise with the action and force his attention to my body. I look up quickly, panicked that he could grab me, tug me back to the bed or touch me again, but as my eyes land back on him I see that he hasn't moved. His hand has dropped to the bed along with his gaze.

My brows knit and my heart grips as I watch him, still unable to speak, unable to piece together anything that has happened, unable and absolutely unwilling to believe any of it. Why? I want to say it; I want to, but my lips have cemented closed and I have no doubt if they could open that I would no longer recognize my own voice.

"You..." his voice startles me and I grasp my suit and step back as a strangled sob fills the air.

I look down quickly, tugging the hem of my shirt down more as if I can make it longer, but I soon realize the cry did not come from me. In fact, no tears fall; I'm in shock, stunned and silent.

Trent moves and I snap my head up to see him looking right at my face. Shadows from the outside trees dance across his face, and it's then that I can make out the pain in his expression. The soft playful happiness he usually carries around is gone. It's replaced with torment and grief, possibly even shame or remorse. I hate him.

"You passed out I think or fell asleep..."

This confuses me. My brows dip lower and I snarl my lip, a tightness forming over the bridge of my nose as it crinkles with my glare.

"A while ago," he elaborates as if he can read my thoughts. "You were breathing so heavy and fast and then you just stopped. I thought you were dead. I thought maybe I..."

His hand pulls back up in a stretch to reach for me. I cock my head back and my eyebrows dart up as my eyes widen.

"Don't touch me," I hiss out before I can think.

He gasps. "I'm sorry. Please," his words come out in a raspy plea. "I just thought that maybe," he pauses, looking down in shame.

He should be ashamed. Venom courses through me and it's the first time in my life that I've felt such a foreign emotion; something so cold and vicious, but it surrounds me, it sinks through my skin and rushes through my veins, filling my heart and mind with one thought. I hate him.

"I thought that maybe it would feel different..." he looks back up at me and my heart stops. The last thing I want to feel is the pain that is in his voice. "I thought with you, it might feel..."

I suck in a startled breath and spin around, not wanting to listen; sickened by what he wants to feel or hoped to feel. Flying to the door, I don't wait, I don't even grab for my shorts; I just run, grabbing the ties that brush across my leg into my hand so that my suit doesn't fall to my ankles.

My hand falls on the door knob and I tug at it before looking back. I stumble forward when I'm met with zero give and quickly see the deadbolt that Dad installed last summer is twisted sideways; locked. My fingers fumble clumsily as if I am trying to escape from a crazed serial killer; escape is absolute. I snap it to the side and fling the door open with such force that it thuds against the wall. I don't even care if Mom and Dad wake up, as long as I am gone.

"Piper, wait," Trent whispers as the mattress creaks behind me. "Piper..."

I run out the door, my feet shaky and unstable, my mind a wreck of images and sounds that I cannot shove aside and my body still crawls with the heat of his breaths on my neck and the touch of his hand on my hip.

I want to forget that it ever happened.

Forget how it felt; erase every dirty detail of this night.

Just forget it all.

Still Here

Evan

ONCE BACK INSIDE MY COZY little hideaway, I drag myself towards my bed with a shiver. My eyes skim over my thick comforter before settling on the small metal radiator between the bed and table. Running my hand a few inches above it, I let out a frustrated breath and drop my hand onto the smooth surface. *Great.* It's warm, but no doubt it is going out. Squatting down onto the balls of my feet, I turn the heating knob just a couple of notches to high and hope that it starts cranking out some heat soon. *I hate being cold. I may not complain about much, but I am a pansy when it comes to cold weather.*

Clasping the fabric of my shirt at the back of my neck, I pull it off in one swift motion and quickly grab the sweatshirt that's wadded up at the bottom of my bed. After pulling on an old pair of gym pants, I slide under the warmth of my blankets and settle in for the night with the springs in my worn out mattress digging into my back. I'm due for a new one, but this bed holds way too many memories; carefree, adolescent fun along with more intimate moments when I got older.

Reaching behind my head, my stomach tightens as I lift my upper body until I find the only thing I have left from all those memories. I pull out a picture of Piper that I've held onto since the second she gave it to me back in the ninth grade. At the time, it seemed like such a small deed, exchanging pictures, but now as I look back, I remember the huge smile she had on her face as she handed it over. I can still see the nervousness in her eyes as I grabbed it and then handed back one of me. Her skipping away with my picture in her hand should have told me right then how much that little gesture did and how she felt about me. Nonetheless, her picture went up beside my bed that night and has remained there, up until earlier today at least.

Flipping my finger along the dog-eared edge that bent one time or another from my excessive obsession of looking at it, I think over everything that was said earlier. Not a damn thing was resolved and nothing was put behind us, but the hostility in her voice dulled; it was drowned out by something else. *Is it even possible that she has missed me too?*

Quickly dismissing that thought, I slide the picture back to its normal resting place in a seam on the wall, careful to not bend or damage it any more. I'm sure it's the last picture I'll have of her. Reaching up, I turn off the light above my head and twist to get more comfortable, sliding one hand under the pillow and the other resting above it in front of my face. Sliding my eyes closed, I breathe out slowly, releasing any unsettling thoughts and worries until my mind is empty and focused on absolutely nothing.

Tap…Tap.

My eyes spring open at the unexpected disruption and my heart slams in my chest with a windstorm of nostalgia. Up on my sock feet, I trip over my shoes and stumble to catch myself with one thing in my head, as if I shut my eyes and slipped into a time warp; it's her. Her presence screams my name. *Maybe she wants to talk some more.*

My head flips through images of her the first time she ever set foot on the other side of this door; one time of many following that night. Once she nervously came inside, I noticed her scraped up knees and puffy eyes, and knew something was off about her visit; not only because it was the middle of the night either. The need to ask her what was wrong burned through me, but something about her frightened eyes told me to leave it alone. Instead, I chose to try and make her laugh. I know that's always what I need when I get in a fight with Dad and brother, so I figured it was worth a try.

My legs fly to the door and my hand falls to the knob with an urgent force as I fling it open, but as soon as I look up, all my hopes fade and all thoughts of revisiting one of those sacred memories we shared are shattered.

"Hey you," Skylar's voice hums in a flirty tone.

Unfortunately, with my head and heart in a different place, this visit comes as an unexpected surprise that borders on annoying and nearly intrusive, at no fault of hers at all.

"Hey," I draw out then look around inside my camper, suddenly feeling awkward at having her here. The same feeling crept over me earlier, but I forced it from the surface of my mind and shoved it down deep to where it may never haunt me again. I was wrong; Piper will always be with me. "What's up?" I ask nonchalantly, still blocking the doorway like a jackass.

She huffs out a laugh and looks around me with her eyebrows arched. "Well, can I come in?"

I instantly look at my wrist like I actually have a watch wrapped around it; hell I don't even think I own one.

"You know what…" *What the hell are you doing? Just invite her in.* My heart and head wage a war that simply should not even be happening. In the end, my head gives up. "It's late." *Lame excuse for turning down a booty call. What am I doing?*

Skylar's hands instantly shoot to her hips like she has them on autopilot for when idiots like me piss her off.

"Late?" she says innocently with a hint of hurt. "I just thought you might want some company, so I…"

Panicked, I bounce down the stairs and let the door slip shut behind me. "Company sounds good. I was actually feeling a bit antsy and thought I'd go for a little stroll. Hang on." In two seconds flat, I spin on my feet, fly inside and throw my phone into my back pocket and hastily shove my feet into my sneakers without untying them before rushing back out to finish up damage control. "I have an early start in the morning, working on those heaters and all, but how about I walk you back to the cabin?"

In the darkness, I can barely make out the skepticism in her glare, but then she relaxes with a soft laugh. For all I know she may think I have some mystery chick shacked up inside.

Her hands fall and she hops over to my side, bumping her shoulder against mine playfully.

"Ok…I guess you talked me into it. Rain check on the visit I suppose?"

I nod, lazily shoving my hands into my side pockets with a shiver. *I hate this cold ass weather.* Clearly reading my mind, Skylar nuzzles to my side with the heat of her hand burning clear through my thick sweatshirt.

"Rain check sounds good. I figured everyone would be passed out over your way." I nudge my head towards Piper's cabin. "Couldn't sleep? Or are you just so needy for all this?" I shift my hips forward with a smirk and she busts out in a laugh.

"Well, of course, I'm always needy for that, but no…they were just getting a little too rowdy and noisy so I said screw this."

Knitting my eyebrows in concern, I snap my head over to look at her. "Rowdy? Did someone get in a fight?"

Breaking into a cough sort of laugh, she pulls closer to my side. "Ahhh, I wouldn't call that a fight, unless it's the making up after one."

My eyes widen as we draw nearer to the cabin and a spark of anger and fury bolts through my veins.

"Who?!" I snap.

"What do you mean who? Everyone except me of course. Single girl here…" She holds her ring finger up, twirling it in the air. "Remember? Kind of an awkward situation staying in a cabin with couples. I mean, who wants to listen to a whole bunch of huffing and puffing from another room and not have…"

"Wait! You mean Piper is…" my voice elevates right as my phone rings. *Who the hell is calling me at this hour?*

Skylar remains quiet as I jerk it out with a frown cemented across my face. Right about now I feel like saying to hell with being out here. I do not need to know when she is so carelessly getting it on with someone else. I know it's jealousy, but damn it pisses me off to know how scarred she was back when we were together and how much effort it was to just hold hands with her. Now, I guess she just hops in bed with whoever.

"Hello," I spit out, not even bothering to look at the screen before answering.

"Evan…" Abby's frightened voice immediately has me on alert and quickening my pace to the door of their cabin.

"What's wrong?"

Skylar follows beside me, saying something, but I'm too focused in on Abby on the other end of the phone.

"It's Piper. She had one of her spells. I know you know what I'm talking about because she told me a long time ago that you always knew how she got and you knew how to pull her out of it when she would…"

Adrenaline races through my body and has me kicking up gravel as my feet pound the ground to get to her side. I cannot even say anything as Abby rambles on. Any amount of thought processing halts, my heart pumps frantically in my chest and the moisture in my mouth dries up, leaving a lump lodged in my throat.

The grip I have on the phone increases to a constricting hold of anger, rage, pain and dread. My hand lands on the handle to the cabin and I fling it open without so much as an invitation to come inside. I immediately search the room, a collage of sounds meeting my ears in an array of confusion.

"I don't know…I don't know…I didn't even touch her!" Chris shouts out in the corner of the living room. "I just don't know what happened..."

"Did you scare her or..." Hayden asks, sounding just as freaked as Chris.

"I don't know...I have no clue what happened like I said."

My legs steer directly in Chris' direction as my fists ball together, one still clasping the phone.

"Evan!" Abby yells and after a quick warning look at Chris and Hayden, I turn and bolt into the back bedroom to find Piper lying on the bed motionless.

The sheets are scattered about beside her and that alone makes all the feeling drain from my body until I'm damn near numb except for the thundering of my heart. She lies on her side with her blanket drawn up to her chin and her knees pulled up in a fetal position beneath the covers.

"Evan," Abby calls out, but my attention is set dead ahead as my feet slam against the wood floor in a frantic pace to get to her side. "I don't know what happened. All I know is Chris said..." My jaw tenses as she says his name. Abby rambles on, her voice trembling, "...that she passed out or something and I remembered her telling me that you..."

I snap my head to Abby, hoping she'll just stop as I shove my phone in my pocket and slide onto the edge of the bed. Abby quiets, pressing her lips together and stepping forward. I look back down to Piper, my heart shattering at how young she looks; like a child that had their innocence ripped away from them in a sick and twisted way by someone they thought they could trust. A lump forms in my throat as I lean down and try to form words.

"Pi..." I clear my throat, placing my hand gently on her cheek. "Piper?" I whisper softly, not wanting to startle her in any way. No matter how timid and sweet she looks, I know she has fight in her and she may very well wake up swinging. When she sees it's me, she may start throwing punches regardless. "Piper." I slide my hand over her cheek to her shoulder and down to her upper arm, keeping my touch light and on the exterior of the covers. "Piper, baby, wake up."

My brows dip as I say words that I haven't said in so long, yet it seems like it was only days ago that I was this close to her; only minutes ago when I last had to face this with her.

I move my face closer, only inches from her mouth. Flicking my eyes down to her lips, I get a knot in my stomach thinking selfish thoughts I should not be thinking at a time they most definitely should not surface.

"Piper..."

I nudge her again, only this time she intakes a mouthful of air and relaxes her body, sending a wave of relief through me. My chest aches just looking at her, being this close yet knowing I have to hold back. Dropping just a bit of my hesitation, I take her face in my hands, softly, and lean down, placing my forehead to hers so I can reach her; reach inside and pull her out of this like I always used to.

"Baby, wake up..." I whisper, hardly able to hear my own words. "Breathe with me. You remember...I breathe, you breathe." Everything I have held deep down crashes against the walls of my chest with each word. "Come on Piper, open your eyes. Take another breath and look at me."

Her eyelashes flutter and she gasps in a quick gulp of air. Pulling my head back slightly, I stare down at her, gently running the edge of my thumb over her cheek bone, over and over again. A smile ticks at the corner of my lips as her eyes slowly begin to open. These episodes have always scared me. This one is a walk in the park compared to some I've seen her have and those were from when I would get too close to her or touch her in a way that took her back. An anger burns in me with the thought of what triggered this particular one.

"Evan," Piper says in a breathy whisper with her eyes only half open.

"Hey, yeah...I'm here. Are you ok?" I lean in close to her face again; so close that I can make out the flecks of violet in her deep dark brown eyes as she opens them wider.

"Hi," she mumbles in a sleepy tone with her lips slightly curving into a smile.

I want to leap up and take her in my arms; bounce up and down with my hands in the air like a prize fight champion, and flip off any guy that's ever made advances towards her, all at the same time. Just as my heart slams in my chest in celebration, her face twists into shock with her eyes wide and she quickly slides out of my hold, back against the headboard. All the hopes and wishes that I've carried around for years where she is concerned take an immediate free-fall from the up-hill climb it was finally on.

"Evan, what the hell are you…"

"Whoa, whoa…I'm just here to help," I point one hand towards Abby, standing defenseless by the bed and the other hand I hold up, trying to calm her from an explosion I feared may happen at the sight of me. "Abby said you had blacked out and I just thought…"

Piper's eyes go wild and she snaps her head around to look at Abby. I follow Piper's gaze and given any other circumstances, I'd probably drop to the floor rolling in a fit of laughter over the completely terrified look on Abby's face. Her wide eyes dart from me to Piper as she opens her mouth. With Abby's feisty attitude and quick wit, for a blonde any-ways, I had always thought she was damn near made of steel.

"Wait…I only called him because you had said that he had helped you through this sort of thing before." She looks back to me in a silent plea for help to make Piper understand.

Her words surprise me a little, just the same as when she men-tioned it earlier on the phone. Even though Abby and Piper have been BFF's since they were nearly in diapers, I thought for sure that what had happened to her years ago was something she'd never tell a soul; well except me and I made sure to screw that up.

Slapping my hand across my forehead and regretting even bring-ing her into this, I turn my sight to Piper who is still focused on Abby. Her eyes are hooded over by drawn down brows and her face a scorn-ful mask that could possibly make someone roll over in their grave. *I always hated when I got that glare. That is the exact look Grandpa always warned me about when he'd say, "Son, if a woman ever gives you 'the look', either roll over and play dead, get ready for the doghouse or go fetch whatever the hell bone she throws at you."*

"Piper..." She immediately flicks her deep dark eyes on me. *Oh hell.* "Abby was just worried. She thought I could wake you up, because obviously she is aware of the situation and how you get." I keep all sarcasm and defeat out of my voice, unable to meet her eyes as I stare past her at the headboard.

"I'm fine!" she spits out, pulling the sheet to her chest, tighter as if I'm someone that would take advantage of her or even hurt her.

That act alone rips my chest wide open and leaves my heart exposed, bleeding and barely beating. *I'd never hurt her. Dammit, she knows that.*

Clamping my jaw, I slowly grind my teeth and stare right into her eyes, wanting nothing more than to reach out and loosen the defensive hold she has on the barrier she's placed between us. She looks back, penetrating every thread of my soul with that look alone. This is the one thing she has always had over me. If she wanted something, was hurt or scared, or even had the slightest hesitation in talking to me, one look is all it took; I'd know exactly what to do, what she needed to make anything better. This look...

God, that look is my undoing.

Her eyes aren't ice cold as they have been the last several years when I've been fortunate enough to be able to look into them. They are emotionless, telling me to keep my distance. They reflect all the hurt I caused her, displaying the deceit that a tiny slip of the mouth can create in a person that you would give absolutely anything for. She stares at me with the eyes that used to say I was everything, but now I'm just another guy she doesn't trust. *Did I really lose her for good?* I relax my jaw and let the defeat course through me, letting out a deep beaten down sigh as I look down.

"Piper, I just..." I start, then pause remembering that Abby is only ten feet away. I'm sure she knows the whole story, but the last thing I want is a bunch of witnesses when I bare my soul.

"Oh wow…Ummm…maaaaybeeee…I should go…you know…I can just make myself…" Abby rambles, but is interrupted as the covers shuffle in front of me and I see movement from Piper.

I glance back up and watch as she quickly motions with one finger held up to Abby. "You don't have to leave." She looks back at me and meets my eyes, the pace of my heart kicking up in dread, hope and fear all jammed together causing it to verge nearer and nearer to exploding. "Evan, I said I am fine. You really should not have come. I don't need your help…anymore." She emphasizes the last word, a method of shoving the knife in so damn deep that my heart may just bleed out right in front of her.

Gulping, I rock my head in a quick repeated nod, a little pissed off that I even took the time to give a shit and more than anything wanting to march right out to the living room, smash my fist right into her arrogant boyfriend's face and then go dive into the ice cold lake to cool off.

"Yeah, ok," I say, pressing my lips together to keep from saying anything I may regret. *How can someone go from staring into the eyes of someone who he always thought would be his future, with his heart wide open, to being dismissed like some stranger that never mattered?*

Abby's feet make a gentle tapping noise as she moves beside the bed. "Piper, I called him. He wouldn't have come if I hadn't called him. I just thought it would help…I mean you were unconscious and I was scared. Chris was scared to death…he had no idea what happened." She points behind her towards the living room and I grit my teeth. Not helping my desire to kick the living shit out of his don't-know-how-to-keep-his-hands-to-himself ass.

"It's fine, Abby. I'm not mad…I just want to be alone."

"Just don't be mad at him. Be mad at me if you want to, but Evan only helped. He woke you up," Abby pleads in a compassionate tone.

Tilting my head to the side, I look her way giving her a half smile with my lips pulled to one side to relay my appreciation. I look back at

Piper with my hands flat on the bed, ready to jump up and go.

"I just want to be alone," Piper announces, emotion cracking her voice and automatically tugging at my heart.

I don't do what I want.

I ignore every ounce of my body that is programmed to respond to the desperation in her tone. Instead, I stand, shoving my hands into my jean pockets and then pause by the bed.

"Piper, just let us help…"

"I just want to be alone! Just leave!" she calls out, a hint of anger taking over her usual sweet and calm demeanor. "Please…" a cry breaks through the wall she's putting up at this very moment, but I listen.

Moving one foot in front of the other, I do as she says, but then stop right before passing through the doorframe. Closing my eyes for a split second as I feel her gaze burning through my skull, I decide screw it; *what do I have to lose?* I spin around on my heels to face her, Abby nearly colliding into me.

"Oh, sorry…" She steps aside, but also pauses, looking at me in question.

I don't say a word, although what I have to say is on the tip of my tongue, lodged there.

"Leave me alone, please!" she fires back at me.

"Evan, let's go. I think Piper needs to be alone for a minute."

Abby nudges at my sleeve, still standing beside me, but I can't move my eyes from Piper. We're locked in a stare-off, my heart hammering and my mouth itching to spit out the words. She stares back, a look of defiance, determined to stand her ground.

Clearing my throat, I swallow down all my expectations and hope that she can take what I'm saying at face value, even though it has more meaning than anyone else could ever imagine.

"I'll leave," I say in a steady tone, barely loud enough for her to hear across the room. "But I'm still here…" I pause, curious if this will even sink in. "I've always been here…all along."

Open my heart

Piper

EVAN WALKS OUT THE DOOR, and although everything inside of me is screaming for him to stay, for him to help me take my next breath like he used to, I let him walk away. The look in his eyes when he said those last words drop my heart into my stomach, but even that can't overpower the tainted, dirty feelings that those memories brought over me. Trent's touch still creeps across my skin, his words echo in my head, and it has always made me view the act of intimacy in a negative, unappealing way.

Looking back towards the door, which luckily Abby shut behind her, the muffled voices of my friends rise into the air and let me know that I am not dreaming. I am not lying on that old hideaway bed in the dark, praying for it to just be over; I am here. I'm in the present, grown up, in control of what happens to me and no longer a measly little girl that cannot muster up the courage to scream *stop*.

Lifting my chin and rising away from the headboard, those thoughts settle into my soul, filling me with a renewed strength and confidence. I can do this; I can move past it all. I relax my shoulder and slowly slip my feet out from under the covers until they are barely dangling above the floor. A creak startles me and nearly has me flinging the covers over my head and hiding like a little kid afraid of the dark. I look up and see Chris peek in.

"Knock, knock…ok if I come in?" he asks in a quiet tone, while pushing the door open further, not even waiting for a response.

Do I say no? Does it even matter? I want to tell him to go away; I want everyone to go away, but the last thing I want is a cabin full of people or any type of witnesses to my insanity. Knowing Chris has always been gentle and kind towards me, I give in and nod. Still uncomfortable, I slide my feet back up to the bed and sink my body against the security of the headboard as if the hard sturdy surface can ground me or lend me strength.

Chris marches across the floor with a pained expression while fidgeting his hands together in front of him as if he has a coin or marble that he is twirling around.

"Listen, Piper…" He takes a seat at the edge of the bed, placing his hand near my feet, but still keeping them to himself. I release a gulp of air I was holding back and go to work calming my heart with deep even breaths. "I just wanted to say I'm sorry. I should have never come in here and just got in your bed. I mean, I just thought…well, I just didn't think. I mean…" He searches my face.

I quickly shake my head to lose the obvious resting bitch face that has surely already masked every feature of my expression right down to a kinked up lip, dipped down brows and squinted eyes. Abby has made me aware of this look on more than one occasion, especially when Evan is around. Sympathizing with the remorse in his voice, I stop him, raising my hand with my sheet clasped into a ball.

"It's ok. No apology necessary." I smile, feeling the panic and fear I felt only minutes ago instantly dissolve.

"Really?" he smiles back, a fun, easy grin that highlights the contours of his square jawline and almond shaped blue eyes. "Ok, cool…" he sighs and immediately I'm on edge again.

"Wait…I mean it's ok now, not that it's ok to…"

"Piper, I know…I know…" he chuckles. "I know what you meant. Don't worry. I shouldn't have assumed. I know I was in the wrong. That should be something we discuss, not just me hopping in and thinking I can…" he stops, appearing almost embarrassed.

I have no intentions of telling him about my past, however, it's not fair to lead him on. We've seen each other off and on for nearly two months now.

Wouldn't I have some sort of desire for intimacy from him if I was ever going to want him like that? I never have that with him; I've never felt it or had it. Well, I haven't since Evan.

Since him, it's like that part of me is dead; shifted back to when I was twelve and withdrawn from any physical contact of any sort, even a hug from my own parents. After what Trent did, I changed. Sure, I was young and I guess that is why Mom and Dad didn't question my moodiness or defiance to any affection and love. They always made the snarky comment, 'that's teenagers these days', when I would pull away or run to my room, so that's how I let myself grow up; absent and absolutely content without love, except with Evan. He filled that void in my heart for a few years.

"Yeah…" I clear my throat, trying to break through the tension in the room. "Well, it happened and it's over now." My stomach clinches on my words, sounding way too familiar as I remember back to what Mom said after she confirmed with Trent that what I said was true…

"Well, it's water under the bridge now. It happened…and it's over." Her eyes burned through me as if she was looking past me or possibly trying not to feel a thing in that moment. But even with the absence of any emotions, her words rip right through me. "All you can do is move on and get over it. There is no reason to drag your cousin's name through the mud and make him look like some dirty old pedophile. Besides, Piper, with all those bikinis you wear around the lake, that was bound to happen; it just gives boys the wrong impression, so you should have known better."

I shake away those damaging words that were said to me; one of the very last conversations we had before she made the choice to choose him over Dad and I.

Working to escape those memories, I redirect the topic, "Actually maybe it's good that it happened. I mean, not good, but I've been wanting to talk to you about something."

Chris looks at me nervously, his hands in his lap, holding tightly to one another as he rubs his thumb across his knuckle over and over again until I think he may grind the skin off. Remorse at what I want to say settles in the pit of my stomach and threatens to make me stop. I've breached this conversation a handful of times since our first date back in November, yet I chicken out every single time; not this time. He remains silent, dipping his chin and lifting his brows expectantly.

Just do it, Piper.

I open my mouth, but nothing happens. Nudging my body forward just a bit, I force out an impulsive blurt that suddenly makes the room seem smaller and much more quiet than before.

"Maybe we shouldn't be seeing each other." It comes out more abrasive than I had planned, so I promptly start back pedaling "What I meant was, do you see this going anywhere?" Gritting my teeth, dread creeps over me. My insides rebel against this conversation as knots form in my stomach and a light thumping begins in my head; it could easily be from my blackout, or perhaps an oncoming headache that is bound to torment me through the night.

His eyebrows fall and his sight drops to the bed, as if he is searching for the answer to my question through the ruffled up sheets and blanket.

"I guess it doesn't seem to be, but I don't know. I just don't think about it like that. I figured we'd take it day-by-day and see where it goes. I didn't really expect anything. I like you and I gathered you liked me; that's about as far as I looked into it."

He looks back up, directly at me like he is cuing me that it is my turn to speak, only I have no clue how to follow up. He has a point; it's not like I was looking ahead to whether I'd marry this guy or anything like that, but I don't think my argument of where this is going was the correct phrase to go with. *Why am I such a chicken?*

"Oh, I do like you," I spit out, correcting him quickly. *Ok, I just need to be blunt and put it out there.* "I just don't see it going anywhere myself." His expression doesn't change, but I'm sure the panic is showing on mine. I open my mouth to elaborate; to maybe change the harshness of my words, but he beats me to it.

Reaching over the bundle of sheets I still have draped over my body and wedged in my fist, he drops his palm onto mine, keeping his touch light and friendly.

"It's ok. I understand. I know you're kind of closed off, which at first I thought was a breath of fresh air; finally, a girl that doesn't go on about her ex-boyfriend." He chuckles and removes his hand, pulling it back to his lap, now free of any nervous fidgeting. "But then I realized that maybe you just had a bad experience or possibly weren't necessarily over someone?" he words it as a question, trailing off with his eyebrows crinkling the skin on his forehead as if he's waiting for me to take over.

I have no idea what to say; I am definitely not going to dive into why I don't talk about myself. Actually, I never really gave it much thought, but I guess I don't ever jump into the, 'this one time' conversations. Come to think of it, I never really say much; I listen and laugh at what everyone else is saying, but I rarely ever take the stage. This is probably why I've always been more comfortable on double dates rather than facing it all by myself. In the short amount of time since Chris asked me out we have been alone twice, and that includes now. I usually don't trust being alone with guys, no matter the circumstances. Darting off into the woods with Tyler this past summer was the most daring I've ever been and that time was abruptly interrupted with Evan walking up all pissed off. I'm not sure he'll ever know how much I appreciated his intrusion even though I played it off being pissy about it.

"Listen, it's fine...I just hope I didn't screw this up by being an asshole and trying to rush things."

My eyes stretch wide open. "Oh no. It's nothing like that. I... well...I ummm..." I stare at him, unable to say what I'm thinking; *yes,*

I do have a bad experience from my past that I'd rather not relive by talking about it and yes, I'm not over someone. I gasp at that revelation as Chris speaks up again, finishing our conversation before I can.

"It's ok. I don't expect for you to talk about whatever you hold back; I get it and I completely understand what you're saying about it not going anywhere. Most of the time we're together it does feel more like we're just friends rather than anything romantic. I try not to push too hard to get past that, but I guess I got a little over eager tonight. That's my fault and again I am sorry." He takes a deep breath and stares me down. "So where do we go from here?"

Squirming around uneasily, I shift my hips to settle back against the headboard, feeling a bit more distance may lessen the tension that question brings over me. I've never really done this before. I have always steered clear of relationships and romance since Evan. I was barely able to drive the last time I crossed this bridge.

Slowly I lift my shoulders, arching them up on an I-don't-know-too-scared-to-say-anything shrug. My head throbs, no doubt from angling my brows into a frown for most of this conversation with my lips pressed together, zipped tight and unable to answer.

He gives me a light-hearted smile and all my worries dissolve. "Friends?"

My chest raises and shoulders drop, as I release a deep sigh and smile. "Yeah, friends."

We continue talking, milling over class schedules for next semester, Christmas dinner, and all that I have to do which probably bores the hell out of him, and other minute topics that keeps the mood enjoyable. He leads the subject into holidays as a child and as much as I try to hang onto every word and laugh on cue, my thoughts wander off to earlier tonight.

Evan's face surfaces in my mind, his brown hair all tousled about as if he had run his hands through it a million times like he always used to. I picture his hazel eyes tinted to match the lake as it laps around the boat dock and his jaw framed in a five o'clock shadow that

I only just noticed for the first time tonight. We were only kids when I last touched that face and at that time, all he did was marvel over the few hairs that had cropped up over his chest, let alone a face full of whiskers.

I snicker at that memory, quickly clearing my throat so Chris doesn't think I'm not paying attention, but it's no use; his face comes back into full view and I can't get that thought out of my head.

Yes, I'm not over someone.

It's been so long since I've thought of him in anything other than anger, yet here he was, swooping to my rescue; something that came so natural to him when we were younger. He was there like not a day had gone by, saying the same words he had always whispered to me when I'd fall into darkness. *Breathe with me.* On that, tiny fragments of a wall I have built up around my heart slowly start to chip away, softening the structure and creating a hole wide enough to let light in again; to feel again. A doorway to open my heart after years of having it closed up and sealed off. *Evan.*

The Look

Evan

"OK, SO THE WORKING IN silence suits me just fine ordinarily, but it's not like I haven't seen you seriously pissed before. You going to tell me what's going on or just keep slamming every tool down like you're throwing some kind of toddler sized tantrum?"

I huff out a laugh and look over at Judd. He's staring down at the clay-colored wall heater that we've been busy installing this morning. Reaching out my arm, I let the metal wire cutters fall from my hand to the floor with a thud. Still nothing; he doesn't even flinch to look my way.

"You know, you're just going to scuff up the paint job that Alyssa and I did this summer," he says in a bland tone with his lips twitching to the side and that pathetic ugly ass pit in his cheek dipping in.

Why in the hell do girls find that so enticing?

"Not that I mind spending a few more hours laying down a fresh coat." He finally glances up with a full on shit-ass smirk across his face. "As long as Alyssa can come help."

I give in to his amusement and smile, shaking my head. "Geez, you're a horny bastard...all of the time. You really need to consider thinking above the waist, just once in a while."

Judd belts out a laugh and I join in, a bit of my anger and confusion over last night's happenings melting away. We quickly get back to business hooking up and affixing the heater to the wall across from the shower stalls. After stripping off a portion of the color coded plastic insulation from around a couple of wires, I scoop up a wire nut and carefully twist together the two circuits. Keeping it clasped between my index finger and thumb, I grab up the black electrical tape and wrap it up before shoving all the capped wires back into the junction box.

"Ok, that should do it. Let's mount this sucker and see how it works…" I swing my eyes over to Judd with a bit of skepticism in my tone. "…if it works." I add with a smirk, knowing full well these units have a limited shelf life, yet still willing to give it a shot.

"You think?"

I laugh, shaking my head. "Who knows…I mean I could be wrong. They may last until I am happily settled or until you're changing diapers. Either way, Grandpa said install them, so that's what I'm doing."

"From the way Skylar looks at you anymore, I'm thinking the happily settled may come sooner than me changing diapers and hey, I am not planning on having kids anytime soon, so you can just leave that out of your lame attempt of a metaphor."

I bite back a laugh, keeping a serious expression. "Whoa, whoa… first off, Skylar and I are by no means getting settled. I like her, yeah, but I don't think it'll go any further, so me getting settled, my friend, is a far-far off occurrence. Second, you keep humping like you and Blondie have been and you'll be sporting a baby swing beside your desk in no time…" I glance at him from the corner of my eyes. He snickers, but makes no attempt to correct me. My eyes go wide and I snap my head up to fully look at him. "Oh, hell…she isn't knocked up already, is she?"

His head pops up faster than mine. "No!" he snaps, "No way. I told you, that's a long way off. Besides, we're not humping *all of the time.*"

Now that's funny. "Oh no, not at all. Come on, puh-leeze…" I press my lips together, holding back a tidal wave of laughter. Pressing the tip of my thumb to my chest, I go on, "I got a front row to you two crazy kids moaning and groaning nearly every damn night you were at the apartment…don't try to tell me that you two don't get it on like a pack of cats in heat all hopped up on catnip on a warm summer night."

I pause and take in his slight grin as he stares back at me, probably about ready to slap me silly or yell out his infamous 'Evan!' in hopes to shut me up; it never works. *I love pestering the hell out of him. I assume this is the path I'd take if I had a younger brother, so why not.*

"Come on dude, you even got another apartment so you could knock boots uninterrupted." My lips twitch as I roll my eyes, trying to appear unimpressed with the lengths he'd go to for a little booty. He knows I'm happy for him, but I can still play that down and make him feel like a dog. "Go flip the breaker."

"Oh, oh…yeah…I would like to have one night of sex where I don't hear you yelling out…" his expression shifts to a painful grimace with his eyebrows drawn down and his forehead crinkled up like an old man. "'Please guys, just let me sleep'…'Just get it over with already'…'Are you guys done yet'…'Yes, yes, yes I want to sleep too', and all the other comments you like to surprise us with in the midst of a moment that your voice does not belong in. The walls in the apartment are thin, man, and damn, some nights, I swore you were right in bed with us." He holds his arm up, bent at the elbow with his fist gripped tight, then quickly starts to drop it. "Nothing shoots a guy down faster than hearing a deep baritone voice mixed with your girlfriend's sexy noises. Wheeeeeew…" He whistles as his hand falls all the way down.

I drive in the last screw to mount the heater to the wall as he walks out the door. A sharp creak sounds from just outside joined by a quiet brushing noise, a loud crash, "Shit" and then a snap.

"Easy now…let's not break everything."

"Shut up, Evan," his voice is muffled, but sarcasm rings through even with the thick shower house walls.

Laughter vibrates through my chest as he walks back in with paint on his boot. "What happened to you?"

"A damn paint can fell off one of the shelves. Breaker is on…try it."

"Probably got your mind on other things, huh?" I mumble, flexing my brows jokingly as I turn the dial.

"Ha…Ha…Ha," Judd groans.

Gritting my teeth as a crackling noise ignites, I place my hand above Grandpa's auction find, then wait. A subtle warmth immediately seeps into the air, heating my skin and sending a wave of chills over me at the difference in temps.

"Well hell, what do you know." I look over at Judd, pressing my lips together and pulsing my head in a quick genuinely shocked nod, ready for the shower house to be flooded with warmth.

Judd laughs and quickly starts gathering tools by the handful before shoving them into the tool box. I follow his lead, a sense of accomplishment oozing through me. *I still say they'll go caput before winter is out.*

After hoisting the tool box and other equipment up to the tool shed, Judd cleans up his paint mess, something I get the feeling he'd much rather invite Blondie over to help him with. Meanwhile, I step inside with a deep exhale, my mouth no longer emitting the usual white puff of smoke brought on by a winter chill. Grasping the fingertips of my left glove, I tug it off my hand and then repeat with the other.

"Hmmmm…" I widen my hand, letting the toasty air thaw my frozen limbs.

I'm blown away that this fifteen-year-old pile of metal works as well as it does. It has actually warmed this building in less than a half hour; unexpected. Unless, of course, the hunk of junk is on the verge of catching fire and burning down the entire place. I glance back to it, a subtle crackle and pop sounding every few minutes that has my nerves on edge. *That would be just perfect.*

"Hey, I'm finished cleaning up the mess. Did you want…" The door smacks against the frame as he walks in and freezes. "What happened?"

"Huh?" I lower my brows, baffled by his question.

"Is something still bothering you? You kinda look pissed or worried. Ahhh…shit, did we hook something up wrong?"

I crack up over his line of questioning and lower my hands from my hips where they must have found themselves during my brief query of whether I was standing in the middle of a soon-to-be inferno. Sliding my arms out of my coat, I toss it towards the sink and look back at him ready to let him have it for walking right into that one.

"Ok airhead, it's warm in here, so how do you figure something was hooked up wrong?" I snicker as he shakes his head, dismissing my comment or possibly agreeing with his dipshit observation. "…and no, nothing happened. I was just a little stunned to see that this contraption works so well. I was prepared to have to lug it all the way up to the dumpsters no sooner than we got the electrical work laid."

"You win…stupid question, but I know something was bothering you earlier. You had that look on your face."

I drop my mouth open on a breathy laugh. "What look? I have a look? I'm not a chick…I really doubt I had a look." Flicking my gaze to the ground, I squint my eyes for a second; *great, I have a damn look.*

"Whatever, you know what I'm talking about." He stares at me, waiting.

I suck in a breath and hold it in. *What the hell; if I have a stupid ass look now, I better start talking.* My shoulders fall and I let out a monstrous breath. Walking towards the wall, I remain silent as my mind shuffles through a million memories of Piper, starting with our very first encounter all the way to the last day we spent together; a day that should have went in the record books for the top five best days, but instead, it ended in a disaster.

Bolting out of my camper like our asses just caught fire, we both turn our heads from one side to the other as if we were caught red handed; caught with our pants down, literally. My heart pounds at a ferocious rate as if

I've been chased by a lion for the past hour. Geez…did that just happen? I look over to Piper, her hand gripped in mine and I see the same anxiety in her eyes.

"It's ok…" I smile a freaking grin that says 'Holy hell, that just happened' and tighten my hold to assure her of my words.

With her best friend staying this week, my intrusive brother and his new best friend that I just can't quite figure out, plus all the other campers, we had to work with a very small window of opportunity and work fast at that. Considering, I've never gone that far, the quick part was not a problem at all. It was all the scary shit that came before and during that had us breaking records for the longest first time ever.

I nudge her hand between us, to move her attention from wildly looking around to keeping her eyes pinned on me. "You ok?" A tinge of guilt settles back in my heart, even though she has told me over and over not to let it bother me. I don't let on in front of her that I secretly would love to rip his arms off so he can never touch another person and I sure as hell don't treat her like she has a broken wing, but every time a simple touch makes her flinch or she holds her breath, it rips my heart out.

"Mmmmhmmm…" she hums nervously, so I stop, grabbing her other hand and facing her.

"Hey, did we move too fast?" I say quietly with a lump in my throat. "I told you, we could stop. I didn't hurt you in any way, did…"

"Evan, no." She moves closer to me, slowly slipping her hand up to my jaw with the familiar gentleness that she has always exhibited towards me. "You could never hurt me. I trust you. Ok?"

I offer a quick nod before she goes on.

"I'm glad we did. It was amazing." She smiles and just that tiny gesture sends my ego through the roof, my conscience brushing off its shoulders and my head passing out drinks in celebration of one more virginity lost in the world. "There is no one else that I will ever trust like that," she sighs, and my heart grips at how hard such simple things are for her, thanks to that douchebag. "You just have to be patient. We leaped the hurdle, but it will still be hard. Just don't give up on me."

I stop her right there. What the hell, is she kidding? We just shared something like we did and she thinks I could skip town due to her panic induced meltdowns? Yeah, sure, some of them; all of them come at pretty precarious moments that leave me understanding the term blue balls right down to the last syllable, but I will not, cannot leave her. She's stuck with me, no matter how annoying or pestering I can be, she's stuck.

Crisscrossing my hand over hers so that my fingertips can softly hold the smooth contour of her chin, I open my mouth and unload it all.

"Piper, I'm not going anywhere. I'm here. I'll always be here. You can tell me to get lost when you get pissed off, because I have no doubt I will piss you off, but I'll still be here. You breathe, I breathe..." I stare deep into her piercing eyes that hold the world for me. "...remember...breathe with me and we'll get through it."

She giggles and crushes her lips to mine. My arms fall around her like they have been molded to her and I close my eyes, my lips slightly opening with her. Her breath is warm, her mouth is moist and sweet and I really cannot get enough of it. Pushing away faster than I'd like, as she usually does, she plants her hands firmly on both of my cheeks. I laugh, looking into her eyes that sparkle in mischief and excitement.

"I love you."

Whoa! She said that...

She really said that...

Holy crap. Do I say it back?

My lips twitch up at the corners, slowly rising to a laugh.

"I..." Not even thinking I begin to repeat it back to her.

"Hey, I have to go to the bathroom. I'll be back. Will you wait for me?" she says, dropping her hands and already backing up to head towards the shower house.

I nod, stunned and dazed by the words she just said. She loves me.

"Ok, see you in a second." She spins and darts off down the hill.

Stepping forward with a strange sense of urgency, I raise my hand and call out to her. "Hey, I'll be right here. I have something to tell you when you get back too." A goofy ass smile emerges on my face as she waves over her shoulder with a laugh. Well if that wasn't plain as day Captain Obvious. I have something to tell you too? What the hell. Hmmmm, I wonder what he wants to tell me…could it possibly be 'I love you' since that is the very last thing I told him; yeah, I'm sure she's even thinking that. Stupid! Why the hell didn't I just yell it. I look at the shower house and see her disappearing behind the building. Shouting it out to her as she walks away would have been one of those lame knight in shining armor stunts that women eat up; damn, I should have done that.

I clear my mind of all thoughts and images of her, then turn and slide down the wall of the shower house. Motioning for Judd to take a seat, I point my thumb to the side and quirk my lips, edgy and uncertain of where to start.

Judd parks himself beside me, quickly typing out something on his phone before slipping it back in his jacket pocket.

"Might as well get comfortable. This could take a while." I bounce upward on a half-hearted chuckle and stare forward, nearly seeing right back to that day as if it was yesterday. "So, yeah…I was a little peeved this morning and of course, you guessed it probably; it's Piper. Honestly, I don't even know what I've told you about our situation." I look over, pondering on whether I've ever told him jack.

Judd belts out a smartass laugh that is usually reserved for me. "That's easy…nothing. You're like a vault on that topic. All I've pieced together is that she hates you…" I cringe at his assessment as he goes on. "…it drives you crazy that she does. Oh and that you must have screwed up somewhere along the way to piss her off. I just figure she can't stand your jokes." He laughs, tilting his head back against the wall.

"Yeah, right…" I mumble, "everyone loves my jokes." I bounce my head back to the hard wall and catch Judd shaking his head from the corner of my eyes. Chuckling, I decide to go back to that day; back to when the drama unfolded, only I plan to keep some of it to myself. I've done enough damage. I trust Judd, but her secret is for her to tell, not me.

"Well you know, Piper and I have known each other since we were kids…right around twelve to thirteen?"

"Yeah, I did know that much."

"Ok…so, the summer I met you…actually the week before you came out here for the first time, that's basically when my life went from freaking awesome to unbelievably crappy in a matter of minutes. Seriously, one second I am about to spout poetry across the damn campground and the next I'm standing there with my mouth hanging down to the ground with no clue as to what I've done." Judd remains silent, hanging onto every word…or so I hope, because I really do not want to repeat any of this. "All I knew back then and pretty much what I still know for certain is that I was waiting for Piper, but geez, I was about to bounce out of my skin. I had something to tell her and it was about to rip my lips in two."

"Ha!" Judd chuckles; I look over, putting on my best irritated expression with my mouth and brows drawn into as deep of a frown as I can muster up. "Oh, sorry…I was just imagining you with no lips and unable to amuse us all with all your unsubtle quips and comments." My face doesn't budge; I remain unamused or try my best. Judd clears his throat. "So what did you need to say?"

I raise my eyebrows, keeping my facial features blank and unimpressed by his attempt at a joke. "Leave the jokes for me, dude. Just listen…what I needed to say isn't important."

Judd's lips wobble as if he's holding back a mouthful of laughter. "So you were going to tell her you love her?"

What the hell; maybe I do have a look. I give in and grin, a bit of heat surfacing across my face that has nothing to do with the newly installed heater. This is a first for me; embarrassment, no way. I flip my head around to face forward.

"I'll take that as a ye…" I cut him off, unwilling to let him have the satisfaction of being right, although he totally is.

"Ok, ok…that's enough. Maybe we should forgo story time."

"Oh come on…" Judd pauses with a snicker that leaves him covering his mouth with one hand. Recomposing himself, he keeps an eye on me, but I flick my sights forward.

Damn I do have a look. Wait, am I pouting?

"Ok, go on."

Screw this. Realizing I'm acting like a flipping girl at this point, wanting to give my friend the silent treatment or whine and cry about him having the last laugh, I finish my story, omitting the whole lame ass, my-heart-is-about-to-rupture-if-I-don't-say-I-love-you-now.

"Sooooooo," I draw out my words as I look back at him and carry on, "I take off running down the hill toward the shower…ahhh…to here," I point down to the floor. "All I have in my head is the stupid ramblings of a sixteen-year-old prepared to bear my soul to a girl that knocks my socks off every damn day. But geesh…I round that corner, nearly collide with her Dad yelling, '*let's go now*' and then come eye-to-eye with the most pissed off woman I have ever seen in my life. I mean, seriously…Grandpa warned me about looks that could burrow right through a guy's willpower and make you do stupid ass shit that you'd deny to every single friend you have, but this look…Ho-Lee Hell." I shake my head, remembering it so clearly. "That look could turn you to stone, shatter you into a pile of ash, and sweep you into the sewer all in a single second. I have never, ever seen that look on her face before." I bring my hand to my forehead, haunted by the nostalgic presence of me staring directly into her eyes that day; seeing that cold gaze that said the exact opposite of what I came to say to her.

The look that said *I hate you.*

Crushed

Piper

I RUN UP TO THE shower house door, hoping I will find him, but stop as soon as muffled voices capture my attention. Evan's deep masculine tone awakens every cell in my body as I close my eyes and remember how just last night I felt that voice against my skin, in my ear and through my hair. Placing my hand on the door, I prepare to open it but wait when his words, ones I know are about me, reach out, grab my heart and take me back to that day. It's a day that I don't really care to revisit considering it's the day I gave up trusting pretty much anyone; however, when I'm around him, that memory burns through me and reminds me why I should keep him at arm's length or further.

"I don't know what happened before I got there but she just started laying into me. I'd never seen her so livid and trust me, I'd seen all sorts of emotions from her at that point, but this was unlike anything I'd ever seen. It was like Satan was unleashed from the gates of hell and took over her body…"

His voice fades so I move my head so close to the door that it may seem to anyone else that I'm planning on making out with it. "Actually, I can play it up or down whatever, but she wasn't pissed…she was hurt…because of me…" The usual always-have-a-comment-for-everything sarcasm is drained from his voice, making my heart tug and my eyes mist over as the pain of that day engulfs me.

My feet race over the old dingy gray concrete as I rush to get back to Evan. Was he really going to say it back?

Several showers run, filling the room with steam and making it sound like a rain storm from inside the suffocating building. No sooner than my hand makes contact with the oblong handle of the door, I have it open, my skin chilled by the sudden difference in temperature. The air is hot and muggy outside, but the brisk wind that rises up from the lakeshore offers a sense of relief that isn't found inside the musty, pathetic excuse for a public restroom.

My heart flies through the doorway, yanking me behind at a nervous and anxious pace. Two steps forward and I see a face I have never been fond of; someone that has always given me the creeps.

"Whoa…where are you racing off to?" Mitch holds up his hand, forcing me to stop in my tracks and take two strides back against the door. "You eager to get back to your mid-afternoon activities?" He smirks, but all I can do is stare.

My mouth goes dry and suddenly I feel violated, spied on during a private moment and very ashamed. I keep my eyes locked on his, looking for any sign of joking or possibly a bullshit grin that says 'lucky guess', but I see nothing. His hazel eyes seem amused, as they usually do, and not at all resembling the charisma of his brother's. The humor is drained of happiness and that ha-ha factor as he puts off more of an aggressive, bullying look that is meant to intimidate. I open my mouth, but he beats me to it as he steps forward and leans closer to me; too close.

"I tell you what…" I turn my head to the side, uncomfortable with the lack of distance between us. "…for someone that I wouldn't have given a second glance to a couple years back, you sure have turned out to be a regular hottie. I sure hope my brother has been wearing it out properly."

I cringe and ball my fists at my side, the urge to swing at him pulsing through my veins. He braces his arm to the side of the door with his palm flat on the wall, nearly blocking any escape I may have. My breathing picks up, coming one after the next and I swear I may very well fall into one of my episodes if I don't find a way to get him to move away from me.

"So I heard this little rumor...I was wondering if you could put it to rest for me..." he pauses as bile rises into the back of my throat and my mouth suddenly fills with saliva, taunting me with a strong desire to throw up.

He knows; Trent told him. Oh God!

"Did you really get it on with your own cousin?"

He says the words that I had already feared and all the blood drains from my face, leaving me light headed, yet a relentless flame in my need to never be treated like shit again still burns inside of me. It dwindles and nears the point of going out, but with every ounce of mortification and humiliation that I currently feel, little-by-little it is revived.

"Did you like it?"

My lip curls into a snarl and my jaw tenses as I turn to stare right into his eyes. He disgusts me. How could anyone be so cold?

"I bet you begged for..."

Without thinking, an adrenaline rush takes over and controls every bit of my body as a crack sound fills the air. My palm burns and Mitch's eyes widen. Looking down at my hand, I realize I just slapped him across the face. I glance back to him with a soothing sense of confidence and pride. He wobbles his jaw before locking eyes with me.

"You little bitch!"

The door behind me pushes me forward.

"That is enough!" Dad's voice booms as he steps out; my mouth drops open.

What did he hear? Oh no, what did he hear?

"What the hell is going on?"

I'm stunned, frozen as Dad speaks. This is something I've shoved down so deep into the pit of my soul and I never, ever wanted my parents to find out; especially my dad. He stares me down then flings his glare to

Mitch, who stands there with a pleased smirk. The only comfort I take in this whole situation is the fact that a flared up red hand print lies perfectly outlined and centered across his cheek. Good!

Dad holds his anger at bay, simply glowering at Mitch and possibly noticing my artwork on his face as well. I look down, pushing my entire back into the door again and hoping that I could somehow camouflage myself within the grains of the wood or disappear entirely.

"You..." He snaps his hand into the air, pointed only a foot or so away from Mitch's chest. "I want to know exactly what was going on out here!" His tone holds no amount of kindness or approachability. "Someone better start talking real fast."

"Or what..." Mitch says slowly, pushing every one of my buttons.

Dad instantly steps forward, right into his face and although Mitch is more than likely twenty or so years younger than him, Dad looks menacing next to him. He makes no efforts to back away, almost testing him.

Dad's hand darts back up, this time digging into Mitch's chest. "Don't try my patience, kid. You may be bigger than me, but you are still just a snot faced little punk. What did you say to my daughter and what would justify her giving you that pretty little mark on your face?"

I cringe at his icy tone and wait, worried that he may turn it on me once Mitch delivers the truth of what we were discussing. Dad makes no move as Mitch coolly looks down at the finger jabbing into him. He moves his hand up and brushes Dad's finger away from his body and finally recedes back towards the edge of the dock.

"We were just discussing how your precious little angel gets around," he says, teeth gritted and a tight face while locking eyes with my father.

"I suggest you reword that. I won't have someone talk about her like that."

Mitch sidesteps, raising the corners of his lips into a somewhat evil grin. My stomach sinks with what he may say the more Dad pushes.

"Dad, let's just go."

"We will go when I say..." he keeps his voice direct, but his eyes never shift to me; they remain still, dead set on Mitch.

Raising his hands, Mitch surrenders. "Listen, dude, I'm not trying to start anything. I was just looking out for my little brother since they are both so young…"

I don't even think. "That's a lie!" My eyes go wide as I step forward and let my words fly. I know better than that. He could really give a crap about his brother.

Mitch looks past Dad to me, a cocky surprised expression on his face. "Oh, you mean you weren't just knocking boots with my brother about fifteen minutes ago in his camper?!

"That is enou…" Dad starts, but I don't even let him finish.

"You aren't looking after Evan and we didn't…" I'm seconds away from denying one of the most life-altering, tender moments of my life.

"Whoa, whoa…careful what you deny, because I'm sure my brother will confide in me what really happened."

"He would not!" I spit out, balling my fists so tight the blood flow to my hands is sure to slow.

"Piper, that is enough. Let's…" dad starts in again; this time Mitch interrupts him.

"Or would he?! I'm sure your dad would be interested in knowing you got a little busy with Trent too." He smiles as all air leaves my lungs.

I shift my eyes to Dad. His eyes go dead, lifeless as his entire face shifts to an indescribable expression that I've never seen before. My head whirls and spins and my heart plummets to the pit of my stomach like a stone being tossed into a river; I'm crushed, in absolute anguish and want nothing more than to run and to keep running until there is no feeling left in my body. Silence surrounds us for what seems to drag on for an eternity before Mitch opens his intrusive, uncompassionate mouth again.

"What, no denying that?" He chuckles and Dad's face goes white as he turns slowly around to face him.

"I suggest you leave now." It comes out as a whisper with the hint of a threat and something about the way he says it scares me more than if he would have screamed it.

"Mitch, hey…" I look past them and see that Mitch's friend Tristan,

decided to join in on my humiliation. "Let's go, man."

He doesn't budge as his friend nudges him, placing his hand on his shoulder. Mitch and my father continue their stand off as I remain frozen in terror of so many people knowing my secret; knowing something that I have worked so hard to shove down into the very bottom of my soul; something I trusted to only one person and one person alone. Oh God. He told him; he betrayed me. He shared one of the scariest and most shameful moments of my life with his brother. Someone that is likely to tell anyone and everyone with no concern of whether it would make me look like a fool, or something dirty and vile for allowing it to happen. Who all knows? Why would Evan have told him? How could he?

Ice surges through my veins and the fluttering sensation that resided in my heart only minutes ago subsides. Mitch's voice interrupts my thoughts and I realize Dad hasn't moved a muscle or said a word.

"Oh what…" He places his hand over his mouth, mockingly. "You mean you didn't know that?" His eyes dart to me, but Dad stays still, his shoulders slumped forward. Mitch looks back to him as Tristan reaches his hand back up to coerce him away from the scene.

"Man, let's just go."

"No disrespect, really," Mitch ignores his friend and starts in with his best performance yet, however, I'm not fooled. He's enjoying this, torturing me, for what reason I have no idea. I think he is one of those sick individuals that only get self-gratification at the mercy of someone else's demise or utter mortification. "I just thought that's something you might want to know about."

Finally, Mitch turns to go with his pal, stepping away slowly in the direction of the convenience store at the end of the dock.

Dad remains in his stance and although I cannot fully see his face, I can make out the same humiliation and defeat in his posture that I hold in my own. He is ashamed of me; he thinks I am dirty and indecent. I look up towards the sky, wishing this whole day away…every…single… bit of it. There is nothing about this day that I do not regret. The stretched out silence that rings out in my ears is disturbed by an array of noises.

All this time, the splashing of water in the distance, skiers darting by out on the lake with a whoosh, yells and laughter and the usual tranquil hums of nature that now just seem like an annoyance, all slam into my eardrums and snap me back into reality.

The shuffling of fabric joins the symphony of sounds as Dad gradually turns to face me. I glance up, straight at his face, scared to death to stare him in the eye, yet I look anyways. His eyes don't even make contact with my face, they focus on the dock below his feet as if he is studying it or thinking.

With a deep breath, he opens his mouth and I cringe. Tears begin to flood my eyes before he can even say a word.

"Piper..." it comes out through what sounds like gritted teeth. He's mad at me. "We are leaving...now." The same whisper he used with Mitch is now being turned on me, free of the threatening tone, but replaced with an urgency.

"Dad," my voice quivers and I barely hold the tears back. "I didn't..."

"I know. We will talk about it when we get back to the cabin." Finally, he looks around, glancing from side-to-side as if he is just now aware that we are in plain sight of everyone in the camp ground. Oh God, who all heard? "Let's go." He moves past me without another word.

I don't move as he walks around me like I'm some stranger he is passing on the street. All I want is for him to throw his arms around me and tell me it's ok. I've kept this pent up inside me for so long, only trusting one person to keep my secret, yet here it is; it's out. Dad knows, but now, rather than the comforting arms of support that I've always hoped for had he found out, I'm hit with the same wave of disgrace that I felt back then, only it's being tossed in my face. I'm being made to feel that it was in fact my fault. Am I misreading this?

I stare down at the dock where Dad's feet had been, only he is now walking in front of me, heading off the dock.

"Dad," my voice vibrates once more. "I need to explain. What he said about Trent..."

"Piper!" he snaps with the tapping of his shoes against the wood

surface of the dock immediately coming to a stop. "Let's go now," his voice cracks, telling me he is not mad; he doesn't necessarily blame me. He knows; he doesn't want to hear an explanation; he already knows I didn't do it of my own free will.

Just as my tears spill over, running down my cheeks and dripping down my chin I see the one face that I have come to look forward to each and every time I am out here, only now, it turns my blood cold. Every fiber of my body tenses.

Evan looks at my dad and although I would think Dad would want to punch him or tell him to stay the hell away from me, he does nothing. He moves off the dock and keeps on his path to our cabin. My gaze leaves Dad and returns to Evan; I look right into his eyes.

Instantly cocking his head back, he shoves his feet into the ground and abruptly stops. Nothing about him looks the same to me anymore. The corners of his mouth tick with the hint of a smile before going blank. Alarm quickly takes over every curve of his face as his forehead crinkles in confusion. Grinding my back teeth together, the subtle scraping sound furthers my craze over this entire situation. I suck in a shaky breath, trying my best to remain calm even though my adrenaline level is pushing me forward. It is urging me to get in his face after having to hold it back with Mitch. I wanted to punch him, not just slap my hand across his face like a pissed off woman in one of those old movies. Now that rush of anger is spilling out of me and directed right at the one who started it all.

"Everything ok?" He seems clueless and that makes my temper flare.

"How could you?!" I hiss in a quiet yet venomous tone that makes him wince.

"I don't…"

"I trusted you." Both of my hands ball tightly at my sides, glued to my hips as I lean forward so that maybe my words will hit him like a punch to the gut. "How could you?" The same words are on constant repeat in my mind, echoing over and over. I don't understand.

The mere thought of him trying to comfort me in any way, or touch me, or even the thought of how we were earlier stirs an uneasy feeling

within me as if I'm back at that night. This whole thing does; all of it...
his deception, his brother's intrusive way of telling me and now my dad
finally knowing the truth.

I hold my hand out to stop him from making contact with any part
of my body.

"Don't touch me," I whisper, squeezing my eyes closed on my words.
I hate feeling this; I don't want to feel this. Why would he do this; why?
How could he?

"Piper..." his voice carries an innocence that I've never heard before.

It pulls my eyes open, but it does nothing to shake the stronghold
that the betrayal, lies and deception have on my heart.

"I don't understand, but I'm sure I could explain if you..."

"Evan...don't talk to me..." I continue in on my line of new rules in
our relationship; on our now non-relationship. That thought rips me in
two. The one person in this world that I knew I could trust and I now find
out that he has violated me and left me with a crushed, more oppressed
feeling than what Trent did.

I open my mouth again as Evan remains completely still with a
pained expression painted on his face. "Don't ever call me or come see
me."

I look at him as his eyes widen, emphasizing the heartache in them.
That would usually stop me in my tracks, but not this time. This cannot
be undone; this kills me.

"What do you mean? What about us? I mean...Piper, what's this
about?"

"How could you, Evan...How could you? I thought you..." I stop,
realizing he's never even said it to me. He doesn't love me.

He shakes his head, still not getting it. I walk past him prepared to
leave as Dad looks back from across the lot, motioning for me to follow
along.

I turn one last time, to make it all clear for him.

"How could you tell anyone something so personal, something that I
only told you? Why would you?"

"What?! Oh, no, no, no..." he looks around panicked, putting his hands up to try and stop me from leaving.

I back away. "This..." I point at him and back to me slowly, clamping my jaw closed for a second with a lump forming in my throat and my eyes misting over. "...is over. I don't want to see you again." I take a deep breath and let the tears fall, hoping they will wash away the dirty feelings. "I will never trust you again."

"Wait, no..." he shakes his head and moves forward but I can't, so I turn and run; again. I run from the pain; from the torment that night brought me when I was too innocent to know who not to trust. I had no idea that someone could be so cruel and vulgar in their actions. I race away with dread vibrating through me for what awaits, facing Mom and Dad; to know that they will finally see this deep dark secret that I've tried to erase for years. Will they hate me? ...look down on me? ...blame me?

My thoughts drift away as I once again hear Evan's voice through the door to the shower house.

"I had no idea back then...not at that moment anyways. I mean, when I first walked up, I thought for sure she was talking about what we had just done in the camper. I was trying to figure it out...searching for answers on how she could think I even had an opportunity to say anything to anyone in that brief amount of time, but when she said those last words and mentioned something she had only told me...it all slammed into me. I knew exactly what she was talking about. I felt like a piece of shit."

Judd's voice chimes in and I strain to hear. "So wait, what was the thing that she had told you?"

The sounds of the wind blowing through the trees right off the dock, instantly stop as if to help me out. I listen, my breath caught in my windpipe. The familiar presence of deceit creeps up on me, waiting. For a second I want to race in and scream at him not to do it again.

He has no right.

Here I am, hoping to run into him and thank him for last night; to apologize for the way I reacted when he in fact came to my rescue like he always had before.

Evan's voice stops me in my tracks and freezes all my fears.

"I screwed up there once before and I will never do it again. That's for her to tell who she wishes."

"So you knew something personal about her and told someone? Who did you tell?" Judd asks and I press my head to the door, not even caring if anyone walks up.

"I did and trust me, I didn't tell anyone. Well…at least it didn't go down as simple as that. My brother has a way of pushing buttons and I usually rise to the occasion like a dumbass. Anyways…"

I pull away, letting him have his conversation. His words make me want to know more, but for now I let it be. *He didn't say anything. Judd doesn't know? He's been his best friend for years and he has never told him?* My mouth gapes open and I walk up the dock, deep in thought. A weightlessness comes over me; one that I haven't felt since that day, before my confrontation with Mitch. It's overwhelming and takes me by surprise.

That day not only changed my entire outlook on love along with ending my relationship with Evan, but it altered my entire life.

Everything changed.

That day crushed me,

But for once, today…

Listening to Judd and Evan talk, it gives me hope.

Hot in Here

Evan

"SO…LAST NIGHT I GET A call from Abby. Freaked me out."

Judd snaps his head around to look at me. "Why… what happened?"

I shake my head, pulling my knees up and placing my forearms across them. Clasping my hands, I carefully shuffle through my wording before letting it fly. Where Piper is concerned, I always think twice before speaking.

"Well, I went over there and tried to help out with a…ummm, just a touchy situation." I glance over and see Judd nod as if not questioning my vagueness at all, so I go on, "For a second I thought everything was going to be put behind us." I sigh, dropping my head back against the wall with a thump. "Then, there she went. She remembered…remembered what a douche I was for opening my damn mouth and telling the one person that would no doubt use the information to do the most damage. Anyways, she ended up getting all pissed off and told me to leave."

"Hmmm…" Judd stares forward, looking maybe like he is half-ass listening or maybe just trying to figure out what I am talking about since I am practically talking in code. "Well, listen…I'd take the first part as a sign that maybe it can be put behind you. Just keep trying." He rises to his feet, brushes off his pants then stretches his arms above his head.

"Yeah," I let out an insincere chuckle at his logic and stand up as well. "Only thing is…it was alright for a minute, because she was half asleep. I think she was a little spaced out when she came to…saw me, a familiar face and didn't think immediately. As soon as she did…she made sure to let me know that I had no business over there."

"And that's what was bothering you earlier? Just another day with her…" he pauses, gritting his teeth before finishing, "…ummm well, hating you I guess."

I flinch at that thought. She did hate me; does, for all I know.

"No, what bothered me is last night when I left her cabin, Abby walked me out and we were talking. Here I assumed that she knew all about everything since she called me for help. I mean, she mentioned that she knew I helped Piper out with this sort of…" I hold my hands up and then drop them, refraining from the air quotes. "…situation. Well…" I blow out a deliberate breath. *What the hell did I do?!* "I freaking had a slip of the tongue…again."

I want to slap my hand across my face and hide in shame, but moreover I look at Judd, wanting his take on it even though he is limited on the detailed information.

"Ok…and she didn't know? She told you?"

My brows shoot up and I shake my head. "Oh no she had no idea."

Judd presses his lips together. "Wow, this is a tough one."

I snicker at his struggle to give me advice.

"No I mean, I don't know much about it, so it's hard to tell you what my opinion is. Of course if that's what you were needing," he pauses, looking for assurance.

I nod, eager for him to enlighten me with some vast knowledge of women that I haven't yet discovered. I seriously am lost when it comes to this. I haven't any idea how to get out of this. There isn't a doubt in my mind that Abby will tell her and then it will be bedlam all over again.

"So what did you say exactly to her?" he stumbles to reword, "I mean, without telling me so much. Did you just say it right out loud?"

I take in a deep breath, thinking it over.

"Thank you for coming. I was so scared. I didn't know what to do." Abby and I trail along back to my camper, her explaining everything that went on from the point she walked in and found Piper passed out.

My least favorite part of the tale is finding out that Chris just so happened to come out of the bedroom and get Abby, telling her of Piper's condition. What an ass! I grit my teeth, scraping them against each other as the sharp sound makes the hair on my arms stand on end. I figured as much from the second I walked in and saw him panicking.

"I don't think I would have known what to do had you not shown up."

"Yeah, I'm glad Piper told you about it so you knew to call me. Has she done this a lot?"

I'm curious for two reasons. One, I'm jealous as hell and want to know if she's put herself in situations to trigger instances like this. I know firsthand, intimacy is the biggest culprit of her blackouts through the night. Two, I'd like to know just how it has been stopped in the past. Has she learned to control it on her own? If so, why didn't she do it tonight?

"Not a lot, but she has a few times. After the first time that I found her, she told me about what makes it happen and then she told me all about you guys…how you used to see each other."

I look over as my feet crunch across the gravel lot not far from Grandpa's cabin. She looks at me bashful, almost guilty from knowing this information. A look that is definitely not very Abby-like. Wow, she knows it all.

"Wow! You must think I'm an ass for everything, but I'm glad she had someone to trust and confide in."

She laughs. "I don't think you're an ass, Evan. Oh...well..." She trips over her words, squinting her eyes and looking up towards the sky as if she is weighing her answer.

I burst out laughing, grabbing my stomach. "Oh well hell, that looks like it's a tough call."

"No, I was just going to say that I thought you were a little bit of an ass, but after she filled me in a bit more and then told me about Mitch basically making fun of her for it...well, then I thought he was the ass. You were just guilty by association."

We both laugh.

"How is she?" the words slip out before I can stop them. I've wanted to ask Piper this for years, but we never have gotten to that point where I can ask something like that before she's telling me to kiss her ass. "I mean has she moved past it yet?"

"Well, obviously not."

I nod my head, but then second guess agreeing. She used to have episodes over the smallest things. One time she blacked out when I ran my hand over her hip. She started hyperventilating and I had no clue what I had done. That was the first thing that made me question what had gone on with her, that and the night she showed up at my camper, looking like she was scared for her life. I hate thinking about that night. I would have hurt him, had I known then.

"I guess I mean more like physical contact and words; do they still make her black out? Or is it just when she remembers what happened due to someone trying to get close to her?"

I look over as we stop in front of the door to my camper. Abby goes silent and I can see the confusion on her face.

"Huh? What are you talking about? Physical contact? Weren't we talking about the nightmares she's had since she was a kid?" her eyes pierce my soul, and I honestly want to crawl under a rock.

No, no, no...I did it again. What the hell...how do I clean this up? Shit!

"Ahhhh...yeah, I meant the dreams about that..." I leave it open ended, sucking at covering up the fact that I was clearly talking about the distress she personally suffered rather than some measly little dream.

Abby crooks her head to the side, reading my expression as I look around, anywhere but her eyes. This girl, I have no doubt could read me like a book.

"No, what are you talking about? Did something happen to Piper?"

"No!" I snap, probably a little too fast.

Great now it looks like I'm hiding something; I am. Damn!

Abby pushes her lips to the side as if she is chewing on the corner of the inside of her mouth. "Evan, I know you aren't talking about nightmares. You know I always thought that wasn't what she was talking about either, when she told me about them. I mean most people wouldn't black out from dreams unless they were brought on from a real life trauma kind of like post-traumatic stress."

"Ahhhh," I have no clue what to say or how to clear this up, so I go for the best I can do. "It's late. I think I am going to hit the hay." I immediately turn and grab the door handle with guilt tugging at my heart. "Abby," she's walking away, but quickly turns in a carefree, out-on-a-night-walk fashion. "Hey, can we just kinda keep this under wraps?"

I look at Judd, remembering all that I said to Abby last night; nope, there is no doubt.

"Oh yeah…no, I definitely told her. Like an idiot, I just let it all fall right out of my trap."

Judd laughs, his eyes filled with a mix of you-poor-damn-sap and wow-you-screwed-up.

"I figured as much. You don't usually think things through before saying them. I'm sure it'll all work out though." His phone chimes and he glances at it before stepping toward the door. "Just keep trying."

I nod once and press my lips together in a somewhat appreciative smile. "Will do. Think I'm going to test these heaters out by seeing if I freeze my ass off in the shower. You better get going before your girl-friend gets too lonely. I'm sure going a whole morning without sex is about to drive you two insane."

Judd stares me down as I chuckle. "Bye, Evan," he says, rolling his eyes dramatically.

Once he is out the door, I toss my sweatshirt and jacket across the sink while I pick up a few tools we missed. The tee I have on sticks to my back like a silent plea to turn the heater down. Damn, that thing can pipe out some heat. Walking over, I stare at the dial set on high and make a decision to turn it down to medium. Maybe a bad decision, especially if I step out of the shower and freeze.

After adjusting the temp, I pull the curtain to the first shower stall closed, strip down and let the hot soothing water rain over me. It doesn't take long to wash off, considering I didn't take the time to go gather my shampoo or body wash, but it's wet and relaxing; that's all I care about right now. Tossing the curtain open, I look down at the bench in the changing space and all I see is my clothes. Dammit; I didn't even think to grab a towel. *Shit.*

I stand there, buck-ass naked and dripping wet, weighing my op-tions.

Shake like a dog and then slip my clothes back on?

Stand under the blow dryer and hope that I get at least a tenth of my body dry?

Turn the heat back up and air dry?

At least the room is plenty warm.

"Evan…" My eyes go wide, not particularly at knowing I'm not alone as I stand here nude, but at the voice itself. "Hey, can I talk to you…" Piper rounds the corner and my heart stops. "Oh God!" she spits out, throwing her hands and her jacket over her face.

I don't move; don't make any effort to dart behind anything. *Is that my sweatshirt?* Placing both of my hands on my hips, I squint at the gray material she has her head buried in. A 'Ro' with a 'C' below it is all I can make out, but I know it's my sweatshirt. Piper no longer went to Rosemore our senior year, and that in fact, is the sweatshirt I got my senior year…Rosemore High Class of 2014.

"Are you decent?" her voice comes out muffled, making me think she may smother if she doesn't come up for air soon.

I look around, before leaning back against the edge of the shower and folding my arms across my chest. *Guess my choice is clear; I'll air dry.*

She slowly drops her hands and my sweatshirt a fraction of an inch. "Oh geez, Evan…why on earth are you standing here naked?" She places her face back in the wad of fabric, sounding like she's in a tunnel when she speaks. "This is a public restroom."

"I was in the shower," I point out the obvious, staying comfortable against the wall. *I don't have anywhere to go.*

Droplets of water still slide down my chest, tickling my skin and letting me know I have plenty of time.

She sighs and drops her hands to her waist, annoyance blanketing her expression now with a hint of amusement in her eyes. I want to laugh, but I keep a straight face, completely serious and confident standing here in the buff.

"Ok, well fine…you can't at least cover yourself?"

I look straight at her face, my lip ticking up at the corners. "I forgot my towel."

"Ooooookkk…" She looks down at my discarded clothes with the exception of the one in her hand. "So get dressed."

Pressing my lips together to hold back laughter, I stare at her hands still gripping my shirt. "I'm trying to dry off first." I glance up to make eye contact and then back to the shirt with a grin on my face. "Is that my sweatshirt?" I nudge my chin forward.

Her eyes dart down to it. "Oh ahh…well I saw it on the sink and I, ahhhh…" I grin as she searches for an answer that doesn't include her hugging my shirt. "Yeah…I just thought…" she clears her throat and straightens her stance, still clinging to it. "Anyways, I was hoping we could talk for a second."

Arching one brow on her words, I remain comfortably perched against the shower wall, not even chilly in the slightest. I level my gaze with her, staring at her hard; curious. *I know she wants to look.*

"About?" I smirk, raising my brows.

She hugs my sweatshirt to her chest, making me a bit envious. "All I wanted to say is…" Her chest rises on a deep breath. "…thank you," she spits out as she exhales, like those words took every ounce of courage she had.

I don't say a word, my playfulness on enticing her to possibly take in an eyeful evaporating along with the shower water that had clung to my body. For once there is no bitterness in her words; it's the voice I used to know.

She gives me a close-lipped smile, igniting a tidal wave of nostalgia. It was never an expression that meant she was happy, not even one that would necessarily open up a gateway to tell me she wanted to talk. It was more of a pained smile, an I'm-going-to-smile-through-the-hurt kind of look. Just that, breaks me. It slaps me down and makes me regret that stupid ass mistake I made back then.

She goes on, "Thank you for helping me last night. I forgot…" she pauses, looking down and taking another profound breath. "…it was nice."

My eyebrows shoot up and I stand up straight away from the wall, my arms still across my torso.

"It was? I mean, yeah…ahhh…you're welcome." I gulp down all the heavy shit I want to say and go for subtle. "I meant what I said…I'm still here…ya know." I dip my chin and grit my teeth, wondering if that may unleash the storm.

Her eyes dart back to meet mine and slowly her lips curve into that bright beautiful smile I remember. *God, I haven't seen that directed at me in what seems like forever.* This is a bigger victory than seeing those dumbass heaters actually crank out heat when I swore they wouldn't. The corner of my mouth slightly raises, mocking her own smile and we both stand there in utter silence. Strangely, given the fact that I am awkwardly standing here completely nude and she is grasping my shirt like she desperately needs a cuddle buddy with no one else around except me, my mind still steers clear of any indecent thoughts. I mean this is Piper, I've had a thing for her since I was fourteen years old. Even after I found out what happened, it never dampened the way I wanted her or the way I looked at her. She always said that was the trait she loved the most; that I didn't see her memories like she did. When I looked at her, I saw her and only her; just like now.

I take a U-turn from the 'I'm always here' statement and try to lighten the entire mood. *Enough seriousness.*

"So you heard the shower going when you walked in and decided *now* was a good time to talk? Like maybe I was over here testing the water pressure, fully clothed or something?" I press my lips tightly together, exhaling out my nose on a chuckle.

She squints her eyes, giving me an evil glare, but I can see through it. This is the playful girl I knew back then; the giggly, trusting personality that usually only emerged when she was around me.

"Evan, don't flatter yourself. I...did...not...come in here to see you naked by any means." She clears her throat again, a sign that she is uncomfortable or maybe even putting forth an extreme effort to look me in the eye.

I know she wants to look.

She quirks her brows, looking sexy as hell in a self-confident stare. "I actually ran into Judd outside and he said you were in here testing out the heaters." She juts her chin side-to-side with a little attitude.

I seriously want to laugh my ass off, but I keep my composure, holding it back for now. "Riiiiigggghhhht," I draw out slowly and deliberately to emphasize the absurdity of her comment. "By taking a shower."

Frowning, she shifts and glances behind her to the new wall unit. She shrugs, not understanding my point.

"I was testing out the heaters by taking a shower. You know...seeing if winter vacationers could trust the heaters to keep them toasty, or if they may freeze their goods off by the subzero drafts when they step out of the shower dripping wet."

I drop all emotion and amusement from my expression and look at her, gauging her reaction. I used to love getting under her skin and riling her up. It was our thing; me teasing and pestering her, and her always giving into my smartass ways with a pissy comment or defiant attitude.

My restraint holds on for so long and then I cave, a huge grin taking over my face. "They work good; don't you think?"

She shrugs, blinking her eyes rapidly. I'm thinking my willpower isn't the only one faltering; this is killing her. I know she's curious.

"I just figured I could gauge the temperature better coming out of the shower, but the boys seem perfectly at ease." I nod my head once as her eyes dart down so quickly I barely catch it. "It's ok…I know it's been killing you since you rounded that corner."

She looks me in the eyes, rolling her own and releasing an exaggerated sigh which only furthers my amusement. Honestly, I really want to thrust my hips or wobble them side-to-side, but I hold back a bit. I don't want her to be completely dumbfounded. It may be too much for her eyes to take in all at once anyways.

"Here, I'd say you need this more than I do." She holds my sweatshirt out, stretching her arm all the way out as if she's afraid to step into the changing space or get too close.

I glance down, making sure nothing unexpectedly pops up during my playfulness. Looking back up, I tilt my head and reach for my shirt. "Thaaanks," I say slowly and pull it to my chest, not bothering to take her hint.

"You can dry off with it, since you forgot your towel." She spins around, then stops. Looking back, her face lights up with a mischievous smile and my body definitely tingles with a subtle reaction. "…and if you ask me…" she glances down and back up. *Ok now I feel exposed.* "…maybe you need to turn the heat up a few degrees."

My eyes widen as she turns back and starts to walk off.

"Oh no, no...get back here and take another look."

"I've seen it before, Evan. It wasn't that impressive back then," her voice is laced in friskiness, but I still bite.

"Oh no way. Come take a better look. That was years ago. I'm older and trust me, all of me has grown up and gotten better with age," I holler, my voice echoing in the room. "Get back here." I race around the corner, slipping my sweatshirt over my head with not a scrap of fabric to cover me below the waist.

As soon as I round the corner, I feel a cold draft and see Piper swing around and take another eyeful with a teasing smile. "Bye Evan...don't forget to crank up that heater."

"Hey, Piper."

I have no time to take cover before Jake is in the door and Piper has fled with a sneaky little grin on her face.

"Oh damn, man, put some clothes on."

I laugh and dart back into the stall.

"Where is your towel?" Jake questions from the other side of the wall.

Slipping one leg into my jeans, followed by the next, I shake my head and relish in the whirling effect that 'the old Piper' had on me. A smirk lies firmly across my face along with a refreshed mood that had nothing to do with the shower as I join him.

"What's up with you?" He looks around and I laugh. "Do I want to know what just happened in here?"

"No," I crack up at his suspicions.

"Because, I actually came here first instead of Judd's cabin. I figured I'd be walking into the middle of something there."

I grit my teeth, knowing exactly what he means. "Yeah...no, good call. Nothing like that has went on here, I assure you, but I can't tell you what has been shaking up at their cabin. I'd stay away for about an hour longer, then it should be safe."

Jake snickers. "So you always install heaters without pants?"

I shake my head, knowing I may never hear the end of this, but still smile. Even though I didn't get the same enjoyment out of the afternoon as Judd is more than likely getting now, it definitely without a doubt, got more than hot in here. *No need to turn that heater up.*

Need Him

Piper

GLANCING OVER, I LOOK DOWN to the shower house, a stir of excitement and exhilaration still revving from my encounter with Evan. I look down at the gravel covered ground as I kick a few small stones and curve my lips into a smile. I have been seriously distracted since Dad got here earlier; I can't get Evan off my mind.

"Ok sweetie…enjoy your Christmas. I'll see you in a couple days, ok?"

Snapping back to reality, I throw my arms around Dad's neck, feeling as I always have, safe and secure, knowing he is the only man I can ever fully trust.

"Thanks, Daddy. I love them." I put on my cheesiest grin ever, turning my head side-to-side to model the new earrings that he gave me for Christmas.

He has never been too keen on the holidays, always using the excuse of his sister running away with some boy when he was a senior in high school and remarking how everything seemed dull after that, like the life was drained from his family. As a kid, Mom, Dad and I always enjoyed big holiday functions and happy celebrations around a decked out Christmas tree. However, after he found out about Trent, him and mom were battling an ugly divorce based on he says/she says arguments. It didn't help that Mom held onto the constant belief that I exaggerated the event.

She was always so protective of Trent; she coddled him like she never had me. From the time he came to live with us the summer I turned twelve, she nurtured and loved him like he was her own. I never thought anything of it until the day we returned back to the cabin after our encounter with Mitch. When Dad sat down to discuss it between the three of us, Mom was livid. She shook her head and screamed for me to quit lying; she fell apart. That is when the journey of changing schools, moving to a different town and living a completely different life began. However, Dad never questioned me or gave it a second thought. He clung to me and protected me from everything. We held each other up, but life wasn't quite the same.

"You're welcome. I wish…"

Widening my eyes joyfully, I nudge my chin forward, a joking reaction to get him to stop his ramblings; ones that I have heard before.

"Don't. I won't hear of it. Quit wishing you would have done more. You do more than enough and I love them. They are perfect and exactly what I wanted."

I pull back, standing in front of Dad outside of his small silver Camry. Warm, sweater covered arms engulf my neck, and I laugh.

"She was just telling me yesterday that she hoped she got a pair of new earrings for Christmas so you did good," Abby pipes up from behind me.

Dad chuckles, shaking his head. "Good deal. I'm getting better at this mind reading since you never tell me what you want." He rolls his eyes, turning to open the door to his car. "You girls got big plans for the New Year?"

I flip my head to look at Abby. "Do we?"

Abby laughs, moving away from me and slipping her hand over her mouth. "We didn't plan a thing did we?" My hair tickles across my neck as I shake my head. She looks at my dad with her eyes narrowed and her mouth drawn down into an exaggerated frown. "We have been so busy planning our first Christmas dinner that we didn't even think of the following holiday. Ummmm…hello…New Years. How could we forget?"

I wave my hand through the air to disregard her worry over a missed celebration. "Oh, we'll do something. Either we can hang here for a couple more days and throw a party or I'm sure something is going on near campus."

Abby crinkles up her nose and nods. "You're right. Have a safe trip home Mr. Shields." She waves and takes off back towards the cabin.

"Come by and visit sometime…" Dad calls out as she races off with her hand held up to acknowledge his comment.

I giggle at her carefree spunk and liveliness. I've always loved that about Abby; probably why we get along so well. We are like night and day, but her fiery, bold, and blunt persona always seems to make up for my withdrawn, somewhat quiet demeanor.

"Sure you won't stay for Christmas? I'm making a turkey and all the sides." I wiggle my brows to add to the appeal of my very first effort in throwing together a huge holiday meal. Sure I've dabbled in the kitchen and made sure to keep Dad fed with more than a turkey sandwich all through my high school existence, but cooking a large bird that takes two girls to hoist it into the oven is not exactly my forte.

Dad shows his teeth, pressing them together in an I'd-rather-poison-myself-slowly sort of expression. I laugh, slapping my hand across his arm.

"Oh, I almost forgot…I have some mail for you." He twists at the waist and takes a seat sideways in the driver's side of his car. Bending across the console, he flips the dashboard open and pulls out several envelopes. "Here…" he looks at me with a weird expression, nervous.

My curiosity piques with this. Flipping my fingertips quickly through the perfectly rectangle, sealed packages, I make no effort to avoid a papercut. I dash past one from the board of education, one I know that is my car payment, another my insurance, but then I stop.

My hand trembles as I look at the carefully swooped handwriting that I always adored as a kid. I glance up at Dad.

"Mom?"

Tucking his lips into his mouth, he presses them together on an apologetic smile. "Yeah...I think so. I mean, it's her hand writing and I believe that is her current address. I haven't talked to her in a while." He sighs and reaches for it. "You know I shouldn't have given it to you. I really thought about not..."

I pull my entire body back, defensively claiming ownership of all the envelopes in my hand including the one from Mom, which has had very little association with me since I was sixteen years old.

"No," I say softly, free of any animosity or regret that I'm holding it now; no fear of what it could say. "I'm glad you did. She didn't tell you she was sending anything?"

"She didn't," he gulps and looks down. "Want to open it?"

Selfishness nips at my heart as I consider how to word this as gently as possible. Not only did what happened to me alter my life, but it turned Dad's world upside down just as much if not more. I've carried around guilt over that and always will. I used to want to lash out at Evan each time I saw the hurt in Dad's eyes. I wanted to scream at him for having a big mouth and not biting his tongue when he had promised to never tell a soul. But now, in the past 24 hours, the constant weight of that anger and bitterness is gently and gradually lifting off my shoulders.

"Would you mind if I opened it by myself?" I hate asking him that, because I know despite how cold she was, he still misses her.

His eyes don't waver in their happiness to see me, though. He smiles and stands, grasping both my arms in his hands. "Of course." Pulling me in for a hug, I grip the stack of envelopes and squeeze him back.

"Thanks, Dad."

He pulls away and hops in his car without another word. I watch him head home, a heaviness settling in my heart as I throw my hand into the cool early night's air for one more goodbye. The envelope lies absolutely still in my hand, yet feels more like a ton of bricks.

My mind speeds through the many months since I've seen her and that was just a random bump into each other at a store, where she maybe said five words to me at the most and then escaped quickly. Step by step, I amble along the bumpy gravel lot to Dad's nearly worn out van that he graciously surrendered to me on my sixteenth birthday. My eyes never leave the letter, and I make no attempts at ripping open the tattered flap of the envelope.

I run my fingers along the dog-eared edge that looks as if it spent a good while nuzzled between the seat of the mail truck. Stopping at the door to my vehicle, I convince myself to take one hand, just one, off the letter long enough to open it and step inside. I cannot even comprehend my own emotional overload; it's like a sacred treasure that I've waited years to stumble upon, yet bitter sweet because she walked away. She shouldn't mean anything to me, or this certainly shouldn't either. Honestly, the first thought in my mind should be to rip it up and just toss it in the trash, burn it? I can't even pinpoint the exact affliction or happiness it holds over my heart or whether it's just peace of mind that I'm not forgotten.

Perfectly settled in the large leather seat with only the dome light to help me out, my hands rest in my lap and I stare at the elaborate way she swoops the curves of the 'P' in my name. Without thinking, I guide my fingertip along the contours of the smudged ink and trace her handwriting. A sense of ease settling into my chest on the thought; that her hands touched this same paper. I sigh as I flip it over, frustrated that I'm even letting this touch me. *Enough of that.*

My fingers frantically pull and tear at the flap until it is a chewed up mess exposing its contents. I grip the folded-up notebook page between my thumb and index finger to pull it free, letting the envelope drop back to my lap. On an unfulfilling breath, I flip the tri-folded paper open and find a completely separate handwriting than what was on it. I grab the envelope back up to look at her writing again; no name above the address, but it's her writing. Dropping it again, I look at the letter, staring at it and searching. The first thing I see completely baffles me and leaves me ready to dart straight to the end. Sort of like a good book that you want nothing more than to just read to the last page; find out whether it's a happily ever after sort of read or if it's going to leave you clasping the book to your chest in utter disbelief at how it truly ended. An eerie, gut-wrenching fear grips my heart; *this is not from mom.* I want to look at the bottom and see who had signed it, but I don't...I read.

Piper,

> *I know your first instinct is going to be to rip this up, destroy it, anything just not to read it, but I'm begging you to read this all when you feel you can. Believe it or not, this is the sixth time I have written a letter to you. I suspect I'll write it a couple dozen more times, then toss them in the trash just like the rest, but I would like to think that one day I will have the courage to send it. That maybe I will get some sort of sign telling me that you are as ready as me to hear this...*

> *I know first off, I should cut to the chase and just say sorry, but there is far more that I need to say to you. Sorry and I never meant to hurt you is not good enough; no words are good enough really. If I had it in my power to erase time, I suppose that may be the only thing that I could do to make it right, but I can't. I'd give anything to do that though...for us both. Piper, for so long I was so messed up...confused, scared and even saying that makes me feel selfish and greedy. I have no right to tell you anything I felt when I tossed all those pains at you in a matter of seconds. I robbed you of your innocence and stole something I can never give back. I cheated you...*

The words blur and my heart stops. My eyes fill with tears and my hands tremble as I dig my fingertips into the paper so hard that it bends little craters into the edges, perfectly sculpted to my fingertips. My breath catches, over and over. I don't need to finish; I can't. *Why would she send this to me?* The tender reflective sentiments that I felt from holding something that had once rested in my mother's hands freezes in my veins and turns my blood ice cold.

Just when I think my bewilderment over him daring to send this cannot reach any higher, I come to a screaming halt on one thought. My heart clutches, racing back to the flawless script handwriting that I remember from when Mom would write letters to her sister in Nevada. I close my eyes, releasing a heart wrenching sigh on the address and writing that was displayed on the envelope: 120 East Elmwood in Rosemore.

"Mom sent this to me…" I whisper to myself, so quiet that the vibrations of my words nearly sound like a whiney hum.

Tears trail down my face and my vision fogs over as more come. It's never ending, and the pull at my heart is excruciating. I always thought with time that she would look at it and come to realize how wrong she was; that maybe she would surprise me with an apology or a 'How could I have ever doubted you'. *Has she kept in contact with him this whole time?* She gave me up for him; for someone that could do such a horrendous act to another person?

She doesn't deserve my tears. She doesn't deserve any of Dad's or my grief over losing her; she never has.

I want to think cold, unfeeling thoughts about her.

I want to hate her like I have hated him all these years, but the heartache goes too deep.

I've carried so much hate with me through the years, that at times, it seemed as if it may eat me alive. Closing my eyes, all strength in my arms fail me as they fall onto my legs with the letter hardly clutched in my hands. I release a breath and focus.

Breathe, breathe…

My head whirls and spins like a deadly cyclone sweeping through all the painful memories that clutter my mind and hold me back from fully living my life. At times the storm is so strong that it blows me down with it and I struggle to get back up.

Breathe...

For years, I relied on Evan to be my reminder of those words. It became a system that only he and I understood. At first it was gradual, the outbursts and scares. It started with him barely touching me, helping me onto the dock when I was thirteen, but when his touch grazed my hips to push me up, I couldn't hold on; the storm swept me away and I woke up to his face chanting the same words over and over again.

"Breathe, Piper...Breathe...Come on...Breathe with me. Take a breath."

"Breathe with me...I breathe; you breathe...that's it."

Just like it has for years, those words echo in my mind; not in my voice but in his. It's always been his voice that I have heard when the memories begin to pull me under. I pushed him away and have done my best to hate him for the past several years, but when he said he has always been here, he has no idea how true that is. He has always been here. I have never let him go. I've worked diligently to shove him from my heart and at moments, even the fact that I still needed him in a way, in any way after his deceit, I hated it.

My eyes squeeze shut tighter, the lids fusing together, but still not stopping the unending flow of tears. They soak my face with moisture, droplets collecting at my chin and jawline until two or three drips become too much and they plummet to my chest.

Dropping my head back to the headrest, it bounces subtly with a hushed thump. The spinning slows and I can finally hear the sound of my own heartbeat slowing; my breathing coming in deep exhales and inhales rather than short gasping spurts. Planting my entire hand along the back of the page, I look down, refusing to read any more. I'm not strong enough yet; I don't know if I'll ever be.

Should I rip it up; wad it up and throw it away? I tighten my grip with my thumbs bent and pressing it forcefully against the edge of my palm. My eyes focus again, and although my mind is screaming, *don't read it*, I stare hurtfully at the first sentence.

I'm begging you to read it all when you feel you can...

An overpowering breath moves over my lips and I stop myself, holding my hands steady and easing my grip. Gently folding one end over the next, I shove the paper back in the envelope and hold it tightly. As I fold the flap over, I struggle to release just a little bit of my animosity, fear of what the rest says and hurt over Mom's part in this. So I pack it all away with the letter. I let all the emotion drain from me on a serene breath, like a reckless energy flowing from the dark parts of my heart, through my veins and out of my fingertips. Running my palm across the smooth flat surface, I press it closed so that the contents will never find me again.

After shoving it into my glove compartment, I sit there lost, not sure what to do. I've always felt when I am around people when my past secrets emerge, that it is written all over my face. I know it's not, but I also know the shame and pain is laced in every word I say and if anyone looks at me for long, I'll burst into tears, believing that they can see it.

My hands slide around the cool, curved steering wheel, clutching it for strength as Evan's face fills my mind; standing in the doorway of his camper the night it happened. He made the difference.

Breathe, just breathe with me...you can do it. I breathe, you breathe.

His deep voice gives me reassurance as I picture him lying beside me the first night we ever even thought about taking our relationship to the next level. Resting on his side, he smoothed his hand over my cheek and calmed all my hesitation and fears in being touched. He made something I had come to see as dirty and indecent suddenly become beautiful and passionate. No one else has ever evoked that in me. With my eyes closed and my entire body melted against the seat, I allow his face and words to bring me back to reality. They lull me into contentment, yet with one desperate plea; I wish he was here. It's not the first time this feeling has come over me. It overwhelms me nearly every time this happens, but I force it down; shove it so deep, then let the hatred over his deception completely drown me until that single emotion is only a memory.

My eyes bolt open and I stare across the lot to his camper, knowing this time he is just steps away. I watch, my insides leaping with a need that I'm not going to shut out this time. All day, our conversation has weighed on my mind, giving me a sense of excitement that I could someday have my friend back; that I could find it in me to forgive and forget, an act that has never been easy for me.

A warmth slowly and softly swells in my chest, making the edge of my lips tug.

I want to see him; I need him.

Go for it

Evan

"**I** CANNOT BELIEVE THIS SHIT," I mumble more to myself. "What?" Jake snickers not too far away as I spread a sheet out on one of the spare fold out cots from the storage shed.

I shake my head, straightening the edges out and flattening the top so that it lays perfectly flat against the mattress. Shuffling sounds behind me and I look back. Jake plops down onto the hideaway bed stationed in the middle of the living room floor.

I laugh. *Of course he's chipper, he didn't have to take the bed right against the wall to Judd and Alyssa's bedroom. I might as well resign myself to getting absolutely no sleep tonight.*

"They don't get that loud, do they?" he asks in a disturbed tone.

Huffing out another chuckle, I raise my brows and look at him in a manner that says, 'Are you serious?!'

"Ahh…yeah. They aren't quiet, that's for sure."

"We are not that loud, Evan." Judd leans against the doorframe to the back bedroom with his arms across his chest and a smirk on his face.

I scowl at him, not even feeling it in the slightest, but I prefer him to think I'm dreading the noise so maybe he'll show sympathy for my poor scarred-for-life ears. He knows I'd never begrudge him the happiness of an all-night booty call or a long life of playing under the sheets.

My mouth falls open as I shove my laughter down. "Yeah...you are. I guarantee the cabins across the lake have heard you sometime today."

Ok, that's a little far-fetched, but if anyone has ever had to sleep through the sounds that I have since he's met Alyssa, they'd surely be begging him to invest in a muzzle or some sort of serious noise filtering device for the entire neighborhood. It's funny how reserved, well-mannered and polite they both seem, almost like a parent's idea of a perfectly raised child, but get them behind closed doors and that calm, pardon-me persona is out the flipping window, drowned out by wild-ass bedroom mayhem; I've heard it, not by choice, but I know.

I stare at Judd, masking my amusement with a shocked expression.

"Evan, you think it's awesome when two squirrels start humping in the yard. We are not that noisy. We keep it down. Maybe you're just on the other side, pressing your ear to the wall."

Jake spits out a snort and I cock my head back, scrunching my face up like I just took a bite of something sour.

"That's gross dude. So you think I want to subject my ears to your kinky bedroom talk?"

Judd's face flames and he looks quickly at Jake. I can't suppress my laughter anymore, dipping my chin and chuckling at his embarrassment.

"I don't care. I brought ear phones." Jake looks innocently down at his bag as Judd stares at him like he just got his pants pulled down in public.

"We are not that loud," he goes on, and now I just think he's trying to convince himself.

I can see the wheels turning; I actually have him questioning how loud he is every night. No wonder he got another place. The awareness of it is probably majorly screwing with his bed play. He probably cups his hand over her mouth while they are doing it, pleading with her to quiet down. *Geez, this is killing me.* Suppose I should break it to him that he really isn't breaking any sound barriers.

Nahhh.

"Damn, I should have brought my earbuds," I mumble to myself. Judd swings his eyes to me and shakes his head. "What? I didn't think my heater would break the second day I was out here and I sure didn't think I'd be shacking up with you and Blondie on your romantic Christmas get-away in the woods." I roll my eyes with a smirk.

"Yeah…" Judd suddenly looks like he's discovered some new information to defend his later headboard-thumping-earsplitting-moans-squeaking-mattress-springs activities. "Let's forget that we were supposed to have this cabin to ourselves, but hey, I couldn't leave your whiney-ass out in the cold camper."

I crook a grin. I will not deny at all that I'm a whiney-ass when it comes to winter temperatures; I get a chill and I will be the first to moan and groan. All these dudes that choose to spend all day in a tree stand waiting for Prancer to dance into their sights, they can have it. I'll huddle up in my apartment or in this case, Judd's cabin, next to the fire in my sweatshirt and jeans. In my book, that's smart. Give me a sunny day at the ball park with sweat dripping down my back from the stifling temps as I listen to the roar of the crowd and the crack of the bat sending the ball into a mob of frenzied baseball fans and I'm there. I'd prefer less clothes, with the boys hanging loose beneath my shorts, rather than layering an army pile of rags on to keep me warm.

"Ok, I'll give you that," I sigh and resign myself to poking fun at them once I hear it later; I'm sure I will. "I'll keep my wise cracks to myself."

Judd shifts his head back, squinting his eyes skeptically. I look down and continue making my bed for the night.

"For now…" I add quietly.

He laughs as the bathroom door opens.

"For now what?" Alyssa says, and I know I better keep it to myself. Sweet as she may look, she will dish it right back; that's what I love about her. I don't think Judd could have gotten any luckier when he found this one.

I move my head side-to side slowly to dramatically mock Judd's response.

"He's giving me shit about the noise again," Judd laughs.

From the corner of my eyes, I catch him pulling her closer. "I would say get a room, but…" I look through the doorway they are standing in.

"On that note, I think I will listen to some music." Jake grabs his ear phones out of his bag, plugging them into his iPod.

"Chicken-shit. A true friend would suffer through this torture with me, you know?"

Jake looks right at me, huffing out a chuckle as he slides the ear phones on. "Good luck sleeping."

I crack up, staring him down and trying my best to relay my thoughts, *you, lucky bastard, preparing for your stay.*

"Whatever," Judd pipes up. "Good night."

"Night guys," Alyssa says sweetly with a smile as she ducks under Judd's arm that firmly holds up the frame to the bedroom as if it may come unhinged.

I wave her off with a genuine smile back, Jake does the same. Looking back at Judd, who now has a sneaky grin, I drop my smile.

"What?"

"Nothing…" he draws out, still looking deep in thought. I have no idea what he's thinking. "I was just going to say good night." He smiles, looking from me then to Jake, who throws his hand up, then back to me. "Good luck sleeping." A lame-ass smile spreads over his face as he ducks into the room and shuts the door behind him.

"What an asshole," I chuckle under my breath then look at Jake. "Can you believe that?"

Jake slides the black headband Princess-Leia-bun looking ear-phones off one ear. "What?"

I shake my head dismissing it with a chuckle as I bounce into bed, quickly realizing I forgot one vital component to sleeping in this stiff vinyl cot that Grandpa calls a bed.

"Man, I forgot my pillow."

Jake shifts in his bed and looks back towards my lame excuse for a room shoved into the corner of the living room. I could do without sleeping on a stiff ass cot, but I have to take what I can get; I'm not sleeping in a thirty-degree camper or under the same roof as my brother. *No thank you.*

"I think they had a couple on their bed. I'm sure they'll give one up." Jake points back towards Judd and Alyssa's room while still looking down at his phone, flipping his finger along the screen like he's scrolling through a social media page or website.

I scrunch up my nose and grit my teeth as I consider the idea of borrowing one for only half a second before rethinking. "That's just gross. I don't know where that pillow's been."

He snickers quietly, focusing on whatever he has going on while I walk across the room, dressed in my Rosemore sweatshirt, sweatpants and my socks.

Glancing to my boots by the door, I say screw it and fling the door open in a dead sprint to my camper to grab my pillow along with an extra blanket, not that it is cold in the cabin, but I might just drape it over me on the way back. The bitter cold nips at my face and the hard ground is like a block of ice sending a splintering pain up my calf with every thud of my feet. No sooner than my hand lands on the door handle, I have the door ripped open and bolt inside in a mad dash to escape the chills that are racing over the surface of my skin. The relief I was hoping to find is somewhat fulfilled, yet not nearly enough. I drape my thick comforter over my shoulders and hold my pillow to my chest, creating a suit of armor against the frosty wind that was biting me in the ass, as I made the trek here.

On the way back, I make double time as if my tail was lit on fire. Jake snaps his head around with a smirk as I slam the door and stand against it like Bigfoot is about to pound it down behind me.

"Cold?" he asks lazily, looking back to his phone.

I let out a breath and allow the warmth to envelope my entire body, goose bumps sprouting up and the hairs on my arm standing on end.

"Yeah…" I mumble, contemplating jumping right into the fire-place.

"Well, I'm out for the night."

I open my mouth but quickly get cut off by a thud. I swing my head around to the bedroom door, but immediately halt all worries on whether one of them slipped on the hardwood floor or if the roof fell in on them, or even if there may be a brewing tornado right outside their window.

"You weren't kidding." I look at Jake as he slides down in bed and pulls his ear phones back over his ears. "Night…oh and good luck again." He sneaks a sly grin in my direction before closing his eyes.

"Gee, thanks." I flip the overhead light off and walk straight across the creaky floor till I am finally to my hovel.

Not even caring that my blanket is half wadded up in one corner, I jump in, sweats and all, tossing the pillow behind my head and pulling the comforter up to my neck. The softness of it is a complete contradiction of the inflexible surface that is boring into my back. In my opinion, this is just an outdated military stretcher. I think back for a minute, and remember seeing them at many of the bases we lived at growing up.

Closing my eyes, my body relaxes and begins to mold to the cot. A heavy weight settles over my lids as I drift off and surrender to sleep.

Thump…

My eyes spring open as more barely-there sounds filter through the air. *Oh great!* A soft girly whine, giggling and another thump and I turn on my side. Digging my shoulder into the stiff bed, I clasp my pillow in my fist and pull the other side over my face to filter out the noise; quiet. I relax again, but as soon as sleep starts to creep over me, I hear a roar of giggles and laughs coming through the wall.

I stretch my eyes open, feeling as though I am back in my apartment all over again. *Thank God their headboard is against the other wall here.* That was a pain in the ass. I cannot even count the times I beat Judd home from work and considered bolting that thing down, desperate for just a solid hour of sleep. If he wasn't knocking boots in the next room, then Skylar was crashing my peaceful evening of sleep. At this point, my body should be used to a max of two hours of rest per night.

Thud…

That's it! I don't even think about Jake sleeping about ten feet away before my fist is pounding on the wall, sending vibrations through my forearm and an echoing drumming sound through the cabin. More giggling rises along with another thump against the wall.

"Cooooome Oooon," I groan.

"Evan," I barely make out my name being called from their room. "Go to sleep. We aren't being that loud."

I hold back my laughter, widening my eyes as usual. *He always says that. Does he really flip all over that mattress all night long, laughing and doing bedroom acrobats that make the walls shake and truly not think he's noisy?*

"Really?!" I rifle back sarcastically.

The bedroom door flings open and the shadow of a head peaks out. "Are we really going to do this tonight?"

I want to laugh at his frustration, because he full-well was supposed to have this cabin to himself. In fact, he had requested complete solitude from me when he asked me to come out and join them. I believe his exact words were, 'You should come join us for Christmas at the lake. Piper will be there…but just know that Alyssa and I would really like to have a cabin to ourselves…like far away from you'. I actually laughed my ass off, but then put his request in with Grandpa. I guess life sucks, because Jake surprises his big bro with a friendly visit that sort of squashed their dreams of waxing the floors with their asses all week long too. Then of course, I crashed the party.

"Do you really not hear yourself?" I smile, although he can't see it.

"We are keeping it down," he points out in a matter of fact tone as he keeps only his head stuck through the opening of the door.

"Geez, are you standing there naked? Go finish what you were doing, but a word of advice...laughing probably means you're not knocking her socks off, dude."

"She wasn't laughing at me...we were laughing...you know what never mind. Just quit pounding on the wall."

I stifle back a laugh, my chest and stomach shaking. "You were pounding on the wall. I just thought it was a game...you know, like you knock three times and I knock three times...Blondie squeals and giggles and I moan and groan..."

"Whatever," he spits out quickly. "And by the way, we weren't knocking on the walls."

"Yes, you were." I challenge, really loving the fact that he is getting fully irritated.

I love aggravating him, of course, he'll get me back no doubt, but I definitely have a bit more aggravation in store for the holidays.

"Evan, we're keeping it down and we will continue...just go to sleep."

"Ok, but I'm telling you, you were..." I start.

Shuffling like fabric on fabric sounds from the center of the room. "Actually, you know what...I can't stay out of this any longer. You were making quite a bit of noise."

Ha! I sit all the way up and point to Jake with a huge ass smile, then point over to Judd, wishing the lights were on so he could see my amusement over his baby brother coming to my defense. Moreover, I'd love to see his face.

"Oh..." I barely hear Judd's quiet response as if he is finally convinced that all night hammering is capable of depriving some of us a good snooze.

"It's cool, I just turned my music back on. I just don't want to hear anything else." Jake slinks back into the bed, nonchalantly throwing his headphones back on for the third time tonight. He's oblivious to the fact that he just made my year by agreeing with me on a four-month argument over Judd thinking he makes no noise and me informing him that any louder and they may wake the dead.

I stare back at Judd, my grin growing along with the silence.

"Told ya…" I say quietly, breaking the sudden peacefulness of crackling logs without the rocking sounds of their bed.

"Ok, well…I'm going back to bed." He slumps back down but not before I hear his chuckle.

Damn those ear phones Jake has; Judd doesn't mind keeping me awake, he just doesn't want to traumatize his little brother, whom he's always viewed as innocent. I know better; Jake and I grew closer after Judd and Tristan's wreck and he definitely is not a sweet, oblivious eighteen-year old; he has some skeletons in his closet just like the rest of us.

"I need my ear buds," I mutter as the door clicks shut. Any second, the noise will start back up I'm sure.

Thirty minutes later, I say to hell with it. My ears are hot from holding the pillow over them and Jake has his music up so loud that I can hear it filtering out from his headphones. The racket from the bedroom isn't too bad, but if I fall asleep listening to "Oh Judd", it may send some very unwelcoming dreams into my subconscious, and I'm just not cool with that. Last thing I want is to be chanting the same thing in my sleep; so I lay here, quiet and relaxed. My phone rests on the floor beside me, lighting up every once in a while with notifications that I don't care to check. I've never been much of a technology buff. I prefer to live in the real world and not on my phone.

A strange noise hits my ears like a twig tapping against the window or something. I stop all thoughts and lie still, listening. Jake's music and shallow breaths come through clearly as I focus my hearing on every sound in the room; nothing.

Shifting onto my side, I glance over to the orange glow of the fireplace which pops and crackles every few minutes as the same tapping greets my ears again, this time louder. I stop everything and sit up quickly. *Is that knocking?* Looking across the room to Jake, he seems to be sound asleep.

Tap…tap.

My head snaps over to the door, now clearly hearing the soft discreet rap of knuckles against wood. I bolt to my feet, half excited that it may be Skylar rewarding me with the opportunity to pay Judd back for all my sleepless nights. Sure Jake may have to turn his music up louder, but it would definitely be sweet revenge.

Flinging the covers off of me, I swing my legs out, then pause. There is nothing but silence until I hear something different. This time it's the barely audible sound of footsteps out on the porch. I jump up, flying to the door with a quick glance in Jake's direction to ensure that he is out for the night. He doesn't move, doesn't register a thing.

My hand falls to the door handle, sending an icy shiver through me as the cold metal sucks a bit of my warmth away. However, as soon as I have the door open and the brisk temperatures hit me, I feel nothing.

"Sk…" I stop before saying anything else as the cold winter chill that I dreaded blasting me, does nothing. I'm too stunned to register anything other than her slinky physique standing still at the edge of the porch, lit only by the distant outer light of the shower house. "Piper," my voice comes out in a raspy shallow garble. Clearing my throat, I try again as she turns my way. "Hey."

My mouth doesn't even shut after my awkward greeting; it remains open, drawing flies and eager to say more if I could find the words. Even though our earlier interaction was fun and playful allowing me to see that sassy, excitable personality that she always had in my company, she is still the very last person I expected to see on my door step. *Wait, this isn't my place.*

"How'd…"

"Hey, ummm…I…oh, I'm sorry," she stumbles around and pauses, her hand dropping to the side railing.

She side-steps, nervously and I watch her every movement as if she's doing them in slow motion. She holds her hand up, pointing; indicating for me to finish my thought, but for the life of me I have no clue what I was going to say. I shake my head, dumbfounded.

The image of her years ago burns into my head and I step forward, taking a quick gander towards her cabin to make sure the creep she's been seeing isn't outside looking for her or anywhere around. I may lose it if I thought for a moment that he had caused her any worry. I come up empty handed, my eyes landing right back on her as I take in her entirety; the way she stands, what she has on, as much as I can make out anyways, and how her voice sounds.

"Oh…ummm…I, I just thought I'd come and ummm…" she stutters, looking around.

Did she not come to see me? Oh yeah, how would she even know I'm here?

A gust of wind blows through the trees, sending a howling sound that echoes around us and gives off a spooky haunted forest vibe. The cool air hits me and this time I feel it. Piper shivers, folding both her arms around her torso to protect her from the weather, or maybe the imaginary ghosts. I chuckle at the thought and move aside as my eyes catch on the fact that she doesn't even have a coat on.

"Come in, it's cold." I wave my hand in front of me as an invitation, but really would like nothing more than to grab her and hurry it along. It's freaking cold, and holding this door open might turn the cabin into a refrigerator, plus I really just want her inside.

She hesitates before giving in, her tensed up posture immediately notating her surrender as her shoulders fall and she lets out an astounding breath that she may have been holding this whole time. Moving past me, she keeps her arms across her, rubbing her hands over them in a frenzy to keep up the blood flow. It used to be that she would get these tiny little goosebumps all along her skin every time I touched her. I loved it; I'd eat up small reactions like that. It was never chills as in she wanted me away, it was a nervousness that came when she was excited, when she wanted more of me. I really doubt that is the case now, but I sure do remember that.

I think carefully before opening my mouth, not wanting to send any signals that I don't want her here or be too rash and blurt out, 'what do you want?'. Lining out a somewhat harmless question, I go for it, knowing full well that I am the king of put-my-foot-in-my-mouth.

"Did you know I was here or have you been stalking me all day after getting that nice view you had earlier?" It's not entirely a foot-crammed-in-my-mouth comment, but it leaves it open for some playfulness, and I'm all about that.

Tiptoeing across the floor as I point towards my corner, she stops and takes her eyes off Jake, which she has been carefully eyeing with gritted teeth as if she was on a mission to be as quiet as possible. She snaps her attention back to me and her expression shifts.

"Don't flatter yourself, Evan. Like I said I wasn't impressed," she whispers.

I hold in my laughter, giving her a wide, tight-lipped smile. "Awww…come on. You could at least humor me and make me think you were."

Her smile grows along with mine and I see a trace of the girl I knew, ready for me to give her hell so she can hand it right back. Shaking her head, she breaks the trance I thought I had her in and dives right back into conversation.

"I saw you run over to your camper earlier then run back here. It was late so I figured you were staying or visiting, either way, I thought I'd come by and invite you to Christmas tomorrow at my cabin."

She goes silent, waiting and watching me. I don't say a thing; I'm too busy staring at her lips as she pulls her bottom one into her mouth, sucking at it like she used to when she'd get nervous. Damn, I wish I were those lips; I'd take being that bottom lip any day. Envy and jealousy claw their way through me as I stare, studying the soft moist skin that glistens under the firelight.

"Oooooorrr…you don't have to. I just thought…"

The movement of her lips and abruptness of her voice snaps me back to reality; the one where I am not devouring her lips like a six-teen-year old virgin that's about to get lucky. Back then, I didn't know half of what I know now and even getting that chance again has faded from my thoughts, up until now.

"Are you listening to me?"

Her hands slide down to her hips as she takes on a defiant stance, but with a light-hearted tone to her voice as if she can read me. I am sure my excitement is written across my face.

"Yeah…"

My footfalls stop as I near my bed. *What the heck now?* I look at the bed and then back to her in question.

"Have a seat," I slide over the cot, scooting my back against the wall and creating boundaries so she doesn't feel apprehensive. I go on, hoping she doesn't think too much about it, "So you weren't stalking me, yet you just happened to be standing outside in thirty to forty-de-gree weather with no coat on, looking this way, huh?"

I raise my eyebrows as she plops down with a little sass in her actions. *There's my girl.* Just like years back, a little distraction and a challenging conversation and she will drop her guard with me and be herself. *God, I love when she does that.*

"Oh, just keep thinking that you're all that, but I just happened to be outside saying goodbye to my dad."

Raising my brows in skepticism, my eyes gleam with enjoyment at her explanation. I know without a doubt that that is not true.

"Noooo…" I draw it out, teasing her, "…your dad left like two hours ago. I saw you saying goodbye earlier right after my heater broke."

She bends her knee, sitting up straight and letting her other leg dangle over the edge. Her arms remain folded across her chest, but this time it's more of a sexy, pouty gesture, not meant to torment or entice me, just letting me know she is fully ready to go head-to-head on any-thing I throw her way.

She spits out a bubbly laugh that makes me grin. "So who is stalking who here?"

"Oh no, no…you still haven't told me how you knew I was here. I know you didn't see me when I walked over then."

"Ok and how do you know that? I think you are the one that was watching me." She arches her brows and cinches her lips together in a kissing-type expression.

I want to grab the back of her neck and pull her to me. My body ticks with the need, but I hold back; a wave of desire swirling through me like a cyclone of wind building and building until it may become a ravenous tornado, ready to unleash all that I've held in for so long.

"Actually, I was watching you." I drop my head back to the wall, looking into her eyes even though the fire is the only thing keeping a hint of light in the room. "And I'm fine admitting that. I looked over and saw you talking to your dad and then I just kept…on…looking."

She stares at me, not saying a word. A sudden high pitched squeal comes from the next room and completely kills the serious vibe we have going.

Piper gasps, looking over to the wall with her mouth hung open and her eyes wide. Looking back to me, she coughs out a laugh, bending at the waist and extending her arm to slap her hand across my knee. I glance down, my abs tensing as I suck in a breath at the sensation of her touch. It's only a second, just a simple flirty smack at my leg, then she is sitting back up, still laughing, but my mind stays right there.

Placing her hand over her mouth to hold back more laughter that has her whole body shaking, she looks at me bright eyed. "Don't you room with Judd?"

I nod, observing the way her hair falls over her shoulders, how her smile spreads into creases across her cheeks and the flicker of the fire in her dark eyes. With so much animosity between us, I'd forgotten how beautiful she is, especially when all her guards are down.

"Oh my Gosh!" she spits out, her eyes wide with amusement. "Do you have to put up with that a lot?" She snuffs out her laughter with both her hands covering her mouth.

Unable to control the overwhelming reaction her happiness has over me, I mirror her hidden smile before correcting my agreement to her comment.

"Oh yeah, I did, but actually they just got their own place together this week." The way she stares back at me has me completely distracted and unable to focus on our discussion.

"Wow, they got their own place?"

I nod once again, slowly keeping my eyes fixed on her lips. They hold me in a trance, my thoughts teetering from the last time mine touched hers, to only days ago when we were at each other's throats. I could go for it; say screw all hesitations, grab her by the waist, pull her to me and taste her lips in a way I never did back when I was only sixteen.

I could, but should I?

"Evan…" she draws out my name much as she did back when we were younger; before anger invaded our carefree relationship. That's all it takes to help me along…

That little sing-song tone in her voice; that says it all.

I'm going for it.

First Kiss

Piper

I LOOK ACROSS THE COT at him, still giggly from my thoughts of what is going on in the next room. *Geez, what am I doing?* His expression is unreadable, not only from the dim lighting and shadows cast over his face, but the way he seems confused and lost in thought.

"Evan," I say, teasingly, a little amused at what has him so transfixed.

The way he's staring at me has me about to go insane. It has my insides bouncing around like a bubbly little teenager with her first crush; or perhaps like the teenager I was…when I was in love with him.

"Ev…"

I don't even have time to get the words out of my mouth when he suddenly scoots across the cot. His face is inches from mine and a soft touch falls to the middle of my back; his hand. My body trembles immediately as I release a strangled gasp with my mouth gaped open. It doesn't scare me like other guys would, because it's Evan.

He knows my fears…

He knows how to touch me…

Where to touch me, and now…

He knows exactly when to touch me, because even though I won't admit it to myself, I've wanted him to all night. I've wanted him to since last night when I had him so close. He was always my security blanket from all the hurt in my life. I need him even if I don't realize it.

"Piper," he whispers my name, his breath moving over my own lips as he moves in closer. I keep my mouth open, my heart beating vigorously as my chest wall pulses in and out, in and out, in a vivacious pace. "Breathe," he utters softly, staring into my eyes.

I look back into his, my thoughts swirling and my heart pounding with an intensity that I've never experienced. My eyes flutter before focusing back on him and I begin to move forward, like a force is pulling me to his lips; beckoning me to see how they feel.

Do they feel the same as they did before?

Another gasp and I close my eyes, spinning, whirling as his hand at my back moves up just below my bra strap. The heat from his gentle caress courses through the thick fabric of my sweater and makes my skin melt like butter beneath his touch. A noise reaches my ears, a quiet whimper that sounds foreign, yet the vibrations of my throat tell me that they are my own.

"Piper...I need you to breathe, ok? Take a deep breath." His words are soothing and hold me steady; they ground me and bring me back to him as he stares intently into my eyes. "Take a breath with me, ok?"

I do as he says, flicking my eyes down to his mouth as I gasp; he smiles.

"That's it....breathe with me, ok?" His voice is so soft, lulling my heart into a steady rhythm. "There you go."

My chest expands as I watch him take in a mouthful of air and let it out slowly. At the same time, a tickle of air moves over my lips and his curve at the corners into that boyish smile I have always loved.

"It's just me." He says words he's said to me a hundred times before, only this time they feel odd. I know it's him; I can feel the difference this time, in his touch and in the memories that ordinarily would sneak up and rob my innocence when I'd get close to someone. This time it wasn't those thoughts that made my mind fuzzy and my consciousness near the point of slipping into a fog, it was a different feeling; one that wasn't awful. It wasn't even bad. It was a sensation that is still driving me forward; making me want to feel him closer.

"I know it's you, Evan," I whisper back.

His eyes light up and his smile widens showing off a mouthful of teeth.

"So..." he grins through each shaky syllable. "This is ok?" he sounds like I feel, nervous as if this is his first time touching someone.

I nod as another unknown sound claws its way up my throat and comes out in a needy, desperate whine.

"Ok..." he barely gets out as his mouth slowly and tenderly touches mine.

His lips mold to mine in a way I've never felt with his bottom lip filling in the gap between my own. I move my mouth with his, my whole body floating as my heart swells and yearns for him to hold me tighter.

All the longing I hold inside of me, must suddenly grip his soul and pull him closer as his tongue grazes over my lips and enters my mouth with a warmth and an unquenchable thirst. I reach for him too, softly moving my tongue and lips with his, mocking each of his movements as if he is instructing me what to do and how to do it. I let him lead as always.

Leaning forward, I wind my hand up his chest and grip the thick fabric of his sweatshirt in my hand. A forceful ambiance floods my mind. I fist my hand tighter as his other hand slides up my back. He pulls me to him and I follow, sliding one leg to the side so that I am nearly on his lap. My entire body tightens and I hold onto him as if he may pull away at any moment; that's the last thing I want. I want him to hold me, I want to taste his lips; I want him...I've never felt this before.

His lips move away and I drop my head back, breathing in and out at an accelerated rate. *Don't stop.*

"Piper...stay with me baby, ok? Breathe..."

I close my eyes as his hand moves over mine that rests at his chest.

Enclosing it in a soft, smooth hold, I lift my head and look at him, seeing everything I've dreamed about since I was fourteen. The boy that
gave me my very first kiss under the moonlight with just the tranquil
sounds of the lake lapping at the dock and a bucket full of crickets
chirping beside us. That was the only witness to where my heart went
that night.

*"Have you ever kissed someone?" I swing my legs below me in a nervous
gesture, the hard edge boards of the dock digging into the backside of my
knees.*

*Evan keeps his pole in his hands with his line cast out far into the
dark waters. He doesn't move with my question; doesn't even look uneasy
as I ask something so personal. For a second I don't think he hears me,
so I look over.*

He stares forward as I resign to reword it.

"I mean…" I start.

*He clears his throat and I stop talking, anxiety rising into the back
of my throat with how stupid this is. Why do I feel this? I don't understand why I get so giddy and excited every time I see him. I shouldn't; he's
just a friend, but sometimes when we take the boat out to our private
swimming hole, the way he grabs my hand to help me back out, it makes
me wish we were more. I know he doesn't look at me that way, but each
summer this feeling inside of me grows. It gets stronger and, I can't help
but wonder…what it would be like for him to be my first kiss?*

*I know I have battle scars in my life and that is definitely something
I've never gone into detail about, but he knows; he knows I've endured
something that has left me scared for people to touch me or get close to
me. He's the only one I let in. I wonder if he would find me ugly if he knew
everything. Does he even find me pretty?*

"Are you going to make fun of me for this?"

He finally looks over, dropping his pole to his lap and knocking me out of my thoughts. I take an uneasy breath, knowing what I really want, but unsure of how to get there. I figure asking him may be the best I can do. No way am I going to kiss him on my own.

Holding my mouth closed, a laugh bubbles up my throat and comes out in a sort of snort. "No," I croak.

He smirks and tosses his gaze back out to where his line is. "Then, no...I haven't ever kissed anyone."

His answer comes as no surprise to me. He's only six months older than me and even my friends that are fifteen have mostly only kissed one guy at this point. I have not ever kissed anyone. I can't even sit in a dark movie theater with a guy let alone let one get that close; well, with the exception of Evan. He and I can go fishing in absolute darkness every night and stay out till Dad is about to flip his mind and I am at complete ease. Nothing about Evan makes me nervous, except the feelings I have been feeling lately and even that is not a nervousness like any other. It is more an exciting nervous not a scared or anxious sensation. The way he is gentle and easy with me tells me he would never do anything to give me pause. I trust him and always have.

"Have you ever thought about it?"

He glances over through the corner of his eyes, then moves his sights back to what he's doing. Chills rush up my spine and my stomach flips.

"Yeah, I've thought about it," he mumbles.

My eyes widen and a strange urgency grips my heart. Now my interest is piqued, yet a part of me doesn't want to know the details of his thoughts about another girl. I've never seen him with another girl at school, but it still makes me uneasy.

"Like you've thought about kissing a girl...on the lips?" I blurt it out, sounding like a rambling fool. I open my mouth to correct my ridiculous question before he can harass me for the rest of my life.

He turns his head as if it's being cranked around slowly. His eyes carry the gleam of hilarity and the grin that always emerges right before he is about to turn loose a round of teasing that I never can quite keep up with, gradually rises across his face.

"Yeeeeessss..." he emphasizes his bland answer and I already know he's going to make me feel like a dummy. "Were we discussing a different form of kissing or did I miss something. I mean, yeah, my mind can get pretty carried away and I can think of plenty of places that my mouth..."

"Oh whoa, whoa, whoa..." I spit out, blinking my eyes quickly like they may erase the stupid question all together. "I just meant...like... ahhh..." he has me all sorts of flustered now, and he knows it. He grins, leaning his head to the side as I go on, my heart all tripped up on his adorableness. "Is there like a specific girl that you think of kissing?"

He chuckles, placing his fishing pole to the other side of him before turning his attention back my way.

"Yes, there is a certain girl that I think about." He raises one finger, his brows drawn up in a matter-of-fact expression. "And just so we are clear, yes it is a girl. I try to keep all sexual thoughts surrounding that gender."

My mind stumbles for a second, unclear of what on earth he's talking about. The confusion must be written all over my face, as I stare at him blankly.

"You asked if I thought about kissing a girl," he clarifies.

I shake my head and blink away my confused state. "Oh yeah, ummm..." I grit my teeth, wanting to ask who she is, but veer away from blurting out another lame question instead. "Is she pretty?"

His face brightens with another huge smile as he snickers, leaning towards me and placing one hand on the dock behind me to support his weight.

"Yeah, in fact, I think she is very pretty."

My body vibrates with nervousness from him being so close. It's not unordinary for him to be near me, helping me onto a dock or holding my hand to pull me on a jet ski but now...

The way he is looking at me brings a whole new level of jitters over my body and causes excitement to bolt through me. I should be pacing the dock or demanding a name, but I don't. I have no right to be jealous; we're only friends. However, the way his eyes keep flicking to my lips, keeps my imagination from running through all the girls back at Rosemore.

"You do?" my voice shakes and I just know I may never live this next question down, especially if he teases me. I gulp, hard, before opening my mouth back up to speak. "Do you think I'm pretty?" my voice comes out in such a quiet tone, that he may not even hear it.

His expression doesn't change at first, he keeps his eyes on me; I almost want to gasp, appalled that he is so blatantly going to think it over right in front of me. Couldn't he at least lie so that I'm not humiliated? My face flames as his fingertips softly close in on my chin sending a rush of goose bumps over my arms, up my back and over my neck.

"I think you're beautiful," he says it in a serious tone I've never heard from him. For a minute, I wonder if I need to wait for a punch line, but then he opens his mouth to speak again. "Are you going to freak out if I kiss you?"

I suck in a deep breath. "Will she be jealous?"

He laughs at me, his eyes dancing with joy. "Who?"

"The girl you've thought about kissing?"

"Well, she doesn't have a reason to be…unless…" he pauses, a hint of a frown crossing his face for half a second before the smile returns. "…unless her answer is no, because then I will be kissing someone else, because these lips will need to be put to good use someday. It would seriously be depriving this world of greatness if I never graced some lucky lady with…"

"Ok, ok…" I blurt out, wishing I would have just said, 'no, I am not going to freak, just kiss me'. "I'm not going to."

He brings his eyebrows together and I believe now he is confused.

"I won't freak out," I say in a little bit more of a desperate tone than I had planned.

"Oh yeah…ok."

I close my eyes expecting his lips to fall to mine, but no sooner than I have them closed and feel nothing, I fling them back open in a panic. Did I misread this or misunderstand?

He's made no move. He's no closer to me and he is still just looking at me, but with a dorky grin that makes my elation climb.

"Piper," he speaks up in a quiet tone that makes me shiver. "Are you ready?"

Now I just want to slap him. He's just playing with me. "Evan!!" I shout, but don't even have time to close my mouth as my playful annoyance is clipped off by the gentle, yet somewhat determined aggressiveness of his mouth consuming mine.

My whole body liquefies against his, melting into a puddle of nerves, fear, happiness and enthusiasm with the soft touch of his arm against my side. He doesn't make any sudden moves as his mouth slightly opens and I'm surprised by his tongue making its presence known. I pull away quickly.

His expression stays cool and calm as I just look at him, wanting to get right back to where we were. Why the hell did I stop it?

Quirking his brows, he runs his free hand up my arm, raising every single hair in its trail. I glance down at his hand as my heart kicks up to a frenzied chorus, slamming into my chest and thumping blood through my veins at a high speed rate. Every cell inside me is on fire, creating an adrenaline rush like no other.

"You ok?" his voice which suddenly seems deeper this summer, brings me back to earth and gently hushes my rapid breaths.

"Hmmmhm," I hum out in a shiver, my chest still quaking and head in a tizzy of swirls and haze that I've come to expect to always pull me under.

"Ok. I just wanted to make sure."

He looks down at his hand, still on my arm and I look too, loving the soft way he handles me, like I'm a porcelain doll or a glass sculpture. With slow, drawn-out movements, he steers his hand along my bicep, then slides it between my arm and waist where it finds a resting point. The pressure of his hand is light and gentle with his fingertips barely reaching around to my back. He keeps his hand there, knowing from past experiences not to lower it near my hip. I continue to stare down as

I take in a deep breath, allowing it to fill my lungs and cleanse me of all hesitation that may take me to a place I do not want to go.

"Just breathe if you get nervous and don't be afraid to tell me to stop."

I snap my head up to level my eyes with his. He smiles and all the excited jitters I had, slowly dull like a camp fire that is lowering from a roaring blaze to a soft gentle flicker.

"Ok?" he says so smoothly, nudging his chin as if he's coercing me to agree; and I do.

Nodding one time, I keep my eyes on him as his face comes back to me. A cloud of dizziness and a storm of unpleasant memories threaten to attack me, but with each strangled gasp, Evan moves away and whispers softly, "Breathe with me, ok Piper...breathe."

It lets me know that I am here and not there.

His voice is my beacon to reality and each of his breaths remind me to breathe as well. To stay here; to experience this just as it is, beautiful and romantic, tender and new, and without a doubt, the best first kiss I could ever imagine.

Christmas came early

Evan

AS SOON AS SHE MOVES closer, there is no holding back. I want nothing more than to pull her down onto this uncomfortable, stiff ass cot and relive some long ago memories, but for her I need to go slow. Once my lips taste hers again, it's like clockwork; she follows my every move as I take gradual nips and caresses at her mouth. Bearing in mind all her fears, I wind my hand up her back, imagining my skin against hers just like it was years ago.

She continues to grip my shirt with a needy passion that I've never seen from her before. The hesitation and the way she held back have lessened. That makes me nervous and practically makes me want to go on a rampage of wondering who has touched her. It was once only me, but I screwed that up in one flash of a second.

Her head falls back, breaking our rhythm but making me aware that I may be losing her in the same ways I did back then. Squinting my eyes to make out her expression in the dim light, I see her eyes closed and her breathing much heavier than normal. With most women, that would be a green light; go for it, make your move, you've got her right where you want her…not Piper. Heavy, quick breathing and her eyes falling shut has always been a big bright red flashing light for me to put the brakes on and bring her back to reality.

"Piper…stay with me baby, ok? Breathe…" no sooner than the words leave my mouth and I bring my hand to my chest to grasp hers, she swings her eyes back to mine, staring right at me in a way I've wanted her to since that day on the dock.

She doesn't say a thing, she just looks at me. I study her, searching her face as we remain silent. Her eyes appear vacant and far off as if she has drifted off to another time. My heart sinks, automatically assuming that I will soon be in the midst of one of her black out spells. It hurts to imagine where her mind could be; if perhaps she has to revisit that night every damn time someone touches her. *God, I'd give anything to take back what that sleazebag did to her.*

Her breathing slows and her eyes flutter shut as she slowly slumps forward. I pull her against me, her body melting in my arms as I slide her to my side to lay her down on the cot. Last thing I want to do is startle her, having her so close and in such an intimate way, but no way am I getting up.

After her head is planted on my pillow, I move to her side with one hand slightly above her waist and the other stroking her cheek. I keep my face near hers, knowing it may take a moment for her to register where she is, but I'll stick with it. I know I can pull her out of this.

"Piper…" I whisper into her ear, my breath gently blowing her hair. "Can you wake up?" I stay level with her, shuffling barely against the hard bed so that I can be close enough for her to hear me.

She continues to breathe and even though her chest moving up and down is a clear sign that she is breathing, I still repeat the words that always worked before; the words that she said always brought her back.

"Breathe with me, ok baby…take a breath with me."

A slight smile twitches over her lips and I crane my neck to the side, pushing myself onto my elbow slightly so I can be a bit above her. Her lips rise more, curving vaguely as her lashes faintly jostle and let me know she's coming to. In a half asleep fashion, she stretches her eyes open little-by-little as I keep my fingertips and palm across her neck and jaw with my thumb busy etching a tender trail over the satiny skin of her cheek.

A soft warm touch eases over my forearm, causing me to look down. Piper's delicate hand wraps around my arm, sending a surge of energy through me that has me bolting my eyes back to hers. Immediately, my gaze meets her somewhat vacant eyes.

"Piper, hey…you with me?" I whisper softly, still focused in on her touch.

She takes a gentle inhale of air, while out of habit I guzzle down a huge gulp and then slowly blow it out. I watch her do the same with me, because that was always our routine; I breathe, you breathe.

I smile. "That's it…breathe with me, ok?"

Recognition finally dawns on her as the features of her face light up with her big brown eyes fully open and the edges of her mouth lifted into a smile.

"I'm ok," she says in a content, soft tone. "I think I'm ok this time," she follows up, assuring me or possibly even herself.

She doesn't push me away or shift around uncomfortably like before. I shouldn't question it, but I obviously don't ever know when to keep my mouth shut.

"So…" I tread softly, skating around bringing up anything that may place us in a sticky conversation, especially one where I am the big-mouth that virtually killed what we had once. "You didn't black out…" I ask it nearly as a question, wondering why she reacted differently to physical contact. My stomach turns a little thinking that someone else may have helped her through it, but I nip that in the bud, knowing that is exactly what she has always needed; help to get past it. I should be nothing short of happy for her. She sucks in a shaky breath and grips my arm harder, her nails like tiny teeth about to rip through my flesh.

"No…did I?"

Nodding slowly, I study her, having not the slightest clue where to go from here. I flick my eyes down the length of her body, nonchalantly, denying the instinct I would follow if this was any other girl. It's ironic; she's the girl I've always wanted above anyone else, the girl who still haunts my damn dreams periodically with that fiery, ice cold stare that she had given me that last day, yet with her, I won't make a move if she does not tell me to first.

Looking back at her, I crinkle my brows, confused on what I want to say; or maybe ask.

"No, you didn't black out like you usually do…" I pause, realizing I have no idea what is usual for her now. I'm sure that douchebag over at her cabin may know. "…or how you used to." My voice fades as my heart clutches with an awkward tension of bringing it up. "You weren't really here either?" Twitching my head to the side with a small grin, I go on, "Where'd you go?" I'm pretty confident by her lack of freak out, that she most definitely did not take a trip back to the night that caused this all.

She loosens her hold on me and pulls away a bit, moving her hand across her waist, below mine. For an instance I consider moving it, but the situation seems under control so I'm not backing away. It's been a hell of a long time since I have been this close without her looking like she may pummel me across the room at any given second. I happen to like 'nice' Piper; I think I'll work on keeping her this way.

"I didn't go there…I know that much. I was just thinking."

Her eyes move down and a bolt of delight runs through me as I take in the fact that she is looking at my lips; staring in fact, like they are a tempting dessert that she's wanting to dive into. *Holy shit.* I literally want to high five myself.

I do a mental celebratory air grind as she goes on, "I was just remembering…" she stops, flipping her eyes from my lips to my eyes and back again as if she is carefully calculating her next move, or maybe mine.

Not thinking fast enough, I move my hand, sliding it over the wooly fabric of her sweater right below her breast when all of sudden the moment is broken. *Dammit.* She looks down quickly, her whole body tensing up beneath my touch and her breath coming in a short clip.

"Hey, hey…I'm sorry."

I pull my hand away swiftly and her composure shifts with it, like a baby being soothed. This was always the frustrating part, and although, I loved every minute of how she depended on me and needed my strength and guidance, I still had bouts of selfishness when I didn't understand why she couldn't move past it. I just always hated seeing the torment in her eyes; nothing would cut me faster.

"No, I'm good…I am."

To my utter shock, she jostles onto her side, facing me. Staying still and stiff as the bed, I lay hesitant as her fingertips slink over my hand, seizing it in her own and moving it back to her body. My brows shoot up and I suddenly have the excitement of a teenager going in for their first feel-up, but the smartass in me holds back from making any comments.

"I like…" She doesn't look at me as she talks, rather looking towards the ceiling with such a low tone that I can barely catch onto every word. "I kinda like having you close…like this."

As if my expression cannot bend anymore in pure shock, my mouth falls and all amusement is thrown aside. *Holy shit!* I seriously never thought I'd hear something like that from her mouth again.

"You do?" my voice cracks, but I quickly clear it away to move on past my thrill and back into the zone. "So how close should I get?" I'm half screwing with her, knowing Piper isn't going to move this fast after years of being apart, but also trying to feel her out and get a grip on where this situation is going.

"Well…" She rests her hand over mine, allowing the pressure of my hand to sink into the thick sweater and feel a bit of her body heat merge with my own. "I liked how close we were a while ago."

There's no holding back now, my grin grows as I shift and move closer until our faces are only inches away from one another's.

"Oh yeah. You liked that, huh?"

Her whole body shivers beneath my hand as she bites out a laugh. At this point, I may have to have my smile surgically removed, because it is plastered on.

Licking my lips, I look at hers, gauging the whole situation. I have one of my hands folded and resting beneath my head, the other is happily settled on her rib cage, then there is the way she's looking at me expectantly as if silently saying 'Lay it on me, baby'.

No more talking.

Leaning forward, I move inch-by-inch so that I can give her every chance to stop me if I'm misinterpreting this in any way, because the fact is, I am going to kiss her; I have to and she needs me to. I stop abruptly, only a millimeter away. Her breath whispers over me, hitting my skin at an elevated rate and meeting my ears. I pay attention to it all as I always had; reading the warning signs. Again, her entire body shudders, but if I had to guess, and that's all I can do, I'd say this is a good reaction. A response she used to always have to my touch. Through curved up lips, I take a breath and go for it; all the way.

My mouth meets hers again and it's not only felt in my lips; the spark shoots through my entire body, zapping every organ in me down to my core, intensifying and causing a pronounced reaction that may hurt later. I keep my hands still, only proceeding on her go.

The plump flesh of her lips lock with mine in a gentle, luscious pace of soft pecks mixed with a few nips until her mouth widens enough for me to ease into something deeper. I tilt my head and use my arm above my head to pull myself up higher so I can fully get into this as I dip my tongue barely in for a more intense kiss that I hope will make her toes tingle. I graze her tongue, thrilled as hell when she joins in, meeting each move I take to taste her. My insides vibrate with need and desire, but I shove it down; however other reactions aren't as easy to get rid of.

She scoots closer and closer, and with each nudge, I pull my lower body back just enough to make sure I don't surprise her with any unwanted 'hello's'. A small whine seeps out of her mouth and between our lips and that is all it takes; I may very well explode. I pull back, not having a choice. Breathing like I just ran a race, I drop my head back to my pillow, wanting to do a major smack down on my body for getting so worked up.

"What's wrong?" Piper's breathing sounds labored as well.

That only makes my situation worse until I have to pull my hand from her waist and use it as a shield to conceal my massive arousal.

She quickly notices my hand not so subtly sitting at my crotch like a waving neon flag to my dilemma.

"Ohhhh…" she breaths out, flicking her eyes down and back to me with a small smile.

"Yeah, well, you know…it's bound to happen," I point out, drawing my eyes wider and putting forth my best effort to joke, although my anatomy is screaming that it should be taking the train to hump-town by now. Shaking away thoughts of how close the necessary body parts are to putting this locomotion into gear, I continue in my efforts of warding off my hard on with humor. "It's really like a dog with a bone. It gets just a taste and it's all in, you know, and ready to devour it."

I shut up fast, widening my eyes and dropping all traces of a smile. That did not help matters at all. My whole body lies lifeless on the cot in front of her, depleted of blood and energy since over half of it is rushing to limbs that aren't going to find any sort of relief anytime soon. *Poor fella; sucks for you.* I have no doubt that in about two-point-five minutes he will more than let me know just how much it sucks with a mind cursing pain like someone is squeezing the hell out of my balls. *Whoo, can't wait.*

Piper remains amused with a smile and bright eyes that form little creases beneath them. She quickly draws her hand over her mouth and spits out a laugh as I scrunch up my face from the intensity of the moment that was lost. My body slowly responds with a gradual ache along with a bit more room in my sweats. I close my eyes and just pray there isn't any sudden movement from her to get closer or even any unexpected moans from the next room.

"I'm sorry," she whispers. "I just don't think I could…I mean I don't think I'm ready for..."

I snap my eyes open and look up at her. "Oh, no...I didn't expect anything. Hell, we were about to drown each other in the lake about a day or two ago, so yeah, it's cool."

"I know, but I just...well, I didn't think we would end up...um... like this."

Shit. My face heats with embarrassment that I decided to move in earlier, but the wiseass in me decides to challenge that thought.

"So you're saying, you weren't checking me out like I was a piece of chocolate cake?"

Her lips twitch, but she simply shakes her head subtly; I call bull-shit.

"Ok, and you weren't staring at my lips and daydreaming about how good they'd feel." I roll my eyes and snicker. "Fantasizing about me again, are ya?" I twirl my hand above my head dramatically, messing with her. "Maybe dreaming up the first time you kissed me, or some sappy thing we did together when we were younger?" I try to tone down my grin the more I say, because I know her thoughts more than likely didn't venture there.

Piper looks at me with a slight smile, not near the one I'm hoping for after my teasing, but it is still a welcoming sight. Her eyes don't leave mine and suddenly this cot seems much smaller and the cabin a whole lot less populated. Glancing down once again, I catch her checking out my lips and a bolt of satisfaction shoots through me, so I go on, pestering her as I always have.

"I mean, come on...after the look you took of me in the shower..." My grin grows and I widen my eyes to dramatize how she looked me up and down. "...I know you've got to be going crazy now." I raise my voice a couple of octaves to mock an excited girl tone, "Oh.my.gosh... Evan has really grown..." I look at her with an over-the-top amazed look and press my hand across my cheek. "...up. I just can't believe how huge..."

Piper bursts out laughing, slapping me across the chest. "Get over yourself, Evan," she barely gets out before looking around. "Oh, ooops."

I grin wider than I have in ages, but don't bother to look and see if Jake has awakened; I really don't care. My eyes don't leave her as an impulse swarms my entire being and catapults me forward until my lips are crashing into hers…again.

Piper's words are clipped on a muffled whine. I don't bother closing my eyes as I let my lips linger on hers, and revel in the silky smooth texture. She closes her eyes as I gently and slowly ease my hand back to her side, feeling my way down her rib cage. Scooting a bit closer, I softly move my mouth in a sucking motion against hers. She responds with the same action, opening her mouth just enough for me to taste the sweet tang of fruit, as if she just ate cherries and pineapples straight off of a Christmas ham.

My body temp heightens on this and I sink fully against her, sliding my hand up her side. Every woven detail of her sweater is felt beneath my touch and if I wasn't concentrating on keeping other things in check, I might very well be able to count every stitch in it. My body is in high gear and attuned to every movement, every breath and every noise she makes. I pay attention to it all, not wanting to push her to a point of panic or fear.

A soothing sigh ignites from Piper and for the life of me I have no idea how it managed to escape. Our mouths are sealed together in hot morsels of nibbles and caresses that has my blood pressure rising, my spirits soaring and other parts of my body ready to take off for flight. I cannot get a grip on it, there is no use trying. I pull away reluctantly, both of our breathing elevated.

Before I can get any sort of excuse out, Piper speaks up, "What time is it?"

I remove my hand from her body where it was leisurely grazing close to a zone I've wanted to be at since this summer when I saw her drop her top out on the beach. *Damn.* Leaning across her body more so I can stay close but also because I remember dropping my phone to the floor by the bed, I press my finger to light it up.

"Ahhhh...you're crushing me Evan." Her fingers dig into my chest as she nudges me off of her, but I stay there, grinning from ear-to-ear.

The need to pester the living hell out of her is alive and rearing to go.

"Evan..." she giggles, huffing out my name in a way that almost excites me more.

I squirm around, my torso laying over her chest with my head hanging down towards the ground. My phone goes back to sleep mode, but I stay comfortable, shifting my ass back and forth in a pathetic attempt to taunt her.

"Ev...vaaaan!"

Fingertips dig into my side, squeezing the flesh beneath my armpit. I grit my teeth and jump, twisting to the side with a burst of laughter.

"Ah ha...I don't think so." Twisting my torso at the same time that I clasp her small hand, I pull up to my knees then thud down against her as she laughs uncontrollably. "There will be no tickling; you know how much I hate that."

"I know that's the spot that gets you every single time," she says through a wide smile and breathy giggles.

She's right; that's the place that she always went for after a silly night of her testing to see if I was ticklish. I had claimed I wasn't, which seemed to inspire her to investigate my declaration by squeezing and pinching along my stomach, the inside of my leg and then up my side. Finally, right above my ribcage she triggered a place that was actually sensitive to her playful pinching technique. I bolted up with a laugh, but I'll never forget the gleam in her eyes as she realized she had something on me. First, she proved me wrong and wouldn't let me live that down. Second, she had a go-to place that would have me unhinged in an instant. I'd muster up my most serious expression and tell her I didn't like being tickled there, but she knew me too well; she saw through that, only making her more relentless in her pursuit of driving me into a kicking frenzy when she'd assault that particular spot.

With her hand still in mine at the side of her face and my other arm supporting my weight, my grin grows until it cannot stretch any further. She twists and squirms, probably assuming she's in for it, but as my laughter dies down, she stops as well.

An easy silence falls over us and I can't help but glance up to our joined hands, a glow of warmth engulfing my heart at how much she trusts me, even though she has claimed not to for years. She may not trust my mouth, and who could blame her for that, but she does trust me with her well-being; she trusts that I will not hurt her and that means the world to me. I swing my gaze down to her lips and pause, not wanting to talk, but needing to keep at a pace she is comfortable with.

"So…" her gentle voice blends in with the quietness of the cabin and jolts my eyes back to hers, which carry that same gleam I had seen back then. "What time was it?"

I really don't want her to leave. "11:15," I force it out, knowing she'll probably use that as a reason to escape.

"Oh wow…it's late. I have a lot to do in the morning."

All of my hopes fall along with the smile on my face. I'm not sure what I was expecting, but her leaving wasn't topping my list.

"Brrrrrr…it's kind of cold, huh?" Piper nuzzles near me with a subtle scoot while lowering both her hands and bringing them onto my chest.

Flurries of tingles spread through my stomach like I just raced down a hill at full speed. Lowering my brows in confusion, yet excited that her follow up words to the time wasn't 'I have to go', I shift to lower the comforter out from under us. Piper lifts her hips as I push it down and then carefully pull it over our bodies, making sure that she is fully covered. A thump followed by another one fills the void of the room and makes me look down.

"Oooops." She grits her teeth and swings her face to Jake as I realize she just kicked off her shoes. *Holy shit.*

A swarm of excitement blazes through me on this. "It's ok. I think he is out for the night."

I pull in closer to her, placing my hand on her stomach. The bottom edge of her sweater lifts as she jostles around onto her back. As soon as one of my fingertips make contact with the smooth texture of her skin, my body springs into action. *I may very well die tonight.* This has got to be tough on the little guy, going from one extreme to the next.

I ignore the obvious which has got to be more than noticeable to her as she nudges her hip against me almost in a sexual, teasing way. *Holy geez, we're gonna be looking at a second Ice age with the amount of cold showers I'm going to have to take after this.*

"Are you doing that on purpose?"

I close my eyes, moving my fingers beneath her sweater, but not pushing the limit. I keep them idle, letting the temperature of her skin combined with her wooly garment at the back of my hand, serve as a glove to warm one of the only places on my body that is still chilled. The rest of me is like an oven with a path of flames raging beneath my sweats.

She doesn't answer, but another shift from her hip and thigh brushes against me and I know; it's fully intentional. Piper has never been the aggressive type, of course, but she always knew how to draw attention to her needs. Suddenly, I feel as though we are years older, knowing each other's movements, wants and desires as if they are our own. I open my eyes.

Her gaze pierces me like an arrow as she presses her lips together shyly with a sliver of mischief and longing beneath it.

"What do you want, Piper?" Her expression changes fast, twisting into a shocked glare. *Shit; insert foot. Dammit.* "I mean, do you want me to touch you?" I just put it out there; no way am I sugar coating this.

A line forms above her nose and her eyes darken into a gloom that shatters the moment. She shrugs, seeming unsure and hesitant as if she is thinking one thing and saying another. I slide my hand up, enjoying the way her stomach tenses.

"Yes?" Smirking, I wiggle my way up her stomach another inch. She sucks in a breath and I pause. "No?" I whisper, trying to read her.

She doesn't make a sound and for a minute, my heart plummets and I search her face to be sure she is breathing. Her stomach sucks in and chest rises on a breath; at that same instance, my panic melts away as my hand slips further up her satiny skin a millimeter or two.

"Hmmmmhmm."

I barely catch her whiney reply giving me the green light and although the sound is damn near equivalent to a crisp leaf falling to the ground in a forest, it's the most exhilarating thing I've heard all night.

I give up the patient path my fingertips have taken and go all in, diving in head first, well hand first actually, as it lands on lace. Surprising myself, I hesitate, running my fingertips to the center of her bra instead of taking in a whole handful like other parts of my body are screaming for me to do.

"Piper." I nudge my face above hers while just lightly tracing the line of her undergarment with my index finger. "Do you…"

My mouth is five seconds away from capturing hers, my heart is on the verge of rupturing and there is truly no more room in this cot for me to be any further turned on. However, even with every fraction of my body propelling me forward, a part of me doesn't feel right just jumping into this sort of thing after years of us not even discussing what all went down that day. I clear my throat and pull my head back a couple of inches.

"Can you stay, maybe for a few hours? You know, like old times?" I smile, not sure how 'like old times' will be received.

The sparkle in her eyes vanish and the barely there smile that was ticking at the corners of her mouth falls. I instantly regret my decision to put the brakes on. *Am I stupid? What man in his right mind would stop right here?* I glance down at her fuzzy sweater and how it rises and falls with each of her breaths. *What am I thinking?*

"I'd like that," she whispers, causing me to immediately snap my head back level with her face.

She has an innocent yet excited grin across her lips; those damn lips that I want to spend the next five hours tasting and enjoying, but I won't. My entire inner being seems to be waging a silent battle of good versus evil. My hand is pleading to jump into this and save the talking for later; *we'll let our anatomy get on the same page and go from there*. However, my mind keeps an idle grip on the emergency brake, remembering that I need to go slow with her, to always go at her pace; exactly the way she needs it to be taken.

To hell with no tasting. I drop my head forward, moving swiftly and capturing her bottom lip between mine so I can savor its sweetness. Her lips reply with an exciting amount of eagerness as her hand falls on my shoulder, pulling me closer and tighter to her. My hand seems to have won that earlier war as it acts on its own, ignoring the barrier of lace separating it from her tender succulent flesh.

A groan vibrates up my throat at the same time that my ears pick up on her amplified breaths mixed with a soft whimper-like sigh. The sound is the exact feeling that is building within me, a *finally* or *Thank God* sensation that makes my own lungs have to keep up with all the air that I continue to suck in at an over anxious pace.

She breathes heavier, shifting to the side towards me as our lips move in sync. My brain starts flashing lights and blaring sirens to throw all gears into park until after her and I talk, but my hands, my lips and my grinding hips that have taken over the act of a crazed dog on the scent of a fluffy little pooch in heat, all of them definitely have not gotten that memo.

Our bodies are nearly cemented together as we face each other, kissing in a way I never remembered us doing before. Her tongue stays idle as I explore and graze mine along the contours of her mouth as if I am scuba diving into unknown and exciting territories. I slide my hand out from beneath her bra, smoothing it over her skin, down her small waist and then stopping. *Shit.*

She pulls back immediately and it's abundantly clear that the moment is lost.

"Sorry." I scrunch up my face in regret; landing on her hips has always been a no-go. *Damn…years and that still does it.* I want to confront the topic; to ask if this has happened with other guys or is it just me that makes her breathing trip up now, but that thought makes me nauseous. I had thought by now that she would have moved past it more so, but then again I suppose that isn't something you ever get past; it sticks with you and emerges when you least expect it.

"Ummm, ahhhh, it's ok. I'm ok, really." She gasps for a breath and just that little bitty thing alone, sends a spark of accomplishment through me; like I just swung the winning hit to bring a teammate around to home plate.

Maybe I can't read her as well as I used to.

"You tired?" Those words feel foreign on my tongue; not so much saying them, but saying it to her.

She nods her head and stays put. *Whoa.*

"I actually came over to invite you to Christmas tomorrow, not to crash with you or interrupt your night of sleep." She spits out a quiet laugh as if she's a tad bit embarrassed.

"Ahhh, I see. Soooo…you're saying it wasn't seeing my goods in the shower that had you running to my cabin when you knew I'd be stripping down to crawl into bed."

Her laughter kicks up and she fidgets around beside me.

"Oh please, Evan. I know you better than that. You strip down? Yeah right. You're a pansy when it comes to getting cold. More like sleeping in footed pajamas, long underwear and about twelve blankets is more your style. Sleeping naked, that'll be the day."

Grinning uncontrollably, I share in her amusement, knowing she is right on, but also knowing if she is beside me, sleeping in the buff against her body would more than keep me warm. The next time I have her clothes off, it will be a furnace between the sheets.

"Shiiiiit…you're just trying to tempt me. Listen, you can go about it like this, trying to get me to take the bait and prove you wrong or you could just be straight with me. If you want my clothes off, just ask."

We both laugh as she shifts around nervously before settling to a still. A soothing calm falls over the room with our eyes locked on each other, but not even I can muster up a single word to ruin this moment. All I can manage is a deep sigh as I savor the fact that she is here; in my arms, letting me touch her.

She came over to ask me to the Christmas get together tomorrow, but from my calculations of how absolutely unexpected and electrifying this night has been since she has stepped foot into the cabin, I'd have to say for me, Christmas already came early.

You never know

Piper

A GENTLE TOUCH LIKE FINGER tips down my arm along with a soft feathery light tickle over my face begins to wake me. My breath steams over my face and I instantly peel my eyes open. The room appears dark with a hint of light bleeding through the fibers of a blanket that is pulled over my face.

"Hey," Evan's voice whispers out beside me and although I know it is him, my whole body tenses with the deep baritone sound that seems so close. I fist my hands and hold my breath, staying deadly still. "It's me…you ok?" his voice comes out tender and cautious, and for a minute, I expect everything to fade out. "Hey…"

The touch over my arm stills, coming to a pause at my wrist, but remaining there. I suck in a breath, knowing it's him; *Relax…breathe.*

As soon as the voice that usually fills my mind begins to speak up, another thought pushes it away and I gasp. *The letter; the letter from Trent.* I didn't even tell Evan about it. How can I? He was furious when I finally told him about what happened; when I finally let the entire story unfold. The pain of it all was mirrored in his eyes, showing me a side of him I had never seen. He was always so gentle and fun-loving towards me, but that day I saw vengeance and rage as if he could physically hurt someone. It was a look I am sure that I had carried for years;

an expression and demeanor that invaded every fragment of my being and transformed me into someone else.

Releasing my pinned up breath that was threatening to turn my face blue, I turn my head at the sound of his voice and allow my body to soften.

The filtered light illuminates his face, and I immediately see it light up.

"We're going to smother under here," I push out, trying my best to hide all my reservations in waking up so close to anyone, even though I've woke up next to him a million times in my life.

He snickers and I melt a bit more, relaxing.

"Nahhh. Besides, it got a little cool in here last night so I figured it was either the blanket over our head or a little more body heat."

I giggle at his subtle suggestion, knowing good and well if I could see his face better, he'd be wearing his signature goofy ass smile with his brows drawn up like a clown and a twinkle of playfulness in his eyes.

"You scared me for a second. Thought I was going to have to break out a little charm. You going to stick with me?"

I smile at his easy, yet frisky way of asking me if I plan on blacking out from a storm of horrific emotions that knock me down like a bulldozer.

"No, you got me," I chuckle out, my chest vibrating with impending laughter and excitement from the heat of his fingers, which gently move back up my arm. "I'm not going anywhere. I think we can bypass the reminder today…not that I mind."

"Me either," he whispers before moving closer until his lips are on mine; sweet and warm, sending tingles down my spine, up my thighs and swirling around in my stomach.

Puckering my lips to his, I give him a slow peck then push my head back into the pillow. I laugh, not sure why I am; nerves, maybe happiness. *I can't believe I'm here with him.* I really had no intention of staying, but it felt so good being here last night. I had forgotten how easy it was being with him; how he could make me laugh no matter what was on my mind.

"What? My breath that bad this morning?"

My belly shakes as I hold in a bubble of laughter before speaking. "No." I barely open my mouth to reply, now aware that I more than likely have morning breath. "What time is it?"

"I don't know. I assume early morning. It's barely light, but I haven't checked my phone yet. I didn't want to wake you."

Shoot...morning already! Holy crap! It's Christmas morning and I have a ton to do.

Panic pulses through me.

"Oh my gosh...I really need to go. I have so much to do today. I need to get the turkey in the oven and start throwing together the casseroles and pumpkin pie and...."

"Whoa! You're making me hungry."

Tossing the blanket from our faces, I sit up and look around, not able to make out the time over the sink in the kitchen, but automatically noticing the spray of sunshine beginning to drift into the room. The bright sunrise barely peaks through the window as it slowly rises in the distance over the opposite side of the lake. The cabin remains silent, not so much as a creak from a mattress or floor board to greet my ears and this makes me happy. I could only imagine the rumors that would fly if I was caught in Evan's bed. That unsettling thought makes me uncomfortable, and a bit of regret rises within me over the fact that I stayed here.

"I really better go," I whisper, flinging the blanket off of my legs.

"Hey, hold up..." Evan's hands close in around my waist.

I twist and look down, right as the full force of his grasp pulls me down on top of him. For an instant, panic explodes in my chest and I gulp down a monstrous breath before his quiet chuckles catch my attention.

"You're not going anywhere just yet."

"Evan," my tone is laced in annoyance, yet I can barely hold back the giggles that tickle the back of my throat. "You're going to be eating a raw turkey and starchy, hard potatoes today if I can't get things ready."

"You stress too much. It'll cook itself, I'm sure of it." He stops tugging at my body as I come to a rest on his chest, clasping his sweatshirt in my hands and staring down into his soft hazel green eyes. "So how can I manage to make you relax?"

I tilt my head back and plaster a genuine grin across my face at his vivacious attempt of always deterring my thoughts and making me feel at ease. An unusual happiness spreads through me and I laugh quietly, completely aware that I need to make an exit before anyone wakes. A gentle, tender touch falls onto the center of my neck, immediately causing a surge of heat to spark through my body. Evan's lips linger against my skin in one place before moving just a fraction of an inch to the left for another soft kiss. I exhale a little louder than I mean to, letting a muffled whimper out with it. He makes my body come alive like no one has ever been able to; with him I feel safe.

"Ahhhhhh," I breathe out, closing my eyes with a heaviness and a relaxation over me that makes me feel like a slab of butter, sizzling in a frying pan and slowly dissolving. "Evan, I really have to go," I mumble, half hoping he doesn't even hear.

"Really." The heat of his breath moves over my neck, then his lips are back on me, torturing me with more nibbles and pecks. "Fine."

A loud obnoxious noise hits my ears as he blows against my skin like I am a five-year-old. The abruptness startles me and has me squirming to get away, but he doesn't let up, keeping his hand clasped around my waist at my back. I can't hold my composure any longer. I crack up, moving side to side on him like he is a balance beam and I can no longer keep any sense of stability.

I don't even have to look at his face to know he has a smile that could match my own.

"You gonna stay?" he murmurs before huffing out a huge breath of air that squeezes out the sides of his mouth and making a very unpleasant sound that I am sure will be the next thing he starts bringing up. No doubt he'll point a finger at me and accuse me of it. *He's still just a big kid.*

"Evan," I sputter, unable to catch my breath.

"You can agree to stay a little longer or admit that you came over here to get another look at all I have to offer." Back he goes, blowing and blasting a roar of laughter from me.

"Ok, ok…"

His lips move away and I take this opportunity to look down at him. The sparkle in his green eyes makes my heart pound.

"Ok what? You came to check me out? Go ahead admit it…I know you're dying to tell me."

My stomach aches and tightens as if I've been doing ab exercises with Abby all morning. I stop moving and look at him, remembering the exact moment that I last felt this sort of overwhelming emotion and joy.

"Merry Christmas, Piper," his voice hitches as he says this in the most serious and sincere tone that I've ever heard from him. The room suddenly becomes quiet again. "Of course, I'll come to the party today."

"Whoa!"

I swing my head around at the same time as Evan does. Suddenly the room feels a lot more cramped and a whole lot less intimate as I look up at Judd and Alyssa, both clearly enjoying their morning findings.

"Whoa…" Evan mocks in my ear as I grit my teeth and Alyssa covers her huge smile.

"You know…I'm real disappointed that I did not get this same sort of invite to the Christmas get together."

I strain to look around Judd and take in a third onlooker as Jake sits up on the edge of the hideaway in the middle of the living room. *Wonderful.* Half asleep, his hair is spiked up in all different directions, his eyes droop as he attempts to widen them and wake up. Glancing back to Alyssa and Judd, they look well rested, still smirking like they just caught us doing more than we were.

"Oh, I…yeah, I need to be going like I said." I jump up, pushing off from Evan and sliding to the edge of the cot.

The playful mood we were in, lost in a rush of anxiety at what they must be thinking. *Should I explain? Deny it? Flee?*

Judd and Alyssa back up a few feet. She lowers her hand, showing off a wide smile as she clears her throat and drops it. Alyssa and I have been around each other for years and even though I'm sure she has seen the level of discomfort and irritation that I usually exhibit in Evan's presence, this has to be throwing her for a loop.

"Sooo, ummm, Piper…" Evan starts, and even though my face is about to explode into flames over the level of embarrassment that I'm feeling, I still want to crack up. My emotions are all over the place, because honestly, right now I could cry out of humiliation, yet a part of me wants nothing more than to bend at the waist, fall on the floor and laugh till I can barely get another breath in. Especially as I make eye contact with Evan.

Evan's hand presses onto mine, which I have braced against the bed so that I can catapult myself to my feet and out of the room if the mortification becomes too much.

"What?" I look over, recognizing Evan's teasing tone. My face heats up; I just know he's going to say something even more humiliating; *don't look him in the eyes, don't look at him.* Luckily he turns his head before speaking, "You afraid we might outdo you two?" He snickers, looking right at Judd.

I swing my gaze around to see Judd's lips sealed tightly together; he doesn't say a word.

Evan's playful voice rises up again as he squeezes my hand. "Don't worry, I think you got the prize for last night's performance. No way, we could keep up."

My eyes widen.

"Yeah, no joke. I wanted to rip my ears off," Jake mumbles, and I think the heat is off Evan and I.

"Oh but we tried to…" Evan challenges, raising his brows dramatically. "We were hitting the walls and shifting on the bed, rocking the…"

I want to die. "Whoa…whoa, we did not…"

Everyone breaks into a fit of laughter as I look around, my finger held up to drive my point home and my face shifted into shock as I prepare to defend the fact that I was not out here bumping and grinding his ass in a game of who can make the most noise. I stop talking, unwilling to holler over the chaos of four people rolling in hysterics.

"We don't believe him, Piper," Judd assures me.

Alyssa bounces and her eyes water. "Yeah, don't worry…we all know he's full of shit."

Jake raises his arms above his head, still perched on his own bed. "I definitely didn't hear anything from this side of the room, so either you suck my friend or she was not very impressed."

My mouth drops open; I snap my head around to meet Evan's gaze as he looks back at me with an easy smirk and confident eyes.

"Don't even. I know you were impressed."

Shaking my head, all my panic melts as I stand there, forgetting for a second that anyone else is in the room. *Two can play at this.*

"Really, I just didn't see much of a change from years ago. I think all that growing up is in your head," I rifle back, teasing him on his 'I'm all that now' assessment of himself.

Scooting away from the bed, I shove down all my laughter and refuse to look at him.

"Ouch!" Judd spits out and I can't hold it in.

"You don't even know what she's talking about, man."

One by one, I cram my feet back in my shoes while quickly taking a glance at Evan. He's still grinning, drilling his eyes through me. I bounce up, stifling the tickle in my stomach that is threatening to spill out.

"Well, I think we can all figure it out, Evan," Judd counters.

He also has a huge smirk across his face, enjoying Evan being on the receiving end, but for some reason I just can't handle tormenting Evan's ego for very long. No way am I going to boost it up and tell him the truth, that I did in fact check him out for a second in the shower. I'll let him sweat that, but I do quickly change the subject to get the heat off of him.

"So everyone is going to be there at noon, right?"

I look around, making eye contact with Jake as he nods, Judd and Alyssa bob their heads yes as they make their way towards the door, then I settle on Evan. His eyes are squinted skeptically, yet one corner of his mouth is drawn up. He doesn't answer or nod; he waits and I have to force down my smile.

Walking towards the door, I join up with Judd and Alyssa.

"We might be just a bit late. We have something we are going to go pick up in town and then we'll be over," Judd says holding the screen door open for Alyssa.

She spins around with an all-too-in-love smile across her face and adds, "That is, if we can find what we are looking for. Is there anything you need while we are out?"

I shake my head, confident that we have everything. "Sounds good. I'll see you there."

Turning around to say goodbye to Evan and Jake, I find Jake gathering up a few things and heading in my direction while Evan still sits on the edge of his bed like a little boy that is sulking.

"I'm headed down to take a shower."

Evan's face shifts and perks up at Jake's words and he quickly darts towards the back room before reappearing.

"Here…make sure you take a towel." He tosses the wadded up piece of fabric directly into Jake's grasp with a smile.

"Yeah, thanks." Jake looks down and snickers. "I think I'd rather towel dry than the method you had going on." He glances at me with a heartfelt grin, then flies out the door.

Evan walks toward me as I catch the screen door so it doesn't knock against the frame. Shivering, he places his arms around himself and I have to laugh to myself.

"So are you coming?"

I step out to the porch, fully expecting him to stay inside where it is warmer, but he follows after me, in sock feet and all.

"Of course, I will," he says sweetly before his face falls. "Right after you admit the truth."

Shaking my head, my hair flies over my shoulders and the icy chill in the air nips at my cheeks.

"I guess you'll never know." I spin around and let my foot fall to the first stair before he grips my wrist to stop me. Turning my head to look back at him, I shiver from way more than the winter weather.

My heart thumps to a familiar beat as I look back at him. He doesn't say a word. Only silence stands between us, because the multitude of what might be happening between us is heard loud and clear and I cannot believe it.

Is this really happening? I must be dreaming.

Remember

Evan

AFTER RACING DOWN FOR A quick shower and grabbing the only gift I cared to throw together for Christmas, I head toward Piper's cabin with an air of confidence in my bones, relief that all the ice cold looks I got from her may be behind me and fully ready to screw with Judd when he opens my gag gift. Passing my camper, the wind picks up, sending a whistle through the trees and a swish over the frostbitten ground that looks like a frosty winter wonderland. The few blades of grass that have stuck it out and stayed put along with clusters of dead leaves here and there are now all tipped in an icy frosting that sparkles as the sun touches down on them.

Grabbing the strings hanging from the hood of my coat, I pull them tight so all that peeks out of my coat is just my eyes and nose. I could care less whether I look like a pansy, an eskimo, or a burglar at this moment; it is cold as a gold diggers ass out here and I am not dealing.

A sudden cough comes from the porch of Grandpa's cabin and I look up to find him cozied up in grandma's old rocker with a blanket over his lap. His nose is as red as a cherry, his thin gray hair is tousled about from the wind and the way he has his hands dug into his pockets makes me want to run him back inside. *What the hell is he doing out here?*

"Grandpa, what are you doing on the porch in this cold weather?"

His face glazes over with annoyance and it makes me want to chuckle.

"Same as you, I figure." He glances out to the lake, straightening his burley white-gray brows into a bland expression before swinging his eyes back to me. "What are you doing gallivanting around in the cold? Don't you hibernate this time of year?"

That does make me laugh.

"Yeah, right…I try to." I point over towards the far cabin. "I'm actually headed to the Christmas ordeal going on." I step onto the porch, sitting my gift bag down on the small wicker table and then take a seat in the other chair near Grandpa. *Lunch can wait.*

"Ahhh, yeah. It's Christmas, huh?"

I bounce up on another laugh, joining Grandpa's gaze out at the lake. The deep dark water is choppy as hell, but still looks enticing, nonetheless.

Sighing, I stare back at him, noticing a different appearance than before; a loneliness.

"Yeah, it is. What do you have going on today?"

After Grandma died, we really stopped celebrating most holidays given that she was the organizer for it all. We all still came out to the lake to visit and get together for the holidays, but the big Christmas turkey and potatoes were replaced with TV dinners or left overs smuggled to us by Dad from the annual military ball. The only trees that were enjoyed this time of year were the leafless ones outside and presents consisted of extra money earned if Grandpa found some odd jobs he needed me to tend to while I was out here. Now that I take a good look, I see that maybe he misses all the hassle of it; the family part of it.

He lets out a big sigh, leaning back into the rocker and stretching his body out of the cramped-up, hunched-over, freezing-his-ass-off position he was sitting in.

"Mmmmm, I think maybe I'll go down and check out that job

you've done on those heaters."

This piques my attention. "What? You don't trust that I got it done or you think those old suckers already gave out?" I grin, looking down to the shower house which I just came out of not even thirty minutes ago. To my surprise, those heaters are cranking out the heat like I would have never expected.

Grandpa lets out a cough sort of chuckle that has me a bit alarmed. Granted, he is the toughest seventy-one-year-old I know, I still feel he pushes himself way too much for his age; someday his body is going to rebel.

He gives me a sneaky smirk, looking at me through the corner of his eyes. "I know you did good, boy. You always do."

Pride blazes through me on that statement. No amount of bad news could shake the grin from my face today, and although, seriousness and sappy sentiments have never been my thing, I get seriously pumped when Grandpa gives me kudos.

"What? You go down there already and turn all the nobs, check the circuit and connections, just to be sure."

He spits out a laugh, knowing good and well that I took his comment to heart.

"So Mitch and Dad take off?"

Grandpa nods, his lips seal together and his eyes squint as he focuses out at the water. My heart grips at him sitting here alone. Every year it seems that it ends up being the two of us milling about the cabins doing odd jobs and what not, all on Christmas day, Thanksgiving or any other holiday that takes place. The fact that I actually have plans today, even if it is just for a couple hours, has a bit of angst running through me and making me want to flip a coin; heads I hang with him, tails I go check out Piper all day long.

Opening my mouth, I have the notion to offer up looking at the piping on cabin seven which was a little leaky this summer, but I suddenly rethink before it slips out.

"Why don't you come with me?" I glance over to the far cabin which should be smelling like heaven right about now, either that or a burnt bird, then back to Grandpa as I rise to my feet. *I'm not even going to take no for an answer.*

He chuckles again, but remains seated.

"Come on old man. Let's go party with the big dogs today." Swiping my foot to the right, I kick at Grandpa's feet, nudging him to get to up. "Better than sitting here and freezing your ass off, don't you think?"

He sighs, pulling his hands out of his jacket and slapping them down to his lap with a thud, before I can even come up with some sort of bribery.

"Well…I suppose I'll come if you're going to keep pestering me about it, all damn day." This makes my stomach quake in laughter; I hadn't even begun the pestering.

Grandpa tosses his blanket into the rocker and joins me in my trek to the party. My entire body vibrates with hints of nervousness that I didn't even know I was capable of feeling. My hands sweat, my heart kicks up to the level it was last night and I keep gulping down every lame ass thing I plan to say as soon as I see her. In my head, I keep running through my hello to her as if I'm rehearsing it in front of a mirror while brushing my teeth. *Why am I even thinking about this?*

As soon as I step through the door, we are greeted with an array of fragrances that I utterly never imagined a couple twenty-year-old girls would be able to produce. A buttery, gamey aroma attacks my nostrils first followed by a sweet and starchy fragrance like sweet potatoes topped with roasted marshmallows. It reminds me of how Grandma used to make this kick-ass sweet potato casserole; I would fill three quarters of my plate with that along with a few slices of turkey on top. My stomach gurgles on that memory.

"Hey guys," Skylar's face lights up as she walks towards us, but I can't help but look over her shoulder at Piper. She has a powdery white substance slung across her shirt, looks like grease all over her hands and her hair in a balled up mess on top of her head.

"Hey, Sky…" I mumble, glancing back at Skylar right as Piper bends to put something in the oven. I think I'll forgo publicly checking out her ass…for now.

My eyes meet Skylar's for a second before she looks back and takes in what caught my sights. She looks back at me with a simple smile as she holds out her hand. "Coats?"

Grandpa and I quickly relinquish the warmth of our coats into Skylar's possession and make ourselves at home, saying our hellos to everyone and mingling about. Skylar escapes back into the kitchen with Abby, saying no more to me and making me feel awkward as hell. *I do need to talk to her.* I have no clue what is going on between Piper and I or if last night meant anything in terms of today and tomorrow, but I still need to shoot straight with Skylar. We've always kept our friendship stress-free, not putting any labels on it or ever having any expectations of each other. Hell, I've never even told her about Piper and I, that we had been an item. I assume she knows as close of friends as they are, but Piper has always been pretty tight lipped, so who knows.

"Ok, everyone…Let's dig in." Abby's voice booms over the chatter in the small cabin. She slaps her hands together as if she's ready to dig in herself, then waves us all to the long fold up table they have set up in the living room. "We have plenty so don't be shy."

A roar of laughter breaks out over us all.

"Honey, you know this isn't a shy group," Hayden hollers out, standing next to the dude I'd like to punch in the mouth for scaring Piper the other night. I never did ask her what was up between them.

"Jake, you hear that. Don't hold back," Judd laughs, leaning around Alyssa as she hands a plate to them both.

"You don't have to tell me twice. I'm here to eat," Jake smiles.

I glance around, tuning out everyone's wisecracks and good cheer, but coming up empty in my search for Piper's face.

"Mom," Alyssa and Abby screech in unison as the front door swings open. They all but tackle her into a group hug as Judd slides to my side.

I look over, checking on Grandpa to see where he took off to. As soon as I find him, my hunt for Piper halts. This time, I say screw the not-checking-her-out rule I fed myself earlier as my breath catches. Normally a girl's appearance wouldn't trip me up, dressed or undressed it is what it is, but after last night, and now with the way she looks, it has my testosterone level belting out a chorus of approval.

Sometime between her shoving a pie into the oven and all of us making a mad dash for the row of casseroles and platters, she must have slipped away and did a five-minute stage change that makes me wonder if there is an assembly of makeup artists and hair dressers in the back room. Flicking my gaze from her eyes, slowly down her body, I begin to respond to how amazing she looks. Her hair now flows over her shoulders in sleek strands of raven curls. Her lips glisten as if she has been licking them over and over as she carries on a conversation with Grandpa. She traded in her messy shirt and sweat pants for a deep purple sweater that hangs down past her hips over tight black pants and boots that stretch up to her knees. Way too many clothes on, if you ask me.

"So, ok…are you going to tell me what's going on with you and Piper now?"

Judd's voice breaks through my thoughts which were quickly steering off the road way past the damn gutter and into the bushes. I snicker, hanging my head down at his question.

"I'm curious, too." Jake sidles up to my other side.

I toss my head back, laughing with my mouth agape and amusement racing through my veins. *They're not gonna let this go.*

"Guys, guys…" My grin deepens just before I dramatically lose all emotion from my face to put off an air of annoyance that I'm not feeling what so ever. I'm actually thrilled as hell that anyone would put Piper and I in the same sentence that does not include the words pissed off, hate, castration or I think she hopes you die. "Are we a bunch of girls here?" I look back and forth from Judd to Jake, holding a stern glare. "Should I go get a carton of ice cream and three spoons? We can go sit on Piper's bed and gush about our love lives."

Jake spits out a laugh. "I'm game. I like it over pumpkin pie. Does that work?"

I keep my expression serious, but quickly swing my eyes to Judd, holding back my laughter at Jake's response. *Smartass. That's my job.*

"Ooooo, that sounds good. I hear they have peach cobbler, too." Judd glances around me at Jake, then back at me with his ridiculously pathetic excuse for a dimple digging into his cheek as he tries to pester back. "What kind of ice cream are you thinking?" he asks his brother.

I can't even hold it back anymore; the corners of my mouth rise into a huge smirk and what I really want to do is wave my hands and yell out 'Enough with the jokes! Don't even think your asses can't keep up!', but I go for subtle. After all, they learned from the best.

"Oh, so you guys think you can one up me, do ya?"

Judd and Jake laugh. "Seriously man…what kind of ice cream are we talking about?" Jake returns, his tone completely free of any humor as he leans his head over my shoulder.

Judd chuckles and I look over, my eyes still and vacant with my mouth now bent into a frown.

"Ha…ha. Let's see who's laughing later."

Judd's face changes and he straightens up his posture. "Ok, in all seriousness. What went on with you two last night?"

"Please tell me you guys weren't getting it on with me in the same room with you? I mean it was bad enough that I had nightmares over the noises that I heard from them." Jake nudges his thumb in Judd's direction.

"We were not that loud!" Judd starts to raise his voice with a defensive tone, but quickly clips it off and looks back at me. "Did you guys really…"

"Ok, ok!" I put my hands out to my sides in an effort to stop all the ramblings of sex and who did who last night. "You…" I raise my brows and nudge my head in Judd's direction. "…need to face reality and admit that you two have a serious problem." Judd's face falls into a sarcastic glare as I go on. "Ya'll are going to have some stiff charges filed on you some day for noise disturbances if you don't get it under control."

"I do not…" Judd starts, but I hold my hand up to stop him, before going on.

"Save it…we've heard it." I chuckle, unable to hold back the storm of laughter that is brewing in my stomach. "And last of all, if I was… shaking boots in the living room last night, don't you think you all would know it." I smirk back and forth at them, then shake my head at Judd. "You're not the only one that can make a girl scream dude. Only difference is, with me, they are going to be yelling for more….not…" I kick my tone up to a whiney sensual whisper and move a little closer to Judd's shoulder so I don't get an audience. Jake moves his head towards me, listening in. "Oh, Judd, wait…not there…oh no, not there either. Wait, go a little slower. Wait, not yet, not yet. Ahhhh, is it over already?'!"

Jake and I crack up, moving away from each other as Judd shakes his head with an eye roll and slight smile.

"Yeah, ok…keep dreaming, Evan."

"Keep dreaming about what," Alyssa says sweetly as she walks up.

We all bust up laughing and move forward to dish up our plates and take a seat.

Christmas dinner goes off without a hitch as we all sit around the table, with some of us dispersed to the couch and the smaller kitchen table, ready to cram our faces with more food than our eyes can take in. I'm delighted when in the middle of the table I see the same casserole Grandma used to make with creamy browned marshmallows bubbling over the top, slivers of pecans sinking into the gooey goodness and a hint of rust tented sweet potatoes oozing over the sides. I dig in, of course filling a good portion of my plate with a sloppy mess of potatoes. Sitting between Jake and Grandpa, another wave of pleasure takes hold as Piper takes a seat across from me. Her supposed boyfriend, that obviously doesn't know much about her, sits clear in the other room with Hayden, and Jessie, which showed up right as we were all filling up our plates.

A couple hours later and after a few interesting conversations over dinner and dessert, mainly from Grandpa talking about the cabins and the property, we all gather in the living room with Judd and I casually huddled near the fireplace. The logs crackle and pop with an orange and red glow as well as slowly filling the house back up with a crisp pine fragrance the longer the food is put away.

"I really wish you'd come." I look over at Judd as he presses his cell to his ear. "Yeah, but we are all still here and probably will hang out all night. You'd make it here by dinner and could warm up a plate."

"Tristan?" I mouth, barely letting a breath out over my lips with the word.

Judd nods. "Ok, that's fine, but can I put you on speaker so everyone can say hey. A couple of people asked about you," he pauses as I make out Tristan's muffled voice at the other side of the line.

"Ahhh, well Jessie, Evan, Abby…everyone basically." Judd stumbles for a second. "Yeah. Why?"

He pauses, looking at me as if he's getting irritated.

Tristan has kept himself MIA since the wreck, supposedly ashamed of the injuries he sustained in the accident.

"Hey, is that Tristan?" Jake leans against the mantle beside me, looking as if he hasn't a care in the world.

I spit out a chuckle at how different all three of them seem for being brothers. Here Judd is the worrier, always trying to please everyone, yet carrying a bit of Tristan's stubbornness when it comes to conflict. Jake is the cool and collected one with a heart of gold and then there is Tristan, a bomb waiting to explode.

"Yeah, it is." I answer as Judd pulls the phone away from his ear to lay it on the mantle.

"Hey guys, Tristan can't make it, but he wanted to say Merry Christmas," Judd hollers out, getting everyone's attention as all eyes turn towards us and several bodies move towards the fireplace.

"I did not want to say Merry Christmas, you jackass." Tristan's annoyance comes out loud and clear through the phone, but Judd doesn't say a word, remaining unaffected. I crack up, tossing my chin forward. "You too, Evan. I hear you laughing. Ha Ha!"

"Hey, Tristan," I manage out through my laughter. "How's it going?"

"Not too bad…just living it up."

"Merry Christmas, Tristan," a chorus of voices yell out, Jessie's screechy tone thundering over them all. "Merry Christmas," a couple more calls stagger in.

"Yeah, yeah, same to you," Tristan says, his voice never changing pitches.

I look at Judd, getting the idea that Tristan would rather be doing anything other than being on a party line with a bunch of happy-go-lucky people ringing in the holidays. I think he's satisfied to just wallow in his grief and throw his own pity party this year, but with good reason. It hasn't been a big year to celebrate for him.

A couple of more questions come across from everyone with a few requests for him to haul his ass five hours out of his way for a plate of food and a short visit before he'd have to head back. *No thank you;* that is exactly the answer they all get, but with much more colorful wording.

"I don't believe I hear Abby. Didn't you say she is there, Judd?" His voice comes out lively and bordering on the desire to annoy the piss out of someone, anyone, especially Abby, who he knows will rise to the occasion.

All of our eyes move to Abby as her mouth drops open and her eyes widen. Her and Tristan's dealings this past summer were about as callous as mine and Piper's had been. There wasn't a whole lot of days that I didn't hear him spouting out some sarcastic, derogatory comment her way with her responding with a quick one finger salute or some insult regarding his manhood. It was actually quite entertaining.

Judd stares at Abby as she folds her arms across her chest and squints as if she is already getting ready for an obnoxious comment, but neither say a word. *Geez, I need to hang with Tristan more; he's good people.*

"Oh wait, wait…I bet she's out skinny dipping. That was her thing this summer, right?!"

I barely catch a quiet snicker over the phone, but I don't miss Abby's eyes going wide as she drops her hands to her sides and snaps her head to the side to look at her mom.

"Abby!" her mom snaps in a disapproving tone with a hint of humor.

Everyone else roars in laughter with Alyssa bent at the waist between her mom and sister.

Abby swings her eyes back to the mantle as if Tristan is standing right there, and she has an arsenal of daggers aimed right at him.

"Oh shut up, Tristan. You never put on clothes the whole time you were out here."

Tristan's chuckles turn to a full on laugh as the rest of us crack up, except Grandpa which is shaking his head, and Abby's mom who looks disapproving.

"Oh Abby." Her mom shakes her head as Abby looks as though she is desperately trying to find the words to defend what now sounds like a summer orgy at the lake.

To think, I wasn't going to come over here today. Hell, I wouldn't have missed this for the world.

"Mom, it wasn't like that. It's not like we were skinny dipping with the guys. It was just us girls when we did."

Alyssa slaps her leg, holding one arm around her stomach at her mom and sister's reaction.

"Alyssa, were you doing this too?"

She straightens up fast, giving her mom a profound look with her eyes wide.

"No way, Mom…that was all them." She points towards Abby, Skylar, Piper and Jessie. Only face that doesn't look downright proud of their moonlight naked swim is Piper, which has a pink glow to her face now.

My chest vibrates and stomach rolls with laughter the more I watch the panic and annoyance across Abby's face.

"Abby, anyone ever tell you that that little birthmark you have on the upper inside of your left thigh looks just like a butterfly?" Tristan chuckles, one-hundred percent hell bent on riling her now.

Abby's face goes pale as she looks around. All laughter stops with everyone's eyes on her, expectant. For a minute, the same question that is probably on everyone's mind rises into my head, but I clip it off; I don't think for a second that Abby would have given it up to Mr. Man-slut himself…too cliché. I'm sure Tristan has a bit of a peeping tom lurking under the surface of that cool exterior.

"Ab…bee…" her mom whisper-yells in a manner that has drifted from slightly disapproving to a what-the-hell tone in a matter of seconds.

Abby looks stunned, pissed, and about to reach through the phone to wring Tristan's ever loving neck. I don't think she gives a damn what sort of injuries he's nursing right now; she wants to murder him. If I were Tristan, I would keep my running shoes handy.

"Ok, Tristan…that's enough," Judd pipes up quietly, grabbing the phone as Tristan roars with laughter on the other end of the line.

"Get it girl," Jessie says in a pleasing tone.

"Ok, wellll…ummmm…" Hayden leans in towards Abby as everyone seems to click all the pieces into place and say what's on their mind. *Did Abby and Tristan get it on out here? No way.*

"Tristan, did you really…" Judd starts, taking Tristan off speaker phone and shoving the phone to his ear.

"Well this is fun," Jake joins in with a calm, not so amused voice. "Here I thought she might be the only one that was immune to his charm."

I quickly glance at Skylar on his words with my eyebrows raised. She sheepishly rolls her eyes. *Yeah, she's guilty. Seriously, is there not one girl that turned him down?* On that note, I snap my attention to Piper; *Oh hell no, she better not have.* She catches my glare, shaking her head slowly as if she can read my mind, and is soundlessly saying, 'Are you an idiot, of course not'. *Well, at least that's what I'm going to go with anyways.*

"Evan, just what the hell gets into you kids when you all get together?" Grandpa leans to my side, seeming a little stunned.

I can't help but want to egg it on though, "Oh, come on Grandpa. You remember what it was like to be our age once? Everything's more fun when you're naked right?" I keep my eyes on Piper as I speak to him, but she just rolls her eyes with a slight smile that tells me she may be up for my subtle invite. *Oh yeah.*

The fun dies down after a good round of questions thrown at Abby, and her shouting towards the phone until Judd clips the conversation to give a public apology for Tristan as well as letting everyone know that he has not been himself. I literally want to laugh my ass off at that one. Anyone and everyone that is familiar with his constant desire to get under a person's skin, can tell that this is the Tristan we all know and love; he always seems to want to ruffle Abby's feathers in particular. He has since the moment he met her.

Piper excuses herself to the kitchen, busying herself with cutting pie and dishing pieces into bowls with a huge dollop of fluffy whipped cream plopped on top of each one. As soon as she slips her cream covered finger into her mouth, my mind is seeing it in a whole other light. My body is ready to get the hell out of dodge with her hand in mine. That simple act of plopping that finger in her mouth is way too familiar. Not to mention, the way she stares me down as she pulls her fingers slowly out from between her lips with a silent smack, it makes me think that she remembers too.

Mine

Piper

KEEPING MY EYES LOCKED ON him, I jerk my finger back out of my mouth. The sweetness of the whipped topping melts on my tongue and circulates a savory sugar rush over my taste buds; I immediately crave the pumpkin pie I have divvied out in front of me…or maybe it's not pie at all. I continue to watch Evan as Skylar sidles up beside him and a vice clamps over my heart, pulling at it with a slice of envy and making me wish I was in another time; another place.

"Is it good?" My eyes widen in excitement as he slips a finger full of whiskey spiked caramel sauce into his mouth.

Watching as he plops his finger back out, his Adam's apple wobbles up and down at his throat while his expression changes, making me rethink trying it at all.

He hands me the bowl with a smile and a shrug. "Try it."

Hesitantly, I take it with an uneasy nod and a surge of doubt rising within me as I keep the bowl between us; I've never had alcohol before. "I don't know," I drag out my words. "And you're sure it has alcohol in it?

I mean will it get me drunk?" Looking up, I can immediately tell Evan is barely holding it together. A grin ticks at his lips as he presses them together and folds his arms at his stomach.

"Oh yeah, one lick and you'll be stumbling your way to my aunt's house, slurring folk songs and handing out hugs like candy," he teases me with a grin that I suddenly feel deep within the structure of my own face as if looking upon his has embedded one on me as well. "You'll be drunk as shit, for sure."

I giggle, smacking at his bicep playfully.

"Ouch...watch it." He shifts his brows up flirtatiously and I immediately glance down at the opened bowl as if it's now beckoning to me, saying taste me.

Before I can so much as make a move or give in to the temptation, Evan's finger quickly comes into my line of sight. Strings of caramel trail from his hand back to that bowl in a spider web fashion. I dodge his sabotaging technique of wanting to shove it in my mouth by dipping my chin down, but instead of a sneak attack, he keeps his hand idle only a millimeter from my lips. As soon as his index finger brushes across the tip of my nose, depositing a nice amount of the sticky goo, I know my efforts failed. Evan grits his teeth, appearing to be holding back a boatload of amusement. For some reason the vision of a dog licking peanut butter off of its nose over and over and over until it's sure that it's gone, flashes through my mind for a brief second. I bust out laughing; I have to look like an idiot, but I don't care. Evan's face breaks wide open with a huge smile and all the laughter he was keeping at bay fills my eardrums with how carefree and simple being around him can be.

"Evan..." I spit out, trying to sound stern and scold him for attempting to paint my face.

"Hey, I didn't mean to get it..."

I don't wait for him to finish before a surge of revenge sends my finger right into the sauce and flinging it towards his nose so that I can see how he likes it. Of course, Evan is quicker than me, reading my moves before I even make them. He nudges his chin forward, but with his mouth open as he captures my fingertip right between his lips. The warmth of his mouth closes in around my skin and although I still have no idea what the sauce tastes like, my mouth also opens and my heart skips to the next beat.

He closes his eyes for a second, as if the flavor of the sticky goo is the best thing he's ever tasted. I keep my eyes locked on his, watching his every move and overly aware of the softness of his mouth as his cheeks dip in as if he's tasted something bitter or sour. The suction around my finger gets stronger as he pulls his head back and reopens his eyes; I can't say a word. The whole moment has my mouth sealed shut, the air in the room is stuffy and hot, my heart is thumping like speakers at a concert and parts of my body are humming like I've never felt before. The moment gets serious real fast and Evan quickly loses his grin, staring back at me in silence. My hand is still held in the air between us with my fingertip resting at his lips. He slowly pulls his head back some more, opening his mouth as I watch him gently graze his teeth over my finger as he finishes his hand-fed dessert.

Neither of us say a word, but I feel strange; confused, yet excited. I have no clue why his lips on my finger has me so hypnotized, but for some reason it is the single most electrifying thing I've ever experienced. My stomach flips, like going down a roller coaster at full speed. His mouth lifts at one corner with a crooked grin and I flick my eyes quickly to shake off the storm of sensations racing through me. Something about feeling this way makes me feel guilty.

Evan must sense a change in the mood; he clears his throat and quickly speaks up. "You gonna try it?"

I bat away the butterflies in my stomach that always emerge when we get close like this. It's been a year now since he kissed me and since then we've kept our relationship PG-13. I'm not sure how I'll react if it ever goes beyond holding hands and kissing.

"Yeah, ok," I say, keeping my eyes on him.

He quickly grabs the bowl out of my hands, which now makes me aware that I was on the verge of dropping it. I lower my hand, swiping my palm across my denim shorts discreetly before bringing it back up, ready to taste this weird concoction his grandpa raves about. On a blink, I lower my gaze to the tan-colored goop that looks a lot like the melted caramels that Mom and I used to use when making a turtle cheesecake or like the caramel syrup that Dad avalanches over a heap of vanilla ice cream. My stomach rumbles with that thought and my saliva glands go into overdrive, prodding me to dive in and sample it.

What the hell. I shove my finger into the mixture which is so misleading. Looking at its soft creamy appearance, I expect it to have that texture, but instead it is stiff and cold, the opposite of what I would expect a sauce to be.

I look up at Evan as I continue to dig my finger into the ooze, tugging and hooking it to capture a nice heap.

He smiles, watching me collect a supply of it on my finger. "It's better when it's warm and a lot less messy."

Pulling my finger out of the bowl, I hold it above the mixture and twirl it to get the threads of caramel to weave around the large drop glued to the end of my finger. It wraps around the blob like delicate strands of pasta stockpiling onto a fork.

His smile grows as I pull it to my mouth and pause. "Is it real strong?"

Shaking his head, he chuckles. "Oh good grief…it's not an insect or poisonous plant I'm having you try. Just taste it."

Here goes. I shove it in my mouth, the flavors instantly spreading over my tongue from a rich sweet buttery taste, a creamy smooth texture and ending with a strong bitter bite. I think his grandpa was planning his own birthday celebration with this batch.

"Wow…" I raise my brows and smack my mouth, still aware of the remnants of caramel between the sides of my mouth and gums. The whiskey wasn't the most predominant flavor; it was more of a butter taste with a briny after bite like a salted caramel dessert. "That's good." I smile, my tongue and belly screaming for more.

"I know I told you and here you were so afraid that you'd be putting one foot in the doorway of alcoholism if you took a teeny-tiny taste."

A squeaky laugh slips out of my mouth as I lean forward and slap at his chest. He instantly grabs the bowl out of my hand, sliding it behind him onto the table and pulling me against him in one swift motion. The suddenness of it all takes me by surprise and a strange sense of dizziness falls over my entire body as if I'm drifting into a black hole while struggling to stay upright.

My eyes fall shut, but I feel them still as if they are being sewn shut; the pull of each stitch tugs at my skin, pulling and fusing them together against my will. I release a breath and dissolve into nothingness.

"Piper...hey..." a gentle pat comes and goes from my cheek, over and over as his voice becomes more clear. "Come on...Piper...wake up," his voice is panicked and strained. "Are you breathing...God, you are. Thank God!"

My eyes flutter and a blurred image comes into my immediate view, only inches away from my face. I open them wide, stretching each lid to break loose the sewn together feeling.

"There you are. Hey," he pulls my forehead to his and it dawns on me that I'm no longer standing. "I just about ran out to get Grandpa. I thought maybe you were having a seizure or..." he trails off as if he knows that wasn't the case, but still wants to get a feel for me. "Do you need me to go get him or call a doctor or to..."

I shake my head, aware of what happened now. It wasn't any sort of medical condition; it was fear; it was memories throwing a veil over my head and overpowering me in a struggle to stay awake or to let them knock me out before I'm there again. It's happened on a couple of occasions, one while I was with Evan, one while at a dance recital, and another while I was in bed sleeping. I've spent countless hours going over each detail and until now I haven't one hundred percent pinpointed the trigger.

Sitting up, I look around taking inventory of where I am and how he is touching me. His hands gently fall from the sides of my face as I ease my way up from his lap. I look over to the kitchen, shocked that I'm now on the couch.

"Did you carry me?"

He nods, a startled look in his eyes, yet he says nothing. I want to ask what happened, but I'm not even sure I want to discuss it at all.

A loud sound breaks the confines of the cabin as his grandpa swishes the screen door open and steps inside.

"You kids ready?" he says in a rush of excitement, obviously eager to get to my aunt's party.

"Yeah…we're ready." Evan jumps to his feet, making the couch bounce from his lack of weight beside me.

His grandpa turns to exit with no more said. I also rise to my feet, getting a funny feeling as Evan walks out without looking back or waiting to see if I follow. My heart sinks and a wave of remorse splinters through me. I should have said more. Shaking my head and dismissing that thought with the excuse that I didn't have time, I quickly follow them out and jump into the renovated golf cart that his grandpa is so proud of.

We both sit side-by-side on the outer seat facing the road and watching as it winds along behind us. The engine is quiet and other than the skiers and boats lapping by periodically, the trip is peaceful and stress free; all except for the fact that a lingering presence of wrongdoing keeps tugging at my heart. It's been a year; a year and I've never told him anything about that night. I glance over and watch as Evan stares out at the rippling water splashing up along the ledge of the shore. The further we get from the cabins, the more secluded the area gets and steeper the drop off into the lakes edge becomes. I look away, turning my head towards the opposite side which is bordered with tall green pine trees and sprinkled with colorful wildflowers here and there. The chirping of birds and crackle of branches beyond add to natures medley of sights and sounds.

I try to enjoy it by focusing on breathing in the sweet fumes of daisies, pansies and daffodils that drift over the subtly humid air. It's no use. I snap my head around to say I'm sorry, to say we need to talk, anything, but before I can open my mouth, his warm hand is in mine and I turn only to meet his stare.

"We're here." The cart stops and Evan bounces out of his seat, tug-

ging me along. "Come on...I want to show you something. Grandpa, we'll be right in."

"Is that your aunt's house?" I ask as Evan pulls at my hand, already three paces in the direction he wants to go.

I keep my eyes dead ahead, barely seeing sections of a tarnished brick red cottage-style home with oversized windows that looks right over the entire lake.

"Yeah, that's where the party is. You coming with me? I wanted to show you something real quick."

I nod, slowly, still looking at the house as my legs follow along after him. Flipping my head around, I look past Evan as he walks toward a row of trees with a huge open space just beyond, blanketed in tiny white daisy-looking flowers that make it literally look like heaven. The sky is still bright blue with streams of light showering the field in an array of beams that make it seem magical.

"Oh wow." I smile with my mouth half open and my eyes dazzled by the view. "How did you know this was here."

"Mitch and I used to play back here when we were younger." He scoots closer, leaning his face next to mine and holding his hand out in front of us. "See that big tree over there?"

I nod, staring at a whole assembly of trees, but one in specific stands out. It is free of branches on the lower half of it and appears to have planks of boards lined up side-by-side along the front, several feet up from the bottom.

"That was our fort...well mine really. I carried every scrap of wood I could find out this way and nailed it together to build a little hangout," he chuckles and backs away a bit. "I just thought you'd think this was pretty or you know..." he shrugs, pressing his lips together as he usually does when he wants to say more, but is biting his tongue.

My heart melts. This isn't the usual smartass Evan that I know, that likes to dunk me under the water when we go swimming or the one that loves to run into the shower house while I'm showering and flip off the light then run off; it's not even the prankster that likes to leave fake plastic insects on my pillow or in my bed so that I freak out, bouncing up onto the highest surface to escape a sudden attack by the creepy crawler.

I pause looking down and around at the soft green grass covered ground before bending to take a seat. I'm in no hurry to get to the party. Evan stands above me, a look of skepticism crossing his face as he lets out a breath and sits beside me.

"So..." he says in a questioning tone.

My chest tightens and I know it's time. Closing both my eyes slowly, a lump forms in my throat, and tears start to well up to the point of spilling over. I reopen them. Evan doesn't look shocked by my tears; he doesn't look panicked as most guys would, he looks relieved, almost as if just seeing me cry has given him some long awaited answers. He already knows. My entire body constricts as all the held back emotion and pain that I've bottled up for so long surfaces. It engulfs me like quicksand, but before I can sink, he grabs my hand, threading his fingers through each of mine.

"Hey," he says in a low raspy grief stricken whisper as his voice cracks. "I'm right here, ok?" I nod again, knowing I can still breathe as long as he's here; as long as he stays right here with me. "You can talk to me or we can just sit here...it's up to you."

He smiles and that alone breaks through all my doubts in carrying this burden around any longer; so I finally open up, I let it all out, crying through every single word until it feels as though my heart may crumble into dust. Evan squeezes my hand, his eyes misting over before he can blink them away and hide the emotion that is swallowing him as well.

After I finish telling him everything up to the moment I came to his door that night, the look in his eyes crushes me. I thought I was the only one that could look that devastated by what happened, but I almost think his heart may have shattered tonight as well. After the summer that it happened, I withdrew from any group activities. Evan quickly began coercing me on duo trips to swimming holes, fishing excursions with just the two of us and my favorite, playing games in his camper nearly all night until a few times I ended up falling asleep beside him. It was always innocent, and it made the loneliness that had settled in my heart almost *go away.*

Laying my head on his shoulder as I finish with the entire story, he pulls me tight towards him like a magic cloak that is meant to transfer all my pain to him; and it works. All that I've felt for so long lessens the more he holds me. With the sudden urge to know what he's thinking, I sit up straight and look him in the eyes. Apprehension begins to consume me as I worry that he may treat me differently as if I'm an injured animal that needs to be handled gently and with caution. That has been my fear forever; that if he found out, everything would change.

He sucks in a breath that may be the first one he's taken since I began talking and gives me a sweet, ordinary smile that I've seen a million times; not a smirk or grin like when he teases me, but the same one he gave me the night I showed up at his door. One that tells me, it will be ok.

"So..." his voice wobbles and he takes another breath. "...when I touch you, you..."

I automatically feel awful, a gut-wrenching guilt twisting in my stomach.

"Oh no, I didn't..."

He chuckles and this surprises me. "No, it's ok. I just need to find out all the road blocks that there are so we can work around them until the road is paved again, you know?" He looks at me, a strange frown on his face, but one that sets me at ease for some reason.

I nod, knowing exactly what he means.

"So when I grabbed you quickly earlier, is that what did it?"

I shake my head, staring forward at a patch of bright green grass, each blade coming into focus right down to the small divots torn away from the edges as if a bug just feasted on it.

"I don't think so." I scrunch up my face, refusing to think of the night Trent did what he did, but conjuring up the times when I've blacked out. "I think it's when you touch my hips or whisper too close to my ear, honestly." A light touch sweeps over my hips and hot breaths sting at my ears, causing me to tense up as a sudden wave of unwelcome nostalgia hits me; I squeeze my eyes shut.

"Ok, so we don't think about that stuff if it makes you think of it, ok?" I nod frantically, tears beginning to form again. "And we won't do anything that…" Evan stops talking and draws his brows down, looking pained before he straightens his face and sighs. "Listen, I'm not in any hurry to get to that point. I mean, let's face it, I'll probably suck at it at first." He laughs, dipping his chin down to my level so he can look into my more than likely puffy blood shot eyes. "And we all know I am not about to do something that I won't do absolutely perfect the first time."

I laugh, the ease of being around Evan flooding my heart and pushing away all the discomfort and heartache.

"So…we'll take it slow, ok? And when that time comes, we'll still take it slow. The most important thing you need to remember is, I'll never force anything on you or do anything you're uncomfortable with."

I keep my head rocking back and forth on an endless loop of agreeing with everything he says.

"If the kissing makes you uneasy…"

I stiffen my head, completely not in agreement with this. "Oh no, the kissing is fine," I spit out rather excitedly, causing a slight smirk to rise over Evan's lips. "I meant, I'm ok with the kissing…now. At first, it was a little different and I worried that I would freak out, but I'm used to it and it doesn't…ummmm…well, I…I like it," I stutter, sounding like an idiot, gushing over a kiss.

This obviously blows Evan's ego out of proportion as he grins uncontrollably.

"You do?" he whispers in a low breathy tone as if he's trying his best to be sexy and alluring.

"Whatever, it's ok." I turn to look forward, refusing to cave to his dramatic methods of luring me in.

"What? No dice? That wasn't sexy?"

I glance over as he keeps his face completely free of emotion or humor. Sometimes him being such a smartass trips me up; I never know when he's being serious or pulling my leg. I shrug, rolling my eyes.

"Oh come on. That was funny."

His fingertips dig into my side and I turn quickly, swinging my head around in surprise that he would still be the exact same towards me as he always has been. Not even a trace of regret or hesitation shows in his eyes, just complete confidence in being himself with me; just Evan.

Everything stops for me in that moment as I stare into his hazel green eyes. "Thank you," I barely hear myself.

"For what?"

I shake my head slowly, knowing what I feel, but struggling to bring up the words that will fulfill the amplified emotional state of my heart.

"For bringing me here…For listening…For being the best friend I've ever had…" I pause, a sensation so much more profound than friendship sweeping through my mind before I go on, "…for being you…for always being you."

"Always." He grins, a smile that I've never seen; an almost bashful expression that is very un-Evan like. He glances down for a second then looks back up, his eyes bright and full of life. "So, what can I do to help?" He shakes his head. "I don't mean to ruin the moment, but I need to know everything."

Frowning, I synch my eyebrows together confused.

"I don't want to ever make it harder on you, and I never ever want you to think of that when we are together, so what can I do?"

Oh ok. "Just do what you always do. Be yourself…that's always worked."

He chuckles, kicking his head back and bringing his knees up in the air as he nearly falls back. Catching himself, he looks at me, seriously.

"So tell you to wake your ass up?" he laughs. "Slap at your face until you come to?"

My smile grow, thinking of how he was patting my face earlier like I was a fragile fainting victim in a movie, but I also remember how worried he looked.

"Tell you, Dammit, Piper…breathe?"

I nod at that, remembering the words he said back when I first flipped out on the dock and he helped me regain control of consciousness.

"Ok...so..." he lowers his voice to a soft whisper, remaining in front of me a few inches, but dropping all hilarity from his tone. *"...maybe just have you focus on me breathing."* He licks his lips. *"I breathe, you breathe, right?"* My heart pulsates with his words, stuck on the fact that he may be thinking about the same thing I am. He moves closer to me, licking his lips again. *"Breathe with me when you think you can't stand on your own. I'll keep you here."*

I'm not even sure he's done talking, but my arms suddenly take over. Wrapping them around his neck, I bring my mouth to his, taking in every breath he has and making it mine; just like him.

Right where I want to be

Evan

SKYLAR CONTINUES TO TALK MY ear off as I watch Piper. I know her mind is exactly where mine is, back to that day. That's the day I knew exactly what she meant to me; for someone to share something that sacred with you, that is something special. She had always kept up this guard with everyone. I think she usually held it at half-staff with me, but that day she trusted me and I knew precisely how extraordinary that was. Although, my heart was singing sonnets in her honor as she spoke, every inch of my body wanted to find Trent and make him pay. I never let on how much anger filled my heart that day; my only goal was to let her know I was there for her.

"Evan…Evan…" Skylar sings, making me completely aware that I may not have joined in on part of the conversation.

"Yeah?"

"You didn't hear a word I said, did you?"

Breathing out a dramatic chuckle, I roll my eyes. "Yes, I heard you…I'm right here."

Cocking one brow and crossing her arms across her chest with a slight shift of her hips, she gets that familiar and defiant, I'm-calling-your-bluff look.

"Ok then, what did I say?" she challenges me.

"Oh good grief, this is Christmas not a trivia play-off. Just go ahead and repeat what you said so I can better assess my answer."

She shakes her head, hair fluffing around her face and flicking her cheeks like a whip.

"Whatever, I know you didn't hear me."

Swinging my gaze to Piper only for a second, my eyes meet hers and all is lost again. *Dammit. I guess I should talk to Skylar.*

"So Piper, huh?"

This gets my attention. "What?" I snap, a little more defensive than I should.

"Oh chill out. I knew there was someone that had roped your ass in long before me, I just wasn't sure who it was. Now I know."

I'm totally lost. "Wha…how do you…"

She smiles, "Oh relax. I've got eyes and I think everyone has seen some type of tension between you two. I just always thought you guys hated each other, not that maybe she was a girl you were still hung up on."

"Ahhh, I…"

She holds her hand up to stop me. *Dammit.*

"You don't owe me any explanations or anything. So don't worry." She smiles and nudges me in the arm with her elbow. "I've been friends with Piper for a while and I always knew she's held something back, possibly surrounding some guy she used to have eyes for. I never put it together really, but I had my suspicions. I just put two-and-two together the other night and then when I saw her leaving your cabin this morning."

My whole body pivots to the side with her bump, all the while my mouth is agape like a landing dock for flies. I start to speak, to try and maybe explain; what, I have no clue, because she just did it for me, but I should say something. *Right…*

"We'll talk later. I've got to head out…Jessie is my ride." She plants a quick peck on my cheek and races away, immediately in a laugh fest with Jessie and Abby.

I stand still, stunned and completely disbelieving that it went down that way. *Is this how it feels when a guy hands a girl a line to break up with her? Bizarre!*

A while later, after Grandpa, Abby, Alyssa's mom, Skylar and Jessie have all excused themselves to head back home, the rest of us hang out and visit. I remain near the fireplace with Jake, feeling as though I'm helping to stabilize it as long as I've stayed in the same spot.

"Oh my gosh!" Alyssa slaps her hand over her mouth on a loud squeal.

Judd sits on the couch beside her, gritting his teeth with a slight smirk. I glance at the container in her hand and chuckle. He's more than filled me in on his gifting ideas, so seeing the small black velvet box with the pink ribbon around it comes as no surprise. Flipping the box open, she lets out another high pitched squeal. I shake my head and look up at Piper, standing behind the couch with Abby. She catches my gaze, looking at me through dark lashes.

"Oh Judd…I love it." Alyssa dramatizes a huge grin with her mouth spread, baring all her teeth while she stomps her feet in enjoyment like a little kid. "Oh my gosh, it matches your arm."

"Yeah, I got it custom made to match it."

He grabs the necklace from her hand, pulling it around her neck as she lifts her hair. Alyssa's hand instantly goes to the white gold infinity symbol with the word breathe etched in its center.

"Ok, now it's my turn," Alyssa announces, clearly pumped about her present.

Jake leans in while Judd snatches a small gift box out of her hand as if it's the first present he's ever received. *Speaking of presents…*

"Here." Jake hands me the small gift bag I brought with me, along with another. "So…when are you going to get one?"

Grabbing the twisted handles of both bags, I glance at the other one a bit confused, then up at him, having no idea what he's referring to.

"A tattoo…" He points over at Judd.

I shake my head, one hundred percent sure of my answer. "Ummm, no…you will not catch me getting one of those in this lifetime. No thank you."

"What?" Judd joins in from the couch.

"A tattoo. No way will I be letting some dude that probably looks like he just served a twenty-year prison sentence, brand my arm by using a possibly dirty ass needle that he just had stuck in some meth head that used his last seventy-five dollars to get a tatt instead of paying child support to one of his twelve children that he actually knows about. Yeah, ummm no thanks."

"Ohhhh…" a thunder of disapproval rings out from Hayden, Jake and Judd with Chris shaking his head and Abby giving me a big ole thumbs down with a frown.

"Now wait a minute…" Judd laughs, ready to defend that act of consciously sinking a needle in your body for no further purpose than decoration.

"While you step outside and do some meth or go check in on one of your little ones, right?" Jake sarcastically cracks in a serious tone, mocking my earlier assessment.

I glance over quickly. *Just who the hell is this smartass?* "What are they teaching you at school?"

Jake jolts his head back, with a small smile. "What?"

"Nothing, you're just a regular wisecrack this week."

He shrugs and nudges the package in my hand. "Open it…it's from me and Judd."

"Well, I assure you…if you ever do get one, I will never ever let you live it down." Judd informs me on something he will have to just make peace with over never being right or getting the last say on. *A tattoo has always been a big ass no for me.*

"Good luck with that," I tip my chin at him and look down at the gift Jake handed me. "Oh well hell," I mutter, more so to myself. Tossing the other gift bag I'm holding to Judd, I snicker, partly nervous about what the hell these two would have gotten me and barely holding my excitement over Judd opening his surprise. "Heads up."

Judd catches the gift like a football, upside down, yet still intact. I smile, glad that I'm so shitty at wrapping that I just shoved it in a gift bag and taped the damn thing shut; he's lucky I went the extra step and put it in a bag when a grocery bag would have sufficed.

"Jake, I'm not much of a gifter so you'll have to enjoy Judd's gift."

Laughing, I look over and catch Jake shrugging, not concerned in the slightest immediately following Judd's release of a heavy breath on my words. *Might not want to relax yet.* No doubt, he's so used to my pranks and wisecracks that he had to be expecting something that would crank up his embarrassment dial. My stomach tightens as I hold in my laughter.

"Evan, I'm almost scared to open it." He glances up, not lifting his chin or moving a muscle as the gift sits in his lap like a bomb waiting to detonate. "I'll open mine, if you open yours."

I nod, but am more interested in his reaction to what's in the package. I relent, focusing on ripping into my gift. My fingers stumble over a gob of tissue paper scrunched into the small bag. Rolling my eyes at their meticulous attention to detail, I give Jake a quick sarcastic look as my hand finds a hard surface at the bottom of the bag.

"Don't look at me…Alyssa wrapped it," Jake mumbles.

Chuckling, I look at Judd and Alyssa as Judd holds my present in his hand. I pull mine out and look down, eager to return to enjoying the "WTF" look he has on his face.

"AJ's Greatest Hits?"

"Oh wow!" I exclaim, a little knot in my throat as I take in the fact that they got me an actual gift. Sure it has sarcasm behind it, but they got me an actual gift. *Well shit.* "These are awesome." I flip the package of the noise canceling ear phones around and gulp. *These had to cost them a shiny penny.*

"Figured those could come in handy, huh?" Jake points to the package proudly.

I nod slowly, not sure what to say. I know they're a gag really, but it's still a damn good gift and hell yeah I can use them.

"Got that right. Almost goes right along with my gift," I mumble with a chuckle.

"I don't know…I've never heard of them." Abby leans over the back of the couch, eyeing the clear CD case that Judd holds in his hands.

"Evan, I'm clueless." Judd squints his eyes skeptically, possibly waiting for a punch line or for me to give away what the hell it is.

"Oh, it's great! You'll love it." I don't even crack a smile, flicking my eyes up to Piper who stands quietly beside Abby with a small un-wrapped present in her hand that looks like jewelry. The jerk off, that I wish would find another party to attend today, stands a little too close to her as she whispers something to him. My jaw tightens. "Piper," I say a little louder and probably a bit more eager than I should, wanting to do anything to pull her far away from that douchebag. "You got a CD player?"

"Oh yeah," she pushes away from the couch, putting distance be-tween them as she makes her way over to a shelf beside the fireplace. My shoulders relax and my anxiety eases. "Let me see it." She grabs the CD from Judd, immediately giving me an all-knowing look with a roll of her eyes as she sees the front of the case.

I wink back; *she's smart.* Shouldn't take a genius to figure out AJ stands for Alyssa and Judd. Inside, I'm rubbing my palms together like a mad scientist about to reveal my master creation to the world.

"Seriously, should I be scared?" Judd snaps his head over to me as a conglomeration of clicks and snaps from Piper's direction fill the air.

Placing my hand over my heart, I throw my best dramatic heart-felt plea out to him, "Now, why would you think that?" Looking right at him, I share a small 'gotcha' look with him as a rapid guitar solo pumps out of the speakers.

Judd flinches a bit, like he is on guard and ready to bolt at any mo-ment. For a second I want to drop to the floor and roll around laughing like an idiot. I wish I could crawl into his head right now and see if he is thinking back to the day he tripped over all that ancient recording shit of Grandpas right outside his bedroom door. I am completely slapping my knee and rolling inside right now.

"Oh wait…this is the best part," I hold my finger into the air and Judd is instantly on his feet, a second before it even starts.

Once Alyssa's muffled moans and a few loud grunts that were ingeniously merged into a techno mix that blends with the drum and guitar beats of a generic song I found, bleeds through the crackling speakers, all hell breaks loose.

"Oh my God, is that you Alyssa?" Abby's eyes couldn't go any wider.

"Holy shit…" Judd bolts to the stereo…

Click, pop and the CD is in his hand, but the noise has just started.

"What the hell was that?" Alyssa looks around, her face flamed in red.

Judd looks at me, his mouth wide and eyes damn near protruding from his head.

"That was you!" Abby exclaims on a laugh.

"Nice," Hayden nods his head with a smirk, holding his thumb up.

Jake spits out a laugh as Piper stands behind Judd, shaking her head with her arms folded. I put on my best innocent face, pointing both my hands towards my chest in a 'who me' sort of expression.

"Evan, where the hell did you get this?" A small hidden smile begins to break through on Judd's face, but I can tell he's pushing it down for Alyssa's sake. *Oh yeah, act like that isn't the funniest shit you've ever heard, dude.*

I open my mouth wide, a little shocked that he'd ask that question.

"Never mind, don't answer that question." Judd points at me then over to Alyssa as she squeals.

"Oh my God, was that us having sex?!"

I can't hold it back anymore. I bend forward with my cheeks about to split and my eyes squeezed shut, damn near ready to spill tears in utter enjoyment.

"You've got balls, dude," Jake whispers, making me laugh harder.

"I'd protect them with my life right now."

I open my eyes and straighten up, seeing Alyssa's face twist from mortification to pissed off.

"Let me see it!" Alyssa puts her hand out, but suddenly Judd pulls it to him as if he's protecting it.

My stomach hurts, already tense and sore from all the hilarious shit going on. Abby snorts and Jake spits out a loud burst of laughter on Judd's reaction.

"Why?!" Judd exclaims as Alyssa darts to his side.

"Because I'm gonna break it." She grabs his hand and he twists and turns away, grinning.

"Well it was a gift…" My mouth drops to the floor as he goes on, now defending my gag gift, "We don't have to destroy it or anything. That's kind of drastic, don't you think?"

Jake, me and Abby all enjoy the chaos as Piper continues to shake her head with a closed lipped smile, occasionally glancing my way. My entire body vibrates while I strain to hear Judd's muffled tone as he wrestles around with Alyssa in the middle of the living room.

"Judd, give it to me so I can break it in half."

"Aren't you at least curious," he spits out in such an over-the-top panic stricken tone that I double over. He lowers his voice as Alyssa turns her back into his chest and looks like she's prepared to rip his arm off. "We could listen to it later," he suggests.

I wish I was recording this; it would get record views in no time if I posted it.

"Ohhhh shit," I say under my breath, the humor of this all damn near shaking me up like a milkshake. I look at Jake, who is in the same shape as me. "Maybe he has more of Tristan in him than we all thought."

Jake leans forward, nearly choking.

"Oh good Lord no!" Abby snaps. "What an asshole." This only fuels our amusement as Judd and Alyssa continue to fight for ownership of the CD.

I tune my attention to Piper, who walks around the couch to join Abby. *Why didn't I think to make popcorn?*

"Boy, your mom sure did get more than she bargained for this year for Christmas, didn't she?" Piper plops down on the couch beside Abby, less than eight feet in front of me, crossing her legs. "So are you going to tell us how Tristan knew about that birthmark, which I don't think I've ever even seen?" she changes the subject swiftly, from the gag gift to putting Abby in the hot-seat. *This oughta be good.*

"Oh, I've seen it," Hayden says in a sly tone from the kitchen.

Abby's eyes go wide, but Piper's question has our full attention now. I think half of us are still wondering.

Alyssa and Judd calm it, becoming their normal sappy ass cuddling selves as they stand in the middle of the room with Alyssa's back to him. I flick my eyes to Judd's arms wrapped securely around her as usual and quickly notice the CD still within his grasp; I snicker. *I guess he won that battle*; I'll definitely be needing these headphones tonight, either that or my damn heater fixed.

"I'm curious on this one also, Abby," Alyssa spouts out and this information sort of shocks me.

I figured for sure her sister would be in on any frisky activities that Abby might have had going on with Judd's brother.

"You really didn't, did you, Abby?" Judd laughs, resting his chin on Alyssa's head and swaying her like there is some unheard music filtering through the air that only they can hear.

Should have left the CD on.

Chris and Hayden walk up to the back of the couch.

Squatting down behind it, Chris folds his arms across the edge of the portion of the cushion that Piper is sitting against, he joins in on the conversation, "Yeah, isn't he a super big man-whore? I mean, that's what I've heard anyways."

Abby's eyes widen on the continued line of questions, shoving her shoulders back into the couch with a spurt of sass that she usually displays when someone fires her up; the usual attitude that Tristan ignites in her.

"Whoooooooaaaa," her voice comes out as a quiet-shocked sort of chuckle laced with a little venom and retaliation as she stares ahead at Alyssa. "Thank you, Chris. Yes, he is a total slut, so of course, I did not get busy with him."

My entire body shakes in enjoyment as I watch Abby point her finger from Chris to Alyssa, cocking her head and opening her mouth, ready to give them all the one finger salute. "And Alyssa, I wouldn't talk now that we have all heard exactly what you sound like in bed, and we all know that happens quite a bit."

I raise my hand. "I know...I know exactly how often it is." My face falls flat as Abby turns her death glare on me. *Oh shit.*

"And Piper..." Abby keeps her eyes locked on me.

Jake slaps his hand into my gut from my side. "Should have kept your mouth shut, dude," he mumbles loud enough for only me to hear.

"Ohhh," I snicker, grabbing the mantle with one hand.

Abby's eyes don't leave mine and if I wasn't so entertained, I may be sweating.

"...just whose cabin did you stay at last night?"

As soon as her words are out with a slight bit of humor behind them, I can't help the slight grin that forms across my face as I stare back at her. Piper swings her gaze to me, looking as if someone just accused her of murder and she's going to face the death penalty. Chris clears his throat and joins in with the entire room that has eyes on me.

"Oh, I know this one," Jake's voice slices through the silence like a whoopy cushion letting out an inappropriate sound right at the precise moment that a conversation has turned serious.

I should return his slap to the gut and tell him to run. Abby is on a roll and taking absolutely no prisoners, but I keep quiet, rather enjoying her laying it on everyone.

Abby folds her arms and cocks one brow, doing a half-ass better job of remaining somber than I could. All I really want to do is bust out into a thunder of laughter that will have my sides in stitches and my stomach about to rupture.

"You want some too," she hisses, turning it on Jake now.

Should have kept your mouth shut, Jake. Damn, I love Abby; that girl can hang with the best of us smartasses.

Jake straightens up fast and this time I hear Judd spit out a cackle-snort laugh.

"Nope." His hands dart up to the sides of his face, palms out in surrender. "Hey, I just came for the pie."

Abby's focus shifts back to me. "So…" she says in a steady tone that is doused in sugar, yet laced in a playful threat. "If we want to discuss details of my private life, we can surely discuss everyone else's activities last night."

Piper shifts in her seat, looking at me and I instantly realize as much as this is fun for me, it may be making her uncomfortable considering I'm fairly certain I'm the only one here that knows the details of her past.

"Well, well, this could be fun," Hayden pipes out with a huge grin.

I flip around, glancing at the bundle of papers that my fingers have busied themselves of flicking over the edge again and again. As soon as I see a photo album, my curiosity piques and I slap it open, hoping to steer the conversation in a new direction and distract the attention off of Piper. I could give a damn if they all think we bumped uglies from dusk to dawn, but I do not, what so ever, want her to feel uneasy.

I clear my throat, basically hoping Abby takes it as me waving the white flag of retreat. "Hey, is this you?" I point down at the first picture I find.

It's a picture of her when she was little and I have no doubt it is her; there is no missing those deep dark brown eyes that look like they have been framed in the blackest lashes I've ever seen.

A shuffle rises behind me and within seconds Piper is by my side. I knew she would catch my cue of avoiding the hot-seat.

"Hmmhmmm, that's what I thought," Abby hums behind us from the couch.

She sneaks me a glance from the corner of her eyes, throwing me a thankful smile on Abby's words. "Yeah, that's when I was one I think." Piper's finger joins mine, grazing against my skin in a barely-there touch that instantly warms my body.

Laughter and conversation go on around us as Jake moves away and as the 'who did what last night' convo lulls into holiday talk and New Year party planning. I don't join in; I'm happy right where I am. I stay put and watch as she points to picture after picture, marveled by the sound of her voice as she speaks softly. The smile she gets as she tells me stories about pictures we come to, has me in awe that I am even here beside her after all this time. *This is right where I want to be.*

Nightmare

Piper

"OH GEEZ, NO I REMEMBER that day," Evan laughs beside me, his legs flat on the floor, extended out as he lazily lies back onto the palms of his hands. He points down at a picture of him and I in one of the many albums that I dug out after the Christmas get-together dies down. "You whined and whined when I threw you in."

His laughter fills the silence of the room as quiet chatter of whoever is left in the living room, filters in. This is something we never really got to do when we were kids, due to my fear of being in this cabin.

"I remember that day, too."

Looking through albums was never a favorite pastime of mine. I was always fearful of coming across the wrong picture. Although, this album does contain a big portion from that first summer out here, the summer Trent was with us. I scramble past those pages.

Sitting on the floor with my legs folded and the photo album on my lap, I nudge into him playfully. "This was the best part of that day..."

Looking back down to the picture we are on, my lips inch up on the memory of such a dark moment in my life being followed up by finding the courage to smile again. I run my finger over the photograph of Evan holding me in a bear hug as he hauled me out to the water. The thunder of humor is written all over his face as I squeeze down on his arm, attempting to stop the inevitable of getting drenched. My breath hitches in my throat as I look at the expression on my face and realize something so insignificant for many, yet huge for me…he was touching me; only he could. That thought warms my soul as I account the events leading up to my plunge in the lake.

Loud thumping vibrates through my ears as a million more sensations come to me. My head pounds and my body aches but not at all in the places I thought that it would. I stiffen up instantly, the memories of all that happened just last night hitting me. My palms and knees burn while my stomach rumbles as if I haven't eaten in weeks. Moving under a bundle of blankets, the muscles in my legs stretch as I point my toes and extend my body to work out any crampy feelings.

Thud, thud, thud, hits my ears again and I flip my head, suddenly confused on where I am and what all happened after I raced away from my parent's cabin. I look over and see Evan curled up on the bench at the kitchen table. His head rests on a pillow that is propped against the camper's side window while his legs are drawn up to his side, bent at the knee and looking very uncomfortable.

Thump, thump, thump.

"Evan!"

The door handle rattles as his grandpa's voice booms from the other side, sounding very on edge and ready to rip the door from the hinges.

I quickly throw the blankets to the end of the bed and race over to his side, pushing on his arm. Dang, he can sleep through a storm I bet.

"Evan, your grandpa is at the door."

His eyes open wide, alarm written into every inch of his face as he throws his legs to the ground and scoots out, swinging his head from one side to the next as if he's looking for a place to hide.

"He's at the door." Maybe he's disoriented from waking up so sud-

denly.

He runs his hand through his hair, which is all over the place, sticking up on one side and matted down on the other.

"Evan?" I look at him, unsure of what he could be thinking. "Your grandpa..."

He cuts me off, glancing over at the door. "I know," he bites in a whisper.

I flinch back at his aggravation.

"Sorry...sorry." He stops, biting the inside of his lip. "It's just that..."

"Evan, boy, you better open this door. Piper is missing and her parents are worried sick."

His eyes widen as all the blood drains from my face. Nobody knows what happened last night except Trent. Oh my God, what if he told my parents; what if they know?

Evan points over his shoulder. "Ahh, yeah, that's what I was going to say," he whispers, "They are going to flip when they find out you slept here."

I shake my head, not even caring. I'd rather be here than anywhere or with anyone else right now.

"Evan, wake your ass up," his grandpa says in an authoritative tone that I've never heard from him before.

"Shoot!"

I watch as Evan struggles, looking around and frantic as if he's going to hide me in a cabinet. This isn't going to be good either way, but at least if I let them know I'm safe, or that I haven't run away, then possibly Evan won't get in too much trouble. I guess I have to face the music eventually anyways.

Grabbing his hand which is balled into a fist in front of him as his grandpa rattles the door knob, I try my best to ease his mind. "It's ok. I have to let them know I didn't run away. At least they'll know I'm safe and I'm sure if you explain..."

Click, click and the door tears open. His grandpa steps up into the camper in one quick stride that makes the whole thing shift and wobble. My heart drops as I take in his expression as well as the one on my father's face, who appears in the doorway immediately following. Evan doesn't say a word and although I know I should come to his rescue as he rescued me last night, my mouth is cemented shut in panic. His grandpa's jaw tenses as he looks at Evan. For a minute, I'm almost positive he's going to grab him up by the earlobe and drag him out of the camper like you see on some of those old family shows that are meant to be funny, but I'm sure that's where parents get all their ideas from.

I open my mouth to speak, but his grandpa beats me to it.

"Boy, you better start explaining now."

"I...I..." Evan's mouth draws open in an attempt to explain, but as he looks at me, I can see plain as day that he has no clue what to say. How could he?

I showed up here last night, unannounced, not explaining what happened to me, but just needing a friend.

"Piper!" Dad's tone comes out firm and demanding. That without a doubt tells me that Trent didn't say a word. "What is going on? Were you here all night?"

I step forward, placing my hands behind my back as I fiddle my fingers together to relieve the fear and anxiety stirring in my conscience; Evan had nothing to do with what happened, so I cannot let him get into trouble.

"Yes, I did," I say, glancing down as a flame of shame washes across my face. I look back up, watching my father's face shift from anger to surprise and his grandpa's eyes flashing with disappointment. Thinking quickly, I open my mouth back up to elaborate and to remove any wrongdoing from Evan's part. I can't let him take the blame for anything. "I had a nightmare last night and it scared me bad." I gulp, my mind going a mile a minute as I spin as good of a lie as I can. "I wasn't even thinking. I just ran out of the cabin since everyone was asleep and when I saw Evan's light, I figured talking to a friend would get my mind off of it." Glancing back and forth, I'm met with a blank stare from Dad and a skeptical expression from Mr. Jansen.

"*That still does not explain what you are doing waking up alone in a boy's room the next day, young lady. Your mom and I have been worried sick. Do you even know what you put us through?*"

"*Evan, start talking son!*" *his grandpa snaps, and my stomach begins to churn with dread.*

"*I just thought...*" *Evan's eyes knit together as he glances at me for a moment in question.*

"*You look at me and start explaining!*" *his grandpa doesn't relent; I have to add more.*

I hate lying and making up a story. One thing my parents have no tolerance for is lying, but I cannot tell the truth. How can I sit here and tell three guys what happened; I don't want anyone to know as long as I live. They'll think I'm dirty or blame me.

"*Daddy. Mr. Jansen...*" *They both look to me, giving me their attention, yet still holding the same expressions as before, so I go on,* "*None of this was Evan's fault at all. The first thing he told me when I knocked last night is that it was too late for me to come over, but I insisted. I was afraid he would laugh at me and call me a girl if I told him I was scared of a dream.*" *His grandpa glances at Evan with a bit of a chuckle and my heart eases.* "*He let me come in for only a minute after I begged and made him feel bad.*" *Taking a quick gaze at the Monopoly board sprawled out on the table, I throw more out there,* "*Yeah, luckily he had some games and I calmed down, but the dream really scared me so when he asked me to leave, I begged to stay just a little longer.*" *I point over to the bench at the side of the kitchen table that has a scrunched-up pillow in the corner.* "*So when Evan dozed off, I laid down on the bed. I didn't mean to fall asleep, but before I knew it, I heard someone pounding on the door.*"

Pulling my hands in front of me, I work my fingers together nervously and wait to see the outcome of my performance. I feel awful!

Dad sighs, glancing at Mr. Jansen as they share a look that almost says that they believe me.

"*Oh Piper, sweetie, why didn't you just wake me or your mom...or even Trent?*"

My back becomes stiff as a board on that name, my heart picks up pace pounding in my chest like a freight train and my teeth clamp down. Dad moves forward, looking sympathetic, but terror engulfs me. Does he know? Is it written all over my face, now that he brought up my cousin's name?

"Honey, relax." He grabs my hand and pulls me forward into a hug; my body remains rigid as my arms stay slack at my sides. "I'm not mad. We were just worried, that's all. Now, let's go tell your mom that you are safe and sound."

He pulls me forward, nudging me gently with his hand at the base of my neck. Looking over my shoulder as I brush by Mr. Jansen, I lock eyes with Evan. His face is a shadow of confusion, sympathy and understanding, yet under it all I see gratefulness.

"Evan, let's go. I need your help with a leaky roof today."

"Bye Evan," I whisper. "Thank you."

A small smile emerges across his lips. "You too." He clears his throat and looks back and forth, clearly regretting his choice of words. "Thanks for whooping my butt at Monopoly. Next game, you won't be so lucky."

I giggle, stepping down out of the camper. Giving one last goodbye, I barely lift my hand before turning to follow Dad back to our home away from home.

"Hey Piper!"

Dread begins to fill my body, starting in my toes like a spray of water filling up a bucket and rising at an unstoppable force, but it stops as his voice meets my ears.

"I'll be down by the dock later getting in a swim…maybe you can come out and join me sometime?" Evan calls out.

Not even wanting to ask permission or think about it, I spin around; just being around him puts me at ease. Last night, all he did was focus on playing the game. After further inspection of my stinging palms, I noticed they were all skinned up, my hair was a mess and my eyes were puffy, yet Evan never asked a single question. Plus, no one sucks that bad at a board game; I know he let me win.

"Ok." *I cast a small smile, that I cannot quite feel through the numbness in my heart and then look up at Dad.* "If that's alright?"

Dad nods as I look back at Evan, a cloud of fear and confusion festering up inside of me on what to tell my parents.

"Piper…" *Evan calls out again, shifting his eyes quickly to his grandpa and back to my dad before going on,* "Come out with a smile and I might just have to toss you in," *he says in a teasing tone that helps to ease my worry some.*

Although, my mind is skipping over walking into my family's cabin and having to face whatever discussions may come up, Evan manages to make me smile. However, in the back of my head the same thing keeps repeating over and over…I wish I had made up the part about having a nightmare last night, because I have a feeling the nightmare has only begun.

A Fresh Start

Evan

"**P**IPER, HEY…YOU OK?"

She shakes her head quickly as if she's brushing off a bad memory. Glancing down at the picture, I'm well aware of what that day was to her; especially the night prior.

"Oh yeah…I was just thinking about it."

Dipping my chin, I narrow my eyes as she looks off into space; a dazed expression that I had come to know quite well, creeping over every feature of her face.

"You gonna be ok?" I ask in a serious tone before trying to flip it into something playful, "…because I can totally give you mouth-to-mouth."

It's not completely a joke, I guess. We had our own version of mouth-to-mouth when she would slip into a fog of painful memories; the way she'd watch my mouth and each of my breaths move over my lips when we would get even semi-intimate; observing, studying… memorizing. It became a pretty natural thing for us.

She finally looks up, rolling her eyes dramatically and sticking out her tongue in a thirsty manner.

"Noooo," she draws out, bringing more emphasis to her eye roll. "I do have some control of it after all these years."

The thud of my heart leaps over one full chord at her words, because this is something I want to know; I need to know. However, I'm not going to be the one that pries. Fisting my hands against the wood floor behind me, I suck in a breath and wait.

"What?"

I shake my head, translucent in my curiosity. "Nothing."

"Ok what do you want to know?" Her shoulders fall in surrender and her face goes flat.

Shrugging, I carry on with no urgency, but keep my eyes glued to her face. "I don't care. Tell me whatever." The corners of my lips arch, thinking of all the smartass things I could slide in there, but this time, I'll let it slide.

A snap and thump calls out and I look down, watching Piper's delicate fingers flip to the back of the album, skipping an entire portion of it. A familiar sensation tugs at me. Some of the pictures in these albums are not going to bring back good memories. I comb through my thoughts quickly, calling up any fun times we had so that I can talk about that rather than anything she's thinking. Staring over at the deep, far off look in her eyes, I want to grab her hand, tear the memories from her mind or rip Trent in two, where ever he is now. *Breathe with me, Piper.*

"Hey…" I start but she decides to talk at the same time.

"I was so glad to see you out on that dock later that day."

This takes me by surprise. I know she's referring to the picture we just saw a moment ago, but for her to talk about that out loud, now… after all this time, and with everything that came between us, all I can do is trip over my jaw which is currently laying on the floor.

I let her go on, not moving an inch.

"Did I ever tell you that I never saw him again after that day?" She looks at me and I nod.

She told me; it was a topic that she avoided at any cost if someone asked where Trent was. It was as if that question sent her spiraling into another time and place. Myself, I always tried to avoid asking anything about her family or home life. I had my own suspicious after that night.

She gazes down at the album which now rests on an old family portrait that looks like it was taken in a trailer at a carnival. I don't recognize any of the four people except for possibly the little boy who looks to be about ten years old. He looks just like Piper when she was younger.

"Mom said he asked to go back to Aunt Kate's house when they woke up that morning."

I direct my attention back to her immediately. She shrugs, keeping her eyes trained on her hands, the same as she did when she was a kid and would get nervous.

"Anyways…" She draws her brows together. "I was so scared he was going to tell Mom and that she was going to come back, you know… asking questions or getting mad…but no one ever asked…"

Gulping, she looks down at the album, obviously with her head and heart on a different picture than the one before her. I want to tell her to stop thinking about it; that it was a long time ago and that it's not important or not good for her to dredge up all those painful memories, but another part of me thinks, maybe this is what she needs. From my talk with Abby the other day, I gather she hasn't confided in her and considering she is her best friend, that leads me to believe she's never talked to anyone. That is a hell of a load to carry for all these years.

So I give her everything, imploring her to go on through eyes that desperately would give anything to carry the weight of this on my shoulders. There is still so much we have to catch up on, and I still need to fill her in on how my asshole brother ever found out about the whole thing, but for now, I'll listen.

I move my hands over hers, capturing them as she fidgets and giving them a gentle squeeze to implore her to go on.

And she does…

"I just never thought anyone would understand…" I watch her carefully, studying the profile of her face as she looks off into space, dead ahead as if maybe the whole day is replaying for her. "I guess I always just blamed myself, then with how Mom reacted once she finally found out." She lets out a heavy sigh; my heart aches for her. I hate that I wasn't there when it all came out. "She was awful after she found out." Piper clears her throat, glancing at me hesitantly and there's no doubt that she's thinking about the very last day we saw each other, because that is what is on my mind right now as well.

I keep my eyes trained on her, hoping she'll go on; wanting to get the discussion out of the way, but if I've learned one thing with Piper, it is to keep my mouth shut. She gives me a warm smile, as if she knows exactly what I'm thinking, so I give her a gentle nudge, nodding my head slightly to urge her on.

As if she can read me like a book, Piper opens her mouth and begins to speak again with tears welling up in her eyes and it damn near breaks me in half. "You know, as soon as we walked through that door and Dad brought up what Trent did to me that day...you know the day he found out..." She pauses as if I don't know exactly what she's talking about; as if that wasn't the most horrific day of my life, the day I lost her. "She refused to listen to everything Dad had to say. I mean it was an all-out war, right there in front of me after I had already faced..." She squeezes her eyes shut, concentrating. It's no secret that this is hard for her to talk about; it's hard for both of us.

Glancing down hurriedly, half in a panic to find something to deter her thoughts from the day everything crumpled before us, my eyes wander back to the picture before her. *Damn that little girl looks familiar.*

Before I can open my mouth, Piper shakes her head and starts again, "Anyways..." She snickers, completely insincere and so obvious that she's trying to cover up her emotions. Tapping her finger against the photo album, she looks back at me. "So, yeah, I was so happy to see you out that day. I thought for sure your grandpa was going to kill you when he found me in your camper."

I smile, joining her on that memory. It's so clear, that I can almost feel the sun's searing touch move across my skin; I can nearly see her as she walked across the ground, right down to the beach, with a smile on her face. I knew she was happy to see me; I was happy to see her. As soon as she left with her dad that day, I thought for sure her ass was grass.

"I thought the same thing," I say with a chuckle.

"So whatever happened?"

My chest vibrates, thinking back to the conversation I had with Grandpa. It definitely went beyond the typical birds-and-bee's discussion that most parents have with their children. Grandpa always cuts to the chase; no use beating around the bush, I guess. "Actually, he told me if I wasn't going to keep my pecker in my pocket, that I better damn well wrap the sucker."

Piper cracks up, tossing her arms around her stomach and swaying backwards on a breathy laugh that catches in her throat. My smile grows as I watch her happiness, relieved that this entire walk down memory lane can go in a new direction.

Snickering to myself, I go on, "Oh he was pissed off alright…said that if he ever caught me doing that again, he'd beat me within an inch of my life."

She laughs harder, clearly enjoying the shit I got that day. Come to think of it, I recall getting reamed about every chance Grandpa got. It was always, 'Get your ass to bed, Evan and don't even think about sneaking any girls in that camper', or 'How'd you sleep, son or did you stay up late, sneaking some girl in there.' He literally acted like I had been doing that for years; like I had been caught countless times with some girl in my camper; like it hadn't just been innocent and someone I was around all the time…my best friend.

"Yeah, I don't think he was ever fully convinced that we didn't do something in there."

Piper's mouth drops open, "Are you serious?! We were twelve! It's not like we would've even known what we were doing." We both laugh, but Piper quickly fades off, looking as though she's thinking way too much into that thought.

I act fast, "Who on earth is this?" Pointing down at the picture, I finally draw her attention to the family portrait that looks to be about thirty plus years old, judging by the kids lame and pretty damn dorky attire. "I know I've met some of your family, or at least seen them here through the years, but that face just looks familiar for a different reason." I tap my index finger over the little brown haired, green eyed girls face.

Her face falls to the picture and quickly scrunches up with concentration, a deep line between her brows and her piercing brown eyes staring at it as if the little girl may just jump up to tell her exactly who she is.

"Well," she draws out her word, possibly still trying to figure it out herself. *Maybe she doesn't know who that is.* "I know the little boy is Dad and these are my grandparents." Her finger moves across to the older couple above the kids. "So I'd have to assume that the little girl is Dad's sister." She sighs looking over at me quickly. "I think she died when she was little or maybe ran away or… I'm not really sure. I know he has a sister. He would always tell me stories about when they were growing up, but he usually changed the subject if I would ask, 'where is she' or 'can I meet her'. I gave up a long time ago asking about her. He has pictures of her up in the house, but it's just a closed-off topic."

I press my lips together, drawing my brows in. *That's odd.* "Hmmmm, she looks awfully familiar, doesn't she?" Staring down at the picture, I thumb through every single thought in my mind trying to process where I could know that face from. I look back up at Piper, considering for a moment that maybe I could be seeing just a bit of that little girl's features in someone that has been on my mind for nearly half my life. After all, similarities do tend to run in a gene pool, but as I study the picture, looking over the deep dark brown tint of her hair and the bronze color of her skin that looks as if she spent every day out at the beach, I come up empty. Piper shares far more traits with her mother than that of her dad, Pete. She has pale ivory skin, jet black hair and even her eyes are a completely different shade. *Hmmm, Pete, did you ever consider that your wife may have been fooling around with the mailman?*

"Who knows," I shrug, "I guess it's just some family resemblance that I'm picking up on..." I stop short, almost seeing an entirely different picture as I look at the girl's eyes; bright green eyes that look almost identical to Tristan's. I focus in on the structure of her face and it comes to me. "Whoa, that's some crazy shit there." Staring harder at the picture, another one comes up in my mind; one of Tristan and his mom from when he was pretty small that has occupied a place on their living room wall from the first day I ever came in their house.

"What is?" Piper sits up, at complete attention, staring down at the picture.

"Doesn't your aunt look familiar at all...think of the biggest smartass you know."

Once Piper dips her head back, scrunching her face up in confusion, I have to laugh.

"You?" She draws her word out sarcastically, and I chuckle. *Oh well, I guess Tristan is the biggest smartass I know.*

"No, no, no. Well yeah, but other than me." I tap my finger to the picture. "Look at those eyes. Maybe I am just making things up in my head or something, but I swear she looks just like Tristan."

Finally, recognition sparks across Piper's face. Her eyes go wide and her mouth drops open. "Oh my gosh, it does. She looks just like him."

"Yeah they even have a picture right in their living room and I swear that is an identical liking of him."

"That's kind of neat..."

Lifting my butt off the floor, I scramble to pull my phone out of my back pocket, scraping my knuckles against the rough denim with a slice and a sting. I grip my phone hard, urgency coursing through me as if I've stumbled upon something undiscovered. *I have no clue if my hunch is correct; I could have this all wrong, but what if I don't.* Moving my phone with the edge butted up against my palm and my fingertips securely holding onto the back of it, I hit the menu button and unlock it quickly before clicking on my photos icon. The very first picture to come up, which is the very last picture I was looking at, is a snapshot of the photo I have laying by my bed; of Piper I glance over at her quickly, barely catching her look away. *Great.*

Swiping my thumb over and over across the screen, I go through what few pictures I have stored on my phone, looking for one in specific. My eyes quickly scan over pictures of the lake, pictures of sites around the property that need to be fixed up, a few screenshots of receipts for purchases for the company, but very few personal shots. I've just never been a big picture taker. I guess if I hadn't lived most of my life right on a dock, I'd probably be soaked up in the technology era just like everybody else. However, seeing how water and phones don't mix too well, I tend to leave mine in the glove compartment of the work truck.

Finally, my eyes land right on what I was looking for: a picture of Jake and Judd wrestling in the living room of their house. Jake had a death grip on his brother, with his bicep bulging around his neck and looking like he was cutting off his air supply. It was a day last summer, when we were all fooling around and having plenty of laughs. Judd started off confident, claiming that Jake could not take him in a fight; Jake proved him wrong. I was busting at the seams, and made sure to get photographic proof of little bro kicking my buddies ass. *It was epic.*

Right now as I look at the photo, my focus is completely pulled to the picture on the wall right behind them. There perfectly framed, just like it came with the house, is the one single image that drifted into my thoughts as soon as I saw the family portrait in Piper's album. Taking my index finger and thumb, I place it on my screen and pull them apart to expand the picture in the background. As soon as it's blown up, my eyes widen. *Wow!*

"Here…" I speak quietly, almost talking to myself as I slide the phone closer to Piper so she can take a look. "This is the picture I was talking about. That's almost creepy how similar she and Tristan look."

"Tristan? The little girl is almost the spitting image of the woman in that picture. I mean, that could nearly pass for what she'd look like as an adult, don't you think?"

My level of curiosity swiftly changes to astonishment as I look closer at the two faces and come to the same conclusion that Piper did. "Damn you're right." I quickly click on the main button of my phone to get out of my photos, then move my thumb up to click on the camera. "What did your dad say her name was, when you'd talk about her?"

"I don't even remember. It's been years since we even talked about her and even then I think he called her by a nickname... Ohhhhh, what did he call her?" She whispers more to herself. Looking down, Piper continues to rack her brain as I snap a quick shot of the family portrait. "Hmmm... I keep wanting to say it starts with an 'A,' but I'm just not sure."

Moving my fingers across my phone to pull up my messages, I add three contacts to the image I'm sending, the whole while wondering if this is a huge mistake. It's probably a simple case of 'everyone having a twin' out there in this great big world, but I just can't help the gut feeling I have. My luck Tristan will probably come back pissed off as hell, then Judd very well might get ticked off at me for ruffling his feathers.

"Do you think that's a good idea? Really, what are the chances."

"So your dad said she died years ago?" I question her comment from earlier. *There's a big difference between dead and ran away.*

Piper snaps her head over, frowning. "I can text him and ask him what her name was and what happened...If you really think there's a possibility that this could be..."

I speed type as she talks, sliding my fingertips from one letter to the next, eager to get a reply back.

Me: Hey guys, stumbled upon this picture in one of Piper's albums and I thought there was just a crazy resemblance between the little girl in this picture and your mom...Not even sure why I'm sending it, just

thought you guys might want to see.

Clicking send with only half of what I wanted to say typed, dread, anxiety and excitement all rush through my veins as I wait to hear back from just one of them. I glance over at Piper, busy typing something on her own phone.

"Okay done," she says, lying her phone beside her on the wood floor with a quiet tap. "I should hear back from him pretty fast."

My jaw tenses as the dread portion of my feelings overwhelms me. *We could very well be opening a whole can of worms for nothing. What are the odds?*

"So do you think that's really her...their mom?" Her voice is flooded in disbelief and it only spikes my nervousness over Tristan's possible reply.

Dipping my brows, I point back at the facts. "Well there is no denying the obvious. I wasn't so sure when I was focused on Tristan, but when you pointed out their mom, I don't know...that's just too crazy of a likeness, in my opinion at least."

"Oh, I agree too."

My eyes wander the image for a minute, before trailing their way back up to Piper's face. Once again she nibbles on her lower lip with a small smile and a gleam in her eyes.

I chuckle, "What?" I breathe out. "You look awfully excited."

Her teeth fully come down on her lip, biting softly as a big smile emerges across her face. "I am." The enthusiasm is evident in her voice. "Well, I guess it's two things that kind of has me...I don't know..." She trailed off. Hoisting my brows, I lean my head forward in a silent nudge for her to go on. *What on earth has her so giddy?* "Think about it. If there is even a chance that this could be their mom, then that's kind of cool for Dad and me. I mean wouldn't it be?" Her eyes light up and her voice kicks up to a squealing, happy tone that makes everything inside of me smile.

Slowly nodding in complete agreement, my curiosity peaks. "And what's the second thing?"

Piper drops her head back, with the huge grin and a girly giggle as if she's gabbing with her BFF. "Nothing." She darts her eyes to me for just a second, looks away then back at me again with a loud sigh. "Oh, all right…" She relents, but I swear this whole time my facial expression never changed. I laughed to myself at how little of a fight she put up. *This could be good.* "I guess I was just a little excited that you had a picture of me on your phone."

Now I feel like her giddiness is contagious. A warmth settles in my chest, causing my heart rate to excel and a shockwave of delight to tickle across my skin. *She needs to be kissed.* I move in, pulling my hand up and placing it beneath her chin. The moment my skin touches hers, the warmth in my chest consumes me, spreading like lava over my entire body. I move in closer, eager to taste her lips; wanting to be just like we were last night, against each other, closer. Her breath catches and as soon as her hand moves across my forearm in an unspoken gesture to keep going…I do. As she slides her other hand across the back of my neck, I move forward in hungry anticipation, wanting to devour her. I'm not sure what's come over me. The guessing game we have of 'What's her name?' and 'Is this the same girl?' should not be affecting me like this, however, with Piper here, there is always the possibility for the impatient python to peak his head out.

No sooner than my lips touch hers, with a warm vibration of an over-anxious need mixed with the softness of her lips, I feel a different vibration and jolt; an unwelcome one at this point. Piper flinches at the chime of my phone, breaking our connection and shooting down all my hopeful horniness like a kamikaze pilot out of the sky. *Dammit; I had to be waiting for a text or call right now!*

Pulling my phone between us, I look down and quickly see Judd was the first to respond.

Judd: Wow! Where did you find this picture???

My phone chimes again…

Jake: Who is that? And yeah, where did you get it?

I can't even type fast enough…

Me: I found it in a family photo album at Piper's cabin. It's a picture of her dad and their parents and his little sister. I just thought it was crazy insane how similar she looks to you guys…Tristan mainly.

I don't even know what all to say. In a way, I almost feel like I'm intruding, but I've always felt a special bond with Jake and Judd; they are my family and if there is even the slightest possibility that this could give them back a little bit of what they've lost, I'm willing to risk the intrusion.

My phone keeps chiming over and over, but no word from Tristan.

Fifteen minutes later, I'm fully invested in figuring out who this is and surprisingly not turned on for the first time in my life while being this close to her, even with her thigh continuously grazing over mine as she leans towards me to be a part of our text conversation.

The three-way texting gets confusing, as Jake and Judd go back and forth, disputing that there's no way it could possibly be their mother. For a minute, I am half-ass ready to end the text chat and start a dang party line.

Judd: Yeah I agree, it looks just like her, but what are the odds?

Me: That's what I said, but crazier things have happened…

"My dad's family actually lives right around here; fifteen minutes from the lake actually," Piper adds, but it doesn't stop my thoughts from climbing and stretching to the probability that my girl and my best friend could potentially be family. "Was their mom from Rose-more?"

Pondering that for a moment, I think back to when I had just started school at Rosemore. Of course, every other kid had been going to school there for years and knew all their classmates; I didn't know a soul after hopping around from military base to military base for half of my existence. However, for some reason I don't ever remember seeing Judd's face.

"I don't think so. Hell, you would know better than me. You went to school at Rosemore your whole life up until your..." I halt on my ramblings, realizing I'm treading on dangerous grounds by venturing onto the topic of her moving after my mouth made a disaster of her life. "Do you remember seeing him way back? Because they could've always moved at some point."

She shakes her head, pausing on that thought. "I don't think so. First time I remember having a class with Judd, was in the sixth grade. I don't even remember seeing him at assemblies, hearing his name or anything, so I bet they did move." Shrugging she looks over at me with her eyebrows arched. "Maybe you're right. Could be her."

I get busy, my fingers swiping from one letter to the next as I type out another question, diving into where their mom is from, but sooner than I can hit send, my phone chimes again.

Tristan: Holy Shit...that's Mom!!!

My mouth goes dry and so does all the sounds from my phone. There's no speculation from him; just a bold statement that confirms what I thought.

I look at Piper, her eyes just as wide as mine. "Oh. My. Gosh!"

"Holy shit!" I think for a minute to question his proclamation, but as the oldest he would probably know. "Wow..." Rotating my face in the direction of Piper, we stare at each other, her with a sneaky grin on her face and me with an equal level of excitement as if I just found out something about my own life. "Looks like you may be having a family reunion soon."

Her eyes light up with the happiness I seriously haven't seen in years and right then my phone starts going off like fire alarms in a house swallowed up in smoke.

"I better take this," I point down to my phone as it lights up with Tristan's name. "This could be good. I mean how neat could this be? Like a fresh start for you and for them." Smiling, I feel it deep in my bones, a penetrating happiness over them both finding something that they haven't had in a long time; a family.

"It is, maybe a fresh start for all of us…" She stares at me, a longing in her dark eyes as she relays far more than her words say.

Let Go

Piper

A BIT OF EXCITEMENT COURSED through me as soon as I saw Evan's phone light up with Tristan's message.

With more than a bounce in his step, Evan waves good-bye, grasping my hand and giving me a sweet, lingering kiss on the lips before he leaves. His phone continues to go off with texts and not even two steps out the door, he has it pressed to his ear in a deep conversation.

"Tristan, hey man...." His eyes relay all the excitement that I'm feeling. "Yeah, no, no, no... Yeah, we were just flipping through an old album of Piper's and all of a sudden, boom." His voice fades as he closes the bedroom door behind him.

Now, I'm eager to hear back from Dad. I called him twice while Evan was busy texting; I skipped the voice mail, but did shoot him a brief text. Maybe they have it wrong, but nonetheless, the proof is right here and it's all pretty exciting. My emotions twist and tangle at all that has gone on, imagining that Dad may be interested in finding out what happened to his little sister; if he doesn't already know.

Peeling back the thin sheet of clear plastic on the old album, I take a glance at the handwriting on the back before sliding it carefully in place. I assume the handwriting is my grandmothers, but there it is in black and white…

Me, Jim, Pete and Hailey 1984

After carefully pressing the protective overlay back against the photos, I slap the album shut, stack all three on top of one another with a thud and walk them to the closet to put away. My heart beats rapidly, in a way that it hasn't in so long, and although I'd like to think most of it has been ignited from sitting so close to Evan all night or even from the possibility of unraveling the mystery that Evan and I have been going over all night, that isn't it. All the memories crash into me as I step onto my tiptoes to slide the albums back on the top shelf of the closet between a dusty box labeled life jackets and another containing an old air mattress.

My clothes from last night lay draped over my suitcase at my feet, calling to me as if they have a voice of their own. Earlier, on the way over from Evan's, I couldn't help the sudden tick of curiosity that started eating at me and driving me to get the letter and keep it close.

Looking down, the corner edge of folder paper peaks out of the top of my sweater pocket like an invisible crooked finger motioning for me to come closer, to lean in and take ahold of it, to simply unfold the letter and swallow every word from start to finish. A sharp shrill sound reaches my ears, startling me out of my thoughts. Shaking my head, I take my eyes off of the letter and focus on what's going on. The vibrating-rattling sound persists driving my attention to the floor, where Evan and I were sitting. My phone lights up and I waste no time thinking about the past or all the fears that were bubbling up inside of me just now; I race over and grab my phone, clicking accept once I see Dad's name.

"Dad," I say in a hurried, anxious voice, excited and partly still caught up in the memories that were overcoming me just a second ago.

"Hey sweetie. I got your message…I don't understand. Why are you needing to know about that picture?" His voice is laced in uncertainty as if just bringing up his sister has opened up a long-ago sealed up vault.

I wince at the thought of even going any further; I completely understand not tampering with a locked up and boarded up room, but bearing in mind that there could be a positive outcome, I forge forward.

"Listen, I know this is a subject you don't like talking about, and I wouldn't bring it up unless it was important, but I was hoping to ask you a couple of questions."

"Okay..." He draws out hesitantly. "Go on... I'm listening." He keeps a defensive tone; one I've only heard when either Mom's name is brought up or his past.

Lifting my chin, I clear my throat, prepared to dive into a touchy subject with absolutely no idea of what the outcome could be. *I don't do touchy subjects very well.*

"Okay," I pause, working to think of the best wording that will help him to not shut down immediately. I guess in that aspect I'm a lot like Dad. He closes down, shuts off and refuses to go any further when unwanted memories start to consume him like an avalanche. "Just try to keep an open mind, okay?"

"Just go on, Piper...what is it?"

Well, no use beating around the bush; all I'm doing is irritating him. "So after everybody left tonight, me and Evan were going through some old photo albums. Now I know this is going to sound totally off-the-wall, but Evan swears your little sister looks like someone he knows."

My father gasps, "Who?! Where does he know her from?!" As soon as I hear the urgency in my father's voice as if he stumbled upon something just like Evan and I did, I know that Tristan could be right.

I go on, filling him in on everything I know, everything me and Evan discussed while he was texting back and forth with Judd and Jake. "Well I haven't found out all the information, but Evan is actually talking to Tristan. I wasn't sure if I would hear back from you until tomorrow morning so he went ahead and left so that he could go find Judd and Jake...."

"Yes okay, but what about my sister; he thinks he knows her?"

Shaking my head even though he can't see me, I hold my hand trying to halt him so that I can finish, "I'm getting to that. Ok, so Evan thought she looked just like Jake, Judd and Tristan's mom. Judd told Evan that she used to live not far from here and that they spent a couple of summers right here at the lake."

"Piper I don't think..."

I don't let him say anymore, "Wait, let me finish. From what Judd said, he had heard from his mom years ago that she had gotten pregnant when she was very young and her parents refused to accept it. Judd said she was only sixteen or seventeen when she had Tristan. He had no idea if she had a brother or where his mom's family was from, but he did remember coming out here a couple of times when he was little." Dad doesn't say anything; silence stretches out. "Dad are you there?"

He clears his throat again, this time appearing to push down a tremor of emotion. "Yeah," but I can still hear it in his voice as he speaks, "I'm here sweetie. Did you happen to catch her name?"

My heart leaps into my throat, knowing this is it. *Should I text Evan first; Judd or Jake? Or do I just find out, then let them know?* I proceed with the latter, "Her name was Hailey."

Once I hear the sharp intake of breath on the other end of the line, no other words are needed. Dad sniffles, and my heart breaks with the realization that there is one more piece of the puzzle that I haven't told him, but just as I'm beginning to speak up he cuts me off.

"Was?"

I slam my eyes closed, grind my teeth together and clench my fists, not believing that I could be so stupid to choose that type of wording. *Dammit!*

"Dad..." Now I'm all sorts of confused on whether I should say anything at all. "Did you want me to have Judd call you? Maybe...

fill you in?" I raise one shoulder, giving a crooked shrug of sorts as I uncomfortably squirm. *I'd rather do anything than be the bearer of this news.*

He takes another deep breath, and I know he is mustering up all the strength he can find. *I have to do this.*

"Honey, you said her name *was* Hailey…" As he stops talking I pick up on every other sound on his side of the phone including a loud gulp as he gathers his courage and his shaky breaths. "My sister's name *is* Hailey."

My freehand slides up to the center of my chest. Clawing gently, I collect a handful of my sweater as a sense of comfort to my heart; or more so Dad's.

I wish Evan was here. "Ummm… You know, I could probably text Evan and he would come back over…" A frustrated huff of air comes over the line; I stop midsentence.

"Sweetie…" His voice carries a smooth eloquent calmness, similar to the day he found out what happened to me. "I haven't seen my sister since she was sixteen years old. I've never known what happened to her, whether she had a family or got married, if she was happy or anything. Nothing. She was just gone one day. Mom and Dad told me she emancipated herself and for me to let it be. I didn't know if she was alive or dead. Our families always came out to this cabin and that was why I started bringing mine. I had hoped that someday, she would be here again and maybe, just maybe I would reconnect with her. So honey, whatever you know, please don't be afraid to tell me. If this girl, your friend's mom is my sister, which it sounds more and more like it could be, knowing anything is better than knowing nothing," the plea in his voice is undeniable and he's right; he needs closure.

A sharp jolt hits me and again, I stare down to the letter that is shoved into the pocket of my clothes; that same thing is true for me. Releasing a breath, I relent on letting him know all that I do until he can meet with Judd, Tristan and Jake; he needs this. Telling him everything may be all it takes to fix what has been broken inside.

Smiling through misted-over eyes, I open my mouth and let it out. "Well, she lived in Rosemore. I went to school with all three of her sons. Her oldest is named Tristan, and he is 21 or 22..." I roll my eyes, not wanting to dive into what sort of a womanizer he is, before moving on. "Then there is Judd, he was a year behind me in school and Jake is a little younger." I collect my thoughts, suck in a mouthful of air and go on, "Evan said Hailey got sick several years back and she passed away the same year he met Judd." I don't hear a sound on the other end as I deliver this dreaded news; nothing. "Dad?" my voice quivers.

"I'm here, sweetie." He stops talking, and I tumble over anything I can say or do to break the silence, but there is nothing I can possibly say; he has to process this, and I get that. "Thank you, Piper." A sound I don't expect sneaks over the line as Dad takes a breath, yet it's not the sort I expect; it's almost a cleansing, relieved breath and that in itself gives me hope for my future as I peer down at my heap of clothes.

"Soooo..." Pushing my teeth together, I decide a new direction is in order; let's turn this into a positive. "I guess a family reunion is in order?" I grin, hoping this will lift Dad's spirits and remind him that there is still a reason to celebrate. His sister left behind three great, wait, two awesome guys and one that is determined to drive my best friend half insane until he gets in her pants. Shaking my head, I get back on track. "I'm sure you all will have plenty of stories to tell each other."

Dad coughs and I cringe, flinching as if his pain is my own. "Yes, that would be nice. I'd love to get to know them all. Would you mind setting something up?"

"Yeah, of course. I'll text Evan when we hang up and see if we can all get together after the New Year."

"Sooo...I keep hearing Evan's name. That's a name I haven't heard you talk about in such a chipper fashion in years. Anything you wanna tell me?"

I hear a hint of teasing in his tone and I automatically go into full on junior high girl mode. "Ohhh, well, we actually spent a little time together and I guess maybe…" I never knew how hard talking to Dad about these sorts of things could be. My stomach dips and turns, making me feel uncomfortable.

He chuckles, "Ok, ok, well make sure to bring him to the house. I'm sure you two have a lot to catch up on as well. I know you both used to be two peas in a pod for as long as I could remember. It'll be nice to get back a little of what you lost."

My body jumps at him saying exactly what I have been thinking. "Ok…I will."

"Well I think I am going to get off here and maybe try to sort through all this. Let me know when and where and I'd love to see some pictures if at all possible. Ummm, I know I'm a little at a loss for words on it, but I do appreciate knowing. It's never good to leave things unsettled in your heart."

I take a deep breath, pushing all of my anxiety that I felt earlier into the pit of my stomach so that maybe, the fears that hold me back in life can once and for all be forgotten, and my scars can heal.

"I love you, honey."

"I love you too, Dad." I hold off immediately on saying bye. "I am sorry, Dad. Bye."

"Bye."

Bending down on shaky legs, I place my phone in my suitcase beside my sweater and reach my hand out an inch closer, and closer and closer, yet as my fingertip barely brushes over the softness of the knitted garment, my legs become concrete. I turn to stone, unable to will myself any further to whatever truths or lies he has fed me after all these years. I fall to my knees onto the hard wood floor, a dull sting splintering over my knee and reminding of that night; pulling up the memories of my legs digging into the gravel as I fled.

My lungs shut down as I squeeze my eyes shut and hear a pained whimper. I snap my head around and look towards the bed, why I have no idea; I know it was me, but as the still blackness of terror and nostalgia threatens to sweep over me like the plague, I'm unable to pinpoint whether the sound is a memory of that night as I prayed it would end, or if it is the fear I pushed down erupting out of me, because it is too much to hold back.

I have to get this under control. I can't let that one-night rule my entire life. It has dictated every fabric of my being from that night on; I've never been able to carry on an intimate relationship with anyone since Evan, I keep everyone at arm's length in terms of trust and closeness, and the slightest things can knock me into a whirlwind of darkness.

Keeping my eyes closed, I listen to the sounds in the room; nothing, only muffled chatter from the next room mixed with a chilly breeze outside and rapping branches against the back window. I push down the feeling that Trent is right there again, invading the present and holding me back from living life. Stiffening my shoulders and drawing them in towards my neck, I push down the impulse to feel his hot breaths in my ear once again. *Breathe, Breathe.*

My mind races, thumbing through carefully selected memories that inflicted further pain and doubt over my heart.

"Piper, do you have any idea why Trent would have wanted to leave so suddenly?"

The question sends ice through my veins. With less than a week since the night he took everything from me, I can barely look Mom and Dad in the eyes out of fear that they will see the truth. However, hearing the skepticism and blame in my mother's tone, tears me apart. She already voiced to Dad that she was extremely against him wanting to go back to California, but she also told us how adamant he was on leaving; I'm thankful for that. No way could I face him day in and day out, or even begin to sleep in the same house as him.

"Well I just found it odd that the last thing he told me is to tell you he was sorry."

There it is. I squeeze my eyes shut and grip the kitchen counter as she continues to scrub a plate for the sixtieth time since we've stood here. I wish Dad was back from fishing.

"So you have no clue why he would say that?"

She blames me; or does she know.

Raising my shoulders till they scrunch against the sides of my neck, I look forward and try to regain my composure by gulping in a lungful of air. My stomach rolls and my head spins as I stare forward. From the corner of my eyes I can tell she hasn't even looked my way, she just keeps scrubbing, brushing her anger off on that plate.

"Hmmmm, well I sure would like to know. He's had a rough way to go and my sister is in no condition to take care of him. I just found it odd that he would beg me to go back, don't you?"

Another gallon of oxygen reaches my lungs and I pray that I can stay upright as she digs, sounding as if she knows more than she's letting on.

‍◦‍

My mind tumbles and scrambles through more memories, feeling each of them like jagged shards of glass piercing my heart.

‍◦‍

Weeks go by and the sounds of laughter from anyone around, at a store, my family, other kids playing outside in the neighborhood, it's all amplified as if it's directed at me; like everyone is pointing at me. The sound hits my eardrums in a series of echoes and murmurs. "Why didn't she tell him to stop?" "Why didn't she scream for her dad or call for help?" I can't stop the accusing sounds anywhere I go.

‍◦‍

My heart stumbles as I remember how helpless those first few weeks were, leading up to the first time my body rebelled and I blacked out.

‍◦‍

I'm alone, surrounded in darkness and it's a dream; no, a nightmare. He's behind me, against me and I can't stop it. It's happening again. I breathe and breathe and breathe until all the air in the room is emptied and there is no more to take in. Muffled words tug at me and I swear I can hear Dad.

"Call 911…she isn't waking up," he cries out, sounding scared and panicked. "Piper, Piper, wake up."

I gasp, not sure whether he is dunking me in water to pull me out of my dream or what. My fist finds something solid and it's then that I realize, I'm still in bed. My face isn't under a faucet or being dunked beneath the surface of a cool bath, but it is soaked in tears and my sobs drown out everything else as I pull myself into Dad's arms, clinging to him.

"Baby, you scared me. Call the doctor," he instructs Mom.

I don't even look around for her. All I can think is to stop them. A doctor will dig and dig to find the answers of why I've become so reclusive, turning away from all school activities, discarding most of my friends and preferring to seal myself in my bedroom alone.

"No Dad, it was just a nightmare. It scared me. I thought I was…" I pause, thinking, searching, scrambling for an excuse. "I was drowning and couldn't breathe," I burst out. That's exactly how I felt, trapped, unable to reach for anything to help me; being guzzled alive as my mind and body felt everything yet I couldn't find the power to say a word.

I squeeze my eyes shut, the memories fast-forwarding through time.

I stand motionless against the shower house door, registering everything Evan's heartless asshole of a brother says about me. My heart crumbles into my stomach and all I want to do is run, escape and never have to look anyone in the eyes again. I squeeze my lids together, wondering if I could possibly will away this moment or my entire being. Then I see him; the one person I trusted with my life, my honor, my heart and my secret. How could he hurt me like this?

My eyes bolt open as I look ahead at the closet, and instantly rip the letter out of my pocket. I have to put an end all of this. I need closure; I need a way to move forward. A part of me wants to rush over to Evan's cabin and demand to know what happened that day. It's something I should have asked him last night, or possibly the other night on the dock or countless other times when I wanted to claw his eyes out from the resentment and anger I had carried with me. However, gripping the paper in my hands, I end on one thought; one thing that helps me to take a breath. It doesn't matter what happened that day, or the day after or even today. What matters is that night; what matters is me finding a way to let it go; to forgive myself and to stop pointing my finger at what I didn't do or say. I have to find closure, and this may very well be the only way to do it. Pressing the now wrinkled up sheet of notebook paper against my lap, I run my palm over it to smooth it out. The words are blurred as I look down and search for the courage to read. I need to be able to forgive and forget; I've got to learn to let go.

Here we go again

Evan

AFTER CHRISTMAS, THE DAYS FLIP by faster than I can count. She and I both agreed that the past is best left in the past, however, I still feel the urge biting at me from time to time to explain how I blabbed to Mitch, but she quickly pulls away from the subject once we head in that direction. I just really hate that she may think that I deliberately told him something so personal. So far so good and we have been carrying on like two fourteen-years-olds that just experienced our first kiss on the shore of the lake. We've made sure to keep it all PG, although our kisses are getting down right R-rated the last few days and my anatomy is on full awareness that we are nearing the month mark in our new relationship status. *Don't women celebrate all that shit?* I'm all for a celebration as long as it ends with a clothing optional party.

"Wait, so Mom was in a band?" Judd laughs as he, Alyssa, me, Piper, Abby, Piper's dad Pete and Jake all sit scattered about in the living room of her house. Tristan seemed to have a bit of a bitterness towards any family reunions in his near future, so none of us could convince him to come. "That's hilarious. She never told us that. I mean, we knew Dad played football, but for some reason I always assumed…"

"What? A cheerleader?" Pete chuckles, flipping through an old album, one of which Piper drug back from the cabin along with a whole slew of other books and keepsakes.

It didn't take everyone long to piece together the ties between Piper and Judd's families, and it's never made me prouder to know that my best friend and girlfriend are cousins. I think they both are due for some family connections. Let's face it, Piper's experience with cousins has resided in the adopted bastard that touched her against her will when she was a kid, and Judd needs any family ties that he can find. His family has been broken since his mom died, and with Tristan on constant excuse mode of why he cannot come talk to Pete or get together with any of us, this development has offered up a great source of distraction for Jake and Judd.

"Yeah...I really envisioned the high school quarterback and head cheerleader kind of movie-like status for them. I don't know," Judd laughs, looking over at Alyssa.

I scoot back into the cushion of the recliner as Piper pivots slightly, brushing her arm back behind my neck as she lazily drapes her body on the arm of the chair against me.

We've spent many evenings lounging in her bedroom after classes or work, however, we keep a nice boundary of hands above the waist for now. We spent a couple of Saturday afternoons at my apartment, but that quickly got out of hand with us diagonal across the couch as I dry humped her like a dog trying to rub the fur off its mate's ass. It was painfully awesome, to say the least, until Piper started to black out and we had to put the brakes on. It's not like I'm not used to it and I'm more than happy with the routine we have, learning to breathe through the flashbacks again, but somedays I do want to shout from the rooftops out of frustration. From that point on, we resigned to have alone time at her house. Her dad seemed to trust me, however anytime we got too quiet, it always seemed like that was the exact moment that he remembered some appetizer that he had in the freezer that we just might want to try. I've started to associate pizza rolls and cheddar poppers with me getting an erection; nothing like shooting a man down with food...

that's never a good thing. That's like using two heavenly possessions against a person; sex and food.

Piper threads herself to my side naturally, as if we've never been apart a day in our lives. I stay put, and of course, glance up at her dad to see if I'm getting the traditional, get-your-paws-off-my-daughter look. Luckily, he doesn't pay any mind. He's way too caught up in learning the details of his younger sister's life.

Pete didn't know all about why his sister left the nest and unfortunately his father has been hell bent on keeping a lid on it as well, but enough was pieced together to learn that she was discarded after she found out she was pregnant. However, from Pete's point of view he was told his sister ran off with her high school sweetheart. He last saw her when she was sixteen. When Judd broke the news to him of her death, I think all of us wished we could shrink down and leave the room. It was clear that he had missed his sister all of these years, but the mist of water that filled his eyes soon evaporated as he came to the conclusion that left behind in his little sis' absence were three boys which he had never had the pleasure to get to know.

"So," I lean towards Piper, speaking in a quiet tone so that I don't interrupt the excitable conversation going back and forth between Judd, Pete and Jake. Today's visit is full of smiles and reminiscing, and they all deserve this. "Grandpa told me that apparently, your dad and my dad didn't like to play nice back in the day. There was some squabble over a girl and I guess they sworn enemies forever," I snicker, dramatizing my words like there may be a shootout at sunset between the two.

"Whoa…" Pete's voice kicks up a notch and projects in my direction, getting our attention. *Damn, I do not know how to keep shit quiet.* "It was not over a girl; it was over my sister. He had the hots for Hailey and I just thought…" he looks down, then over to Judd and back to us. Judd grits his teeth as if hearing that his mom was desirable back then, hits a sour note. "Well, I thought he was arrogant and didn't want him around my little sister. He had a bad rep and I knew how my mom was with that stuff."

I raise my eyes and look at Judd. "Arrogant, imagine that…my father, really?" I say sarcastically, in complete agreement of his assessment.

Judd snickers and they return to their back and forth, did-you-know-this chatter. Myself, I'm about ready to abandon the family talk and spend some alone time with Piper.

Glancing past the clock that reads a little past 7:00, I look out the window at the dark night and sigh about the half hour drive still ahead of me.

"So what would you say if I suggest both of us ditching the family reunion and heading back to my place to…" slowly letting a smirk rise over my lips and across my cheeks, I add the part of that suggestion that I usually leave out, but not tonight. "…for the night?"

Her head snaps to attention, and the abruptness of it is so noticeable to me, that I immediately glance at her dad to make sure that my whisper didn't come out in my regular voice for all ears to hear. I clamp my jaw down expecting to find all eyes on us with expectant expressions and probably a shitty ass grin from Jake and Judd, but fortunately, their idle conversation has them all fully engrossed.

"Ok," her calm, quiet voice reaches me before I can look back, but that word has me spinning my neck her way so fast that it may possibly pop right off.

Our eyes meet and there is no *maybe,* or hesitation or even nervousness in hers…just a simple *ok* with something I'm thrilled to see; excitement. *I do not think I can get to the door fast enough.*

After what seemed to be a ten-second flee from her house, that had to be noticeable by everyone, plus a thirty-minute drive home, which I believe I shaved down to about twenty, we get to my apartment and speed upstairs.

"Evan…" she laughs, clinging tight to my hand as I fumble for my keys. "Is there some movie on that we're going to miss or do you just have to pee really bad?"

Shoving the door open finally, I turn my head slowly, rather proud of her sarcasm, suddenly dumbfounded on whether I should just throw her down as soon as we walk inside. *I sure the hell hope she wasn't being serious though.* She looks at me with a slightly held back grin and a sparkle in her dark eyes, but I play it cool, remaining nonchalant as if I haven't a care in the world; especially one where I have years of pent up sexual frustration for her, that is currently beating its fists across my pelvis region and begging to come out to play.

"Just glad to have you to myself." *Come to think of it maybe I should've peed before we left.* At this point, I'd practically have to stand on my head to make sure I aimed that sucker straight.

Pulling her along on my heels, I make a beeline for the couch and plop down. To hell with any more talk and I'm definitely not in the least concerned with what could be on TV. Piper drapes her body across the couch with her legs lazily flung over my lap; in an instant my body's on alert. Placing my hand gently at her kneecap, I run my eyes up the length of her legs starting at her ankles, all the way up before pausing at her thigh. *To hell with this.* Reaching forward, I slip my fingers into the belt loops of her jeans to pull her onto my lap. She laughs, shifting and wiggling as I tug her, enticing a whole lot more stimulation beneath my jeans than she's bargaining for. She finds a comfortable spot, settling down with her legs folded calf against thigh, but I can't help the grin that creeps across my face as her eyes widen and she stares right at me. With anyone else, and given her past trauma, I'd bite my tongue on this one, but this is Piper; we've never been that way with each other. I say what's on my mind and she's come to expect that from me.

"Oh, don't act like you haven't felt that before," I chuckle, raising my eyebrows mischievously.

A small smile instantly tugs at the corner of her lips, but the sexiest thing of all is the slight tent of pink in her cheeks that flame all the way around the contours of her face as she tries to hide her embarrassment.

"Don't worry it won't bite…" pulsing my eyebrows, I pause and she grins as I finish my statement in an over-the-top alluring tone that nearly makes me crack up. "…hard."

Her hand comes up and she bursts out laughing as she smacks my chest. I catch her hand, using it as leverage to pull her closer until my lips are on hers, tasting what I've been craving all afternoon. A needy, impulsive desire sparks in my chest, practically igniting a hump reflex in my hips as I shift toward her in a rhythmic motion that matches the steady and tender pulse of my tongue.

Closing my eyes, I'm zoned in on the kicked-up pace of my breaths, the rapid beat of my heart and the sweet satisfying touch of her lips against mine. One of my hands sits uselessly against her clothing, still clasped in her belt loop, while the other remains at my side. This is where we usually put on the brakes, however, my engine is revved up and my brakes are so erect, I think it would take an army to stop me now.

Slowly opening one eye, I take in Piper's demeanor, but as her tongue caresses mine and her lips pucker, and as needy sighs slip out of her mouth every few seconds, I realize it's really not needed; she may want this as bad as I do.

I pull away just enough to be able to say two words, "You ok?" They aren't necessary seeing as she was just about to burn a hole through my jeans too, but I ask anyways. I need to always walk softly when it comes to moving too fast with her, and this is definitely moving fast. In the last month we haven't so much as made it to second base and here I am fantasizing of how good sliding into home plate will feel with her body crushed up against mine.

She gulps down a few shallow breaths, her chest moving in and out, like it's beckoning for me to dive in. Spreading out my fingers as my hand rests at my side, I fight the urge to go for a rather large feel up.

"Yeah, I'm ok," she gets out with a heavy-winded gasp. "Are you?" Her eyes flick down before meeting back up with my gaze.

I want to laugh, in fact my lungs burn with the desire to crack up, but this is not the damn time for laughing and playing; I'm on a hell of a mission and I need to keep my head in it.

"Ohhh, I'm good." I raise my brows, putting forth my best serious tone while gulping down that little voice that's saying, *maybe we should just wait. Screw that voice.* "Will you feel comfortable if we go in my room?"

Drum roll. This will be the deciding factor, because even if I get the slightest idea that she is hesitant, I will not push it; I won't. I may be eager as hell and about to get a serious groin injury if I get any more turned on, but this has to be completely ok with her.

She doesn't say a word, and a tinge of dread fills my heart thinking this is the end of the road for today; all I'm getting tonight is a whole lot of snuggling and a serious case of blue balls, but before I can even finish my thought, she is off of my lap with a smile and a slow backwards, sexy-as-all-get-out trip into my bedroom with her eyes locked on me. *Holy shit, it's happening!*

I bolt upright, practically face planting into the coffee table. I don't even wait for her as my feet lead me blazing past her and right to the bed. The only dilemma on my mind now is, do I start the show without her by throwing myself onto the bed, like here I am, come get me or do I rip off my clothes like a horny teenager and wait for her to take matters into her hands, at her own pace. *Oh geez, that sounds good.*

"Evan…Evan!"

Shaking my head, I look around. I'm frozen right beside the bed, with my hands securely holding all of my assets. Piper stands in front of me with a silly grin on her face. I keep my hand right where it is, the tightness of my jeans about to cut off my circulation to all of my lower extremities if I don't let the beast out of its cage soon. Raising my brows to let her know I'm now back on Earth rather than drifting off to Planet Boning, I hold back my smile and wait to see what she has to say.

"Ummm, are we…"

She looks around, her eyes searching my unmade bed, then running down to my hand. Ok, I can't hold it back; I snicker, releasing my hand and bringing it up to the small dip at the side of her waist. She shivers beneath my touch and all humor is set aside.

"Don't worry, I think we can warm the room up pretty quick."

Her eyes widen impishly; I take that as a green light as I move my hand straight across to the center of her back, joined by my other so I can slowly but surely pull her sweater up. I'm always careful to keep my hands away from her hips after we figured out that is what triggers her black outs. Squeezing my eyes shut, I push that thought away and nudge my chin forward. I reopen them, staring into her eyes, to search for any signs of distress or freak out.

No sooner than the sweet, moist flesh of her bottom lip is between my lips, I reach my hands beneath her sweater, making a steady incline to the hooks of her bra. It may be backwards to keep her clothes on and take her bra off, but I figure it may keep her a bit more comfortable and help us ease into it. A short trembling gasp escapes her and my fingers stop, holding the straps of her bra in my fingertips, which I already spectacularly unhooked, like it was second nature.

I pull away, again....

"You ok?" I huff out in her face, unable to keep my ragged breathing under control.

At this point, testosterone is blazing through my body and I can barely hold back. Piper nods, bringing her hands up between us and shuffling them around inside her sweater. I watch, my hand still remaining under her shirt and holding tight to the back of her bra, but as soon as the delicate threads of fabric get pulled from my hand, I know what she's doing. *Oh yes!*

All I really want to do is pull her sweater off, fall back on the bed and let her press those puppies all over me. I'd also like to thank her, because back when we were younger, those things were under lock and key for the longest time. I could understand why, but it didn't dampen my urge to see them any less. I even tried to convince her that all boobs were just fat and that maybe, just maybe I could give them the proper exercise that was required if she let me fondle them for a bit; *no dice.*

Keeping my hands at her back, I wait, all the excitement in my body rushing below the waist right where I thought I could not swell any further; I was wrong. A slight rustling sound as she pulls the bra out from beneath her sweater and a subtle tap on the top of my shoe as it gets dropped to the floor, is all it takes before my hands are burning a path back to the front of her waist. I make sure to skim over every bit of soft delicate skin as I can possibly touch until they rest below the prize. Still wishing her sweater was out of the way, I look at Piper, pausing, but no sign of this stopping; those are up for the grabbing.

Her eyes glimmer as she looks back at me, fearless and ready. *Me too.* Quirking my brows, my fingertips move, quickly reaching their destination. Taking as much as I can into my hand and nearly ending it all as her nipple skims my palm, I release a lungful of air and quietly mumble, "Boy have they missed me."

Piper's nervous grin grows to the point of spilling into laughter, but a shaky breath tells me that her nerves may be pushing away all humor.

"I meant that in all seriousness." I slowly bring my hand up to join the other, this one also getting to indulge in the pleasure of touching every inch of skin that it can, as I move my fingers over each rib as if they were keys on a piano before scooping up another warm, soft handful of flesh.

"They have been aching for me to touch them again. I know these things," I inform her.

Keeping my face serious, I slowly and reluctantly use my wrists to lift her sweater so that I can visually devour her. I stay a few inches away so that we can take baby steps, but still looking as I raise it further up her body. This is actually the furthest we've gotten the entire month we've been dating.

She moves her arms as if she may pull it off, but I'm getting anxious. I cut the chitter-chatter, not making a sound as I slowly spin her around as if we are slow dancing, then carefully ease ourselves down onto the bed. As my right knee sinks into the soft mattress, she slowly scoots onto her back, grazing my inner thigh with hers. We never lose momentum and as always my ears stay locked in on the picked-up sounds of her breaths. As our bodies find a comfortable spot, forming an indention into the pillow top section of the mattress, I mold my lips back to hers with my hand soon finding its own resting place which seems to have been designed to fit it like a glove.

Her hands trail my back, tugging and pulling me against her and my lips know absolutely no boundaries as they fall from the corner of her mouth to her jaw onto her neck. A small whimper greets my ears as my pelvis shifts and moves against her in a hungry plea to have the rest of our clothes off.

"Ah…"

I move my face away from her delectable skin as I hear a tone in her reaction that sounds a bit different than pleasure.

My chest expands on a deep breath. "Are you ok?"

Normally, I wouldn't ask her this half a dozen times, however, this is like starting over with her; approaching it all as if it were our first time again. Back when I was inexperienced and new to it all, plus with her delicate situation, I always worried about doing anything without her ok first. That's when we really got things straight between us and I realized that she didn't need me to change how I was; she just wanted me to go about it naturally so that I wasn't drawing up bad memories. This is different; if I, for even a second, think that she is in distress or wanting to stop, I stop.

Smacking her lips together on a heavy gulp as if she's thirsty, she wiggles against me with a bit of a pained expression. I lift my weight off of her a bit, looking down between us as she readjusts her position.

"I'm sorry… It's just…" she stops talking, sucking her bottom lip in between her teeth, a nervous habit she's had for as long as I can remember. "Your jeans were just…" She presses her lips together and looks at me hesitant to finish; she doesn't have to.

"Oh shit I'm sorry." I grit my teeth, realizing that I was probably damn near rubbing her raw with the way I was dry humping her like an over-eager dog in heat. Glancing down, and gently lowering myself back down onto her, I shift to the side so that I'm not bearing all of my weight on her. "Is this all right?"

She nods, and for a moment the only thing circling in my head is *let's get right back to where we were*, but I have a better idea. Scooting back in a flash, I bolt to my feet, keeping my eyes on her as I slowly lower my hands to come up with a better solution for both of our problems. My jeans are about to cut off the blood flow to the rest of my body, and they're obviously not aiding in any sense of pleasure for her if they're about to give her a rug burn. Besides, this way it'll cut out any hazards of me starting a fire; that would really put a kink in the intense moment that we have here.

Piper keeps her eyes glued on me, glancing down to my hands as I unfasten my button, lower my zipper and shove my jeans to the floor as if the fire has already started. No sense in drawing it out; I'm not looking for a new profession as a stripper and I'm sure as shit not taking my pants off for sex appeal. Using my toes, I shove off both of my shoes, then step on my pant legs one at a time to pull them off in two tugs.

I flick my eyes back to her, raising my brows mischievously with plenty of ideas for my next move, but for the first time, probably ever, I'm at a complete loss of whether I should continue. Normally I'd be like a damn magician in this sort of situation, snapping my fingers and all of our clothes would drop to the floor so that we could get the real party started. However, this is her; this is us.

This is something I've had in my head on constant replay for years, imagining how it would go down again; fantasizing about what she would look like and always keeping in the back of my mind, that those dreams were probably all I was ever going to have. But here we are, so I'll be damned if I'm not going to take it slow…

Savor every touch…

Relish in every brush of her skin against mine…

Consume her lips as if it's the last thing I'll ever taste…

And make the most of every single second as if it's our last…

But with all that sappy sentimental crap aside, I sure as hell plan to get my freak on and show her what grown-up Evan is capable of. Then, we can reiterate our conversation from the shower house. Of course, I'm planning to do all of this in an orderly, calm, gentle fashion and as always, I'll let her call the shots, because I'd never do anything to hurt or scare her.

Standing steady at the side of the bed, I search her face, not letting my eyes fall any further just yet. *I am ready for that shirt to come off though; who am I kidding, I'd much rather see all of our clothes in a pile on the floor.*

Grabbing up a healthy handful of the hem of my shirt, I rip it over my head and toss it aside with a swish, then pulse my brows as I look at her again. She laughs, dipping her chin down.

"Your turn. By my count, I'm quite a few articles of clothing ahead of you."

Her eyes sparkle and broaden, as if she didn't expect that remark from me. *Has she forgotten who she's dealing with?* To my surprise, she doesn't even hesitate. With a smile, she raises her butt off of the bed and shoves her tight black pants over her hips, and down her thighs to her knees.

The saliva glands in my mouth go nuts, filling it like a cartoon character drooling into a pool at its feet. I never knew fabric could be so damn arousing, but yet, as the thud of her shoes hit the floor and as she goofily flips her calves and feet back and forth like she's paddling through water, her pants drop to the floor as well and my third leg suddenly feels like it may rip through my boxers. *Holy shit!*

She lays there only in a soft red knit sweater, with white lace panties barely peeking out like an invitation to a black-tie event that you know you're not good enough to go to, but you also know that if you got the invitation you'd be stupid to pass it up.

The corner of my mouth rises into a smirk as I look her dead in the eyes. I put my hands out to the side, standing there proudly in a pair of navy blue boxers and white socks. Glancing down my own body and back to her, I quickly make note that the socks are not sexy by any means. *One article of clothing would be best at this point.*

"I'm still ahead here," I say, using the heel of my foot to step on the opposite toe of my sock as I jerk it backwards, then repeat till both of them are off.

She leans up onto her elbows, taking in my attire one inch at a time, running from my face, down slowly and back up again. The whole thing probably took one second, but in my head it went in total slow motion.

The grin that's already painted her face for the past few minutes since this exchange of clothing began, grows to a full-on smile. As if I'm the mirror image of her, my smile rises as well.

"Okay, you want to even the score?" She sucks in a deep breath, plopping back down onto her back and dropping her hands to the hem of her sweater faster than I can keep up. She tears that thing off and throws it over the side of the bed as if it just sprouted wings and flew south for the winter. *I thought I was eager to get my clothes off.*

My mouth drops open, un-hinging from my jaw with the rest of my face paralyzed in awe. I look her over, her soft delicate skin bare except for the white underwear. My hands twitch, wanting, no, needing to be all over her all at once. This is literally like dangling a juicy, mouth-watering rare steak four feet in front of a lion's mouth, yet I'm not moving; *where the hell did this restraint come from? I never knew I could be so disciplined!*

My heart does a couple hundred laps, pounding like it may rupture at any point while my hard-on contracts in eager anticipation with the strain and motion of doing a 100-pound bicep curl. I suddenly feel like a little boy who has just discovered there's a bone in his willy; I'm amazed, fascinated, confused and downright concerned. *Why am I not making a move right this second?*

I step forward, but stop in my tracks as soon as Piper's thumbs tuck beneath the small itsy-bitsy straps of white fabric at her hips.

"And..." she draws out seductively, turning my mouth into Niagara Falls. "I'll one up you." Once again her hips rise off the bed, but this time as her fingertips flawlessly flow down her legs, over her knees and to her ankles, she does indeed beat me at this game. Her last article of clothing drops to the floor, delicately without a sound and she is left completely naked for my eyes to devour.

I draw my hands, patting at my boxers to make sure I didn't end this show before it even got started. She giggles, no doubt knowing exactly what I'm checking for; luckily all I find are dry boxers and a steel crowbar ready to pry open Pandora's box. Grabbing the waist of my boxers, I shove them down in a much more rushed, less appealing way than she did. *I'm not aiming for swagger here.*

I look down, kicking them off, then quickly back up to catch her eyes widening. *She's impressed.*

"Looks like we are even." Winking, I slide down, slowly on her, letting the erect portion of my body remain on her leg and away from where it impatiently wants to go.

She pulls in a shaky breath as her body trembles and tenses. *I hope this isn't a mistake.* I freeze, keeping my arms where they landed, at either side of her head.

"Piper," I practically mouth so that I don't startle her anymore.

Her eyes close and her breaths stop. *Here we go again.*

Let's do this

Piper

THE MOMENT HIS SKIN SLIDES over mine, my body tingles and pulsates with a million sensations like an electrical board with circuit after circuit lighting up until the entire thing is illuminated. I shut my eyes tight; just feeling.

"Piper."

His voice grabs me, letting me know it is indeed him, yet I'm already very much aware. I am sure he is sensing more than there is, but all I can do is lie here, silent and still, willing for the first time in a long time to venture further. I have no idea if I can keep it together, if a dark cloud will drift over me and pull me down, but I need to try; I want to. A rush of adrenaline circulates through me on that thought. *I want him.* I open my eyes.

"Is this too much?" he asks gently.

Letting a positively ridiculous smile overcome my face, I stare at him, more sure of myself than ever. I haven't changed anything in my life, I still haven't read that stupid letter and we haven't even so much as seen each other naked until now; well, with the exception of Evan strutting out of the shower in front of my eyes a few times. Today... and now, a flood of courage has been released in my head and heart, pushing me forward. Maybe it's him; he was the one and only boy that

I ever let touch me. It's like I have found my place again…with him.

"No," I breathe out quietly and it's then that I realize, the frenzy of passion I felt as soon as he was on top of me, stole my breath. "It's not at all." I try to smile, but I can't. As excited and certain that I am, I'm still glued to the bed and unable to will my arms to feel their way over him.

He lowers his brows, looking at me questioning as if he doesn't know whether to trust my words or my actions, which are definitely saying two different things right now.

"Really?" Smirking, he turns his head from one side to the next, glancing down at my immobile arms at my sides. "So I take it that it's going to be me doing all the work?" he jokes, chuckling, yet having a hint of worry in his eyes.

"Yeah, ummm, well…" Here goes, a topic we have left out for the whole past month. We have never even breached half the things we need to talk about. There is little to tell on my end and I don't even care to hear what or who he's been doing in the past few years, but nonetheless, we've never brought it up. Bad timing, I guess, but it should be said. "I haven't done this." I spit it out, slamming my eyelids shut; waiting.

"Piper?" he speaks so calm and even without looking, I can hear the smile in his voice.

I open one eye, still very aware of the hard mass on my left thigh which doesn't make me too uncomfortable. More so, it makes me want to move around and squirm. Evan has a small grin on his face, looking as though he may laugh at me any second. Scrunching up mine, I make a quick mental note to relax, slowly slacking up all the muscles in my hands and pulling them both around to his back.

His eyes immediately light up and his grin widens, displaying a mouthful of teeth as I softly scratch my nails up and down. *It's just a backrub, just a backrub; not sex, not foreplay…all innocent. Breathe Piper, Breathe. God, I have no clue what I'm doing!*

"Wow." Smirking, he shifts, and at the same time I move my leg so that his crotch isn't digging into me. His hips fall between my legs and parts of him graze areas of me that I had forgotten even exist.

Oh.My.Gosh!

"You still with me?"

I flinch, looking back at his face. For an instant, I was so caught up in my head with my heart hammering like a drum and my body vibrating like a washing machine, that it almost happened. I'm not sure I even know how to process all that I'm feeling. I want to scream, moan, whine and close my eyes tightly. My mouth goes dry and suddenly there isn't enough moisture in the world to quench my thirst. Licking my lips, I look at him; he takes note quickly.

His lips fall to mine, instantly filling my mouth with his tongue. I move mine on cue, swiping it with soft tickling caresses as I run my hand hungrily up his back and into his hair, letting thick strands thread between my fingers. Gasping from an extreme mix of sensations, I drop my head back onto the cluster of tossed aside blankets. Evan's mouth falls to my neck with gentle, wet, soft kisses before moving to a new portion of my skin. I open my mouth and whine as the rest of him moves, forcing my lower body to ignite into a fiery spasm.

As his moist lips continue to tickle across my skin, I seal my eyes shut prepared to enjoy the sheer exhilaration of this, yet, just then a disturbing vision flickers through my head. My blood freezes and I release a whimper as an unwanted touch slithers over my hip and painfully grips my skin. The sensations I was building only moments ago turn to an icy chill in my veins; I unseal my eyes in a flash, staring through the daze with my breath coming out faster and faster. A head of brown hair comes into my vision and I know it's Evan. One kiss, two kisses, three, land along my collar bone as he descends further down my body with his hands to both my sides. I glance around, taking in my surroundings and trying frantically to ground myself. *Breathe.*

Slowing my breaths, I flutter my eyes, all in an effort to focus on where I was; it's a euphoric state that I desperately want to return to, a place where it is just Evan and me again and no harsh memories or blackouts or ghosts of the past sneaking up on me.

"Piper," the whisper meets my ears and my arms both stiffen, dropping to my sides like a pebble being tossed into a stream. *It's not him, it's not him…it's only Evan…Breathe.* "Piper, hey, it's me. Open your eyes."

His voice pulls the black veil from my consciousness and I look ahead, making out his tan oval face and warm hazel eyes that stare back to me, encased in concern and doubt. Managing a small smile, I am completely happy to be here with him, comfortable being totally bare beneath him and annoyed that my mind will not cooperate with my body right now. *I want this.*

"Hey, there you are." I smile deeper with his words. *Yes, I am.* "Did you leave me for a minute?"

he says that so matter-of-factly, like we never left this point and it occurs to me just why I could never let anyone else touch me like him.

"Right there?" I scrunch up my face as I feel him pushing; he grits his teeth in return. "No?"

I nod, unable to get any words out. Closing my eyes, it's as if I have no control over my body, like I'm slipping backwards from an elevated surface, dropping…dropping into an endless shadow of darkness that assaults my body on the way down.

"Ok, open your eyes." I hear his voice and I do as he says. I know it is Evan and that alone knocks the horrendous memories out of the way, as if he personally stepped into my head and shoved them aside. All movement from him stops, yet I can still feel that we have gotten further than we've ever attempted. "I'm not going on until I know you can keep your eyes on me," he whispers, his eyes a mask of reassurance, covering up his worry for me, and maybe even the desire to stop before it gets like it has so many times before.

"Ok." I take a deep breath, then push it out along with all the nasty thoughts that keep invading on this intimate time.

"Ok," Evan mimics me, lying still above me and not daring to move a muscle or anything else of that nature. All I can think about is how this is it, we are actually going to do this. "Just listen to my breaths and keep your eyes on me, ok? Watch my mouth, I breathe; you breathe, remember?" I nod again, a flame of blush creeping over my cheeks as if he can hear my thoughts as he goes on. "Breathe with me, Piper and if I need to stop at any point, tell me...ok?"

Nodding, I tense up, waiting as he slowly moves his body, arching his back like a cat. A strong painful, yet amazing sensation rolls through my pelvis, electrifying my inner thighs and stomach. Drawing my mouth open in need of more air, my eyes intensify with the urge to slam shut on the feeling.

"Open your eyes and keep your eyes on me, ok?" Evan huffs out through a muffled grunt.

That sound alone, more so than his words, have me widening my eyes and looking at him in total fascination and curiosity. His chest moves up, sliding against me as small tingles spark through me and make me even more anxious, yet excited. Not even realizing it is on the tip of my lips, a gasping whimper makes its way up my throat and out my mouth before I can stop it. I'm not hurt; I don't want him to stop, but I still could not help it. It's as if the warmth of his body combined with the subtle, slow movement of his hips into mine, shove the air in my lungs up and out of my body in a whiney sigh. His eyes widen and he stops, keeping his body pressed firmly against mine and us locked together.

"Do you need me...

...to stop?" Evan's voice is so close, yet slowly begins to pull away. "Piper..."

Hot breaths hit my ear drums, and a weight moves away from me. It's a different feeling than I'm used to and my fear lessens.

"Open your eyes," Evan's voice comes through loud and clear, and until now I had no idea I had closed my eyes again.

Opening them as if I'm peeling a wrapper off a delicate package, I look up and see him kneeling on the bed with both of his knees between my legs. I pull my hands to my chest instantly, almost embarrassed and weirded out that I'm laying here with nothing on while he's above me with a full-access view.

He smiles, scooping up one of my hands in his. A piercing, electrifying tingle moves over my skin as his hand brushes over my breast in the process.

"Ok, we haven't even started and you are doing what you used to." He presses his lips together, looking me in the eyes in a more serious manner than I'm used to. Linking my left hand with his right, he holds our hands suspended in the air between us as he continues, "I'm not sure this is a good idea as much as I want it." He grits his teeth, but my heart is immediately up in my throat in a panic I've never felt.

"No, I'm fine. I'll be ok. I can do it…" I plead, pulling my hand out of his and sitting up in front of him with both of my knees bent and on either side of his hips.

His face scrunches up with his brows dipped low and his bottom lip tucked into his mouth in thought.

"Honest, I can do it," I throw out one more plea, nearly begging; I really want to laugh at how I sound like he used to when he'd beg for me to try, insisting that he may die a virgin if not. He always knew how to turn the moments when I was scared the most, into a playfulness that took my mind far from the pain and tragedy. He's always put me at ease and made me feel safe.

Squinting in skepticism, he opens his mouth to speak then pauses for a second. "You sure?"

My heart jumps, an intense palpitation like I just had paddle boards shock me back to life. "Yes!"

He chuckles with a sincere, adoring grin that makes his eyes glimmer as he cocks his head to the side and reaches his hands behind me to pull me closer. I look down, extremely aware that he is still plenty ready for what is going to take place.

He laughs louder. "Don't worry, it's not equipped to take matters into its own hands. I'll have to do the work."

My head snaps back up to look at him, humiliated that I was just inspecting the manner of his arousal when all sorts of things on my body have come alive including my nipples which could currently etch my name in a sheet of glass.

He goes on, making sure that my embarrassment is well deserved and fully pointed out, "He's just an innocent bystander that is forced to take the plunge."

I shake my head, dropping my chin as his hands tug at my waist until I am into his lap, straddling him. He shifts, pulling me along with one of his hands now behind him on the bed as he directs us to the headboard. I lift further into the air, sliding against him and his completely ready anatomy as he straightens his legs out beneath me. Now it seems like we may go somewhere.

He clears his throat and lifts my chin. *I cannot believe it; I was staring at his penis again.*

"I'm sorry," I say quietly, now staring at the silly smirk plastered across his face.

"It's ok. You were always fascinated with that."

"I was not!"

"If you say so," he snickers, pulsing his brows up in an adorable flirtatious way that makes my stomach bounce with laughter.

He's right, but it's time to knock that cocky grin off his face.

"Do you have a condom?"

His eyes widened in shock and sure as I thought, his smile relaxes into a stunned expression. I know he doesn't think it, but I am ready. *Let's do this.*

Tears

Evan

MY EYES WIDEN AND I damn near cut off the circulation to my hands as I grasp her waist.

"…Oooo, ouch…"

I look down, immediately loosening my grip, but nearly having little to no control over any of my body. My ego instantly swells along with other parts of me that may very well explode at any given moment. Subconsciously, I'm completely stunned and my brain is screaming at my hands, *Rip the damn drawer of the nightstand open and get one of those suckers on.* I can't do it fast enough; but I pause, needing to be sure.

"Okay, so you're ready for this? Because I'm gonna tell you right now," I point my thumb at the nightstand, still looking at her with a bit of held in laughter as I start to joke, "I think I only have one non-latex condom in that drawer, and I sure don't want to waste it."

Her lips rise at the corners into a bright beautiful smile as she leans back and her chest vibrates on a small laugh. It's pretty damn enticing. As her eyes light up in recognition, I can see the wheels in her head turning; *I know exactly what she's thinking.*

"Didn't think I'd remember that, did you?"

"I didn't know if you would or not," is all she says.

The first time we tried, as soon as I ripped that condom open, the smell reached her nose and reality was history. That was the worst blackout I had experienced with her. She was in my arms in a matter of minutes with me reciting the words I've always had to say to bring her back.

"Of course I remember." I'm not so sure it's a good idea for her to see I have a drawer full of condoms, but what else can I do? *I'm not taking this journey bareback; perhaps a little explanation beforehand?* Reaching over with one arm as I hold tight to her waist so that I don't bump her right off my lap, I awkwardly twist my wrist and pull the dresser drawer open. "Okay so don't flip out and over analyze this, or anything that you chicks do."

"You chicks, huh?" She folds her arms across her chest, covering a view I'd rather see.

I pause for a moment. *Am I putting my foot in my mouth again?* I ignore that small technicality and go on, nudging the drawer all the way open exposing a shitload of condoms.

"This is not what it looks like," I annunciate my words dramatically. "About 90% of these are from Judd's room… He had a ton of them after this past summer and well, they just sort of made their way into my nightstand."

Of course, I exaggerate the truth. It's not like they sprouted legs and walked their way in here; I had a big part in that. It would've been a travesty to let all of these go to waste. Although now I'll just need to pitch them all. I will never use a latex one with Piper again and as long as I have her, I don't have a need for the others. *She's all I want.*

As soon as she chuckles and shakes her head, her usual reaction to my bullshitting, I relax my worry on inserting my size elevens into my big mouth. I don't waste any more time. Quickly flipping my finger through foil package after package, my eyes land on the one purple square amidst about forty mustard colored wrappers. I dig it out and use the back of my hand to shove the drawer shut. Pinching the package between my fingertips, I can make out the raised, circular edge of the rubber as I hold it up before our faces and try my best not to look too eager.

"Okay…" I stop, meaning to go on and tease her some more, but my mouth goes dry as every part of me becomes aware that this is going to happen. It's almost an emotional overload, realizing that the first girl I ever touched, the first girl I ever felt this way about is right here with me now; naked. I glance down taking in all of her curves before my eyes go back to her face. I forgot how beautiful she was.

"Okay," she says so sweetly, interrupting my thoughts and disbelief on what is actually going on.

Just like always, my brain and mouth get mixed up, "We're really going to play hide the salami, aren't we?" I say out loud, totally thinking it and not meaning to say it.

Usually when my mouth runs wild, I have this instant reaction to slap my hand across my face and shake my head, but it happens so often anymore, I just skip that part.

She laughs, "I think we are," not skipping a beat.

My smirk grows to a shit-eating smile as I keep my eyes trained on hers and the condom package between us as if all of this needs to be done at eye level, just in case she would decide against it. She doesn't say a word, watching my hands the whole time; the quiet, subtle ripping of paper rises into the air and she still doesn't look away or even show me the slightest sign that this may not go down today. Holding the torn off piece to the floor, I lower my hands to continue on my mission of practicing safe sex. It takes less than a minute for me to toss the trash back onto the nightstand and get the raincoat in place. Piper stays entranced the whole way. *She says she wasn't impressed before, yeah right.*

"Ummm, so…ahhh, do I…" she looks around for a place to sit or lay or go or maybe hide, but stays straddled over me.

Placing both of my hands at her waist gently, I stay absolutely still. I don't want to scare her off. Now that I'm sitting here, casually with my back against a propped up pillow that rests against the headboard, plus with my erection on full salute wrapped up like a present, it is all more than real now. *This is gonna happen, but only on her go ahead.*

"Look…" I start up, shoving down all of my sarcasm, teasing and playfulness for just this second. I have no clue what she is thinking or what could be racing through her head. This was tough before, so it may always be a hurtle for her to jump each time.

Placing her hands against my chest, I flinch at her touch but instantly stop talking. "No, don't," she says through heavy breaths that make me wonder if she may be beginning to have a black out episode, but I listen anyways; keeping my mouth shut. "I need to tell you something first. I haven't done this with anyone; no one…since you."

My mouth falls open and a tidal wave of pride washes over me. All I truly want to do is close the space between us and feel her again. *Only me; how?* A million questions threaten to surface in my mind, yet I refuse to think any further than her words. *I'm the only one; the only one.*

"Ok…" I say in a husky tone that sounds as if I badly need a drink of water. I smile, licking my lips and preparing all of my senses to be alert and fully aware of everything through this. "Come here."

She allows me to pull her forward, her breaths already gaining momentum as she nervously looks down and uses her knees to rise up a bit.

"Oh…like this" she stutters out, looking down and back to my face all the while her chest is pulsating in and out with each labored breath. "Oh…"

"Hey," I stop her, ready to send the mothership into orbit, but I can already tell this position may be uncomfortable for her. "We can lay down if that would be better…I just thought this way, I can help and well," I search for the right words, needing to be serious, yet easily wanting to spew out a smartass remark to balance out all the sappiness; of course I take the road less traveled at a time like this, "Show you just how this bull likes to be ridden." As soon as the words are out of my mouth a goofy ass smirk forms across my face, covering the sudden thought that has crossed my mind. *WTF is wrong with me; think before you speak, Evan, think before you speak!*

She shakes her head, all the tenseness beneath my fingertips and at her waist relaxing on that motion; and so do I. It's not very often that I become aware of my non-filtered mouth, but when I do, I give it a rest for a while.

"Seriously, we can do this a different way, if it'll make you more comfortable."

"No," she says slowly, moving her hands up to my shoulder and using that momentum to gradually lower down; I'm suddenly speechless.

I know what I'm supposed to do, I should be helping her out, but I'm in too much shock that she is making the first move.

"I'm a little scared," her voice trembles.

I immediately react, opening my mouth to speak, but she keeps going, easing down. Before I can even get a word out, a wave of heat, and lightning bolts of sensation wash over me. For a brief moment, as my head knocks backwards into the headboard with a clunk, my eyes roll back from the euphoric rush, and all I can wrap my head around is how damn good she feels…that is until I hear a sharp intake of breath and nothing else.

Shoving aside the blanket of bliss that has fogged my mind for a second, I bring my focus fully to her.

She's down…on me, I'm in, ready to move and feel everything I've thought about for the past few years, but she has to be one hundred percent on board. I stare at her, gripping her waist firmly and holding her steady. Her eyes are squeezed shut and I can already tell she's not here with me; her mind is undoubtedly floating back to a dark time where it does not need to be.

"Piper," I move my face forward, a breath away from her as I whisper, "Open your eyes and look at me." She does, her lids peel back in slow motion, like a scared animal dreading the view of her possible predator. "It's just me; stay with me, ok," I tell her, speaking in a soft tender tone that I've only ever used with her. Once I have her attention,

I hold dead still, even though I am being slowly electrocuted with a throbbing sensitivity in every major organ in my body and a burning desire to move; to thrust back and forth until we are both catapulted into a fiery coma of ecstasy.

Her chest lifts, grazing over mine as she sucks in a gulp of air.

Smiling, I start in, just like it was our first time again. Slowly and securely, I roll, using my arms at her back to brace her as I flip us over and onto the mattress. My hand stays at her back, keeping us locked together as I softly find a resting place with me crushed on top of her and our faces only inches apart. She keeps her eyes on me the whole way, still struggling to take a breath as if she's back and forth between here and another time, and that's exactly what is probably going on.

"Piper," I say again gently. "Don't close your eyes, okay? Listen to my breaths," recognition sparks in her eyes as I speak, so I go on. *She's with me now.* "…keep your eyes on me, watch my mouth…" Her eyes flick down to my lips as I keep talking, "…and Piper… Breathe with me." I gently kiss her lips, softly, then lean back enough to go on in a soothing whisper, "Do I need to stop?"

She shakes her head frantically, her breaths coming quicker as she looks from my eyes back to my mouth, watching each swallow of air that I suck down.

With that, I go on, slowly pulling my pelvis back; she opens her mouth, heaving in another deep breath. I move at a leisurely pace, my body ticking with the need to push harder and faster, but I stay steady and deliberate in my pace as I pulse my hips forward. Her mouth opens wider and her eyes flutter.

"Keep looking at me," I keep going, back and forth, slowly and meticulously with my heart thudding its approval. "I breathe…" I place another tender peck against her lips, "…you breathe." I look into her eyes and she looks back at me, a pool of passion and longing appearing in them, that signals me to pick up the pace; I do.

I rock forward, holding tight to her body as her soft skin melts against me like a warm pat of butter. Another deep thrust and her eyes flicker shut as her head pushes back into the pillow on a whimpering exhale of pleasure. I start to speak up, to instruct her to open her eyes, but they do automatically and fall back to my lips. Unable to keep any sort of control for too long, I crush my mouth to hers, devouring her lips and tasting her as I move excitedly in an overanxious pace now, knowing the finish line is right around the corner. Her tongue and body moves with mine, her hips pulsating to the same rhythm that my body is rocking to as the level of exhilaration within me builds and builds to the point of exploding.

Lowering my brows and pulling back to look at her, my abdomen contracts and stiffens, my biceps tense up and my ass turns to stone as I push forward one last time with all the zipping sensations centralized and releasing like a cork being popped off a champagne bottle.

My vision flicks to her face, taking in her elated expression with her mouth still open wide in excitement before it blurs; I collapse, trying vigorously to replenish my air supply. Closing my eyes on a deep breath, my body vibrates in an epileptic-type shockwave every couple of seconds as I work to bring myself back to earth.

"Whoa," I breathe out, barely able to form words and my body ready to hit the hay, but a sudden, unexpected noise has me on high alert.

I jerk my head back, startled and pleading inside that this didn't turn out as it did so many times before. She holds so tight to me, clinging with her arms wrapped fully around my torso. As soon as my face is above hers, my fears are confirmed. I look down at her tear-streaked face and puffy eyes. Regret, pain and a truck load of un-relinquished sorrow hits me all at once. *How did I miss her crying?*

She sniffles, her brows bowed and crinkled above the bridge of her nose.

"Oh God, Piper…" I hoarsely say in a quaking voice that sounds as if it has just broken in two. "I'm so sorry. I didn't know. I would have stopped. I looked at you and I thought…" I ramble on, only stopping when she presses her lips to mine. I kiss her back, a soft, sweet, gentle kiss, devoid of lust and any sexual intentions.

"Stop it," she whispers through a weepy tone and another onset of tears. "I didn't want you to stop. I wanted to, no, I needed to…" she trails off and the regret in my heart amps up.

I'm not even sure how to feel about that. "No…" it comes out quickly before I have time to think. "I don't want you to be…like *that* with me, because you need to move on or need to…" I nearly say the word fixed, but that's wrong; I've never viewed her as broken. I rephrase it, walking softly on my words; a feat I didn't even know I was capable of. "…listen," I clear my throat and go on, "I think we should only do this if we are both one hundred percent sure, no doubt and most of all there should be no regrets afterwards…"

"Oh, no, no, no…I don't regret it…" She raises her voice, anxious to be heard and frantic to let me know where she stood through it.

Furrowing my brows, my chest tightens. She may not regret it, but I refuse to do this if the end result is tears. In my opinion, if a girl's crying then something hurt her, and I will not be the cause of that; years ago, every time we would try to get handsy and act out what most would consider a normal puberty-stricken and un-chaperoned teenage activity, nine times out of ten it ended with her crying and the guilt I felt from that was unbearable.

I want to tell her that me going into that with the mindset of two people wholeheartedly wanting it, and her entering into it as a form of therapy or a means to get past that tragic memory, in a way it's not fair to me. Her heart is in it, no doubt and it's obvious that she wants me, but just like back then, sometimes I believe there is still so much healing that is needed; I don't know how to do that for her. It's something she has to figure out on her own, unfortunately.

I continue to tread softly and compassionately over the subject, but there are some truths that need to be voiced. "I know you don't regret it and I hope you don't ever regret any time I've touched you because I've always tried to make sure and be absolutely positive that we were on the same page, but when you cry after I just get…" I stop myself, keeping my words respectful.

Closing my eyes for a brief moment, I grit my teeth. What I need to say may come out as harsh and she may totally misinterpret it at first, but we need to be clear in order to move forward. It was a long road before, and after so much time there are sure to be tons of potholes in need of being filled before we can smooth it out, but we'll get there again.

I go on, deciding to say just what I'm thinking even though I'll probably have to iron out the edges afterwards. "When I see you cry afterwards, in a way, it almost makes me regret it." I move quickly, doing damage control as soon as the words are out of my mouth and as soon as I see her eyes widen. She's not mad, but with any woman's overactive imagination, regret is not a good choice of words. "I do not mean I regret what we just did. It kills me to see that something that felt so amazingly out of this world to me could make you cry." She keeps her mouth open as though she wants to say something, but I keep talking, "I know I'm always playing around and teasing, but you mean the world to me..." My heart pounds fiercely as I think about how I want to word that, knowing I should be saying something different; something I meant to say years ago to her. "It just... crushes me to see you hurt and when I think about what is in your mind when we are having sex." A lump forms in my throat and I swallow hard to get past it. "...you crying makes me feel like I did something wrong," I just spit it out.

Her expression softens as she tips her head to the side and brings her fingertips up to my face, smoothing them over the back of my jaw up into my hair. The touch relaxes my anxiety and sorrow over not stopping earlier.

"Oh, Evan, you didn't do anything wrong."

I raise my brows, scrunching my forehead up and doing my best to mask all my apprehension and go back to my smartass self. "Wait, I know I didn't do anything wrong, let's just be clear on that. I said felt, but I know without a doubt I did everything just right." Plastering on my best grin, I lean down and give her a quick, soft peck on the lips then nudge my head back to look at her. "You get what I'm saying, though, right?" I return to seriousness, unable to keep up my usual façade of playing.

"I do…" She smiles, but a few small trickling teardrops bear as a reminder that tonight I may have taken it too fast; back to square one. "It was just an overload of emotion, I think."

Biting her lip, she looks at me as if she's gauging whether I'm buying her excuse or not.

"Well whether either of us like it or not there's a lot of things we need to talk about. I can only help you through this if we're open about everything and so far we've kept the door to the past pretty closed." I shift subtly, the added weight of my raincoat making its presence known as all hysteria and thrill of excitement in my body dies down. I chuckle, trying to stay brutally somber, but also knowing this condom may very well be glued on by the time this conversation concludes.

She shifts as well, of course for a different reason, looking uneasy on the topic. Any time this has been brought up, she doesn't seem too thrilled to talk about the happenings of our break up years ago; I assume thinking that I ran my mouth isn't a fond thought of hers, but I do need a chance to explain, only not while we are lying in bed together.

"Maybe we can get cleaned up, then discuss why I'm the only one along with some other need-to-know subjects. Sound good?" As hyped as I was about knowing she's never been with another dude like this, it's something we should have discussed long before now, as well as the day everything fell apart.

Sighing, she nods her head with a relieved look in her eyes.

"Deal."

"Ok, deal then, now let's move onto more important 'to dos' for the night. I need to take a shower…you wanna take advantage of that? I have it on good authority from Judd that showers are meant to be a joint effort with your girlfriend. Besides, I have some hard to reach areas." I crack up, her squealy laughter mixed with mine as she closes her eyes on a wide smile with no trace of any more tears.

Perfect Day

Piper

THE NEXT FEW DAYS SLIP by and Evan is adamant about not being intimate again, no matter how I explain that I did not mean to cry. It was more of a reaction that I could not even control. Honestly, I cannot even explain why it happened. One second I would flip from his face to a flicker of a bad image and immediately back to him. My nerves were on high alert, my body was revved up in a way I could not even remember and it all kind of intertwined into a flood of heart-shattering emotion that had me wanting to smile, laugh and cry all at the same time.

Stumbling over my own feet, I hop over a crack in the sidewalk. My emotions are on the verge of going wacky all over again as Evan brings up the dreaded topic that I try to avoid. It's been weeks and we haven't discussed what happened on the dock back when we were kids. I also haven't finished reading the letter and now we are reduced to Evan's 'no boning rule' as he puts it so eloquently.

"Well I know I was feeling pretty damn studly coming out of that camper that day. Sun was shining, water looked perfectly inviting and the birds were chirping out 'let's get freaky…Piper and Evan got freak-ay,'" Evan sings out in a mockingly unattractive female tone while grinning from ear-to-ear.

I shake my head, hoping to avoid talking about that day, despite him always trying to slide the topic into a conversation. It was so bittersweet for me; to feel that amount of closeness to him and to take that step, but then to have it all shoved in my face as some vile act only to find out that it was because of Evan that my secret was out. I tense my jaw on that thought and flip through anything I can say to divert the conversation, even if I have to talk about it. I just don't want the anger, hurt and feelings of hate that I felt that day to fester back up. I fear opening the lid on that would unleash too much, so I bottle it up, tight.

I gasp loudly, opening my mouth as what to say hits me, "Speaking of freaky, you looked surprised to know I hadn't…" I glance around quickly, a little weirded out about it. "You know, been with anyone else…when I told you the other night."

Evan keeps his familiar smartass smirk pasted on his face as he turns to look at me with a comical gleam in his eyes.

"Nahh, I wasn't," he starts, but then quickly stops with a frown. "Well yeah, I was a little bit, but I was more impressed with myself than anything. No one else could measure up, huh?"

I giggle, thankful for the turn in conversation and amused at how much well-due praise he gives himself.

"Oh yeah, that was it…" I joke back with a grin as Evan flexes his brows flirtatiously. "I just never really got to that place with anybody… I guess I just didn't trust anybody… "I say sincerely, gritting my teeth with a shadow of awkwardness sneaking up on me over talking about this with him. He is, in fact, the only one I've ever been with, but to talk about other guys just seems off. "I guess the desire for that form of feeling was not something I really thought about a whole lot. "

I can practically hear the snap of Evan's neck as his attention is fully on me now.

"Whoa, whoa, whoa…you mean you never like strummed your own banjo?"

I gasp, flipping my head around fast, all my hair slapping me in the face in the process. "What?" I gulp down all my nervousness approaching this topic. "I can't believe you're asking me that. "

"What?!" Evan's voice comes out in a shocking manner with his eyes wide and his mouth drawn open. "I can't believe you're not just answering it. Come on, own up to it. Everybody does it."

His face lights up in curiosity as he jabs my arm with his elbow. "What...so do you go for one or two times a day? Probably a lot, huh?"

I seriously cannot believe he's talking about this. I stare over at him, trying my best to act aggravated but I really want to crack up.

"You got one of those electronic devices or you just go for the ol' fingers?" He snickers nudging me in the arm again, but this time I giggle.

"I...ahhh, I," pausing, I think hard, strategizing how to compile the appropriate words to answer his question, but Evan doesn't wait.

"You probably use your fingers? So do you go for one or two? "

I tilt my head to the side, giving him my best sarcastic glare. It's no match for his, but it'll have to do. He chuckles, glancing down at his feet then looking back up to me with his eyes squinted. Tilting his head almost to match my own, he opens his mouth, nearly hesitant to speak for what may be the first time in his life.

"You know I'm only joking and teasing when I say things like that, right?"

I roll my eyes with a laugh. "Evan, of course I know that. That's what I've always loved about you." The words come out quicker than I can even think. We were kids the last time I said that word out loud.

His eyes widened and he might be just as surprised as me, maybe more so, but as his smile grows all the way up his cheeks, I can tell that was a slip that he was pleased to hear.

Straightening up my posture with the little pride in my step at being able to say it out loud, I finish what I was going to tell him, "I'm comfortable talking to you and I don't ever want you to treat me like something's wrong with me. Dad walked on eggshells for so long after he found out and that's one thing you never did."

Evan gently nods his head with a small grin, but subtly looks away, shoving his hands into his pockets.

"I know… I just wanted to check, to make sure…" Taking a breath, he clears his throat before looking back at me with an obnoxious grin that immediately informs me that all serious talk is over. "…before you answer my questions. How many times? Oh and one finger or two?" He draws his eyebrows up, wiggling them for added dramatics.

My whole body shakes for an instant as if he will physically see me doing the deed if I admit it out loud. Breathing out a small laugh, I look down while shaking my head and rolling my eyes. Only Evan would want to talk about this like two old ladies swapping casserole recipes.

"Oh well, ok…" *I cannot believe I'm going to admit this.*

Quickly following a quiet swish and thump, I turn my head to find him nowhere around to hear my confession. *Really, he picks now to run off. Where is he?*

Just then a mass of thunderous barking breaks through the tranquil vibe of this abnormally warm February afternoon. Twirling around on the balls of my feet, my sneakers grind into the sidewalk. I look to the house we were passing just as Evan bolts over the chain linked fence with his hands braced against the top metal bar and a crazed look in his eyes like he just did something he shouldn't have. His other hand stays midair in front of him with something small clasped in it.

"Whoa, holy hell!" he hollers out, racing towards me. "There is a seriously big dog back there!"

The barking gets closer and closer until suddenly a giant dog the size of a pony, with droopy eyes, a mass of hair and a mouth that sags at the corners even as it rifles out bark after bark, pops up over the fence. The bag of fur would look harmless if it wasn't baring teeth, and big enough to clear it. He looks ready to pummel both of us.

Evan's hand falls to my lower back as he runs past me pulling me with him. We both take off, sprinting for our lives as if a lion has just stumbled upon a pack of gazelle, and it truly sucks that we are the prey in this particular case.

Rounding the corner of my street on our small Sunday stroll

through the neighborhood, my lungs burn and Evan is about five feet in front of me, his hand occasionally going to the back of his jeans. Slowing to a stop with him, my lips curve into a small smile while my brows kink in confusion at how ridiculous he's being. *What's he doing?* He cranes his neck, straining to run his eyes from his back down to his ass and back up several times.

"What are you doing?"

Evan looks up quickly, clearly out of breath as he huffs and puffs with a panic stricken look still on his face.

"I swear I don't have much of an ass, but that dog may have just took a chunk out of it."

I take over the task of scanning for any possible dog bites, but all I come up with is a trail of muddy dog footprints up his back pant leg as well as a portion of his back pocket torn away from his jeans; I laugh.

"What on earth were you doing... why did you jump over that fence in the first place?" I shake my head knowing full well there's no reason to ask him this type of question; it's Evan.

He looks up, a serious expression on his face and no sign of a smile. "I...Ahhh..." Looking back down as he stumbles for words, he raises his hand between us, "here."

My gaze drops to his hand and I gasp. Pinched between his two fingers is a small flower with delicate white petals and a tiny yellow center bright enough to look like the sun.

"You picked that out of those people's yard?"

He bobs his head while raising his shoulders in a yeah-sure, whatever, I-guess sort of manner.

"For me?" I say excitedly, sounding like an absolute dork.

Evan puffs out a chuckle of air as he responds, "No...I picked it for the dog so we could play fetch." My eyes flip from the flower to him and back as I let that thought settle in my heart. *He hopped a fence in broad daylight, nearly got mauled by a monster dog and picked a tiny little flower that had to be hard to see from the sidewalk, all for me.*

No matter the minute, hour or day, anytime I see a daisy, whether it be on the side of the road, in the window front of a floral shop, or even in someone's yard, my mind ventures to the day I first told Evan about what happened to me; I think about the first time I let someone in. Making a quick decision, I refrain from playing back and accept his sarcasm as a cover to avoid getting too sentimental.

"Evan…" I draw his name out in a playful, adoring fashion, feeling every bit of it in my soul; feeling him.

With that I take the tiny flower from his hand and twirl the fragile stem between my fingers as I stare at it, so grateful to have a second chance. Looking back up, I truly know what they mean by feeling warm and fuzzy, because a volcano of heartfelt warmth bubbles up through me, making me want to run into his arms.

"OK, so one finger or two?"

I burst out in laughter; only Evan. Taking a breath, I figure what the hell. *A flower for a pervy confession…I can do that.*

"Fine…" I grin, fully prepared to take part in this raunchy topic, but before I can slam right into the gutter, I glance over and watch as he kicks a couple pebbles like a little boy…so nonchalantly and possibly oblivious to just how I feel at this very moment. My heart soars for him; it is doing ten thousand cart wheels at how lucky I am.

Keeping my eyes trained on him, I go on, continuing in on his preferred topic, but as the sun shines high above, illuminating all signs of the soon to change season, plus with him by my side, I can't imagine how much more perfect a day could ever get. My heart skips as his green eyes return back to me with an expectant look. *Well two can play at this game…let's go for shock appeal since I'm sure Evan is waiting for a bland, embarrassed answer.*

With extreme effort to not laugh, I bite down on my lip and cock my head, trying my best to take a page from Abby's book on sass. I raise my brows and stare him down confidently as I spit out in a slow, drawn out tone, "Three," and then walk ahead of him.

Sneaking a quick glance back, I watch as Evan stops, almost like he's calculating what I just said. My luck he won't even get it.

"Three?" he mumbles, "Wait, I..." His eyes instantly widen and his head snaps forward to look at me. "Three...whoa...hey wait," he races to catch up.

I laugh to myself, returning my gaze back to the sidewalk in front of me as he goes on excitedly.

"...three...wow...we can work with this. I think we may need to take our relationship to the next level..."

I shake my head, my stomach bouncing in laughter as I bring my hand over my eyes as if this topic is just too obscene to dive further into.

"So like do you..."

I peek out through my fingers, cracking up over how fast this conversation has amped up to a triple X-rating from my simple answer, yet there is something comforting that I can be completely myself with him, and him with me; free of fear or nervousness. Evan rambles on, asking more and more as I laugh, but all that repeats through my head is just how perfect of a day this is. I couldn't ask for more.

I can't wait

Evan

"YOU KNOW WHAT I THINK is sexy as hell?" I smirk, squeezing my arms around Piper right outside Academic Hall.

She quirks one brow, probably wondering if I may turn this into some sort of raunchy convo. I've been landing in the gutter a lot lately since she teased me last week with an answer I was not expecting. I'm not sure what gives me more pride as a boyfriend, her coming back with a smartass comment like that, the fact that she's cool as hell or that she wears a size Double D and I can see those suckers any time I want now.

"My boobs?" She jokes as if she is tuned into the satellite signal that my brain runs off of.

I chuckle, looking down at her chest that is currently crushed against me and overflowing upward towards both of our chins as I hold her tightly and securely in my arms; it gives me the perfect view.

Flicking my eyes back to her seductively, I smile ridiculously with a warm sensation shooting through my body.

"Ahhh, yeah those too," I pause, sighing. "I think the fact that you are so simple and don't expect me to be taking you on big elaborate fancy dates complete with all these stupid ass gestures like flowers and chocolates…" I nudge my chin to the side as a girl walks by carrying a fluffy ass teddy bear that reads 'I love you' across it's chest with a huge 'Be my Valentine' heart shaped balloon floating above it. Piper looks over and giggles as I go on, "But…I was thinking I just might want to take you out tonight."

She's never been one for going out on the town, just like me. Fast food and a movie is our idea of a perfect Friday night.

"You want to take me out for Valentine's day?"

I draw my chin back, along with lowering my brows and mouth into a frown to mock my best offended expression. "What?! I do know how to be romantic…once in a while."

Softening, her mouth twitches at the corners and her eyes brighten to a lighter brown like she just dialed them down.

"So just the two of us?"

I pulse my eyebrows upward, hoping she catches onto where those words lead my mind. *Just the two of us.*

"If it is, do I get a reward at the end of the night?"

Her internal dial goes haywire with her eyes deepening and gleaming in exhilaration. "You just might," her voice alone is enough to make me drag her off campus in true caveman fashion, minus the club. "If you play your cards right." As always, her cool confident façade drops as if she's scaling a high wire and suddenly lost her nerve. She zips it and goes into a shy smile with her lips pressed together and her eyes wide.

I squeeze her tighter, letting my fingertips linger at her waist between her shirt and jeans to soak up as much of her skin as possible. *This dry spell has got to go.* Since the last time we tried to cross that bridge, I've been practically playing the girl in this relationship, reciting phrases such as 'no procreation' or 'I have a headache.' She knows I'm just screwing with her, but it sure has been a swap in the needy department.

We've taken it slow, played around and had plenty of fun, but going all in is something I've held off on. There is still too much to discuss, and somedays I think it'll never come up. She thinks she's clever, switching the subject any time Trent's name pops up or the day she shut me out of her life, but when she is diverting subjects, she's totally on my turf at that point; I'm usually the king of avoidance, so she can't fool me. I'll respect her wishes and always go along with it. I keep hoping that there is a way to break through the wall she has built up over the years; a way that she can learn to let go of what happened and know the difference between the past and present. I wish I could help her with that, but I can't.

The last few days I've been thinking about it and have decided to go with the flow. Used to be that when we tried to be a typical couple and give in to our horny little ways, it would result in her blacking out, halfway hyperventilating or soaking my sheets with a hysteria of tears. That in turn causes a wrecking ball sized knot to form in my stomach and a colossal cloud of guilt to roll over me like a ravenous thunderstorm about to wreak havoc on my conscience.

"Oh well if there's something I do know how to do, it's play cards. There's no way I can lose. You better just plan to wear some edible panties and no bra to dinner tonight."

Piper looks at me as if I just told her to chow down on a juicy ass cheeseburger and fries right in front of a homeless person. A grin breaks out over my face; *maybe I should swing by that gag store on the corner of third and Marshall Street and pick up a pair of actual edible undies; sure beats the hell out of teddy bears and balloons. Screw it; I'm not going overboard like Judd.* I left her something in her car that'll make her smile; I'll give her a real present later tonight.

The shock wears off her face as she speaks up, trying to match my sarcasm, "Well, let me get a pen and paper here and tell me where I can find this item. I assume you bought edible underwear before?" She tucks her bottom lip in as if she's almost fearful for me to answer that question.

I kick my head back on a laugh; no way am I answering, instead I go for a more dramatic response, leaning in quickly to devour her lips.

"Wait just a minute…" Judd's amused tone comes barreling at me, stopping me dead in my tracks just as I'm about to take a nibble of my Valentine. "I seem to recall you always telling me, 'Oh, get a room, Judd'…'Stop making out in front of me, Judd'…'Don't you two ever get enough of each other, Judd'…'Geez, why don't you guys just throw down right here on the ground, Judd'…"

I roll my eyes, turning slowly to level him with a glare; it is possibly the same one he's given me a time or two with that ridiculous excuse of a smile and that ugly ass dimple digging into his cheek.

"You need to have that damn thing surgically removed, you know," I smirk, ready to kick up the sarcasm as Alyssa and Abby walk up behind him.

"No way," she slides her arms around him from behind, staking her claim for all to see. "That is my favorite feature on him."

I crack up. "Damn, burn!" I look at Judd, about to burst into stitches over her seemingly innocent and sweet comment. "Alyssa, even though that crater-like dip in his cheek may very well be the biggest feature on him, give the others a fair chance. I mean, he may just stop putting out if you don't give the others equal attention."

"Oh shut it, Evan," she pipes up with the same sass that her sister usually exhibits.

I look over at Abby, currently clung to her phone in deep conversation.

"Evan, I give plenty of attention…" Alyssa stops midsentence as Abby hangs up the phone.

"Sure you do," Abby giggles, teasing her sister.

"I thought you had to work," Piper speaks up, looking at Abby. "Did you end up getting off after all?"

Abby bounces up on her toes like the Easter Bunny on speed, squealing and smiling like a fool. "Yep! I traded shifts with another girl, buuuuut…" She draws out her words, obviously super excited. I chuckle as she goes on, "I just got a call that I got a delivery of a huge vase of flowers." She tilts her head side-to-side, sticking her tongue between her lips and doing some goofy ass dance.

I roll my eyes looking over at Judd, who's got his arms wrapped around Alyssa as usual. *The sap level is turned up way too high here. What the hell am I talking about?* I just deposited a huge bouquet of roses in Piper's vehicle a few moments ago; I have no room to talk.

"So what are your plans for the night?" Abby's delight over the flowers that she has at the hospital seems to have made her millennium.

I hope the ones I left for Piper have the same effect. Actually, I hope they have a better one...like a super big reward at the end of the night. She looks over her shoulder to me, pointing with her thumb as if she's preparing to hitch a ride.

"Going to dinner as far as I know. Evan, isn't that what we're doing?"

I release a huge sigh, dramatically rolling my eyes to the top of my lids and around, in what seems to be the entire perimeter of my eye socket, frustrated and knowing what the outcome of this will be. Sticking my tongue to the roof of my mouth with a smidgen of annoyance, I dart my eyes to Judd and Alyssa then back to Piper. "Yeah," I breathe out.

Piper and Abby both begin to speak up, but Judd beats them to the punch, hopefully to my rescue.

"That's what we are doing tonight too. I figured we'd keep it simple...dinner and that's it. Everywhere will be packed more than likely. I made reservations at that new restaurant on fourth, Julianne's. I heard it's pretty good."

My eyes widen, that's the same damn place that I made reservations at. "Seriously?" What time are your reservations?"

"Is that where we're going?" Piper asks in a giddy tone.

So much for surprises. How is it that Judd and I discussed stupid shit like sending them flowers and things we would prefer to get them, but never discussed the place we were taking both of our dates? I cast Piper my best smart-aleck look, then turn back to Judd as he answers.

"Six o'clock tonight. You?"

I look quickly to the sky; *Why me?* Dropping my chin and shaking my head with my hands on my hips, I choke back the urge to laugh at the turn of events. Judd snickers and I look up. I don't even have to say anything.

"Same time, huh?"

I nod, smiling about the odds of us planning the same thing, at the same time, and the exact same restaurant in town when there are a million others.

"Julianne's?" Abby announces in an over-the-top enthusiastic tone that automatically makes me aware that this is going to turn into one big non-touchy-feely date. "I heard it's awesome too. I bet I can get all of our meals comped." She holds her phone up with a huge grin on her face, but all that's repeating in my head is: *our. Yep, it's gonna be a party.*

"Oh yeah, that's Lanie's mom's restaurant." Piper's eyes gleam as she joins in on Abby's excitement.

"Yes and I guarantee if I tell her we are all coming, she'll do us a favor. She's been trying to get me to come try it out for a while now. Sound good?"

Well, at least this is getting better; free meal, I can handle that. I look at Piper, who is obviously on board, then to Judd, who glances to me with the same look in his eyes as I'm feeling. Pressing my lips together, I shrug. *It doesn't matter to me; might as well.*

Judd shrugs as well, cocking his lips to the side and emphasizing that stupid dimple. "Sounds good. So, six o'clock at Julianne's?" He looks back and forth at each of us, getting us all on the same page as we nod our heads in agreement.

"Cool. I'll call Lanie then." Abby announces, turning to Piper. "Ok if I swing by to get ready at your house?"

Piper snaps her head to me, skeptically as if I might have a problem with this. I want no part of girls getting prepared for a date. With all the junk piled on the counter of the bathroom at Judd's place, makeup, hair contraptions, way more personal hygiene items than I thought one person would need and things that personally scare me. Unless it involves a long period of nakedness, leave me out of getting ready. I will be happy to wait for the finished product. I urge her on with my eyes, widening them with a go-for-it, have-fun sort of grin.

"Ok, yeah. I'm headed home now."

That reminds me. "Judd, hey, before you run off, I need you to swing by the worksite with me. Grandpa wants me to bid my own job and the clients are swinging by at 4:00. It shouldn't take too long and then you can go…" I pause, taking note of how all over Alyssa he already is before going on. "…do whatever you plan to do before dinner."

Judd snickers, unashamed of his affection and love for Alyssa. *What a sap!*

"Sure." He glances from me to her and back as if he's unsure. "You mind heading home and I'll meet you there?" He looks back to me. "Can you run me home?"

"Yeah, sure. I'm picking you up right?" I ask Piper. She nods as Abby waves her goodbyes, already on the phone.

After kissing Piper goodbye, I head off with Judd, expecting to receive a text as soon as she sees the surprise in her car.

"So group dinner, are you on board or are you just going along with it?"

I laugh at his question. "It doesn't matter to me really. I mean, I was sort of wanting to enjoy the rare occasion of going out with her alone since I'm such a cheapskate and don't take her out very often, but she'll have fun either way and so will I." Judd stares at the ground as we walk back to my truck, gently nodding his head in agreement. "And I know it doesn't bother you or Alyssa…" I pause, waiting for a reaction from him, but he keeps nodding. *He's already thinking about after dinner, I'm sure?* "…it's all about what happens after dinner? Before dinner? Maybe in the bathroom during dinner? You guys have probably already snuck a couple of quickies in today, right?" I chuckle and he finally looks up, quirking his brows as if he's joined our conversation for the first time.

Lowering his eyes into small slits as if he's studying me, he keeps a straight face and for a minute I think he's going to roll his eyes, brush me off or stress my name as a means to get me to shut up, but then he speaks up.

"Come on, let's hurry." He pulls the door to the truck open and hops in, slamming it quickly behind him; I follow along, then slipping the key into the ignition and cranking it up as he finishes his thought. "I need to get back to the house so I can get in one of those quickies."

Snapping my head over, I crack up at his smooth wit on that one, pressing my lips together and try to add to the lovey-dovey Valentine's day humor. "Oh yeah, no romance required…just bumping and grinding all night long."

Judd throws his head forward on an exaggerated laugh. "Whatever, I saw the huge bouquet of flowers you left for Piper. I was there, man. 'Do I get red ones or pink ones or should I get the ones that are multi colored since I have no clue what her favorite color is? I'm not getting chocolates; I don't think she even likes…'"

I cut him off right as my phone chimes. "Ok, ok, I get it…I was acting like a girl. Well that was definitely bound to happen you know, since I hang out with your sentimental, sappy, I-have-to-get-her-a-black-box-gift-for-every-holiday themed ass. Besides, so much for romance, we're having a whole threesome party at the restaurant from what it sounds."

Rolling up to a stop light, I push my foot down on the brake slowly and glance at my phone, swiping it to bring up my messages.

Piper: OMG! I love them! You really shouldn't have, but I do love them. TY <3

With a wide grin on my face as if I just won a million dollars, I glance up to make sure the light is still red before typing out a quick response.

> **Me: All for the reward later, baby...all for the reward.
> Lol**

I hit send, then quickly type out a secondary message, feeling my smile right down to my bones as if she was right here beside me.

> **Me: Jk
> I'll text you when I'm on my way.**

Her message back is nearly immediate and does nothing to dull the smile on my face.

> **Piper: Ok...I can't wait! ;)**

Another spit of laugher comes from Judd and breaks up the happy coma I had dissolved into for a moment. "Oh sure, so much for romance, huh? First roses, now you are smiling at your phone like a thirteen-year-old girl getting a tweet that her fav band is on tour."

I shake my head, looking to my right as I turn the wheel into the lot of the nearly finished mall. *He's absolutely right.* I was smirking like a cheesy teeny-bopper trash talking in the locker room about their first feel-up; actually I doubt it was that manly, I probably resembled Judd when he's looking at Alyssa. *Oh shit, it's turned into that; I'm becoming a girl.* Even with that revelation, I give Judd a quick glance, then return to my phone, brimming with the same delight as I reread her message and answer both of them back.

"Prepare yourself. I may have just been struck by that little fairy's arrow and shock you all tonight."

Judd laughs, "Cupid?"

I crack up; *He would know the name.* "You're such a girl," I tease, "But I believe that would be the fellow."

Getting back to my lame-ass smile as Judd snickers at me, I move my fingers to return her sentiments.

Me: I can't wait either...

How could you?

Piper

"OK, I'M HERE," ABBY ANNOUNCES as she walks into the room as I'm brushing on one last stroke of mascara, a task which took much longer given the fact that I could not stop sneaking glances at the beautiful red roses which now occupy a vase in the center of my dresser.

"Hey," turning, I see that she's already dressed in a black dress, with her blonde hair tossed up into a messy, yet adorable updo and makeup applied to perfection. "I thought you were getting ready here?"

Abby holds her hands to the side and looks down as if she's taking in her appearance for the first time. "Oh yeah, well I ran by the hospital to get my flowers and my supervisor wanted to speak with me about joining the staff full time. Soooo...I'll be taking on my first patients this week." She scrunches her shoulders up excitedly with a huge grin, showing a whole mouthful of teeth.

"That's great."

"Yep, no more giving tours and sitting in on therapy sessions. I'm so excited." Glancing past me, her eyes light up. "Ooooo, I see I'm not the only one that got flowers. Your dad?"

"No," I laugh. Evan doesn't exactly fall into the usual sentimen-tal-type that would give flowers, but then again I've always seen a side of him that others don't. "Evan left them in my car today."

"Wow," Abby widens her eyes and lifts her mouth into a surprisingly pleased smile. "Go, Evan." Raising her arms, she pumps them in the air, cheering him on.

"What? He can be sweet." I sneak a look over at Abby as she rolls her eyes. "He can."

Abby laughs, plopping down on my bed and placing her arms to her sides to lean back. "Yeah, when he's not being a smartass."

"Oh yeah, he can definitely be that; you never know what's going to come out of his mouth…."

"That reminds me. I have been meaning to ask you…" Abby starts as I finish my original sentence, mumbling the last part.

"… That's what I love about him…" I trail off.

Abby jumps in quickly, "Love?!"

Her eyes go wide as she exclaims the word that I didn't even mean to say out loud, let alone in that context. I do feel that way; I know I love Evan. I always have. It's just something I tuck down deep inside for a long time; denying it and afraid to let anyone in.

She goes on, nearly the same as Evan would do, pestering and hell-bent on teasing me. "Love?" she emphasizes the word again, in an ooey-gooey sort of tone that makes the corners of my lips curl uncontrollably, and laughter to bubble in the back of my throat and spew out of my mouth. "See you two are at that 'I love you' phase?" She tilts her head side-to-side, rolling her eyes and batting her eyelashes dramatically as she says the words *I love you*.

Giggling with a huge I-sure-am smile, I swiftly redirect the conversation to shine the spotlight on her, "Speaking of love…so Hayden sent you flowers, huh?" I do my best to wiggle my neck and be as dramatic in my actions and tone as she was, but as soon as the words are out of my mouth, Abby's face falls into a gloomy expression and quite the opposite of the giddy girl she was when I brought up the roses earlier. "Uh oh, what happened?"

Folding her arms across her chest, she sits up straight, quirking her lips to the side and dipping her brows on a deep frown. I wait for her to answer as she stares down at the floor, but I don't say a word; I just wait silently.

After a delayed pause in our conversation, Abby looks up with a startled look in her eyes as if she had no clue that we had stopped talking.

"Oh," she says in a baffled tone. "Nothing is wrong really....not with me and Hayden, I guess." Her nose crinkles up on the words and gives way that there's a deeper meaning behind what she's saying.

This is when I cross my arms over my chest, making her aware that I don't believe a word she's saying. I've known Abby long enough to know when she's holding back. I'm the one that's mastered the art of not saying things; bottling everything up, but Abby, she says everything that's on her mind. It's very obvious when there's something on the tip of her tongue that she's dying to let out.

"Okay spill. What's going on with you and Hayden?"

Abby's face softens with a smile as she bounces out of her deep thoughts and looks back at me. "Nothing really. We are fine. I mean, we're not in that I love you part of the relationship, but then again, I don't know if we ever will be." This surprises me, and it must be written on my face as she goes on, quickly explaining, "Don't get me wrong, I'm crazy about Hayden, but I just don't feel *that thing*, you know."

"Okay, yeah I get what you're saying." And I totally do. "*That thing*...is pretty vital to a relationship, if I'm hearing you right." Abby nods her head quickly, in complete agreement of what I'm saying, but there was more to her expression earlier; like she's worried. "So that's that? You looked worried earlier...when I brought up I love you..."

She snapped her head up to look at me, lowering her eyes again with way more thought behind them than I've ever seen. Abby's always been a fly by the seat of your pants type of girl. She's never been one to sit and analyze or overthink any situation, rather she is blunt and lays it all out on the table.

"Abby?"

"Yeah," she finally joins in. "I'm sorry. I was just thinking."

I laugh, a whole lot of smartass comments entering my mind. *Great, I'm turning into Evan.* "That sounds dangerous."

"Shut up," she jokes, "No, it's just…" she pauses, bringing her hands together nervously flicking the tips of her thumbs back and forth across one another. "Well it's no big deal, but you know how I told you that I've been sitting in on a lot of the physical therapy patients?" I nod, genuinely intrigued as she continues, "Okay so, imagine my surprise in January when I am walking up to watch one of the first sessions and Tristan ends up being the patient."

This surprises me. Not many of us have heard much from him or seen him since the wreck last summer. We all figured out gradually that he was just fine, but I think all of us have been curious one time or another to know what happened to him; what made him drop off the face of the earth? I nod my head frantically, urging her on with her story.

Abby makes a funny face, crinkling her forehead for only a second before returning back to her story, "Anyways, so today…well, for the first time since I've seen him in the wing on his appointments, I actually ran into him," she stops, looking at me, hesitant in her words which is not a normal thing for her. "I don't know…it was just really strange and kind of…" Abby closes her eyes for a second before reopening them to go on, "…it's just, he used to be so playful and like to screw with me. You know, like at Christmas. But today, he rounds the corner…" she pauses again, biting the inside of her lip and thinking before moving on, "…he was just really bitter and angry and acted like he hated my guts. I didn't do anything, even say anything. I had my roses in hand and he lets out this loud sigh and becomes this huge asshole. I mean, more than he ever was."

I'm all sorts of confused. "And that bothered you?" She hasn't really told me anything; I have no clue where this conversation is going. "More importantly, what happened to him?"

My door creaks, drawing our attention instantly in that direction.

Evan's face appears in the doorway, and I can't help the girly grin that comes over me.

"Hi," I draw out in an over-the-top adoringly happy tone with a huge smile.

"Oh brother!" Abby rolls her eyes, before looking back to Evan.

He cocks his head in a questioning manner. "What'd I do?"

"Nothing!" I stand up, quickly walking towards him. "We were just talking about…"

Abby quickly clears her throat, cutting me off. "Well I guess I better get going. I'm meeting Hayden at the restaurant. I'll see you guys there in a little bit."

I take her subtle, yet abrupt exit as her not wanting to discuss Tristan in front of Evan. I'm not sure why, but I go along with it, dropping it.

"Oh wow, yeah…that thing…" I raise my eyebrows as she looks at me with a smile, nodding her head and completely getting my joke about what we were talking about earlier. "…definitely need to get some of *that thing*. I'll see you there."

Winking, she throws her hand in the air to wave us both off.

"Catch you later, Abby," Evan says before turning to me. "Ready?" He snaps his attention over my shoulder to the roses on my dresser, looking pleased that I have them proudly displayed in my room.

I bounce up onto my toes, excited for the night and everything that's yet to come. I'm hoping tonight will be a new beginning for us. Everything inside of me is eager to move forward, to let go of the past and just live; enjoy him like I've never allowed myself to before. I'm ready to get everything we've held back out of the way.

"So are you ready for this super private, romantic, alone-time, triple date we are going on tonight?" he smirks, sarcasm lacing his every word. "Maybe we'll get a group rate."

I smile, knowing something he doesn't and hoping to cast a small shadow of thrill into his thoughts about the private and alone-time part; I've never officially celebrated Valentine's day with anyone, but my dad, so the romance part is already in high gear.

"Actually, Abby texted me a second after I left campus…it's on the house. Lanie is going to comp and she said for us to go nuts." I pulse my brows, feeling a surge of confidence that I just one-upped him and am gearing up for my next eye-opener. "And I think we should…go nuts that is."

Evan's whole demeanor over the group date night perks up, "I sure hope you aren't referring to us ordering two of every appetizer or then again," he slyly waggles his eyebrows, making my toes tingle and my stomach tighten. "Maybe we'll just count dinner as the appetizer for the night?"

Every organ in my body zings with nervousness, yet sweet excitement and anticipation. *Enough talking; now I'm thinking like him.* Nodding, because I'm way too giddy to speak, I frantically swipe my purse off the bed and grab his arm to urge him out the door.

"My thoughts exactly."

My smile stretches to the point of making my cheeks ache as we make our way down the hall and to the front door, caught in a flirtatious game of him wiggling his brows and me in turn giggling uncontrollably. My belly quakes and my entire body shakes in a happiness that only he can ignite within me.

Before I can reach for it, the door swings open. I take a quick look at the clock; *5:30,* then fling my gaze back to the door as Dad walks in with a massive collection of kaleidoscope roses running from yellow to magenta to multiple purple tones and on to a deep blue like tropical waters, interchanging from petal to petal all the way to the center.

Dad smiles as I take in the beauty of the same arrangement of roses he has gotten on Valentine's Day since I was sixteen-years-old.

"Hi sweetie…Evan," he looks from me to him with a nod then back to me as he stretches the vase out between us. I wrap my hands around them, extending my neck so that I can hold my nose over the bouquet and take in a healthy sniff of their perfumed fragrance. "Couldn't let a Valentine's go by without getting them." He looks to

Evan sheepishly, as if he feels somewhat bad about still trying to be my Prince Charming for the day.

Slipping Evan an indirect look, a bit of guilt and awkwardness creeps over me. He stares at the flowers just like I did, a less enthusiastic look in his eyes as he had before and all playfulness dropped, but he quickly covers it up with a breathy snicker and a crooked grin.

"Well, I clearly need to do some research on this kind of stuff and until this afternoon, I thought roses were just red. I just went by the little rhyme…you know, roses are red…" he trails off with a laugh and I jump in. "Wow, I just feel like royalty tonight. A dozen beautiful red roses this afternoon, now these and then dinner at Julianne's. You may create a monster if I get spoiled like this, every day," I tease them both, glancing back and forth as they share a genuine smile.

Placing his hand gently on my shoulder, Dad draws me in for a quick hug and a small peck on the forehead. "You deserve it sweetheart. And Evan… Red roses?" Dad cocks an overconfident grin that I've never seen before. "Not too shabby."

We all laugh and the typical icy chill of a father and boyfriend competing for a girl's affection, the same one that makes me feel like I am trapped in some teen drama movie, instantly melts away.

Looking back down at the roses that are still firmly held in my hands, I'm overwhelmed with warmth and adoration.

"Thank you, Dad. I love them." I turn quickly to Evan, more as reassurance, even though I know he doesn't need it. "I think I know the perfect spot to put them."

Swiftly, I move across the living room to the TV center that's against the back wall and place them right in the center, between the family portrait from the album that Evan and I discovered and picture of me at graduation. I step back slowly and admire their beauty one more time before spinning on the balls of my feet to hurry back to Evan. *We have reservations.*

Just as I look up and am ready to say goodbye to Dad, the door swings open and bumps him in the back.

Abby pokes her head in. "My car won't start."

Dad moves away stepping forward as Abby pushes the door open the rest of the way and joins us. "You should've said something. I waved when I was coming in, but I thought you were already headed out."

"I really thought I'd be able to get it started, then I was texting Hayden…" Abby starts rambling on.

"Do you want me to look at it?" Dad offers and panic begins to slither through my veins, wondering if she'll want us to wait.

"Abby just hop in with us," Evan begins, looking quickly at me probably for an answer, but I believe my expression is enough of one; he doesn't even wait for an answer. "That way we can all be on time and Hayden can just run you back home after dinner or whenever…if that sounds good."

I slump my shoulders, wanting badly to frown and rebel against her riding with us. She's my best friend, but I really wanted to talk with Evan and get a lot of things out in the open that we haven't discussed; things we've set aside for far too long. I want tonight to be perfect. Seeing as my options are very limited at this point and I can't leave Abby sitting here at the house or even ask Dad to give her a ride, I relent, nodding my approval with a smile. We've got all night; I suppose we can talk after dinner to get things warmed up. A zap of excitement shoots through me at that thought.

In no time at all, and after a quick suggestion for us to take my vehicle rather than his dusty old work truck, we all bolt out to the car, ready to get the night on its way. Evan makes a pit stop at his truck, then hops into the driver's seat, shoving a small box between the door and seat on his side. Leaning my head, I make a spectacle of letting him know that I'm aware that he's hiding something. I love surprises, but I'm way too amped up tonight. Going to a fancy place to have dinner on the most romantic night of the year, for me, is more like stepping onto the red carpet at the Oscar's. It just never happens and I can barely contain myself.

"Ok, Evan, what's in the box?" Abby speaks up on the same thing

I had planned on pestering him over. This whole time I've been giving him obvious looks and drumming my fingertips across my knee to show my impatience; my mouth goes agape on her bluntness. His face goes blank as he stares at the road. Now my curiosity peaks.

"Abby, you just worry about the lame ass tattoo of your name that Hayden will probably have stamped cross his bicep; I'll worry about what's in the box."

She rolls her eyes, giving me a sneaky wink before reaching forward from the backseat to where Evan shoved it. I grit my teeth and shake my head subtly, trying to get her to stop. I'd hate for her to ruin anything he may want to surprise me with.

Abby sits back up straight, her eyes widening in amusement. "Evan! Really!"

I look to her hands and see the dark gray and white box he hid now in her hand.

"What?!" He twists his head instantly, back to the space between the door and promptly back to her again, straining to see her sitting in the backseat directly behind him. His eyes flick from the rearview mirror, to me, then her and back to the road in a flash.

"What in the heck?! Are these made of iron or something."

I narrow my vision in on the box, scanning quickly for what on earth could be in it.

"Abby! Give it back! It's not what you think..." Evan reaches to the backseat, the car shifting as his hand wildly fumbles around her legs.

She laughs, moving speedily and pushing herself all the way against the door with the box held high. I glance again as he steers and blindly wrestles for it. I make out a bold black print across the front that reads Edible and I stop, my mouth wide and my eyes about to pop out.

"Abby, dangit..."

I swing my astonishment to him and he instantly notices, stopping his attempt at getting it back. My heart beat ramps up into my throat, but yet, a sense of intrigue starts to overpower any nervousness

I feel. I'm plenty used to his teasing, pestering, gags and pranks by now, so anything edible that he may want to happen tonight can be discussed and thought over, but what has my interest rising more, is that he seems to be embarrassed; Evan, embarrassed by someone finding a gag gift of undergarments. He usually would live for this shit.

"Ok, you got it...the secret is out. I'll be muff diving later and gobbling up those suckers. Now hand them over and Piper can open them later," he says casually, but I still catch a hint of something unrecognizable.

"Oh come on!" Abby urges him, holding the box tightly. "This has got to weigh fifteen pounds. What did you get, a lock and key with them?"

"Oh, familiar with them, are ya? Hayden do a lot of deep sea diving? Does he go for the hard candy thongs or the red licorice G-string? I'm more of a fruit roll up sort of guy myself...strawberry."

I look at the box again and see a picture of a strawberry in the corner that reads, scratch and sniff. *Oh.my.gosh!*

They carry on back and forth as my anxiety level over wearing them increases until I cannot stand it anymore. Evan carries his usual cool and confident facade as he tries to rile Abby up. Of course, she rises to the occasion, her fiery attitude giving way as she defends her sexual preferences with her boyfriend.

"...He's all big and buff, but I bet he's all thumbs..."

"He is not and we have not..."

"Oh would you give me this..."

Pressing my knee into the seat with a twist, I snag the box out of her hand and infiltrate their ridiculous squabble. As soon as I have it, the weight pulls down on my arm, surprising me as I plunk back down on my butt. Both of them stop talking and Evan concentrates on the road. I stare down at it, the flat, smooth texture of the box seeming foreign as I study the picture of the very small pair of bright scarlet colored string bikini panties. Gasping, I flick my eyes up to Evan and back down before he notices.

"Just open it…it was supposed to be a joke, but I have a feeling you are looking way too far into this."

I stare at the round circle sticker that seals the package shut, that appears to have been ripped open once before. *Abby probably already looked inside.*

"Go ahead, open it," he urges me again with a more tender, less sarcastic tone.

"Yeah, open it up so we can see just how kinky Evan here can get. Feels like they may be brass underwear rather than a fruit roll up pair."

"Strawberry…" Evan peeks into the rear view mirror, clarifying his flavor of choice to Abby. "It's ok. Abby can give me shit the rest of the night…"

My attention snaps to him.

"Oooooh, yes! In that case, definitely open it."

Abby's impatient excitement over a gift she single-handedly let out of the bag, so to speak, and the tenacious enthusiasm in her voice as if she's the one that has a date with the panties, has my stomach stiffening on an onset of laughter. I dip my brows, trying to hold back my over-zealous impulse to tear open the box and probably rip the fragile candy gift inside in the process.

"Well?" Evan nudges his chin forward to implore me, all while keeping his eyes on the road.

I do as they say, a portion of my heart expecting him to have something even raunchier waiting inside, just to see my face go red; he knows how to do that too. The other part of me knows that by the heart-felt way he said I'm looking too far into this, it may not be what's pictured on the box at all. A little bit of my excitement drops on that thought; not like I fantasize about exploring new and quirky methods of playing in the bedroom. I don't even know how to lay there and do the actual act, but it is somewhat thrilling to imagine.

My fingernails work to free the clear round sticker, peeling it up with ease and ripping it off. After pulling the flap of the box open, I slow down, staring down past a clear plastic interior package and spotting a hint of bright red; and it even looks like a fruit roll up. *Oh.my. gosh…he did.*

"Pull it out." I don't even look up when Evan speaks, but I assume he's watching my reaction.

"Piper, open it all the way. I wanna see what these things look like," Abby says in a rush of excitement.

I laugh and automatically squeeze my fingers between the box and plastic piece inside to pull it out; *it's heavy…weird.*

"You seriously want to check these out so you can go get your own, don't you? You're a little kinkster, aren't you Abby? I knew it!"

"Oh shut up, Evan!"

A squealy sound rises with every millimeter that I slide the plastic out until at last, I drop the box to my side and just hold the small, cratered-like clear holder for the garment. Above the candy-wear sits a whole handful of arrowheads. *What on earth?!*

"Ok, wait…" Evan starts.

"What is it?" Abby stretches to get a look, immediately scrunching up her nose like I have mine. "Whoa, ok, Evan…you are into some seriously weird stuff here. Why?" She points her finger to the assembly of carved rocks, crooking her head as she speaks as if she is more stumped than me.

"You seriously don't get what that is about?" Evan speaks so directly that I know there has to be something here that I'm missing.

I circle through my mind, searching for the meaning behind the gift. Combing through them like a mall of windows into my memories, I come to a halt on one particular moment that at the time, didn't seem too important.

"Wow…I thought they only had these in museums," I say wide-eyed, staring at the huge display of arrowheads sitting in Evans grandpa's bedroom.

The large wooden display case is about the size of the window in my bedroom back home and has rows upon rows of these small carved little stones.

"Yeah and he found every single one on this property, back before they bulldozed some of the hills to put in the cabins. I found this one," Evan's voice goes high with excitement as he points to the display case at a tiny black shimmery stone that has tiny curved etch marks along the edge, making it look fragile and delicate to the touch, yet somewhat lethal down to the precise tip and sharp border. "... This one too...Oh," his voice kicks up a notch, anxious to show me more and more. "... And this one." His finger moves to another one. "... This one I found one day when I was helping Grandpa replace the boards along one of the docks down by the end cabins. We stopped for lunch, and no sooner than I sat down, I looked and there it was...just buried in the dirt. I could barely make out the tip of it."

My eyes move from one rock to the next, admiring the designs and different sizes; the intricate way someone spent countless minutes or hours whittling out shavings of the stone to create a perfect arrow shape; the precision to detail at each curve and corner and how not one shade of color is the same, ranging from pale beiges to earthy browns, a few blacks and even some whites and creams mixed in, but not one exactly the same; they are amazing. Dad used to take me to nature centers and museums when I was little, and ever since then I was always fascinated with the things people could do with their bare hands and a mind full of creativity; I always admired it.

"Wow. I've never even found one, and we've been coming out here for forever."

"I haven't found one in years, but if I see one, I'll get it for you."

I look over at him, a tingle of color rising into my cheeks and flaming up over the bridge of my nose until I'm well aware that I've turned bright red.

"Ok," I whisper hesitantly, my heart thumping over the fact that he would do something like that for me, while my hands shake and body *floods with nervousness from acting so silly; it's just a rock.*

Evan drops his hand from the display case and turns to me, brushing his fingers over mine; maybe it's not just a rock.

As soon as the memory comes clear to my mind, I straighten up in my seat and level him with a sentimental stare.

"I've never found one," I squeak out in a quiet and gentle whisper, my heart still tripping over the fact that he remembered that small insignificant moment that I had forgotten. "You found one for me?" my voice barely rises above the sound of the engine and the wind buzzing by outside the windows.

Evan cocks a huge grin, twisting in his seat and putting his arm behind mine after he shoves the vehicle into reverse. I look up, realizing that we are at the restaurant and it only seems like one minute ago when we left.

"I found you nine, actually."

Glancing down, my eyes take an exact tally of the arrowheads before I swing my sights back to Evan with a question in my head, but at a loss for words.

He goes on before I can say anything, "I'll be damned if I didn't look for one of those suckers every single time I helped Grandpa, when I'd be out at the beach, swimming, doing whatever and nothing for years."

I finally speak up, interrupting his train of thought and story, "That was when we were fourteen," I point out the absolute obvious, still stuck on the memory of the two of us standing there looking at rocks after we had snuck in to borrow some change out of this huge glass jug he had sitting in the corner of his bedroom.

Evan throws the van in park and looks to me with a nod. "I remember how old we were," he chuckles.

"That was the same week you kissed me for the first time…" I keep up with pointing out unnecessary facts as if he wasn't the other person in the memory.

He shrugs, "I had it all planned," he says with a quick wink, his smile never fading as he glances from the arrowheads and back up to me.

I'm still sitting here in awe. "When did you get these?"

My eyes flick to his throat as he takes a large gulp before answering, "I found the first…" he moves his hand to my lap, pressing his index finger to a dark brown arrowhead no bigger than an inch in length. "…the summer I last saw you…and several after," he pauses; I gasp, my mouth open wide as I stare down at the tiny thing which now looks far more significant than rocks. His fingertip hops two stones over to a creamy ivory stone that is much bigger in thickness and size and currently carving its way through the fruit roll up underwear. "This is the last one I found. I found it this summer down by the ninth cabin after I was cleaning up a mess of shingles from the roof we put on."

My head is still set back to him finding it the summer he last saw me, "You looked after I left?"

He lets out a sigh, looking out the window and sitting very still in his seat, very un-Evan-like. "I combed every inch of those grounds for one of those for you and even more so after you left. I figured when school came back in session it would give me a way to break the ice; a reason for me to approach you and explain how stupid I had been." He turns back to me, remorse and regret etched across every feature of his face as if someone had carved it out just like the stones. I start to speak up, to say I forgive him for whatever happened, but he beats me to it, "When the first day of school came though, I found out you had moved…that you had transferred to Fairview High," he stops, pressing his lips together with a shrug as his mouth twitches to the side. "So I hung onto it and more found me."

My mouth hangs open and my eyes feel as though they are drooping with sympathy and an ache in my heart for years wasted. There is no way to turn back time, to erase my stubbornness, but I want to say it; I want him to know I wish I would have just asked him what happened instead of acting so rash and reacting without giving him the benefit of the doubt.

"I should have called you. I should have…"

He shakes his head. "No. You had every right to leave. You didn't owe me anything. I should have run after you and explained what happened. I really should have just learned to keep my mouth shut," he smoothly tries to change the mood with his usual sarcasm and humor. "Someday, I will learn when to keep my mouth shut."

"That'll be the day," Abby's voice comes from the backseat and we both jump, looking back. "Oh yeah, I'm still here and can I just say…wow," she hisses in a playful, dramatically sarcastic tone as she holds her arms across her chest, lounging back in the seat comfortable. "You're a softy, aren't you?"

Evan shakes his head again, a slow grin popping up over his lips and curving up to his cheek bones. "Yeah, you got me Abby. But, in my defense I did throw some edible undies in with it."

Abby cracks up, leaning forward and spitting out a loud laugh as my body bounces in my seat, feeling every bit of her amusement, more so from nerves and a rush of emotion.

"Ok, yes and what was with that? Too afraid to just lay your heart out there? Gotta butch it up a bit to overshadow the sentiment and sappiness of truly loving someone?"

Abby's words come out like bullets and it is written all over Evan's face as he snaps his eyes to me, his grin dropped, but a serious expression cast upon his face with his lips motionless and his eyes a deep tone as if he's looking inside me. She could not have said is better.

The seriousness flies away as Evan turns back to her, but not before giving me a small smile that whispers to my heart that every word she said was true.

"Well some people use tissue paper. I use edible undies."

Abby spits out another laugh; so do I.

"Ok, whose hungry? I believe there are two appetizers each with my name on them." Evan smirks, pulling the box out of my hand and placing it on the console between us.

"That's what I'm talking about," Abby says in agreement, throwing her door open as a rush of wind sweeps over my ankles and makes me shiver.

"We'll talk about it all after dinner, ok?" Evan's voice goes back to the tender tone he reserves for me and honestly now, all I want to do is skip the red carpet and go right back to his apartment. This night is already perfect.

He flings his door open and I release a sigh, my lungs screaming as I sit there on that breath before I'm forced to draw in more air. Maybe if I hold my breath, my heart will calm down and learn patience tonight. No sooner than Evan's door slams, mine is opened with his hand outstretched before me. *Ok, so maybe I'll enjoy being spoiled and just let the entire evening build and build to the best part.*

Stepping inside, arm in arm with Evan and on Abby's heels, we quickly see everyone already seated at a table. I glance around for a second and laugh to myself, making a mental note that the entrance is adorned with a bright red runner along the floor and big plush red drapes swung to the side of the huge front windows. Through the doorway into the dining area, more splashes of red catch my eye from small droplets of red crystals that hang from the center of a huge glass chandelier in the center of the dome shaped ceiling, red napkins and candles strategically placed along each table and even a huge velvety rug in front of a large grand fireplace at the back of the room. The place is dripping with elegance and class.

"Wow…and you're sure she said we'd be comped or was that just our waters we might want to order?" Evan mumbles through the corner of his lips as we walk to our table.

"Look, look, look what he got me…" Alyssa jumps up towards Abby, squealing and holding her wrist to show off a gorgeous diamond bracelet.

"Don't worry, Lanie will come through. Her parents can afford it,"

I whisper back to him as everyone says their hellos.

"Hey, what no tuxedo?" Evan points to Judd who takes a quick look down his body from his black dress jacket and button down white shirt and black slacks. "This isn't prom, you know."

"What?" Judd looks back at Evan, studying his attire and probably ready to rifle back over Evan's much more casual wear of jeans, an untucked navy blue button down and a white tee peeking out near his neck.

Evan laughs, cutting up with Judd as I look back over to Abby and Alyssa, 'oooing' and 'ahhhing' over her most recent piece of jewelry.

"I should have gotten you some jewelry, huh?" Evan's voice startles me as he whispers right by my ear, and I snap my head around, a dumbfounded feeling in my actions as if I'm expecting someone else to be standing there. "Whoa, I'm sorry." Panic takes over his face, as he puts his hands out towards me.

"Oh no, it's ok." I brush off, refusing to let it ruin tonight. I have to learn to control it. I swallow any sense of anxiety that traveled into my consciousness just now, and respond to his last question, "And no, I love what you gave me." I hold my arms out slightly and raise my chin. "Do I look like I wear much jewelry?"

Evan looks me over and chuckles. I probably look like a department store mannequin right now.

"Well, you're not going to wear much jewelry, if you don't own much."

I shake my head again, completely disagreeing with where his thoughts are going. I've never been a big 'diamonds and pearls' person; simple and meaningful is the way to go.

"Oh my gosh, you're kidding me," Alyssa exclaims. "Ooooo, Piper," she says quietly as Evan sparks up more chatter with Judd and Hayden.

I turn back and forth prepared to answer Evan, yet curious at what Abby is telling Alyssa. *Oh no, she's telling her about the underwear.* Mortification sweeps over me.

We all take a seat and the chaos of several conversations all at once continues all around me, reminding me of Christmas Day at the cabin and many times this summer when there were a big group of us all clustered together; it makes me anxious and uneasy; maybe it was the wave of memories that hit me a few minutes ago.

"Red roses, huh?" Alyssa's voice chimes from across the table as a pair of feet subtly kick mine.

I look up, a bit off on my social appetite.

"You ok?" Evan leans to my side.

"Yes…" I answer him, then pull my eyes across the table to Alyssa. "Yes," I say with a smile. "He did." *I hope this is all the questions about my gifts.*

Alyssa smiles, apparently pleased with my answer, then turns to join in on a conversation between Hayden and Judd.

The night goes by in slow motion, dragging on possibly to torture me or to draw out the turn of mood I've felt since we got here. I munch on bread sticks off and on, analyzing it all. *I was happy, on top of the world and blown away with the arrowheads*; my heart thuds on just that thought alone; *then I walked inside, still thrilled to be coming here for the first time…*

I pause in my thought process. It's like I'll never escape it. The letter surfaces in my mind and I have no earthly reason for thinking about it, but I do; just then every lively thought I've had for the night flies right out the window.

"Piper?" Evan says softly, leaning into the table and giving me a concerned stare. "You're quiet? Is everything ok?"

I quickly grab my napkin, swiping it across my face, then toss it onto my half eaten plate of food. *Doubt I'll eat anymore.*

"Yeah," I assure him as I push off from the table to stand. "I think I might use the restroom. I'm just feeling a little…" I give him a regretful look, knowing I may ruin his night if I don't get this in check. "Just a little off for some reason. I think I'm just tired. I'll be back."

"Ok," he speaks softly, hesitant as if he's blaming himself.

"Oh, wait…Piper…I'll go with you." Abby hops up and flies

around the table to join me just as I give one last reassurance to Evan.

"I'm alright, really." I smile, before joining Abby.

Five minutes later, my eyes are closed as my hands press against the cool flat surface of the granite counter, chanting to myself. *Breathe, Piper, Breathe. What is going on with me?*

I take a deep rejuvenating breath, my shoulders rise and my diaphragm tightens as I draw it in and slowly release. *Breathe.* Opening my eyes, my sight blurs with remnants of that night. The mirror, the reflection of me standing there in only my t-shirt and skinned up knees and hands, pale white in fear and nauseous. I've got to get past this...I have to, but every little thing takes me back to that day; back to square one. I squeeze my eyes closed with a pool of tears building behind them.

A swish of the toilet being flushed behind me brings me back to my senses and I instantly jerk my eyelids open as Abby flings the stall door forward, looking down at her feet.

She looks up, right at me as she straightens her dress in the back. "Toilet paper check," she laughs. "I just know everyone would let me march down the street with it hanging out of the back of my dress or stuck to my shoe."

Scrunching my brows at her joke, I give her a hint of a grin before looking back down to the sink.

"Especially Evan, right?" she chuckles again then pauses, sitting back against the counter so that she can face me. "Hey, did that gift make you nervous?"

I look up quickly, a little taken aback by her question. *Why would the story and memory about the arrowheads make me nervous; that was amazing of him.*

"The strawberry underwear..." she points out the obvious, which I clearly did not even think of. "You know, since you really haven't had a whole lot of..." Abby trails off, but she has my attention now.

She's my best friend and although I have pointed out to her that Chris and I never went all the way and never so much as played around, as I also did when she asked if I fooled around with Tyler this summer, I have not told her everything. I have kept a lot to myself and don't indulge in much talk about sex and hot guys, and Abby has always got that about me. Granted, she does know that I lost my virginity to Evan. I needed someone to talk to after all that; the end of that day didn't go like I had hoped and I had to play my depression off to everyone as something. Going all the way for the first time was all I had to give as an excuse and I hated even sharing that with anyone. After what Mitch said that day, I felt so violated. My body tenses and I cringe, regretting even going down this road.

"Piper?!"

Her voice shakes me out of my trance and I flinch, my shoulders jerking and jostling my upper body.

"What's going on? You have been in la-la-land all night."

Taking a deep breath, I drop my head and peer down at the sink, gazing at the browns and grays swirled through the granite in an untamed pattern. *What's wrong with me she's asking. What is wrong with me? Why am I thinking about so much tonight?* I should be living this night up with a smile that could outmatch anyone's; I'm here with Evan, I got roses from someone other than Dad, he gave me the most prized present anyone could ever think of and I'm surrounded by all my friends; life should be grand.

"I don't mean to pry, but you haven't been real talkative on the whole thing…have you two done anything? I mean, besides just the basic messing around or did it go back to how you guys were when you were younger?" Abby flexes her jaw as I look her in the eyes, concentrating on figuring it out myself.

It's all the stupid memories of that day. The fear of finding out how Mitch knew. Hesitation of whether I can get through and enjoy later tonight without it ending in tears. It's a flood of overwhelming emotion from all the wonderfulness of this day, and it may even be a bit of nervousness brought on by considering to actually wear those stupid, red underwear and how that means Evan will get them off. A buzz of exhilaration zips through my entire body starting at my toes, zapping up my inner thighs, swirling through my belly with a kick of flutters, causing an extra hundred beats of my heart and making my head spin with visions of him somewhere I've never imagined before.

"You don't have to talk about it if you don't want to, but…"

I snap out of it fast on her words, remembering her comment about me being in la-la-land only moments ago. *What the hell; she's my best friend, if I can't talk to her, I'll never be able to talk to anyone.*

Sucking in the deepest breath of courage I've ever taken, I turn and lean against the counter with my hands tightly clasped in front of me as a sort of barrier for my nervousness and the threat of a possible emotional outburst.

"Ok, well…" I suck in another mouthful of air, slowly releasing it before speaking again. "At first we just kissed. Well actually for the first month, that's all we did."

"Wow, you're disciplined," Abby says in an exasperated tone.

I may be in a sharing mood, but I'm not sure I'm ready to take a trip all the way to the beginning of memory lane. That's a dark road; I'll just stick to the present.

I snicker a little and continue, "Well, I've always been sort of cautious in that department, you know that," I spit out so matter-of-factly as if she knows the whole story. All I told her years ago is that I had nightmares when I was a kid that made me have the blackout. In a sense she knows what happened, kind of, just in a simulated sort of way. "But the other week we did end up…" I look her dead in the eyes, suddenly uncomfortable to say the word sex out loud, like it's such a dirty word; only with Evan it's not. I still can't say it.

"Ohhhh, wow. So you two had sex again for the first time since…" Abby looks down, squinting her eyes as she quickly calculates. "…since you were what? Sixteen or so?"

I nod.

"And?" She nudges her chin forward, hope and curiosity all over her face.

Stumbling inside to figure out what she could want to know, my mind comes to a screeching halt. *This is Abby; she's the female equivalent of a smartass male...basically Evan with a vagina.*

Half stuttering, I blurt out, "Oh, yeah it was good...it was great...I mean wow, but..." I throw the but in there causing Abby's eyes to widen and her jaw to tense. "No, it was amazing, but I ended up crying afterwards because I was so nervous and scared, but excited and wanting to so bad at the same time. I don't know, I guess I just got overwhelmed with it all, plus then I thought about those nightmares I had when I was a kid..."

"Did you black out?" Abby interrupts.

"No," I say quietly, lowering my voice as if we have an audience. "I was fine during, I just was partly relieved that it was over, afterwards, yet so happy that I didn't blackout, then excited that it was him there..." I shut up quickly, almost saying too much...but would that be so awful? Shouldn't I just tell her? *I was molested...*I cringe, a huge knot forming in my stomach and every muscle in my body stiffens. *Or was I raped? Maybe raped sounds less wrong or God, I don't know how to do this. What if she looks at me like I'm sick or twisted or gross or...?*

"Piper?"

I dart my attention back to her.

"You zoned out there for a second again."

Breathing in and out calmly to brush off all the anxiety that is rising in my conscience, I take a turn from my earlier thinking. *I'll tell her, just not now.* I need to brush this off, enjoy tonight and start the healing process tomorrow. Opening my mouth, I decide to elaborate and redeem Evan's bedroom skills. I'm sure she is wondering why the hell I would cry about an eight-year-old dream when I'm making out with the one guy I've longed for and missed all these years. Just as my words hit my tongue, Abby speaks up again.

"Ok, you are my best friend and I need to know the truth." Abby stands defiantly with her shoulders firm and straight, and her face dead serious; my heart sinks. "What happened to you back then and don't tell me it was a dream?"

I breath in and out and in and out, my chest and pulse accelerating with what she wants to know. *Why is she asking this?* I rationalized that she probably is skeptical by now about the dream story, but she can't be asking this. *Why would she? Not now, not tonight. I can't get into this here.* Fisting my hands together, I think and think and think. *What can I say? How do I get out of this and come back to it at another time?*

"I know back when we were younger and you had your first black out spell in front of me, you said you had nightmares about someone coming into your bed at night and raping you, and of course I believed you, but is that really all there is?" Concern and pain laces her every word. *She's just trying to be a good friend.* "I saw how hard every one of those black out spells were on you and even how you seemed to lock up when guys got too close to you, but something just doesn't add up. You know a dream isn't real, so why haven't you got past it after all these years and why on earth would it affect you with Evan? I mean, you trust him and you know he would never hurt you..."

My head is spinning and I just want her to stop. "Ok! Just stop!" I shout, huffing out breath after breath till I feel as if I might hyperventilate.

"I'm sorry, Piper," she whispers in a gentle voice that manages to calm me a little and bring me back down from my escalating adrenaline rush. "I just want to be here for you and if you're holding back, you need to talk to someone."

Listening to the sweetness and need to be there for me tone in her voice of wanting to be there for me, I lean back against the counter not even aware that I had bolted forward when I yelled. My shoulders relax and I open my lungs to another heap full of air as I suck in and back out, hoping it will have a peaceful effect on me. Silence stretches out. Abby looks startled by my outburst and now I have absolutely no clue what to say. I search the room, desperate to move forward and get back to normal girl gab. My eyes land on her purse hanging from her shoulder.

"It's ok, really," I assure her. "Hey, can I borrow your lip gloss. I left mine at the table." I try my best to be cheery and give her a big smile, a fake, say-cheese sort of one. "I need to make sure to look hot for later, ya know?" I wink as she digs in the front pocket of her bag and hands me a pink cylinder container with set of lips painted across the front; I pinch it between my fingers and spin around, thankful for the distraction. "Thanks."

After unscrewing the applier, I pluck it out with a moist suction noise, pout my lips and bring the soft spongy tip to my bottom lip.

"Besides, during Christmas break when you blacked out with Chris," Abby pushes forward; I cringe and continue to focus on making my lips shine as she goes on, "…after Evan had woke you up…well I walked him out and we started to discuss how it happens. He more than confirmed my suspicions. I've wanted to ask you about it ever sin…"

As soon as the words are out of Abby's mouth every fraction of my body ices over and freezes. I stare forward, my hearing shut off and my hand a block of ice still holding the lip gloss to my lips. I can't even feel the beat of my own heart, yet slowly a tidal wave of tremors begins to come over me beginning in my hands. Ferocity festers in my veins as if I am standing right back on that dock, against the door of the shower house as Mitch fires bomb after bomb right into my soul over a memory that is so violating that it's as if he's making it happen again. *How could he?!*

The lip gloss falls to the marble counter with a clank. Before I can think to put one foot in front of the next, my body is in over drive. The handle of the bathroom door is in my hand and I seriously am not sure when I crossed the room. All that is on my mind is putting this to rest. *Why would he discuss this with someone without confronting me first?*

"Piper, wait! Let me explain. Oh shoot, I didn't mean that he…."

I don't even let her finish; *I don't care.* He's done this before and it destroyed everything. Flinging the door open, I let the fire that ripped through me years ago blaze into an uncontrolled anger that may never subside. *He had no right and he needs to learn that my past is not up for social gathering discussions. How could he; how could he??!* It's the only thing that keeps repeating in my brain, because I cannot fathom why he would.

My face twists as I scrunch my brows into a veil of pain and confusion, while keeping my lips glued shut by a thin sheet of gloss. He looks over to me the second I walk out of the bathroom as if he can sense my very presence as I enter a room. It's something he's always done, whether I'd walk out of my cabin, enter a classroom or pull up in Dad's car, he would always look up, knowing I'm there. It was always a comfort to me that he could feel me even without the sound of my voice, yet today, it is not a comfort at all. I draw my brows down further, the urge to zap lasers or fire from my eyes if I had the power to, burning through me. Just like years ago, his usual smartass smirk shifts and changes to something more, confusion just like I'm feeling maybe; a hint of fear or dread, but this time I see something more…recognition.

I don't even wait for him to say a word. "How could you?"

Damn my mouth

Evan

WHAT THE HELL?

Piper bolts out of the door of the restaurant with Abby mumbling behind her, "I didn't say he told me…Piper I didn't mean to cause…"

Shit! Dammit! Son of a bitch, I knew we should have talked about this in the beginning; all of it.

As Abby tries to explain herself in a remorseful tone, I shoot up from the table, refusing to let her storm out of my life for a second time. I don't even feel my feet as I fly towards the door seconds behind her. I'm reliving the worst and most regretful moment of my life, because I know without a doubt that her thinking I told Abby, has her doing the same thing as before. *I should have never spoken to Abby about it. I should have known I'd put my damn foot in my mouth.* My hands fall to the cold hard surface of the door as I shove with all my force to get outside as fast as my feet will carry me. Cold air sweeps over my skin as I hear a tap tap-tap on the pavement as Piper races down the sidewalk.

"Piper, would you wait!" I call out, knowing she's pissed as hell and not going to even care to hear an explanation. *This feels like a repeat of years ago.*

I shake my head, the rage from that day beginning to rise within my veins and bubble to the surface. I literally wanted to drop my brother into the deepest hole in the world when he came off that dock not too long after Piper had stormed off, but then he surprised me with what had happened.

"Dude, your chick is history, I think."

My fists wound up tight as my chest constricts and my jaw damn near feels as if it may crack in half. Spinning around, I feel an ache and loss that I've never felt before; something deeper and more horrifying than I could have imagined. I've lost her; all because of him, I've lost her.

"What did you say!" I roar out my words, not caring who hears at this point. "What did you say to her, Mitch?!"

Tristan quickly steps up, siding up to me as if he is ready to pen me down in case I lunge at him; and I will.

"Oh boy, was she pissed off at you." He presses his lips together, but all I have running through my head is me driving my fist right into them and how good it will feel when I do. "I'm thinking you weren't supposed to tell me that info, little brother."

That's it, I've had it. Raising both my hands, I reach for him ready to tear him limb from limb. Tristan's arms fall around me as he holds me in a bear hug that locks me in place.

"Whoa, hey just let it be. He's just trying to rile you up."

Mitch cocks his head back. "Whose side are you on, man?"

Tristan holds on tight, having a death grip across my chest that I cannot penetrate, no matter how I squirm and fight.

"Let me go, Tristan," I say through a clamped jaw.

"Hey, I'm not taking sides, but," Tristan gulps. "But I do have little brothers and I don't think yours in any way asked for this."

Mitch starts laughing and it shoots anger right through me. I kick my legs, clipping his in the process and knocking him off his feet.

"Whoa…" Tristan mumbles.

"Let me go…" I yell out, wanting to tackle him while he's down.

"You little shit." Mitch quickly picks himself back up, looking around to make sure his precious image is safe.

Everything was perfect that day, just like today; I had no warning. My mood was sabotaged, and I was robbed of ever explaining how it all went down. Then when Mitch proceeded to tell me all the cruel and horrible things he said to her, even Tristan couldn't hold me back. I wanted blood for that. I ran to her cabin, but when I heard her parents yelling and saw through the window as she sat at the table in utter ruins, I was a coward. I walked down to the dock with tears in my eyes for probably one of the first times in my life. My mind flipped through it over and over until I finally convinced myself to go back and just talk to her, to explain, but by that time she was gone; packed up and had drove out of my life.

Piper's feet still pound pavement as she makes it to the same old ass van she's driven since she was sixteen.

"Just let me talk to you!"

She spins around fast, her eyes wide and looking like she's damn near ready to lay me out. I stop, surprised by the venom in her expression; it's not something I was used to before. She puts her hand out fast and I just know it; *here it is; she's going to finally deck my ass. I deserve it.* I stare at her, expecting to feel her fist slam into my nose or eye or possibly even get a painful as hell blow to the groin, but instead her hand lies palm up between us.

"Give me my keys, Evan," she hisses, her lip snarled and brows drawn into a diagonal slope above her deep dark brown eyes that look nearly black at the moment.

Patting my hand over the outside of my jeans, it falls on an odd shaped object jutting out at my hip that I know are her set of a million keys with at least five different frilly girl keychains to decorate it. At first thought, I flinch, moving my hand to the top of my pocket, but I pause. *She can't go anywhere. Hell no, I'm not giving her the keys.* I drop my hand to my side and level her with a serious look that I'm hopeful will tame her guarded, about-to-throw-you-right-in-front-of-a-moving-vehicle expression that she's giving me.

"First let me talk to you. Let me explain what happened with the whole Abby thing, because it is not…"

"Not what!" she cuts me off, hollering at a level I've never even heard her voice reach. "Not you opening your trap again and telling someone something you have no business telling them?! What, Evan?!"

Opening my mouth, I prepare to calmly explain the situation, but she does not wait. She's mad as hell and in full on argument mode.

"Is it not the same as before?! You just don't know how to keep your mouth shut! You did it back then and now you did it again! It will always be like this, because you don't care, you don't…"

"Whoa, whoa, wait just a minute…I don't care?! You think I don't care?! Seriously!! Piper, come on!"

"You always have to have the last word, don't you Evan?! Always got to have a comeback for everything with some smartass comment or joke about…"

I cut her off; no way am I listening to this. "Since when did this become a dig at my personality. How does that even have anything to do with what's going on here? Yeah, sure I like to lighten up shit and joke around. Big freaking deal!"

"It's how you are; it's how you will always be. You have a big mouth, Evan, and you need to learn how to control it."

"And that is where letting me explain everything would help out a little," I widen my eyes trying my best to drive home that she is damn well overreacting and not even giving me a chance here.

Piper, turns on her toes and starts frantically pulling at the handle on the passenger door as if it will magically come open despite the fact that it's a solid metal car door that is locked tight. Shoving my hands in my pocket, I feel around until I find the little square lock remote. I pull it to the edge of my pocket, enough to see which button is the lock and which is the unlock. Zeroing in on the tiny picture of a fully sealed lock, I push it, a beeping ringing through the air immediately; giving her a sound confirmation that it is indeed locked.

"Arrrrrhhhgghhhh!" Piper instantly stomps her foot and kicks at the door then turns to face me. "Just unlock the door!"

"And what? Are you going to get in and lock me out, all while I have the keys right in my pocket and can unlock it at any point and talk to you?!"

Bouncing in a tantrum sort of fashion, Piper grinds her teeth together as her face twists and turns into angry frustration. "Just give me the keys then, Evan," she urges me with a pained glare that nearly makes me give in.

"Hear me out?" I don't give in, pleading with her right back to do something she never did before; let me tell her the whole story. "Just let me tell you what happened back then and with Abby. If you're still pissed off, then I'll give you the keys."

She pauses, pursing her lips. "Fine," she spouts out, still pissed off as hell.

Suddenly I have no clue where to start. Closing my eyes for only a second, I replay the entire frustrating moment of when my tongue slipped and I betrayed her.

"I would love to get a slice of that piece of pie," Mitch says eyeballing Piper out in the distance with a smug grin on his face.

"Don't talk about her like that and stop looking at her."

"Or what?!" he snaps in warning but I ignore him.

He's looking for a fight; he always is. If there were ever two brothers that detested each other with every ounce of their being, it would be us. After being dragged from military base to military base, you would think we would cling to one another for support, but it had the opposite effect on us. Mitch grew up following around all of the guys on base, longing to be just like them. I, on the other hand, wanted more. I wanted a home, friendship and a stable environment that didn't include bouncing around the country. That ultimately pushed us apart as brothers; the need for a future so different.

"So what is she like in the sack? Those shy, quiet types always seem like the most enthusiastic and wild ones between the sheets."

He's still trying to bait me, I know it and honestly, with this burning sensation blazing through my chest and the quickening of my pulse, I can tell he is slowly succeeding.

"So does she let you talk dirty to her or does she just like you pound..."

I can't take it!

"Shut up, just shut up." *I turn and slam my fist into his shoulder, sparking loud laughter from him.*

Gritting my teeth with my jaw wound so tight that it may shatter, I glare, daring him to push me more; I need to calm down.

His smirk grows with my anger, so I look away, sliding my gaze out to the lake dock where Piper and Abby are in a splashing war. Piper laughs with her wet hair flinging in all directions and just that simple vision soothes my furious heart, but of course, my brother doesn't know when to lie down and let it go.

"I have to admit when she first got out here, she wasn't much to look at, but this past year has been gooood to her. She's filling out in all the right spots."

Keeping my eyes on Piper, I remain calm and steady.

"Mitch, could you just pay attention to your own girl and keep your shitty ass comments to yourself," *I plead.*

Knowing what happened to her makes me feel like the slightest sexual comment towards her is like putting her through it all over again. I joke with her and touch her, but that's for me and me alone. She trusts me and I would never, ever hurt her.

"Hey guys. What are we doing?" *Tristan walks up looking as glum as I feel right now.*

He is pretty cool, however, I have no idea what he sees in my brother. I'm sure he will turn into a douchebag just like him soon enough.

"Fixing to go join those sexy ladies down on the beach." I tense at my brother's suggestion.

"Leave Piper alone!"

"Why you so touchy about her anyways? Maybe she'd like to try someone a bit more experienced."

I don't know what I'm thinking and I barely say it, but I say it, "Ask your pal Trent."

He flinches and belts out a laugh.

"No way! Whoa are you saying…holy shit, I can't believe it!"

Every ounce of color drains from my face and I turn, wide-eyed in alarm at what I may have so carelessly divulged.

"What's true?" Tristan jumps into the conversation and I swing my attention out to Piper, so carelessly having fun and totally oblivious to what just slipped out of my mouth.

"Trent and Evan's gal out there did the deed." He points out to her; Tristan's eyes widen as he looks at me, but I just snap.

"They're kissing cousins, man…"

I lunge at my brother, fury engulfing me and taking over every limb in my body as I pound my fist into his chest.

"Whoa, whoa, whoa."

Tristan rips me off of my brother, but Mitch just laughs, wiping at his busted lip. "Come on, Evan. Just go down to the beach. Mitch is just screwing with you," he says in a sympathetic tone while pulling me down off the porch.

My chest heaves in and out and the air in my lungs feels like fire as I fight to calm myself.

"Don't ever talk about her. Ever!" I shout and pull myself away from Tristan.

He puts his hands up in surrender as I turn my angry eyes to him for a split second then back to my brother.

"If you ever, ever talk about her like that again, I swear I will kick your ass…I don't care if you're bigger than I am or not. I will kick your ass and make sure you look like the biggest pansy there is." I pause and

turn to walk down to the beach, behind Tristan."…and tell your friend, Trent, to keep his damn hands off her!"

Flicking my eyes back open, I stare at her, hoping she understands that it was just a sense of protectiveness I was feeling over her when I said it. It was a reaction and I've regretted it ever since.

"I know I should have kept my mouth shut. I had no right to say anything, I know I didn't, but believe me when I say, I have kicked myself for it every day since."

Her defensive stance doesn't give way at all. Her hands remain balled at her sides, where they fell shortly after I refused to hand her the keys.

"No, you didn't have a right to tell him. So Tristan knows too?"

I drop my head, my chin nearly slamming into my collar bone as I realize what I just told her. *Wow, do I ever learn.* Looking up sympathetically, I nod my head slowly, the dread of my words catching up to me and biting me in the ass harder than that dog did.

"Perfect!" she snaps, all her of fury, is now blazing through her at full steam.

"So it was just some sort of game I guess…macho talk, huh?" She raises her hands into the air and deepens her voice, mocking much as I do, but she's dead serious and fuming. "Just go ask your pal, Tr…" she stumbles her words, stopping at his name as if her tongue will not finish that particular one.

"What?! No, it wasn't a game! Did you even listen to me? He was putting you down and pressing my buttons. All he was doing was egging me on to get me to say more. He knew what he was doing. He's my brother; no one knows better how to piss me off to where I can't control my damn mouth and even form a reasonable thought. I didn't tell him intentionally; it was more to protect…"

She raises her hand to stop me. "Yeah, yeah…I got it. Protective, right! You told two guys who are the biggest assholes in the world that I'm damaged goods."

This infuriates me. "I did not and I've never thought that. How the hell do you figure you are damaged? It happened, Piper; it happens to people, but you have to find a way to get past it."

"Oh spare me the therapy lesson. Do you know that after that day, my parents fought day and night?! Mom refused to believe me until Dad could not take it anymore. They filed for divorce, we moved and I had to change schools. Everything in my life changed because of you opening your mouth," she stops, the whites of her eyes bright red. Clearing her throat, she regains her composure and straightens up. "Besides, I am perfectly fine now, and getting through it." She glances around, caution and hesitation suddenly taking over the anger and bitterness. "We had sex didn't we and I've even said that I wanted to again. You're the one that keeps putting on the brakes, not me," she whispers through a tight jaw with all anger reappearing.

I lower my tone before speaking, respecting her casual way of pointing out that she doesn't want to draw attention right here in the middle of downtown. "Hell yeah, I've put on the breaks, because every damn time you cry after we fool around, it's like shoving a knife through my heart. It's like a reminder of what happened and it makes me think that you feel in a way like I'm taking advantage of you. I hate myself after, don't you understand that?"

"Oh great, so now I find out that you hate yourself after we do that?"

"Oh.my.gosh…no! Would you stop being such a damn girl, Piper. Stop trying to turn this into a fight!" My temper flares. It really doesn't matter what is said at this point, it's going south one way or another if she has her way; she's in flight mode and I don't think I can do a damn thing about it. I go on, trying to finish everything I planned to explain, "…and the thing with Abby…"

"Oh yeah, you opening your mouth again?"

"Dammit, Piper!" I huff out, about to prove her big mouth theory right if I don't cool it. *Geez, she is frustrating the hell out of me! How the hell did this night go so wrong?* Shaking my head at her stubbornness, I go on to explain the situation with Abby, "…and no, I never said a word to Abby. She was talking about what you told her I assumed and it sounded like she knew. I was just telling her that I was glad you had someone."

"Piper, he's right. I just came to my own conclusions."

We both swing around seeing that we have drawn Judd and Abby outside with the way we ran out. Judd hangs back by the door, his head hung low, focusing on the ground as if his ears can't hear a thing as long as he doesn't make eye contact with us. Abby, stands only two feet away, behind me, nervously fidgeting her hands together. She looks straight at Piper, the sympathy and remorse in her eyes plain as day. *No doubt, I'll catch slack on that too.*

I pivot back around to face Piper, who swings her gaze from Abby to me, without saying a word. She slides her hands up, folding them over her chest and dipping her eyes low into a penetrating frown that makes it clear that this shit is not making a turn for the better.

"Wonderful…so now everyone knows I guess…" she mutters, keeping her voice quiet, but direct.

"Oh yeah, because I'm the one that stormed out of the restaurant and wanted to argue on the sidewalk…"

She jumps back in, "…and everyone thinks I'm some sort of filthy, damaged…" tears begin to stream down her face and her words come out with more anger the more she talks.

Any amount of frustration and irritation that had made its presence known melts away. What she's saying is aggravating as hell, but not so much at her, more so that she can't bend her thinking on it.

I lower my voice to a near whisper, "Ok just stop it. Piper, that night should not define you. It happened and it sucks ass…bad." She shifts her body, looking even more defiant than before, her jaw flexing and a deep crease embedded between her brows as she glares at me through misty eyes, but I keep going, "That was then, this is now. The past needs to stay where it was or there is no hope for..."

"Evan, just stop! Just stop! Give me the keys..."

I snap my mouth closed, clamping my teeth together and taking a perturbed breath as I close my eyes for a second. *There is no getting through to her; none.*

"...now! Just give me the keys please..." what started out as a bitter, enraged attitude in her stance and voice, dissolves into a painful plea. "Please..." she whimpers as huge droplets of water spill from her eyes again.

She shivers, running her hands up and down her arms and it's then that I notice she didn't even grab her jacket. My fingers lock on the keys, hesitating for a second. *Will she come back if I let her go?* I don't know if she will; it took so long last time that if I let her walk away now, it could be goodbye.

"Please..."

Her pleading whispers reach my ears and everything inside me goes numb with what I may be giving up as I pull the keys from my pocket and hold them between us. I could say the same to her; *please...* but I won't. If this is what she needs; if this is what will heal the broken parts inside of her, then I'll let her walk away. Squeezing my eyes shut out of dread, the metal ring gripped between my thumb and index finger slips away and I, without a doubt, will be kicking myself for this later.

I reopen my eyes and look right at her. "Piper..."

She holds her hand up immediately, stopping any attempt I have to turn this around. "Evan, just don't." She clicks the locking mechanism dangling from her keychain and a red light flashes in my peripheral vision. "For once, just keep your mouth shut," she says it gently with not one trace of anger or resentment in her tone, keeping the level of her voice low and calm, but she might as well have thrown a fast ball right to my chest, because it nearly knocks me down.

No amount of explaining myself can undo what happened when I told Mitch her secret. I screwed up so bad that day. I press my lips together and take a step back, signaling that I will do just as she says. However, every bone and muscle in my body is hollering at me to stop her, to rip the keys out of her hand and say, 'Screw this shit! It's time to get over this and stop running from the pain and from what has always made you feel good; me'. I don't move an inch, though.

"Piper," Abby calls out, running past me. "I'll go with you."

Piper doesn't say a word as she walks around to the driver's side and jumps in. Abby pulls at the handle of the passenger side, twisting her head to the side to look over her shoulder at me. I can't even force a smile and neither does she, instead she scrunches her face up, crinkling her nose and creasing her brows together in a remorseful expression.

I have no desire to watch her leave. After turning, I look around quickly making eye contact with Judd, who also stands in the freezing cold without a jacket. *I cannot think of a shittier night.*

"Man, is everything ok?"

I don't even know how to answer that and I don't really want to. "Hey, I'm just gonna take off. I'll catch you tomorrow and ummm... would Alyssa mind taking Piper's jacket back to her? She might have her purse hanging on the back of the chair also."

Judd looks down the street, swinging his eyes side-to-side to take in where we are as if he didn't already know. "Where you going? I can drive you home at least."

I point forward down the street, shaking my head. "The jobsites just a block away, figured I'd walk it. I can do with the fresh air anyway."

One foot in front of the next, I start the trek to the work trailer, for the first time not a bit fazed by the cold air blowing right in my face. Judd opens his mouth as I pass, but clamps it shut before saying a word. It's not often that I'm at a loss for words; he knows I don't want to talk.

The trip goes fast and all I can think about the whole time is where I made my first mistake. *Was it the arrowheads? The stupid ass gag gift? How did we end up here? Why and how do I get back to where we were, if we were ever even there in the first place?* She will never get over that part of her life and I don't know how to move forward if she can't. There's no way to make her; there's no way to help her and as much as it hurts her, it hurts us and it pains me to see her like that. She was so wrong when she said I don't care. I care to the depths of my soul; I care.

Once I get to the fence, expecting it to be locked tight and free of visitors, I look up and see a work truck in the parking lot and the light on in the small trailer. *Shit! That's all I need is someone that wants to talk tonight.* I move fast continuing in on my initial plan to just stay the night at work, not that I'll sleep at all.

As soon as I fling the door open, my eyes land on someone I did not expect. Turning his head just as quick as I opened the door, his expression shifts damn near to the same one I'm probably sporting at this moment. He looks about as unhappy to see me, as I do to see him.

"Well here I came late at night, hoping I'd have time to myself and put in a little overtime uninterrupted," Tristan's annoyance comes across loud and clear

I glance around to the wall beside his desk where one crutch rests. Heaps of papers are strung all over his desk, which took up residency once Grandpa gave him the job. I look to Judd's desk chair, sitting empty and calling my name only a couple feet away.

"Well I was thinking about the same thing. I guess great minds think alike. You know you don't have to keep taking on so much. Most of the jobs aren't even scheduled for this year."

Walking over to the chair, I grip it in my hand and pull it out before plopping down. My ass hits the firm, uncomfortable cushion and a truck load of regret is pushed from my lungs on a heavy sigh; everything that happened tonight suddenly bites down on my heart.

"I like to keep busy." Tristan keeps his eyes down on his work, shuffling two papers back and forth. Glancing over with his brows etched with curiosity, he studies me for a second before speaking. "Well that looks familiar. You get dumped?"

I chuckle, knowing this expression should be very familiar to him considering he was there the day it took place or the first time it happened at least.

"Ahhh, don't act like you know so much about it. Who's ever dumped your ass?"

Tristan face never changes, keeping a somewhat bland unemotional expression and a vacantness in his eyes that is usually lit with the desire to pester and aggravate everyone around him.

"I don't usually give anyone the chance to dump me. Rough day?"

I raise my brows. "Do you really want to know about this? Is it share time?" I say it sarcastically, but honestly, I could probably go off like a woman right now, minus the emotional outburst of tears. Although, the walk here, I did get a bit misty eyed just thinking over the fact that she may blow me off for another couple years. *This sucks.*

He blows out a breath, staring forward past the dim lit desk lamp to the jobsite map tacked to the wall with a million different small colored ball-tipped pins stabbed into it in various spots.

"What the hell, try me. It's better than sitting here and sulking about my own life." He turns his head, remaining tucked beneath the desk.

I look down at the base of the chair, hesitating on laying any of my garbage on him, when he's dealing with much more, I'm sure.

"Yeah, don't go there," he snaps.

Swinging my sights back up to him, a pit forms in my stomach. *He must get that shit all the time; dumbasses staring. I did the first day he came onto the jobsite.*

"Ok," I snap out of it, going right into rambling mode. "I'm not good at girly-ass heart-to-hearts, so you'll have to bear with me. Let's see..." Rolling my eyes up to my lids as if I'm searching my brain for the words, I come up empty. *I am not a talker when it comes to this crap.* "Plans for a mind-blowing exciting evening turned to the shittiest night ever with an extra scoop of shit and a cherry on top to round it off." I bob my head in victory of a well explained evening. "Yep, that about covers it."

Tristan leans back in his chair, raising his arms to fold behind his head into a relaxed position.

"You don't say. So you did get dumped." He glances over from the corner of his eyes. "...and I suppose she stormed off and left your ass and you had to huff and puff it all the way here."

I jostle in my seat on a laugh. "Correcto," I say, bobbing my head again with my lips pressed together and my eyebrows raised in surprise of his quick assessment. *Right on the damn money.* "Good job, Freud...and here I always took you for an arrogant asshole that never knew the difference between a heart and a hemorrhoid. I just figured you considered them both a pain in your ass."

He spits out a laugh-type sigh, looking back towards the map. "Yeah, well today's a joke anyway. I never took you for the type to ring in overrated holidays like today. Please tell me you didn't go buy your gal roses and a box of chocolates." He glances over and I look at him sheepishly, holding back an all-knowing smirk. Swinging his eyes back to the wall, he shoves another sarcastic breathy laugh from his nose. "Figures. Well I guess that didn't help, huh? Should've saved your money."

I twirl a quarter of the way around in my seat, keeping my heels pressed to the same area of the floor as I anxiously finger a pencil, picking it up and dropping it down and repeating.

"Nahhh..." I start, then stop what I'm doing and snap my attention back to him. "Today's your birthday, isn't it? Judd mentioned it this morning when we went to get Piper and Alyssa's flowers."

Even from the corner of his eyes I can see I-don't-give-a-damn fester up in his expression as he rolls them and bounces up subtly on a sarcastic laugh, before turning to look at me.

"Piper, huh? So you guys are still a thing? I thought you two were history years ago. So what happened this time?" His tone turns serious.

Holy shit! Finally, someone that knows. "We were..." I stumble, tripping over my thoughts and veering from the obvious topic of what happened to her even though he knows. I'm keeping my damn mouth shut this time, regardless. "I thought some things could be forgotten, but she chose to dredge them up and punish me for them again."

"Ahhh, well, I don't know the whole story, but that has to be a tough one." For the first time in years, he sounds sympathetic to a situation.

"Well Abby seemed to help it along this time."

His sarcastic, down-played chuckle from before moves to an all-out laugh as he jolts forward, lowering his arms. "Well hell, she just seems to have brightened everyone's day, didn't she?!" I frown in confusion, but he goes on, "She looked giddy as hell carrying around that ridiculously huge bouquet of flowers today. Hmmm, maybe I got her in a pissy mood," he goes on practically talking to himself, then suddenly snaps out of it, turning back to me. "Probably better off."

A lot of good talking to Tristan is going to do. "Well, I'd like to fix it, but with her..." I sigh, "It'll be pretty impossible."

Tristan's brows dip and he cocks his head back incredulously. "That's pretty harsh, given what it seems she's gone through."

I blink my eyes in a bit of surprise, because it's not every day, or any day for that matter, that this discussion is breached, not even with her. It's somewhat encouraging, yet still a cause for caution; I'd like to limit myself to one screw up every couple years.

"No, it's not that. I mean, yeah, that's the reason she does what she does, but she just hangs onto it...she lives there...in the past and lets it dictate every major part of her life. Then when faced with it, she runs, takes off, hides from the damn issue instead of realizing..." I gulp, fuming the more I say, because dammit, I wish she'd find a way through this. If I could knock that wall down, I'd tear through it and make sure there wasn't a fiber of fear left in her. "...that it happened. Yes, it is horrible, it sucks major ass, it's even downright traumatizing obviously, but if she lets it beat her, if she just lets it hold her back her whole life then..." I stop, not sure where I'm going with this, but a bolt of livid frustration is thundering through me. She couldn't even hear me out. "I think she's so scared of facing what happened that she thinks of reasons to run. She's not even mad at me, she just needs an excuse to not face it head on. She's running," my voice grows quieter as I go on, picturing her at my doorstep the night it happened. *She's still running; she ran out of that cabin that night and she never stopped running from it.*

"Damn..." Tristan murmurs, also sounding deep in thought. "Yeah, but sometimes that's all a person knows to do. Sometimes, that's all they've got to save them, because if they stop..." His face twists into a painful understanding and for a moment I wonder; *Is he thinking of his own life: his mom, his wreck, his own unrelenting traumas.* "It might bury them alive," he pauses, looking me dead in the eyes and shocking the hell out of me that he can be serious and make some damn sense. "Listen, I think everyone has a trigger. Something that can free them from their personal demons." He shrugs, continuing on, "Some find it, some don't. Maybe you're hers, but...maybe you're not..." Pursing his lips, he goes back to a straight bland expression as if he's not talking about himself; *maybe he's not.* "I guess all you can do is wait and see if she comes back? Or just say screw it and move on." He shrugs, sounding more like the same antagonizing Tristan I know. "But the pain in the ass you spoke of...I wouldn't worry about whatever she said to tip this off."

Kicking my head back, I suddenly do not follow. I referred to a hemorrhoid being a pain in the ass, but I don't remember it saying anything. My face goes slack as I stare at him in question.

"Abby...I'm talking about Abby."

Ahhh, pain in his ass. Got it. I always thought there was something going on there.

"Yeah, I'm sure she's a pain in a lot of people's when she gets going." I go over all that went on tonight as I pause. "Ahh, I guess Abby's a lot like me. She just doesn't know when to shut up," I say, refusing to elaborate anymore on the night.

"I'm sure I could shut her up," Tristan's confident tone which has been lost since the wreck, comes through loud and clear as he turns to get back to work.

I chuckle, "Well I'll let you use whatever preferred method on her, I'm good. I'm learning on my own that I need to keep my mouth shut."

Tristan and I both quietly laugh to ourselves, neither of us sounding real genuine or invested in a happy mood or night of talking. Jumping up, I head for the small blue sofa in the break room for a restless evening of no sleep. My head goes over where I should be right now and I slam on the breaks, in full on 'kick myself in the ass' mode for the stupid careless slips I've made. *Damn my mouth!*

I have to do this

Piper

FTER A FEW DAYS OF deep thought and time alone, I came
to the one-time-halting conclusion that is, I have to read the
letter. I already had this talk with myself, convincing my heart
that it could bear whatever he had to say and ensuring my mind that it
would help me move on, but in the end I still put it off.

Not any more!

Flinging my legs off of the bed, I sit up with my hands digging
into the mattress on each side of my hips to hold me steady; to give me
strength to do it. I stare ahead, my vision set hard on the top drawer of
my dresser where I had hidden it as soon as I had returned from the
lake. My body trembles, and my eyes bear down to such an extreme
that they should be able to penetrate the solid wood piece of furniture.
I can do this. I spring forward, off the bed and to my feet, bolting across
the surface of the carpeted floor as if I'm on ice skates. My hand falls to
the brass knob and I pause, a deep breath moving over my tongue and
down my throat to fill my lungs and give me courage.

Pulling it open, I automatically set my eyes on a sliver of notebook
paper at the bottom of the drawer beneath a pair of red and white pol-
ka-dotted pajama pants. I move quickly, not wanting to lose my nerve.
After slamming the drawer shut, I walk back to the bed and slowly ease

down, because standing up seems too hard right now. After a deep breath, I begin to read.

Piper,

I know your first instinct is going to be to rip this up, destroy it, anything not to read it, but I'm begging you to read it all when you feel you can. Believe it or not, this is the sixth time I have written this letter. I suspect I'll write it a couple dozen more times, then toss them in the trash just like the rest, but I would like to think that one day I will have the courage to send it. That maybe I will get some sort of sign telling me that you are as ready as me to hear this.

I know first off, I should cut to the chase and just say sorry, but there is far more that I need to say to you. Sorry and I never meant to hurt you is not good enough; no words are good enough really. If I had it in my power to erase time, I suppose that may be the only thing that I could do to make it right, but I can't. I'd give anything to do that though...for both of us. Piper, for so long I was so messed up...confused, scared and even saying that makes me feel selfish and greedy. I have no right to tell you anything I felt when I tossed all those pains at you in a matter of seconds. I robbed you of your innocence and stole something that I can never give back. I cheated you and I can never change it.

That night changed everything for me. It made me look at my own past in a different light, because I had shoved a burden that I had carried for so long to someone else; to you. I made you feel helpless, violated, alone, afraid, powerless to control your own life and with so many unanswered questions that you knew you'd never get. I hurt you and the only thing I can offer you is some answers, although I fear I'll never be able to give you the best answer and that is why. All I can offer is a bit of understanding, yet never enough or what you deserve.

I started seeing a counselor shortly after what happened. I thought I was screwed up, demented, beyond repair. I was ashamed and wanted to die for what I did to you, but also for what was done to me. I felt that pain for years before, I felt it every single night that my innocence was taken from me. My counselor fed me all kinds of crap about how that act was imbedded into my mind and when a child watches and experiences an act that is made to seem like it's routine or possibly even normal, that it distorts their view of life and that act, almost makes it seem ok, but I can tell you right now, I always knew it was wrong. It made me feel like I was guilty, it made me feel ashamed. I won't go into the details in this letter, but as clear as it reads, I was molested. It happened to me from the time I was adopted at 8 years old till the time I came to live with your family. No, it wasn't by my adoptive mom, which spent the majority of her life bouncing from rehab facility to rehab facility, it was by her cracked-out friends that would come to party every week. I don't know why, and I know now that I will never get answers for that, but I know that it changed everything in me. It made me withdraw from any sort of friends, it made me think twice about any type of functioning relationship, it made me live my life closed off and shut down, until I got help and faced it; until I finally opened up and realized that I was holding back an ocean of pain and suffering that was only aiding in my self-destruction. I don't think I would have ever lived, if I had not found a way to open that door. That's one of the reasons that I'm writing this letter.

Years ago, my counselor told me that the steps to healing included acceptance, remembering, anger, change, moving forward and so many others, but one thing she did mention was forgiveness. I didn't know how, not with what I had done to you. She suggested me healing through opening up further, by explaining to you what had happened to me; offering you a small resolution to the "Why?" that I'm sure you need. And I know, I know this whole letter will never give you healing or most importantly allow you to forgive me; I truly don't feel I deserve your forgiveness, but you deserve for me to show you my scars, no matter how it hurts to open them back up.

If you found a way to read this letter, to finish all the way to here, then maybe you will find a way to respond. I know I don't have a right to even ask that of you, but honestly, even if you want to send me a letter reciting every hateful thing you've ever thought of me, I don't care, do it. All I know is that for years I held it all inside and until recently, I didn't realize the impact it had on me could have very well affected you in the same way. My hope is that you found a way to talk about it; that you got help before it even dawned on me that I needed some. I know there are a million things that I've forgotten to say or go over, but maybe someday I can tell you more. You deserve that at the very least. I wish I could change the past, I do. If you find the courage to talk, hear more and let me explain, write back or email me…anything.

Trent

Trent_sr@globalnet.com

Every nerve in my body tenses in an emotional effort to save me from drowning; from blacking out. I clamp my eyes shut tight, squeezing my fists around the letter and half tempted to rip it to shreds. Anger courses through me at what he did. *He's sorry? He wishes he could take it back?!*

My blood races through my veins, flowing like molten lava. Pressing my teeth together, I tense up more, my shoulders tightening and my back rigid. My knees and calf muscles tense, although I suddenly feel the need to jump up, run…flee from the feelings that are overcoming me; but I don't. I don't move at all and the most unbelievable part is, no tears come. *I hate him; I wish he was dead. How could he try to compare anything that happened to him, to what he did to me?!* Anger like I've never known before scorches a way through me, causing my heart rate to accelerate and my head to throb. A sudden ball of ferocity forces its way from my chest, up my throat and out into the still, silent confines of my bedroom in a sound-shattering scream. I fall back onto my bed, my body wracked with a hate and hurt like no other.

Curling my knees to my chest, I pull the letter to me as the fury slowly bleeds into pain and the tears finally come…and they come and come. I cry long and hard, twisting my head into the soft, pillowy fabric of my comforter and then cry even harder.

I lie there for what feels like an eternity, letting the anger from it all consume me, eat me up and burn through me until I cannot even keep my eyes open. This time as the lights go out in my mind, the whole night is replaying; every second, every touch, every dirty feeling I felt, but this time I fall asleep from pure emotional exhaustion; no blacking out, no hyperventilating, and no need to remind myself to breathe.

My eyes slide open slowly, and the first thing I notice is that I didn't sleep away my entire Saturday. The sun still streams through the window, casting iridescent strands of light over my desk. I look down, my fingers shuffling against the crinkled-up notebook page in my hands that I obviously hung onto in my sleep. Flicking my eyes back to the desk, I stare at my cell phone resting silently beside my laptop. I could look him up; look Mom up; email him or write a letter back. The lids of my eyes close, a heavy weight dragging them down even though I'm not tired. In a sense I am tired, but not physically. I'm exhausted from carrying around the pain of that night. Restless from worrying that it may sneak up on me during every exciting and heartfelt moment of my life. I'm emotionally drained from feeling the fear and confusion of it all, over and over again. I'd do anything just to have peace from it.

Pulling the letter away from my chest, I finally sit up, the bed making a creaking noise in the process. My hands fall, bringing the sheet of paper to my lap as I study the bottom.

trent_sr@globalnet.com

My chest expands on a deep breath, but I can't move. *What would I even say?* All that comes to mind when I think of running into him, is a string of profanities and gestures that would scare most onlookers. I'm the one that's gone through this, and I've dealt with it for years, but I still have no idea how to handle it. But now, looking down at the letter, my eyes focus in on the center portion of it…rereading it to myself.

…it made me live my life closed off and shut down, until I got help and faced it; until I finally opened up and realized that I was holding back an ocean of pain and suffering that was only aiding in my self-destruction. I don't think I would have ever lived, if I had not found a way to open that door.

Could writing him, talking to him, or even seeing him actually help? Knitting my brows, my stomach swirls in unease at the thought of being near him again. I haven't even faced him since that night; not even to hear his voice. A few times, Mom would call him and she'd ask if I wanted to talk with him, assuming we had some sort of cousinly bond, I guess. She would usually drop the line and get off, stating that he had to go a second after she hollered my name. I pause on that. *Was he just as scared and pained by what happened as me?*

I look down for the hundredth time, the letter suddenly taking up more space in the room; a ghost that has come to haunt me over a past left unsettled. *I'm not sure I can do this.* But just as that thought seeps into my mind, a surge of strength lifts me to my feet and straight to my laptop. I'm not even sure what has come over me as I pull the chair out and plop down, still grasping his letter; the same sheet of paper he held in his hands at one point. I drop it to the desk and stare at it, gazing long and hard and pulling my hand away up to my computer. *I have to; and maybe it will even be like it was for him. I could write something and then have to rewrite it half a dozen times. I might write it and never send it, but I have to try. I'll never get past this if not and I'll continue to screw things up in my life. I'll keep trying to push people away.*

Evan's face comes to mind, and instantly, I suck in a breath. *Breathe, I can do this.* I have to do it or I'll keep trying to blame him for the fact that I cannot even talk to anyone about it. I should have never put something so huge on him and expect it not to burn through him. He cares about me and always has. If this hurts me so greatly, how can it have not hurt him for as long as I've had him carry it around too? I owe this to myself mostly, to get closure, but I also owe it to us.

My fingers pinch the edge of the laptop, pulling the screen away from the keyboard as I continue to look back over to the paper, studying the words and committing them to memory so that perhaps it can fill my head with the words I need to reply.

After clicking the power button, a slow hum sounds and my screen lights up. It takes me seconds to have my email open and type his address at the top. The thoughts of waiting for a response, when I only check my email about twice a week, is almost like waiting for a bomb to detonate; a slow torture, however, instant messaging him makes me sick to my stomach. At least this way, it gives me time to catch my bearings and think of what to say.

My fingers run over the keys, typing frantically, the simplest and easiest thing I can think of; the only words I have the courage to say at this point.

I'm ready to talk.

I hit send before I can even think to forget about it or stop myself. A swoosh goes off and my stomach plummets. *I did it.*

Sitting there, I slowly close my laptop and shove the letter beneath it, waiting. It's not like my laptop is going to announce a new message or that I'll receive a satellite signal to my brain that he replied. I will have to find the courage to open it back up and check to see if he answered later, but I still wait, a sense of resolution overpowering the nausea that was taking root in my belly. It gradually unravels each knot that had settled in my subconscious.

Breathe with me.

I close my eyes; imagining myself back in that small little camper with Evan slid all the way against me, whispering those words in my ear and my heart stops. It was always when I knew I wasn't alone that I had strength; that's when the pain stopped and I was free.

He knew…he shared my grief over that night. I could face it and fight away the fear and heartache when we faced it together. I think about what the letter said, my mind reeling around what has been missing this whole time.

She suggested me healing through opening up further, by explaining to you what had happened…

I recite the words silently then repeat them again. A more profound sensation moves through me than I've ever felt before; a sense of strength, courage and confidence that barely gives way to light at the end of this dark and lonely tunnel that I've been trying to claw my way out of for years.

Can I do this? Can I?

My hand falls to my phone and I rip it up, urgency pulsing through every cell in my body with the need to face it all, to open up, to free fall into a place I've never ventured. Evan's face comes to mind; his laugh, his smile, his voice. *Breathe, Piper, Breathe with me.*

I pull up the first name on my phone, the most recent contact and begin to text.

Me: Hey, I know you're working today, but I need to talk to you. Would you want to come over and hang out here at my house later?

After hitting send, and as always, it takes only seconds to hear a chime.

Abby: Sure! Sounds great. Everything ok?

I sigh, knowing everything will be ok, even though this will be the hardest step I've ever had to make in my life. *Can I even do this? Can I finally open up to everyone?* The fear of possibly chickening out once it's upon me rises within me as I read her text, so I nip it in the bud so that I have no choice.

> **Me: Everything is fine. I need to talk to you about what went on at the restaurant...about what you brought up in the bathroom. There's a lot I need to tell you and a lot I should have told you a long time ago. No worries, but I'm just ready to talk. :)**

> **Abby: I'm always here and yes, I will head right over after work. I'll bring us some greasy cheeseburgers and fries and we can talk all night. Sleep over? ;)**
> **I love you! <3**

I smile at her response, braver by the minute.

> **Me: Ok...see you later. Make mine a double cheeseburger. ;)**

> **Abby: You got it. :)**

I don't stop at that, pulling up Dad's name and shooting him a quick text as well, knowing I probably won't hear back from him as fast.

> **Me: I was hoping we could chit chat when you got home. Love you, Daddy.**

Placing the phone in my lap, I know I won't worm my way out of this. Abby won't let me forget it after I said I need to talk. She should have been a detective; she's pretty dang persuasive and has a pretty sick ability to sense when someone is holding back. I'm surprised she didn't ask me years ago about the blackouts, but if she had any sort of a clue what may have happened, I know Abby has the heart enough to respect my privacy. No more...I'm getting all of this out. First Abby, then I'll tell Dad that I want to talk to Mom, then whatever comes with speaking to Trent. I can't hide from this anymore. It's only fueling the fire and turning my life into a mess. *I can do this; I have to do this.*

Never Again

Evan

THE COUCH SHIFTS AND I look over at the pain in my ass that has the same lack of restraint in opening her yap as I do. I'm six beers into my second week of moping and I really don't care to stop myself this time.

"Abby, tell me something…do you plan to be in the passenger seat for every major break up moment, or is that just a coincidence?"

All eyes swing to me sitting lazily on the couch; the same place where I planted my ass two hours ago when I showed up at my best friend's house, hell bent on drinking my sorrows away. Judd's mouth drops open, Alyssa's eyes grow heavy with remorse, and Abby, she just flat out looks like she may knock my lights out.

"Evan!" Judd's eyes spring open and he looks from Abby to Alyssa.

"No…no, no. I'm fine. It's fine. He's pissed at me," Abby snaps, stopping Judd from scolding me like I'm a stupid teenage kid mouthing off to their parents. "Just let him get this out. I'm sure he's been waiting the last two weeks to say it."

I snicker, kicking my head back into the plush cushions of the couch. Abby stands up from the arm, pulling her hands up to her hips; I laugh harder, the vibrations moving from my stomach up into my chest and spewing out my mouth in a breathy chuckle.

"You know, you remind me of a cat," I slur out, pointing my index finger with my thumb and other three fingers wrapped around my half-empty beer bottle. "Like right now…" Abby lowers her chin, glaring at me through her lashes. "I'd imagine if you were a cat, you'd have your fur all raised and be doing one of those high arched back stances right now as a form of intimidation. Like 'Hey, I'm bigger than you so give it your best shot.'"

"Are you finished?" she snaps, looking unfazed and completely unamused.

"Me?" I yell out dramatically, nudging my chin back sarcastically with a smirk. "Hell, I'm just getting started. I've got a huge ass mouth on me, or haven't you heard? I'm sure you have. I mean with not taking any of my calls or responding to my text messages, Piper had to have plenty of girly gab time on her hands." I take a couple more gulps of my beer, the hard circular edge of the bottle pressed to my lips as a flood of bitter liquid slides down my throat. "But you know, I think that's why I like you so much, Abby. You have a ginormous freaking mouth too and neither one of us know how to gauge when we should keep the damn things shut. I mean, you just spout off and…"

"Evan, really?!" Judd tries to shut me down, but Abby once again stops him.

"Oh no, seriously Judd, let him keep going," she bites out, shifting her hand across her chest and slowly drumming her fingertips against her left bicep.

Alyssa spits out a laugh; Judd and Abby turn her way, causing her to stand up stiff as a board and stop.

"What?!" Her eyes widen as she walks towards me and plops down on the cushions. "I like drunk-Evan. He's even more entertaining than smartass-sober-Evan."

I wobble my head to the side and smile, looking at her through hazy eyes. "You're alright too, Alyssa. Any girl that gets her freak on with my best friend as much as you do, has to be cool…"

"Oh geez, Evan…" Judd starts again, persistent on quieting me, which cracks me up.

I never look over at him, keeping my eyes trained on Alyssa and my case of beer on the table behind her. "You hand me another one of those?" Quickly, I raise the one in my hand to my lips and guzzle it down.

She complies, twisting at the waist and grabbing a beer with a subtle pop and fizz sound.

Once I have a new beer in my hand, I carry on, determined to fire Abby up.

"Speaking of the difference in siblings, I ran into one of your admirers, Abby, the same night that you opened your mouth. You know, the one that you so graciously helped out with?" I raise my brows, waiting for a response, maybe even for her to lunge at me. A slow rumble moves up my chest and comes out on a growl type chuckle as I take several more gulps of my beer.

Abby shifts, pushing her lips to the side as she bites the inside of it.

"Ooooo, an admirer? I wanna hear about this."

I snicker at Alyssa's enthusiasm, even though Abby's mood is slowly altering from playful annoyance to a fiery volcano of f-bombs and obscenities that is sure to explode on me at any minute.

"Ooooh yeah," I holler out, not sure if my words are coming out in one long mass of slurs now or if I'm pausing long enough to separate them. "We had a long chat…"

Judd steps forward, glancing at Abby every other second. He's more than likely expecting Abby to lose her cool and claw at my face like some rabid animal, but she's a mountain of restraint tonight.

"Evan, hey, why don't I take you home and you can pick up your truck tomorrow?"

Abby doesn't even acknowledge him. "Is that so?" she pauses, genuinely curious. "So who was this admirer?" She pulses her eyes, widening them then quickly drawing them back to a perturbed squint.

"Well, I'll give you a clue…" I stop before going on, "He said you are a pain in the ass. Ohhhh…ouch. You? A pain in the ass…never." I mock, snickering to myself, nearly ready to crack another beer open. "Oh hey, did your boyfriend ever settle on getting that tattoo of your name across his bicep? He could always get Abby spelled out creating an ass out of the two B's…" I put my free hand up in the air, creating a letter 'C' with my thumb and index finger, then carefully doing the same with the other while keeping my bottle tightly grasped in my hand. "It'd be perfect and very fitting."

Abby stands still and the room goes silent, everyone looking over at her. *This is no fun; she's not even letting me pester her.*

"Ok, finish up your beer and I'll take you home," Judd suggests again.

"I'm beginning to think you don't like my company," I tease, knowing the threat of a woman going ballistic is making him nervous as hell.

Judd shakes his head, but Abby beats him to the punch, once again.

"Oh no, Evan…we are all enjoying watching you make an ass out of yourself."

Snickering loudly, I point back at her, my grin unable to stretch any further. "Oh no, we can give all the credit of being an ass to you, remember? Come on Abby, I thought we just established this. Tristan clearly pointed out that you are the biggest pain in the ass."

"Tristan?! Oh well, there's someone you wanna listen to on saying someone is a pain, not to mention, he was talking to you. I am sure you both could lap me in the 'ass' department."

I crack up, about to slide off the cushion as I lean forward, my arm slung around my torso to keep my stomach from busting in two.

"And if anyone should get a picture of an ass tattooed on their body it's you or you know, there are more suitable body parts that you could get. I'm sure some of the shops could draw a penis across your forehead…"

"Penis!" I burst out, my abs damn near about to rupture. "Such polite language, Abby. Are you saying I'm a penis head?"

"You're a d…"

"Ok, let's go!" Judd intervenes, keys already in hand and leaning down to grab my arm.

Abby switches gears fast, still eyeing me a second before looking at Judd. "I'm leaving too…I thought you two were going to see the late show?" she says, already sounding calm; her voice sounds as if it's in a tunnel.

With a little help from Judd, I make my way to my feet, the room spinning and my whole body swaying as I try to steady myself from going head first to the ground. I chuckle. *This'll be fun.*

"No big deal…" Judd mumbles, keeping a tight lock on my upper arm as I wobble one foot forward followed by the next.

"You know what? I'll take him back to his apartment."

I look up, amused as hell just as Judd and Alyssa snap their heads to look at Abby as well.

"Whoa, you plan on dropping him at the dump or just throwing him out of the car while you're doing 60 down the highway?" Judd's voice carries a trace of concern hidden beneath the sarcasm.

Nudging my chin his way as I side step, smile and congratulate him, "Nice…good one."

Abby sighs, moving in beside me. I look over, watching her face as she draws one brow up with a small smirk. *She's up to something.*

"No, seriously. You guys get to the movie and I'll take him home," she pauses, looking around at all three of us staring at her, me trying to hold back my laughter. "I promise. The penis head will arrive home safe and sound."

No holding back on that one. As I bend forward, I slide out of Judd's grasp and face plant right into the floor on a gut wrenching laugh.

"Come on…"

"Are you sure? He can barely walk. How do you plan to…?"

"I got it, you go…"

Moving slowly, all chatter merges into one garbled voice, my vision gets hazier and my mind spins. I try to concentrate, hearing a steady rhythm of a vehicle starting up and other background noises, but it all soon blends together. I fall, my ass and back hitting something solid, then a pressure bears down on my left thigh near my knee.

"Well, help me out here…get your feet in the car…"

I snicker again, knowing Abby is having a time with me. *Oh, this will be fun.* A door slams and I jolt to the side, then another click and another door slamming. *I wonder if she has a tarp and shovel in her trunk.*

"Abby, you're just a saint, taking care of me like this…" I laugh. "You still think I'm a penis head?" I fall forward, spitting out a lungful of laughter and not sure if I can even sit back up. "So, what's that friend of yours up to tonight? Maybe we can call her, from your phone, she doesn't answer my calls…" my mouth suddenly feels as though it may be hinged open this whole time and my sentences just one big conjoined word. Closing my eyes, my whole body grows heavy as I remain bent forward in a touch my toe position.

"I have a better…" Abby's voice trails off…

The ringing of a phone goes off. *Is that mine?*

It sounds again, this time louder. *Geez!* Stretching my hand out to the side, I reach for my phone, expecting to find it in its usual resting spot on my nightstand, instead my hand finds something soft and fuzzy. I keep my head buried in my pillow, the likelihood of me smothering growing more imminent by the second as I sweep my hand side-to-side, getting more frantic with each swipe. *Holy shit…what the hell…is that hair?*

I raise my head in a panic, the nostalgic remnants of some girl laughing at me in my drunken haze last night, creeping up in my head and causing me to freak out a little.

Bam…

My head cracks on something solid sending a shooting pain through my skull and making me extremely aware that I am in fact, not in bed at all. A dull throbbing sensation continues as I turn my head to see what my hand is on. I squeeze my eyes shut to ward off the discomfort right as another sensation sparks in my ass. *Geez, what did I do, sit on a broken beer bottle while I was drunk?* Opening my eyes, I feel like the biggest dingbat around as I view my outstretched hand grasping at the rug. I begin to chuckle, the vibrations of a light laugh jogging my body just enough to send another throbbing sensation through the back of my head to the top of my scalp and making me cringe. *Oh I need some Aspirin.*

Slowly and steadily, pushing up onto my hands and bending back, I sit up with my heels below my ass. *I'm never drinking again.* My eyes scan my surroundings, trying diligently not to make any sort of quick movement that will spark more hangover pains. I usually don't get sick the morning after, but I drank a hell of a lot last night. I don't remember anything after leaving Judd's apartment. I continue to look around, my eyes landing on my phone on the floor, exactly where I had heard it only minutes before. *Geez, this is going to be a doozy of a day.*

Throwing myself forward to grab it, I immediately regret my quick movement and feel that my head is not screwed on very tight. A sharp stabbing sensation burns through my ass and my head nearly sends me back to bed for the remainder of the day. *What the hell!* I grab it and waste no time.

Just what the hell did I drink after I left his house. I trip over snippets of my memory, Abby's face coming up time and time again from pissed off to cracking up to nearly gloating. I click on Judd's name, hoping he can fill in the blanks.

Ring, ring…

Pulling the phone away from my ear, I check the time; 12:31. *Well hell, everyone should be awake by now.*

"Hello," Judd picks up on the third ring.

I jerk the phone back to my ear, working hard to put my left foot out and use the bed to stabilize myself enough to stand. Another pain pierces my left cheek. *Geeeeez! What the....*

"Hey," I try my best to mask my agony over the ferocious conglomeration of aches and pains in my body.

"You survived?"

I snicker, dipping my brows, scrunching my face and holding my other hand over my ass.

"Of course I survived," I say in a tone that doesn't send a shock wave of aches through my head as I make my way into the bathroom. My legs feel like limp, dangly noodles that may not be able to hold me up. "I *have* been drunk before, and even drunker than last night, I'm sure."

Judd laughs, "No, I meant I'm glad to see Abby didn't kill you."

After rounding the corner into the bathroom, I turn with my back to the mirror and start unfastening my pants button and zipper with the phone pressed into my shoulder. I tug at the waist band of my pants and pull them down, immediately finding a white bandage over my asscheek. *What.The.Hell!*

I grab the corner of the gauze and look up, a memory of me signing some document while Abby ranted about how I was not drunk to some long haired dude behind a counter.

My eyes draw up to the mirror and I stop, holding my fingertips to the corner of the bandage and my phone securely pressed to the side of my face as I stare.

"Abby, huh?" I mumble practically to myself, putting the pieces of the puzzle together as I read the bright red letters written across the mirror in either marker or lipstick or something:

WHO'S THE PAIN IN THE ASS NOW, BITCH!! :>

My mouth falls open and I barely register Judd's voice at first, "Hey...Evan! You got home, right?!"

I shake my head and look back down at the bandage that is still covering up what I fear may be completely permanent.

"Ahhh, yeah, I got home. Hey, I gotta go."

Judd says something, but I click end call before I can say another word, pull up Abby's name in my phone and hit call with my pants still pulled down below my hips. My eyes stay glued to my covered up cheek in the mirror; *you've got to be kidding me!*

The phone rings once and I start to peel the corner of the gauze, squeezing all the features of my face together into a scared-to-look sort of frown. Another ring and I peel it more, making out bright red, inflamed looking flesh surrounding dark black ink that is fully embedded into my skin. *You're kidding me!* Another ring and I rip it off, killing the suspense with a blaze of pain and a sting that doesn't even measure up to what I am feeling in that general area. *Holy shit!*

"Hello, sunshine," Abby's voice comes on the line pert and chipper like she just destroyed someone's life that she hates with a passion, then continued on to win the lottery and go on an all-day girls shopping excursion to blow it all; gratification and satisfaction laces her every word. "How are we feeling today?" her smile drips off of every word.

My mouth, which currently sits on the floor, hinged open in shock and disbelief as I look over every swoop of the tattoo that now takes up residency on my very pale white butt cheek. I begin to trace the letters, mentally following along each cursive letter as if I have an invisible pencil, then stop. My eyes move pain-stakingly in astonishment to the heart above the letter 'I', to the grass that adorns the bottom of the word, onto the small frilly flower behind the 'R' and then up to the dainty damn butterfly that sits on the capital 'P'. *Son.Of.A.Bitch!*

"Abby, what the fu…"

"Hey…" she cuts me off, a cocky tone that is ready to let me have it even more than she apparently already has. "I just figured that would be a change up from the lame-ass tattoo that Hayden may get on his bicep. Seemed pretty fitting…don't you think?"

"Ohhh Come On!" I holler out, staring longer at the tattoo, with the phone now crushed in my hand. "Are you serious?!"

Abby laughs. "Yeah, I think that is exactly what the tattoo artist said when I showed him what to put on it."

"What the hell was I doing the whole time when you were discussing this particular design?"

She lets out a squeal, enjoying the hell out of my agony, "Oh, you were right there, talking with us. You had a ridiculously huge smile on your face the whole time."

"Geez! You mean, I didn't see the freaking flower and say…Oh whoa, whoa, hold up…lets butch this bitch up and add a skull and cross bones or a baseball bat or a damn hammer or something?" I whine, sounding like a girl now with a pleading tone and hoping that I at least spoke up.

"Oh no…are you kidding! You couldn't even see straight at that point. You probably thought the tulip was a bat," she says in a matter of fact way. "Oh, but hey, it's better than my first idea."

"Well just what the hell was that, dolphins and gold fish jumping through the 'P'?"

"Oooo, that would have been good too. Nope, I was going to have them tattoo a penis to your forehead, you know, given the fact that you are now a penis-head…your words not mine."

I imagine Abby on the other line, painting her nails or doing some nonchalant, every day thing while I am freaking out that I am now branded across my ass with something that makes absolutely no sense to have on my body.

"Well, you should have gone with the dong on my face, because she won't even talk to me and now…"

Abby spits out a loud laugh. "Well I really didn't think you'd go for that one, but not to worry, I saved the sketch. We'll do that next time we go out."

"Oh hell, no, woman. My drunken, ink covered ass will stay far, far away from you."

"Well, I think there is only one solution here, don't you think?"

I stare ahead, unable to unlock the trance I have on my new found body décor.

"What's that…skin grafts? The makeup shit you girls put on your face across my ass every time I have a date? Butt implants?"

"No, Evan…maybe rather than being a pain in the ass, maybe you need to just go and get her. I mean it looks like your ass belongs to her now, after all."

My eyes focus on the curve of every letter, ignoring all the lame frilly garbage that makes me look like a tree-hugging, nature-loving dude or extremely secure in my masculinity. *What the…*

I don't even respond to what she says, I don't need to. I know she's right and what better to remind me to get my ass in gear than this.

"You know I'll get you back, right?"

"Well you know that I have that other tattoo design handy at any moment I need it."

I chuckle, looking at the blades of grass along the bottom of the tattoo, "I guess my ass would be grass if I tried anything to get you back anyways, huh?"

"Yep so you better get your ass on the move."

I shake my head; there is no getting one over her. "Bye, Abby."

Clicking end call, I set the phone on the counter and slide my jeans up, nearly jumping out of my skin as they brush over the red, irritated flesh. I grab my phone and bring up a text to her.

Me: Please tell me there are instructions for taking care of this thing?

Abby: Hahahaha…It's not a puppy, Evan!
But yeah…they are in your nightstand drawer. And wth is with all the condoms? Good grief! Maybe we should get Whore branded across the other cheek?

Shaking my head, I crack up at her feistiness.

Me: No! Never Again!

A Long time coming

Piper

I GET TO THE RESTAURANT, almost ashamed that I lied to Dad when he asked where I was going. I'm not even sure why I didn't just say I was going to get a bite to eat with a friend. *Whoa, well a friend he definitely is not.* He's family, but I don't even consider him that. He's…

I don't even want to think about it.

"How many?" the hostess greets me.

"Ummm." I look behind her, not even sure of whether he will be here yet or what he would look like now. *Maybe I should just take off back home.* I glance at my phone, nervously clutched in my hand as if it can shield me from what will be said today. *11:38, I'm early.* "I'm meeting someone so I guess two."

"Right this way…"

I follow along, not particularly paying attention to where I'm going, my feet are on autopilot as I flip my head from one side to the next, nervous that he's here, yet scared that he may not come. When he answered my email almost immediately, before Abby even got to my house, I instantly panicked. Lucky for me, Abby is a terrific mediator and helped me through talking to him and setting up a time to meet with him. The last two weeks have been an emotional roller coaster, however this is something I knew I had to do alone.

"Will this be ok?"

Looking around, I'm not even certain when we stepped back outside to the front patio. "Yes, thank you."

The hostess leaves. Wrapping my fingertips around the cool steel back of the outdoor chair, I pull it out and slide down, swinging my purse over the back of it. People walk by on the sidewalk, going about life as normal and all the while I'm screaming inside and on the verge of running back home. *I thought I could do this, but maybe I can't.* I turn around, the need to flee fully alive and burning through me to a point of nearly shooting flames right out of the heels of my feet to get me to the door. Standing, I reach for my purse.

"Trent…Hey, wait…" a female voice hollers out by the street.

I freeze, my eyes wide and pointed in the wrong direction. Moving in slow motion, I turn my head to look towards the street, afraid to even see. My chin barely brushes my shoulder. *Is it him?*

"What, I gotta go," a dark brown haired guy with his back to me calls out. He stands beside a gray SUV, dipping his head into the passenger window. "Oh geez, thanks. I can't believe I almost forgot that."

A pretty young blonde sits in the driver's seat, leaning over and handing him what looks to be a wallet. I glance to the back seat and see a little boy busy playing with a toy train, oblivious to anything going on around him. I stare, hypnotized, still unable to see the guy's face as he darts to the back window and taps on the glass. The window goes down and he bends his head in, quickly spinning around and darting to my left towards the entrance of the restaurant.

"Bye Daddy," the little boy hollers.

I snap my head in the other direction to the guy that I still have not gotten a good enough look at. He stops at the door, holding it open and turns directly in my view.

"Bye baby."

My eyes go wide and my mouth hangs open in astonishment. His big brown eyes dart right past me, clearly unaware that I am here or perhaps not recognizing me, but I'd never forget his face. I lower myself back down to the chair, slowly, because at this point I'm not sure my legs will even move. Turning, I plant myself back down and I place my hands in my lap, bowing my shoulders and leaning my chest in towards the edge of the table, to get as close to a comforting fetal position as I can get.

Commotion sounds past the doorway to the patio. My heart picks up pace and my breathing comes out in quick huffy spurts.

"I'm not sure, but I might know if I see…" I stop breathing as the same voice comes in behind me and then stops. "I got it. Thanks."

My ears pick up on the rustling of fabric and soft footsteps and my whole body quakes. I can't even look up. My mind flicks to that night; I squeeze my eyes shut, a wave of fear crashing over me and making me spin, as I start to feel the bed dip beside me and the sheets above me stir.

"Piper?"

I flinch, an earthquake of panic flashing through me. Goosebumps shoot over my skin, but I'm fully conscious. The tremor of darkness that crept over and threatened to engulf me, passes by as I open my eyes.

"Piper?"

I look up, fear, remorse, anger, hurt and pain all taking a backseat as I stare at his face. My heart beats at a normal pace and my breathing slows. I have no clue how to feel at this moment. A weepy sensation hits the back of my eyes and pushes forward under my lids and until I may cry, yet my heart doesn't ache. I don't say a word as he continues to stand, looking around and fidgeting his hands like a little boy. Staring back up at his face, I quickly find the same kid that came to stay with us after his mom checked into some drug rehab program; the same square jaw, a hint of freckles over his nose and dark brown eyes that made him look like blood relation rather than an adopted cousin. I pause, looking back over his eyes that seem worried and lacking confidence as his brows dip in regret.

That alone makes my voice reemerge, "Yeah, it's me." I press my lips together, not sure of what else to say.

He looks around, seeming lost, but I don't even have it in me to tell him to sit.

"Can I get you two something to drink?" a waitress calls out, coming as a surprise, because I didn't even see her walk up.

He jumps too, swiftly pulling out a chair and taking a seat. "Just a water."

I nod, "Same for me." I could really go for something stronger, but I'm not sure I'll even have the desire to drink or eat.

She leaves and it's just us again, awkwardly looking around the surface of the table as if there is some hidden treasure that we are eager to find, but we both know better; it should be shameful for him to look at me and I just can't bring myself to look at him for long. I suck in a breath of courage and pull my eyes shut for a moment.

"Thank you…" he mumbles and my eyes spring open, staring right at him, fearlessly.

"What?" his words hit me wrong and a bite of anger takes hold as I grit my teeth.

"For meeting with me. I know I'm the last person you want to sit across from." He looks around at the few tables that are occupied around us and it suddenly occurs to me just how uncomfortable this is for him too.

"You have a child?"

He swings his attention to me, looking shell-shocked by my question, then flips his head around to look at the sidewalk only a stone's throw away from our table.

"Oh…yeah." Pointing his thumb over his shoulder, he goes on, "My wife, Sarah and son, Jax."

He clears his throat, still looking uneasy, but I keep my eyes locked on him, unable to look away now. *He has a family?*

Just as I think about it, but before I can open my mouth, he speaks again, "I met Sarah a few years ago and it took me a long time to open up to her about my past, but I finally did. I honestly never saw myself having a family…" he pauses, his throat bobbing as he looks to the side.

The same waitress as before places two glasses on the table and pulls out a small notepad from the black pocketed apron at her waist.

"Are you ready to order?"

"Oh, ummm…" he swings his eyes to me, dumbfounded as if we aren't sitting in a restaurant. "Yes, can I have a coffee and then just a bagel?"

She jots it down, moving her pen quickly, then looks at me.

I put my hand up. "Nothing for me, thank you."

She darts off, and he goes on, "Before I told Sarah, our relationship was all over the place. I think we broke up about every couple of months. I'd just get freaked out, almost scared of myself," he stops abruptly and I look around, expecting the waitress to already be back. "Is this ok? I mean, I figured you wanted to know about…" he stops again.

Shaking my head, I'm not sure how to respond. I don't want anything from him; I know I don't want to hear I'm sorry, but I'm not sure what I expected from today. I'm just here, hoping for some sort of peace from my own chains; the chains he gave me all those years ago.

So I say the only words that make sense, because I sure have nothing to say at this point. "Go on."

His brows shoot up, crinkling his forehead. "Ok…ummm, well, I finally told her and it helped. It was almost a relief to share it with someone. I never told anyone up to that point, except for my counselor. I didn't really think there was anyone else that knew."

This comes as a shock, because last week I finally got the courage to call my mother. The reunion wasn't peaceful. I ended up crying and telling her exactly what I thought of her abandoning me at a time I needed her most, but what ignited more fury than I knew I could hold is when she told me that her sister had told her about Trent years ago. That's why she took him in, yet when her own daughter accused him of doing the same act, she immediately went into denial. Nothing ever ripped out my heart more than to know that; she knew it was true, yet still left me.

"But my mom knew…" I enlighten him with info I'm sure he didn't know I was aware of.

His eyes go wide in surprise. "Yes…she did," he says it slowly. "I didn't know she knew for the longest time though. I wasn't even aware of what had happened in your immediate family. I moved back out here when I was eighteen and I reconnected with her. She told me all that had happened in a brief summary and how she felt it was her fault that she let me stay with you all. I felt even more ashamed after that."

I crinkle my eyes on his words, an onset of tears coming into my view. Taking a deep breath, I instantly push them away, but cannot make my tongue work. A lump settles in my throat and clogs up any sound from coming out.

Trent stares at me for a minute before going on, filling the silence at our table.

"Listen, the same as I told you in the letter…I know this won't take away anything, but I want to tell you what happened to me. It doesn't excuse it or make it right or…"

He stares ahead at me; I flinch and then nod my head, nudging him to go on. I'm having a hard time viewing him as being too nervous or afraid or worried to approach this subject considering he was the one actually bold enough to execute the same act upon me. I just want to sit here and listen, because I don't know how to join in on this type of conversation; just give me all the information and let me process it.

"Yeah, well, I…ahhh…" he fidgets his hands, placing them on the table and flicking his thumbs back and forth against each other as he looks at them, concentrating as if he's twirling a strand of yarn around them. "So, I guess I'll just…"

For some reason, my heart dips, watching him struggle; I'm not sure why. I owe him nothing. He, however, owes me everything, my youth back, my innocence, courage to move forward, more than he'll ever know. *Or does he know?* I dip my brows, compassion filling my heart, tears blurring my vision, yet confusion over why this is even coming over me.

I speak up, without even knowing I had any words to say, "Trent, just tell me...I'll listen," I say it like he's my friend, like he's someone that did not wrong me. I offer him the shoulder he didn't have before his actions were directed at me; I offer him what I have had little of because of my own fears.

His fingers stop their slow dance with each other, and he looks at me, a disbelieving, touched emotional look glazing his eyes. Crumpling up his face into a pained frown, he pulls his lips together into a straight line before opening his mouth with a gentle nod.

"Ok..." he squeezes his eyes shut, then back open as he lowers his voice, "It started when I was 8 and not too long after she adopted me. I was already situated in my new room, a new school and tried to get in the same routine that came with going to a new home, but then she started having parties. She and her friends would drink and get high, I even got up in the middle of the night to go to the restroom and found one of her friends shooting up. A couple of weeks later it started."

A knot forms in my stomach and although I don't even have to ask, I do. I need to hear. "What started?"

He gulps, nudging his chin upward and looking to the sky for a brief moment.

"The same friend of hers that I walked in on, came into my bedroom in the middle of the night." He presses his eyes shut and I do the same, a revolting nausea coming over me. "She told me to stay quiet and that it wouldn't hurt. I stayed quiet just like she said. I had heard things from other kids that had dealt with sexual traumas, but I never thought it would happen to me. I guess, I was in shock and too scared to say a thing. I just laid there." He takes a huge breath, his shoulders rising as he glances over my head.

I look down, seeing his coffee and bagel at the table, having absolutely no idea when it was delivered. I'm not even sure he notices.

"She did things to make my body cooperate and honestly at that point, I never even knew anything about that sort of thing, how it worked, what was done, but I hated it the whole time. I'd start to sob and she would tell me to be quiet…"

Holding my hand up as tears stream down my face, I stop him. I can't listen to it all. My heart aches and my whole body shakes in pain, but not for me, I hurt for him; for him. *How could I feel anything but hate for him?* There's one thing I need to know and it's the hardest thing to ask.

"I'm sorry. Should I stop?"

I shake my head, then nod, pausing before shaking my head again. "I understand." I don't fully, but I get what happened to him. "I just…well, it's hard to hear…" gritting my teeth, I halt, focusing on my breathing and trying to control my trembling hands as I see that tears also glisten in his eyes.

"I know. I'll skip those details. That just went on for weeks, then months and soon it turned into years. Not always the same girl, but each one knew the drill like it was a scheduled event," He lets out an incredulous deep gurgle that comes across as an insincere breathy chuckle. "They always made me promise not to say anything and what did I do, I listened. I knew it was wrong, I knew what they did was not normal and wasn't supposed to happen, but I still kept to myself, too scared to speak up."

Listening, I think back to my own reasoning for keeping it to myself, for not yelling when he did it. I was scared; I also knew it was wrong, but I stayed silent.

"Does that make it our fault? Because we said nothing?" Looking past the table to the ground, I say the words out loud, but saying them more to myself, partly unaware that my voice has even carried to him.

"No," he whispers, startling me with the alarm in his voice. "It's not ours at all. Wait, it's not your fault. You did nothing."

I look up at him, the only question I can ask resurfacing in my head and I know I need to ask it.

"If you knew it was wrong and you knew how it affected you, why did you do it to me?" I ask it in a whisper, the tears fully coming now, welling up and falling in huge droplets down to my chin.

His chest vibrates in two quick bounces as he seems to trip over a sucked-in breath.

"Ummm," he stumbles, returning to fidgeting. "This was the hardest part of my therapy, acceptance of why I did what I did."

"So why did you?" Suddenly the compassion I felt starts to ice back over to anger and hate, as if I heard nothing of what he shared.

"I…I was curious." His eyes seal shut and I watch as a small single tear rolls in slow motion down his cheek, leaving a wet mark on his skin like a scar for his sin. My eyes continue in on their rain of tears and the vice on my heart lessens. "I wanted…" his voice cracks before he clears it in a growly grunt. "I had it happen so many times by girls that were older and that I didn't know and then there was you and I guess I was curious. I felt ashamed the second it happened and hated myself for it. I ahhh…"

I put my hand back up again, stopping him, but he opens his mouth again, "Piper, did you talk to anyone? Get help? I know I have no right to even ask, but after Jax was born I thought about it more and more, knowing I had left you with something I could not even handle for myself. I just always hoped that you had."

I shake my head, wobbling my chin back and forth quickly to answer him. "Not until I read your letter, that is."

A breath catches in my throat and I hold it. He gave me the courage to move forward, to get it out, to open up. Had I never received a word from him, I may have held it in forever and never had the strength to face life normally. Just being here shows the potency that finally knowing had over me; a sense of closure. A peace that I've longed for settles in my chest and spreads out within me and I let out the breath I was holding.

"I finally did," I tell him confidently, no longer afraid. "…and it was a long time coming."

This time

Evan

I RAP MY FIST FRANTICALLY on the door of her house. *Please be here, please be here!* I knew it wouldn't do any good. She'll probably look out the window and refuse to answer the door, have her dad give me some lame excuse of her being gone or just text *go away*, while I stand here foolishly. Abby told me to wait a day; it's been the worst one of my life.

I pound my fist on the door again, this time hard as the solid wood surface sends a splintering sensation through my knuckles, right to my wrist. I go to slam my hand against the door, looking back into the driveway and seeing no sign of her van, but still hopeful.

My hand falls forward and so do I; I snap my head back and kick my leg out to catch my fall.

"Whoa, Evan," her dad calls out, already clamping his hands down on my shoulders.

"Oh shit…I mean, damn it…ahhh, crap, sorry," I trip over every word, making a lousy impression of coming back into his daughter's life after a two-week hiatus. "Is Piper here?" I spit it out, trying to cover my tracks from a slur of cuss words and silly ramblings.

Her dad slides his lips to the side in a sly sort of smirk and subtly shakes his head. *Great!*

"She's not, but…" he opens the door wider, waving his hand to the side to invite me in.

I don't need to come in if she's not here. "Do you know where she is?"

I'm sure my urgency is coming across in my tone, but he remains unaffected, keeping the door open and stepping to the side on his own invitation. I do the polite thing, stepping through the door and into their living room with a slow burning fizz of adrenaline working its way up my throat as my anxiety over finding her increases. *My mouth might very well get the best of me today.*

"Sure, well ok," I mumble.

Pete rolls his eyes chuckling, then shuts the door. "She has a calendar that she writes down her appointments and schedule. I was going to offer to look and see if she wrote it down, but you're welcome to just comb the town if you'd like."

I cock my head, genuinely impressed. *Now who doesn't appreciate a good ole smartass; that deserves some patience.*

"That'd be great," I chuckle out.

Pete laughs and motions for me to follow. "Rooting around in a girl's stuff isn't something I would recommend, but she's brought your name up a few times and I just so happen to like you, so I'm more than happy to help you out." He glances over his shoulder and a step of pride tugs at me as I follow.

A dad that likes me? Who would have ever thought? Awesome!

"Hey, I can use all the help there is. She has shut it down pretty tight. I think she even has my number blocked or something."

He snickers, "Probably. She can be pretty bull-headed when she decides something."

I grit my teeth, losing a bit of confidence in worming my way back in there, ass tattoo or no ass tattoo.

"Yeah, she can."

We both round the corner of her bedroom, and he knocks the door open with a worn-out creak. I pause, staying in the doorway and looking around as he walks over to her desk. I look over her perfectly made bed with a ridiculous amount of fluffy and frilly ass pillows across the top, a small folded-up blanket slung across the bottom then over to her dresser, decorated with an arsenal of lotion and perfume bottles like she's trying to keep the department store in business.

"I do know she was meeting with a friend, but not sure where. She actually just left a bit ago so you probably passed her on your way into the subdivision."

I swing my attention over to the desk, which seems out of place in her seemingly neat and tidy room. Her laptop is slung open with the sun highlighting a weeks' worth of dust; with the sheen of the wood on her dresser, it definitely stands out. A crumpled sheet of paper that looks like it's been through hell and back sticks out from beneath her bright white laptop, photo albums sit stacked behind it, a few with pictures sticking out from the corners and papers strung along the top one. Then there is a small notebook resting to the side, which Pete now runs his finger across.

"Ok, looks like she must be having a late breakfast with that friend in Rosemore. I hope you didn't come all the way over from your place."

I don't even care about the wasted gas or time. "Where at?"

"Sonny's Café, that little place over on the…"

"I know where it is." I spin around abruptly before thinking, then turn back to face him. Pointing my hand as if I'm staging an armed robbery as a kid sporting my finger gun, I relay my gratitude, "Thanks. I'm gonna go get her," I say slowly as if I'm asking for permission to leave.

"Well get your ass in gear then."

Dipping my brows, I subtly place my hand over my throbbing new skin graphic, a bit of awkwardness easing over me that I'm standing here with his daughter's name on my ass. I throw him a thumbs up so I don't burst out laughing at the sheer irony of his words, then take off.

My pickup still drags with my foot pressed to the floorboard as I come into Rosemore and make a right, heading to Sonny's. As soon as

I get there, frustration starts to throw me into a frenzy of wanting to flip everyone off to get out of my way. I park around the corner and choose to walk up rather than fighting for a closer space, but just as the restaurant comes into view, so does Piper. She's facing the sidewalk, but my eyes quickly dart to the person she's looking at. *What the hell?!*

My step slows and I stare. The dude's profile is all I can make out and although I can't see his full face, something about him is familiar. I walk closer, close enough for Piper to see me, but she is so caught up in the conversation that she seems to be oblivious to everything around her. I look closer at the guy, coming up to the left of the black wrought-iron fence they have gating the patio dining space off from the street.

"I never did, no…" his deep voice reaches my ears and I step closer, ready for Piper to see me at any moment, but kind of feeling a little weird about it.

"But Trent, didn't it just…"

I watch Piper's lips move, but all of my hearing stops shortly after I hear the name. Whipping my head back over to him, I step all the way up to the fence, placing my hand against the metal frame with an iron grip. My blood boils on that name as I grind my teeth in a hateful fury.

"Evan!" Piper calls out my name and he turns to look at me; I can't look away. I want nothing more than to lunge over the fence and attack him.

"What the hell are you doing here?!" my voice comes out through a clamped jaw.

His eyes go wide and he stands, Piper jumping up a few feet behind him.

"Evan, what are you doing here?" she returns my question back to me.

I ignore her, strangling the fence as if it is him.

"Evan…Mitch's brother, right?"

He looks back at Piper, appearing comfortable around her and this completely screws me up. She steps forward, closer to me, yet even closer to him and I can't help but stare back and forth from her to him, enraged. She can't take my calls for the past two weeks, yet she can find the time to come meet with the son of a bitch that stole so much from her. I squeeze harder on the steel bar, feeling as if my fingerprints may be permanently embedded in it. I flick my gaze back to her.

"Why are you here? With him?"

She puts her hand out, but my elevation of anger has far surpassed calming at this very moment. "How did you know where I was?" she counters my question with another one and I shake my head, not sure whether to just grab him or to be pissed off at her for putting herself through something like being around him.

How in the hell is he here? Why? How could she do this? It makes no sense.

"Listen, Evan…"

I toss my attention down to the bar I'm holding, flinching at her effort to patronize me.

"Piper, why?! Why?" I look up, pissed off at everything right now.

Trent uncomfortably glances around and a spark of satisfaction shoots through me. *I hope he is uncomfortable as hell.*

"Evan calm down. It's not what it looks like and it's hard to explain…"

I cut her off, annoyed that she won't explain this to me; when she's here gabbing with him like he's some long lost buddy. "I came here to tell you I'm sorry for having a big mouth, but now all I want to do is use it to tell him just how despicable and low he is. I don't understand how you can just sit here across from him like this is ok, like he didn't do anything."

Piper looks around. "Evan please. I don't need you coming to my rescue right now. I have it under control; I know what I'm…"

"Obviously not!"

"Just quiet down. I don't need you to protect me right no…"

"Oh you don't need me to protect you, huh?!"

"Evan, I didn't mean…"

"Listen, I know I used to be this guy that made you laugh and I always tried to make you forget all that happened. I thought forgetting was the only way to protect you, but I was wrong. No more jokes and no more standing back and allowing someone to hurt you in any way. They will have to deal with me and I'm not going to be nice about it."

"Evan, I know, I know..."

"No, you don't. I spout off plenty when I shouldn't, but I cannot fix this or help you if you keep..." I call out, my voice getting louder, and Piper looking around more and more.

"Listen, I'm going to go," Trent jumps in; we both turn to look at him, my lip curled and eyes squinted in an untamable rage.

"Is everything ok, Miss?" A waitress walks up, but I can't take my eyes off of Trent. He makes a wrong move and I will...

"He was just leaving." I snap my head to Piper as she stares at me; her words deliver a punch to the gut that softens the rage that was building inside of me.

"Piper..." I plead.

"Evan," she begins firmly, looking like she has been crying, yet a strength behind her eyes that makes me think she may not need me at all.

I try to break through the wall she's putting up to shut me out, "I just want to help. I can fix this."

"But you can't fix me," she whispers, gently without a trace of anger or bitterness.

I hang my head on her words, a raw sensation tugging at the walls of my chest and pulling them in on my heart. Looking back at her, I nod, pressing my lips together. I glance over to the asshole that stole her from me before she was even mine. He's the reason she's struggled all of these years. He's the one at fault for taking the most fragile pieces of her life, like trust and security and desire; feelings that were foreign to her at that age so they never even got a chance to develop and prosper.

Continuing to shake my head, I'm in total disagreement of her not allowing me to intervene here, yet, I will respect her wishes. I know what is best; what she wants. I won't try to fix this or her or whatever she views this as.

I'll keep my mouth shut this time; I'll be the one to throw in the towel for now.

I won't say a word to him no matter how sick and twisted I think he is.

I'll keep my distance and let her shove me out of her life and this time…

I'll be the one to walk away.

I'm free

Piper

I DON'T SAY A WORD as he walks off, looking defeated. I didn't even mean Evan when I told the waitress that he was leaving, I meant Trent. A part of me is shouting out to go catch him, to stop him from going. I haven't seen him in two weeks and it has without a doubt been the longest two weeks of my life, but right now, I have to finish this. I have to get full closure and, this is the final step before I can be completely whole again and ready to be a part of someone's life; a part of Evan's life. I won't walk out on him again and I refuse to give up on him like I have in the past.

"He cares about you...a lot."

I spin around, mystified by Trent's words. "He does?"

I already know the answer, but I ask it anyways. Every part of me wants to punish myself for torturing him with my incapability to cope for all these years. I should have been clinging to him for comfort and strength since he provided me with the will to keep breathing, but instead I shoved him as far away as possible.

"That's obvious. He didn't want to walk away. He should want to knock my teeth out. He should want to hurt me as much as I hurt you, and that alone is an infinity of pain. He does know?"

My stomach churns and I look back down at the sidewalk, not

even able to see him any longer.

"Yeah, he was the first person I told. He was the only one I told for the longest time," I say, regretting everything that just happened. *He wasn't hearing me. He was so angry by seeing Trent that he couldn't see straight.*

"Piper?"

I glance over to Trent, still standing near the table.

"Didn't that help? I mean, it seems you both care pretty deeply for each other, otherwise he wouldn't have been so angry and well, I don't think you'd be so determined to talk to me after all these years unless there was a reason behind it or maybe a person. I know, for me, Sarah was the flame that fueled my fire to get closure. Seems he's yours maybe?" I look down as a hand gently falls to my shoulder. "I'm sure he'll listen once he cools off."

I stare back at his hand on my shoulder and he quickly removes it.

"He is," I mumble out quietly, answering his initial question, but still focused on the fact that I didn't flinch; I didn't pass out. I sat here today and met with someone I was frightened of for a third of my life. *I did it.*

"He is…" a surge of relief and acceptance pierces my conscience and spreads out, urging me to go after him. "I have to go." I spin around, a smile in my heart as I dart to my chair to grab my purse. "Good luck with your son and wife."

I stop, a few paces away from him and for an instant want to hug him. Not to thank him for talking to me, but over a shared heartache; over a trauma that shaped and nearly destroyed both of us. I want to hug him for the little boy that he didn't get to be; for the fears he had to endure alone. He was the cause of my pain, yet also the undoing. *Who would have ever thought?*

Slowly, I reach my hand out, extending it between us. It catches his attention and gratitude fills every corner of his face as he grabs mine in turn and gives it a gentle shake.

"Good luck to you and your guy as well."

With that I sprint off, a sense of freedom I've never felt swelling within me.

Feeling more confident and less hesitant in my life by the second, I drive straight to Evan's apartment, but come up empty. I swing by his work and then onto Judd's to check there, remembering how Abby called me just yesterday and told me about her run in with Evan; I turn up unlucky at both. I stumble through my mind, my head an encyclopedia of information when it comes to Evan, yet still not able to think of a single place he could be.

But then it comes to me; the lake.

I drive and I drive, my heart on fire with the desire to bear my soul before him. A four-hour drive and I have plenty of thinking time, going over everything Trent said, finding forgiveness in my heart for what he did, imagining what I'll say to Evan and knowing one hundred percent that everything will be alright from here on out.

I pull into the gravel lot, parking directly behind his grandpa's cabin and his camper so I can get there faster. I barely even connect with the handle of the van door and already have it open, my feet taking the lead as I run to his camper.

Only fifteen feet or so, but my chest heaves in and out from my hurried pace and large leaps that got me here in two seconds flat. I lift my hand, ready to knock, not even thinking anymore of what to say. It'll come to me. Suddenly, a presence hits me; a feeling or sensation, and I look over.

The sun is setting over the lake, casting gorgeous beams of light over the waters that make it shine like ribbons of gold. But not even that amount of beauty captures my full attention. The dark hair and slumped over guy sitting at the edge of the dock grips everything within me and pulls me forward. Suddenly, I don't just see the twenty-year-old man that I'm so in love with, I see a little boy sitting alone on a dock with his fishing pole in hand; the same little boy that eyed me as I arrived at this place that first day, innocent and unaware of life's challenges and all the weight it can put on you. I see the little boy that looked so badly like he was in need of a friend to share all his secret hideouts with.

I race forward, running with a joy in my heart like I did after the first time I told him that I love him, running down that same hill. As soon as my foot steps on the dock, I expect an uncomfortable nostalgia to wash over me; for remnants of the past to sneak up and pull me into darkness. *Breathe?* I look at Evan, still with his back turned and know that those words will never have the same meaning. They won't have to save me anymore, but they will always be a part of me; a part of us; the bond that started it all. He lets out a heavy sigh, his entire body rising, then falling back down as he stays slumped forward. He looks as if he needs those words today, because now, I'm free.

Breathe with me

Evan

SITTING ALONE ON THE DOCK, the same place that I had my first kiss with Piper, I stare out at the rippling water and feel nothing but loss and emptiness. I never realized how much I need her; I love her. Squeezing my hand over the pole that has nothing but a cheap ass lure attached to the end, a gentle breeze blows and I catch the flowery perfumed scent that I'd know anywhere.

"Catching anything good?"

The words flow through the air before I can even turn, and I am suddenly cast back to the memory of a twelve-year-old girl walking up behind me while all I cared to do was catch some fish. I turn, holding tight to my pole when all I want to do is toss it into the water and run to her.

Looking over my shoulder, the sun shines over my head and across her, making her black locks of hair shine, the stuff she has on her eyes shimmers like glitter and her skin glows in a soft milky tone. My eyes pulse open wide in delight at seeing her standing there, completely unexpected.

"I caught some ink on my ass recently. No luck with the fish," I joke as always, but too caught up in a river of emotions to laugh.

I start to apologize, but she laughs, a carefree, calm and confident sound that I haven't seen in a long time; I stop all thoughts of not being myself.

"Maybe you should put their names on there and they might bite. You know, let them know your ass belongs to them, too."

This cracks me up, igniting an ache in my ribs as I heave out a laugh. *Abby, Abby, Abby...you sure as shit don't keep your mouth shut either.*

Piper, moves forward, not even gauging each step like she usually does; I regain my seriousness, still unable to shake my smile though. She takes a seat beside me, hanging her feet off the dock just like she has done a million times before, just to be beside me. I smile, a warmth filling my chest. I look down to her hand on the dock, wanting desperately to take it in mine.

"Evan, I'm sorry."

Looking up, all sentiments and longing jolts to a stop. "About what?" I barely get the words out, unable to fathom what she could be sorry about.

"About everything. About putting so much on you. About blaming you. For making you carry this and never having anyone to talk to." Her eyes mist over as her soft skin grazes over the hand I have in my lap. She pulls it into hers, wrapping it in a desperate hold, just like I wanted to do. I let out a disbelieving breath, ready to tell her there is nothing to be sorry for, but she goes on, "Most of all I'm so sorry that I pushed you away instead of pulling you closer. I can stand on my own two feet and I know now that I'll be fine, but I can't imagine a life without you in it. I want you in my life...big mouth and all."

I chuckle, sliding my hand around in her grasp so that I can softly squeeze it to show how much I want her too. Her skin nuzzles to mine, fitting my hand like a warm glove as I easily slide my fingers between each of hers.

"I'm not scared anymore, Evan. I want you, in every way...no tears, no worries and no holding back anymore."

My heart leaps, doing the wave and sparking a whole lot of attention from my other extremities; I keep it at bay though, wanting to take this step with her slowly and savor each courageous movement from her. Even I know moving forward has never been easy, yet here she is, ready to take that plunge; and I believe her this time.

I want to ask what changed. I want to ask what she talked to Trent about, but all of that doesn't seem as important now. She's here; I'm here; we're together and she is saying she's ready. Looking into her eyes a memory flashes before me, her hair still black as night, only shorter and her eyes dull with a fear hidden beneath them as she asked, *have you ever kissed someone?*

My shoulders rise and I suck in a deep breath, a sense of newness in the air.

She shifts her body, twisting at the waist to get closer to me. As soon as she moves our hands into my lap, I flinch, a rush of desire zipping up and down and circling all perimeters of my body.

Moving slowly with a hint of a smile, she whispers so softly, "Evan, you breathe, I breathe, remember?"

Every muscle in me relaxes as I move my other hand to set the pole down. I need to have my hands on her. Her eyes sparkle as she looks at me, and I truly don't think my life has ever felt so full. I suck in a breath, keeping my eyes locked on hers.

I whisper back, ready to feel her lips, "I remember."

Her lips fall to mine, but not before she utters three more words that have come to mean more than words alone; three words that mean more than any 'I love you' ever spoken, because when I said it, that's exactly what I meant.

I pause before tasting the sweetness of her lips and listen…

She recites them to me for a change, setting my heart at ease and letting me know that I have her forever.

I listen as she whispers, "Breathe with me."

Epilogue

"**N**O, SON OF A BITCH!" I yell out, digging both of my hands along the sides of the reclined black leather seat that I'm lying in. "Ooooouuuuuch!"

Piper's hand comes over mine as I flick my eyes to her, catching sight of the guy that is hell bent on inflicting the max level of pain possible while giving a tattoo.

"Why the hell did I let you talk me into this?"

Abby's quiet snickers meet my ears and I just know she has the same shit-eating grin I usually have when I tease the piss out of everyone.

"Stop being a wuss," Abby laughs.

I look up at Piper as the needle sinks into my flesh again. "Oh geeeez!"

"Another couple swipes and we'll be done…chill dude." Ozzy, the long-haired, heavy-metal looking tattoo gun slinger throws out there like its everyday to have your ass branded.

Sure, I'll just chill.

"Oh shit-damn-mother…"

Piper clears her throat, squeezing my hand harder. "Well maybe if you hadn't complained like a little girl every two seconds since you got it, I wouldn't have even suggested butching it up."

Abby cracks up and I strain my neck to try to see her. *Is she staring at my ass; great!*

"Hold still," the tat-tyrant pipes up.

"And fortunate for you, she asked my advice," Abby says, sounding way too chipper over my agony.

"Oh yeah, feeling real lucky here, Abs," I mumble in a sarcastic tone while gritting my teeth from another sharp, searing pain that flies over my skin.

"Plus, Piper wanted to make sure if you decide to start wearing thong speedos to the lake, that you at least look manly doing it," Abby keeps rolling out the jokes while I'm being tortured one swipe at a time.

I huff out a breath and roll my eyes even though no one can see.

"Oh, I bet that one shop has a pair you could get...hey, they may even have flavored ones, huh, Evan?" she goes on, trying to get a rise out of me.

Piper laughs, throwing her other hand over her mouth.

"You guys are enjoying this shit aren't you? Ha...ha! Let's all joke while Evan's butt is being shredded one swipe..." I strain to look back at the needle jabbing fellow. "Swipe is the word you used, right?" I direct my question to ole Oz, not waiting for an answer from the only dude I know that could be truly that focused on confidently staring at another man's ass. "...yeah, one swipe at a time. Feels like I'm getting the worst shave of my life with a rusty old razor and hot sauce."

Piper bounces up and down, clearly entertained by me being on the receiving end.

"Strawberry...don't forget to get the strawberry ones," Abby adds, keeping a serious tone and throwing my smartass comments back at me.

Pipers whole body vibrates and shakes more, tears spilling from her eyes as she tries desperately to hold back her laughter.

"Yeah, yeah, laugh it up." I look at her with a smirk, not an ounce of happiness over me sitting in this chair, but psyched as hell to see her happiness, even if it is at my expense.

"Ok, all done," Ozzy announces in a bored-as-hell tone like he just finished taking his ACT's.

Holy freaking shit, thank you!

Abby and Piper both crack up as I sit there, still exposed, my ass on fire, dumbfounded by how two girls could convince me that this was a good idea and wondering what the hell this is going to look like now.

The drive back to my apartment is less than desirable, with me hiking my left ass cheek halfway up in the air while pressing my face all away against the door. Piper drives, glancing over at me every few minutes while huffing out breathy giggles and telling me to suck it up.

"You try getting your ass stabbed with a needle over and over, for nothing more than a decorative design that nobody will ever see…well except you."

She laughs, shaking her head. I guess I am whining like a little girl.

"You know; I was really hoping this would stop once you got it all butched up." I sneak a look at her from the corner of my eyes, amused by her playful irritation. "I mean, what guy gets tulips and butterflies painted on their rear-end anyways?"

"Ask your best friend! Not me, that wasn't my idea! If I was of sound mind, I would've never gotten a tattoo at all. Do you have any idea how much crap I will get for this from my friends?"

She glances over, her eyes squinted and her face devoid of any laughter or humor.

"Evan, you are completely sober today, yet you got a hammer above my name so that you can tell everyone you like to bang me…" She rolls her eyes and I crack up.

Yeah, a hammer above her name with splinters of sound shooting out around it and over the girly garbage as if it was just slammed down on her name super hard, was absolutely ingenuous. I mentally pat myself on the back for that as she goes on.

"So yeah, give me a new line. You have no excuse today."

I snicker as we pull up to stop in front of my apartment.

"My excuse is, thanks to Abby, I had no choice. It was sink or swim. Make the damn thing my own or never show my ass again," I say, completely serious.

I'm confident in my manhood and am all for nature and outdoor life, but there is no reason to have all that woman stuff marked on my backside. That's typical high-school-notebook-doodle-art-stuff right there and it has no business on my body. At least this I can explain; I like to bang Piper...simple.

Piper jumps out of the car, no sooner than she puts it in park, and runs around to get my door. I let her help me out, kind of enjoying acting like a baby and getting spoiled by her. She sneaks me an all-knowing smile and shakes her head once again, a reaction I'm getting used to when she has to put up with all my bullshit.

"Sooooo dramatic," she teases.

She's right...I'm not even going to argue that one. I pestered Abby about this tattoo from day one, however, that is not my fault. This tattoo has been the topic of conversation from Judd giving me endless crap, to Jake pointing out how I said I would never get one, and then to Abby of course, who lives for the fact that she got one over me. I'm still dead set on never drinking around her again.

We make it into the apartment and where I'd usually have no bigger goal than to kick off my boots and plop down on the couch, today is different. This particular tattoo may have been my idea, well not technically, but I got to say the when, where and what. However, unlike the last one that I was pass-out, barely-know-my-own-name drunk, this one I got to experience the full amount of head-spinning pain. *Why do people get these willingly?*

"Where you going?" I ask, as Piper makes her way to the bedroom.

I follow, somewhat excited as she glances back to me without a word. Keeping my eyes locked on her, I watch as she spins around seductively beside the bed and starts to undress. *Whoa!*

In the past few months since we got back together, physical contact and intimacy has become normal. I wouldn't say we're the hound dogs that I would like us to be, but the need to remind her to breathe and stay with me, has become a rare thing.

"I don't know," she says innocently, but with a glimmer in her eye that tells me that she does know; *yeah, she wants me.* "Guess it's just something about you getting a hammer on your ass today."

At the risk of ruining the moment, I spit out a thunder of laughter at her words. *Now that's my girl. Wow!*

Flicking my hand to the button of my jeans, I swiftly unsnap them, tug my zipper down in a flat second and push them down to my hips as I enlighten her with my own words, "Well, well…I definitely have a hammer for you…Owwwwwwwww!" I holler out, fully killing my mood and shooting my happy-humper down as a fiery stabbing sensation blazes through my cheek.

Piper pouts her lips, frowning as if she feels my pain. "Awwww, hurts pretty bad, huh?" she says sincerely. "Let me help."

Oh yeah, I could get used to the spoiling.

She makes her way to me, slowly, with a sneaky grin on her face while maintaining eye contact the whole way; suddenly my butt isn't the only body part throbbing. I stare back, surprisingly with my mouth shut. *I got nothin'.* Instead of trying to think up some lame smartass joke to throw out and potentially kill this awesome vibe, I grab the hem of my shirt and tear it off in one swift motion. Helping her out is the best solution here. I toss it to the ground and look back at her just as her hands touch down on my skin, raising the hairs on my arm, *and other things*, from the sudden warmth.

Sliding both her hands down to my waistband, we keep up our silent charade of 'Come here big boy' on her end and 'Oh yeah, come get you some' on mine. Pulsing my brows, our spell is broken as soon as she breaks into a fit of laugher, tossing her head back and pulling me down onto the bed with her. *I don't think she had that planned.* We both land with a quiet thud. She lets out a forced breath mixed with joyous giggles while the waist of my jeans scrape over my bandage and instantly have my skin on fire.

"Ahhhh…" I scrunch up my face.

Hers, in turn, dips in pain as well. "Here…" She slides one hand in each of my back pockets and immediately the denim is pulled away from my sore flesh as she wiggles them back and forth.

Again, I help her out and get them off, kicking them to the floor along with my shoes and boxers. Piper wretches and slithers beneath me, tugging her top and pants down as well. The whole ordeal takes way longer than need be, and I'm thinking a pair of scissors is what may be needed next time; clothes are over-rated anyways.

After all of our clothes lay in a pile at the side of the bed just like I prefer them, I get comfortable finally, only sporting a bandage on my ass. Her skin melts like butter against mine, lighting up every cell in me and hugging to my frame like we were custom designed for a perfect fit. I lie there…we lie there, completely memorized by each other.

For weeks, this is how it has been. It's like we're two horny, googly-eyed virgins, too nervous to say a word, wondering who's going to make the first move and me about to blast off with the grand finale before we even get to the main event.

"So what's next?"

I narrow my eyes, having no clue what she is talking about. "Well, if you haven't figured that out by now, I am clearly doing something wrong."

I lean up, careful to not send a wave of shooting pains through my backside. Flinging the night stand drawer open, my eyes instantly light up from the reflection of a purple box of condoms; all the latex, mustard colored ones made their way back to Judd's place. Piper may be mostly healed and able to shake away all the nostalgia from before, but I prefer to take one thing at a time and not press it. *Non-latex all the way from now on.* I pick one up, before doubling my hand back for a few more. Tossing them to the mattress, I situate myself back against her with one arm bracing me from bearing my weight down and the other enjoying a slow trail up her side to the Appalachian Peaks.

She shakes her head on a shiver. "I meant, what's next in terms of your butt?"

I smile. "No thanks, I'm not into that."

She rolls her eyes this time and goes on, ignoring me, "Maybe a drill on the other side?"

"Mmmmm, I do like to drill ya…"

She moves her eyes to the top of her eye sockets as if her next comment will be found written on her forehead. "A screw driver?"

"Oh yeah, even more fitting, because you know I like to…"

She spits out a laugh, cutting me off, "A bat?"

"Hmmmm…" I think on that one. "Let's start with…" I move my hand up, up and up, feeling every ounce of her silky smooth flesh until I find my resting place; the rest place. "…second base."

This ignites a slow whimper as she tosses her head back, pressing it into the mattress. I watch her, trailing my hand down in search of new territories. Her eyes close and I suck in a breath before she opens them and looks back at me, meeting my gaze.

"I like second base," she heaves out a deep breath before sucking back in another gulp of air as my hand moves over her waist and downward.

I smile, ready to tease her in all kinds of ways tonight; some involving my mouth in a whole new way. "What about third, how's that base looking?"

She closes her eyes again, whining and gasping as my hand takes slow, sensual pulses. My whole body thunders on a wave of need and want. *I don't know how long I can carry this on. I want her, now.*

Leaning down, I crash my lips into hers, swiping my tongue into her mouth to taste her, to take her, to consume her. She complies with a needy whimper and a surprising amount of passion as she pulls me fully against her, completely clipping off my mission of getting her to home plate with my fingers alone. I slide down, pulling my hand to her side to gear up for what's next. This pilot is ready to fire down the landing strip and take off for flight. My hand fumbles along the bed, searching for the condom package, about to slur profanities between our lips as our tongues tangle and pulse in a heated kiss.

My hand finally finds what I'm looking for. I clasp a package between my fingertips, bring it to my mouth and tear the corner off in one swift motion. Right as I lower both my hands to her sides to push myself up, she unexpectedly laughs. *That's not always a good sign.* I look up fast, my eyes meeting her. The look that she has on her face is the most beautiful thing I've ever seen. She looks happy, truly happy; she looks complete, content and unafraid of anything. Her eyes hold an enjoyment of life that I've never seen; peacefulness that she's never gotten to experience. I slide back down, pulling both my hands up and around her head, still clutching the torn open condom wrapper; that can wait.

I don't even smile while I'm looking at her, I just look; I stare, in wonder. I'm completely awestruck that I could screw up so greatly, telling the biggest ass I know something so sacred, yet, she would still find her way back to me. She fought her demons in a dangerous game of tug-of-war for years. We both held on tight, but in the end she was the one that was strong enough for the both of us. So I look at her...

I finally smile, because my heart is pounding so fiercely that it is felt in every muscle of my body, lifting, tugging and pulling my lips till they spread across my face.

"Well?" she says with a grin.

I don't come back with some quick witted response; I don't even care that the condom wrapper is open. I just nod my head.

Nonetheless, after a brief pause, I comply, wanting to feel her just as much even though this connection is way more than bats and hammers and screwdrivers and drills; this is time we are together. I feel it deep in my bones, throughout my body, in my mind and most of all in my heart.

Moving my hands down I position myself upright and secure the snug safety coat on before sliding back on top of her. She immediately lets out a large gasp, from the pressure of my body or maybe the thrill of the moment. Sucking in another breath, our eyes meet as I dip my head closer so I can speak.

"Hey, breathe," I whisper across her lips, seconds away from feeling them.

She moves her mouth closer to mine, only a millimeter away until I taste her. "You mean breathe with me?"

I slowly…shake my head as I lock our bodies together with an exhilarating slow thrust that takes her breath away.

"That's not what I meant at all," I huff out as a shockwave of electricity shoots through me. "That's never what I meant," I say in a husky tone, pulsing my pelvis forward again at an unhurried pace.

She opens her eyes wide, her mouth gaped open as if it is ready for me to devour it. I thrust forward, gently, slowly as if she's fragile, as if I want this to last all night, because I do.

Her eyes light up and she raises her head up just enough to place a soft, tender kiss against my lips, then she pulls back just a little. I bob my head forward to taste her again, eager, antsy, but she nudges back with that same sparkle in her eye.

"I love you, too Evan,"

My mouth twitches and begins to curve into an uncontrollable grin. Speechless and ate up with an extreme amount of pride, my whole body lets out a soothing sigh on her words and I breathe….

Damn, I love her too.

Releasing Fall/Winter 2016:

Just Breathe

Book Four in The Breathe Series

Tristan's story

Acknowledgments

Thank you to everyone who makes it possible for me to do this every single day; to write to my heart's content and create stories that become a part of my heart, mind and soul...so that I am able to dream up character's that feel more like family than a person living in a fictional land...to build plots and events that bring my imagination to life. I absolutely love being able to write.

Thank you to my two handsome sons, that put a smile on my face daily. I hope someday when you have a dream, you go for it, grab it and bring it to life. My advice to you both is don't wait, don't get discouraged if you don't succeed at first, have faith, have confidence and most importantly don't give up. You both ignite a desire within me to strive for more, to go for my dreams and make them happen, and that is what I did when I started this series.

Thank you to my editor, Jeremy. What would I do without you? Your insight, opinions and feedback on my books is always right on. My absolute favorite part of meeting with you is when we brainstorm, get on the same page and run with an awesome scene. Although for my next book, I fully plan to bring a rolled up newspaper for you to keep on hand...you know how I get. Be ready to knock some sense into me if I start over-analyzing, not thinking or losing faith in my writing.

Thank you to a fabulous cover designer, Daniela with DCP designs. Your work is beyond stunning and with each teaser, bookmark, rack card or cover that you create, I am truly amazed with their beauty. You deserve all the success in the world and I cannot wait to see what all my future covers will look like.

Thank you to K. Keeton Designs for the lovely photography that fits my characters perfectly. Dusty and Gabriela make a great Piper and Evan.

Thank you to Stacey with Champagne Formats. The end of this process is always my favorite...seeing the interior of my books match the beauty that was created for the cover is always something special and I look forward to it each and every time.

Thank you to a wonderful group of beta readers, proof readers and beta group. I could not do this without you. I count on each of you more than you know and I'm so grateful that you are willing to take time out of your busy lives to help bring my book to a close, so that readers can enjoy it. Thank you: Ashley Schoen, Brandi Ackman, Billy Wilson, Cori Wray, Deanna Richardson, Heather Lesch, Heather Cavanaugh, Jaclyn Keller, Jesica Schultz, Karrie Zschille, Lisa Icard, Tara Dameron and Zack Koeller. Each of you have helped so much to bring this book together.

A special thank you to Karrie Zschille for all the long hours, heart and preciseness that you put into helping with my books. Your faith in me, means more than you will ever know and I am so grateful to have found a friend like you through this journey.

Also another special thanks to Heather Cavanaugh for all the time and effort you put into promoting my books, advice on all the ins-and-outs that I have not yet figured out and for your creative eye in whipping up a quick teaser or banner when I need one. You have helped out so much and I look forward to meeting you at a book signing very soon I hope. You've become a great friend.

Thank you to Billy Wilson for all the promoting you've done to help me out, thank you to Cori Wray for quick advice and input when I run into a snag or get overly stressed, thank you to Deanna Richardson for all the quick trips next door to let me read a chapter or go over an edit with you and also thank you to Jesica Schultz and Brandi Ackman for the extra help with Beta.

Thank you to El Sol in Cape Girardeau for letting me take up your dining area for seven hours to proofread and finalize my book. You're awesome.

Thank you to my mom and grandma for all of the love and support you've given me for my entire life. You've always encouraged my writing, telling me to go for it. If only I had listened to you twenty years ago (haha). This has been a rough year for our family and at times I didn't think that I would get the book finished. We've been overcome with grief, but in the end, I think the best tribute to grandma was to put another piece of my work out into the world. I know that would have made her proud.

Thank you to all the readers that have eagerly anticipated Evan's story and have contacted me or become avid readers of this series. I hope you love book three and I cannot wait to share the next one with you, and many more after that. All the feedback, reviews and personal messages that I receive only further my determination to continue writing book after book after book. I truly appreciate you all and am truly humbled when you say that you love my stories.

Most importantly, Thank you Lord for blessing me with the ability, heart and mindset to put my thoughts into words. When I was little and life seemed to weigh me down, I turned to writing as an outlet for someone that liked to bottle up her emotions. Through poetry, short stories and now novels, I am so grateful for this talent and gift that you have blessed me with.

About The Author

Wendy Wilson is an independent author. As a little girl on through adulthood, she has dreamt of writing and has finally put that dream into action with the release of her first book in a series of novels called *The Breathe Series*. She enjoys spending time with her family, hanging with her friends and reading. She also has a passion for running and has found it is the perfect time to create and think up more exciting plots and characters to add into her books. She currently lives in Chaffee, Missouri with her husband, two adorable sons and two cats.

Visit my website at:
www.wendylwilsonauthor.com
www.facebook.com/wendylwilsonauthor

Other Books

www.ingramcontent.com/pod-product-compliance
Lightning Source LLC
Chambersburg PA
CBHW050903250626
47155CB00001B/83